STEALING THE SHOW

Christina Jones

An Oriel Paperback
First published in Great Britain in 1998 by
Oriel
a division of Orion Books Ltd
Orion House, 5 Upper St Martin's Lane, London WC2H 9EA

A CIP catalogue record for this book is available
from the British Library

ISBN 0 75281 605 5

Typeset at The Spartan Press Ltd
Lymington, Hants
Printed and bound in Great Britain by
Clays Ltd, St Ives plc

For *Uncle Sam* and the Prefab Memories

ACKNOWLEDGEMENTS

As always, to absolutely everyone at Orion for all their hard work, help and friendship. Very special thanks to Jane Wood, Selina Walker, Sarah Yorke and Susan Lamb who put up with so much and are still lovely to me.

To Sarah Molloy for being much more than an agent and far more than a friend.

To all the Showmen who made my childhood so brilliantly happy and unusual, and who gave me so much help. Especially George and Mary Irvin, Bill and Benny Irvin and *Uncle Sam*; all the Pelhams for the transport details; everyone travelling with Masons, particularly Lee Jones (painter, fairground art expert, and restoration genius); and to Rosie and Harry Hebborn for their help and encouragement. Many thanks also to the Hatwell, Williams and Smith families for making it possible.

To Peter Barnes, lifelong friend and *World's Fair* reporter, for taking up so much of his time with so many questions, and for not minding the late-night phone calls.

To Joan Hibbs, Secretary of the London Section of the Showmen's Guild, for her invaluable help.

To Percy Dearlove for the endless research and information – and for being lovely.

To Rob and Laura – as always – for supporting me with love and endless cups of coffee.

I would like to add that, while everyone connected with fairgrounds mentioned here gave me accurate and correct information, as this is a work of fiction I used their facts only to suit my story. Any inaccuracies are me bending the rules to fit the plot, and in no way reflect their expertise.

CHAPTER ONE

She was never going to cook bacon and eggs for seven starving men in the early hours of the morning ever again. Young, muscular, and exceedingly grateful they may have been – but it played havoc with her sleep.

Aching with exhaustion, Nell punched her pillows and snuggled down further beneath the duvet. There were plus points, of course: no matter how dishevelled and dirty or cold and crotchety she was, the plate-scraping appreciation helped to make it worth while. The fact that two of the plate-scrapers were her brothers dimmed the delight a little, of course, but then life was all swings and roundabouts.

'Nell! It's half-six!' Danny's voice bellowed into her brain from somewhere beneath her window. 'You up?'

Rotten dream, she thought drowsily. Danny's voice – he probably wanted feeding. Everyone always seemed to want feeding. She curled her toes into the warmest part of the bed and started to drift.

'Nell! Are you awake?'

'Yes . . . no . . .' she mumbled, fumbling for the bedside alarm. 'I've only just gone to sleep.' She peered at the clock. 'Oh, hell.'

Showering, cleaning her teeth, dragging on jeans and sweater, and making a mug of tongue-stripping black coffee, took a little over ten minutes. Most of this routine Nell managed to complete with her eyes still shut. Prising one open, she went through the process of packing every remaining movable object into the cupboards, securing the doors, and dismantling the gas and water-pipes in record time. Danny would scream at her to hurry again at any moment, she knew he would. She could happily disembowel her brother on mornings like this.

Pausing in the doorway she risked Danny's wrath, retraced her steps, and struggled into her long black coat. The April sun was deceptively warm through the leaded windows of her bedroom, but she knew from experience that the cold Cotswold wind would whistle through the thickest layers.

'Nell!' Danny pounded on her door. 'Get a bloody move on!'

Muttering curses which should have shrivelled her elder brother to a warty toad, she managed to open both her eyes. 'Have a heart, Danny. We've got ages yet.'

Danny's enraged shout indicated that they hadn't. 'We should have been out twenty minutes ago. Shift your butt and get down here!'

He ought to have been a Butlins Red Coat, Nell thought, peering into the mirror to check her early-morning face, in the good old days of campers being awakened by a blistering cheerful Tannoy and plinkety-plonk muzak. Or a GMTV presenter. Or even a prime minister. Danny seemed to thrive on three hours' sleep. She would have loved the chance of six.

Her early-morning face peered back at her with some trepidation. Red-gold hair escaping in silky strands from a haphazard scrunchie displayed Nell's freckles at their absolute worst. No matter that she was tall and slender, with sleepy slanting eyes and the high cheek-bones inherited from her nomadic ancestors, those damned freckles ruined everything. Who could possibly look sophisticated covered in smudges and splodges? To Nell, the tiny golden speckles were each a yard wide and glowed like beacons.

'You've been kissed by the sun, my love,' Adele, her

mother, used to say as she watched Nell scrub her face with lemon juice. 'They're nature's blessings.'

Nature was more than welcome to them, Nell thought. With her endless legs and long eyelashes, she had total sympathy with giraffes.

Danny, stocky, weatherbeaten and seven years her senior, grinned with all the smug superiority of a lark over an owl as Nell opened the door. 'About bloody time. Me and Claudia are ready to pull out. Sam's coupled up, and the Mackenzies were set ages ago.'

Nell staggered down the steps of her living wagon and shivered. She had been doing this all her life and still loathed the early starts. 'You back the car up then, and I'll do the hard work.'

'Do you want one of the lads to help you? Hold your eyelids open?'

With further anti-sibling invective, Nell slithered across the damp grass and stepped over the living wagon's drawbar as Danny slid into the driving seat of her Volvo estate and began to reverse.

He twisted round behind the steering wheel, looking as irritatingly wideawake and golden as a breakfast cereal advert. 'Stop yawning and grab the coupling. And you have secured everything inside this time?'

'Yes, of course I have. Most of it last night. *After* I'd fed everyone, washed up, checked the water tanks and the gas.' Nell took a deep breath and heaved the ball-and-socket coupling into place, then snapped the electric wires from her trailer into the Volvo's connections. Once – only once – had she left the Crown Derby and Edinburgh Crystal still on the shelves, but Danny never let her forget it. 'And *before* I went over the loads, paid the lads, and made sure that Sam had put the takings in the night safe. Somewhere in there I also managed to get about five minutes' sleep.' She straightened up and glared at Danny. 'OK. That's fine – now stop being so unbearably cheerful and go and nag someone else.'

Nell stretched, pushed her hair more firmly into its achorage, and rubbed her eyes. By midday she'd be human, and by ten o'clock tonight she'd be the life and soul. By ten o'clock tonight she'd be in – oh, yes – Broadridge Green. Fifteen miles south down the A34 and into the leafy greenery of Oxfordshire. Bradleys' Mammoth Fun Fair was moving on.

This start to the working day was as commonplace to her as the mad commuter scramble for city-bound trains. Packing up, travelling, arriving, unloading, building up, spreading magic, packing up again . . . And people thought it was exciting and glamorous. Nell knew. They'd told her so. But then they only saw the glittery lights and the gaiety; they weren't there on cold wet mornings when the lorries refused to start, or the trailers were bogged down, and your hands were frozen and your feet saturated. Or at night when the crowds had gone home to snug beds and there were still three hours of pulling down, dismantling and packing away before you could grab a cup of tea. She sighed happily. It was her life – and she absolutely loved it.

The bark of a Seddon-Atkinson's diesel engine blasted into the early-morning silence and Nell side-stepped the load-towing lorry. Danny, still functioning on fast forward, leaned down from the driving seat. 'Go and ginger the lads up, Nell. They're probably still asleep – and we need to move. Now.' He revved the engine impatiently, making the towering two-tier trailer stacked with dodgem cars tremble.

Nell, who didn't blame their workforce for clinging to oblivion for as long as possible, headed across the slippery field towards what she and her brothers irreverently referred to as the Beast Wagon.

'Danny's on the warpath,' she yelled up into the battered, dark-green truck. 'We're pulling out now – and if you don't shift this instant, I'm not cooking when we pull in at Broadridge.'

Muffled curses, a colourful oath, and one declaration of immediate suicide later, five unshaven and rather unkempt figures stumbled into the morning. The Bradleys' regular core of gaff lads were fiercely loyal, extremely hard-working, and, as far as the authorities were aware, didn't exist. Like most casual fairground workers they were there because it was preferable to their past. Some were ex-prisoners, some perennial drifters, some running away from debts and tangled love-lives. As long as they were generally honest, worked well, and didn't cause any trouble, no one pried too deeply. Casual staff members were recruited on a daily basis from wherever the fair stopped, but the regulars laboured long hours for cash-in-hand wages, three meals a day, and a bed and basics in the Beast Wagon. They all seemed happy with the arrangement.

Relieved that this morning there were no dishevelled teenage girls sliding coyly from the depths of the Beast Wagon, Nell stopped in mid-yawn and tried to be business-like. It was difficult when her body still yearned to be beneath the duvet. 'I knew that'd fetch you. See you at the other end.'

'With sausage sandwiches?' Terry, the youngest and most recent addition to the gaff lads, who looked like a fallen angel and managed to seduce a new girl every night, asked hopefully. 'And brown sauce?'

'OK.' Nell nodded. She'd promise them anything to keep Danny off her back in the early hours – and sausage sandwiches seemed a small price to pay. 'And brown sauce. Now scarper.'

They did. Within minutes the eight-legged Foden trucks containing the dodgem tracks, the bulk of the paratrooper, the painted rails, and carrying the generators, chugged choking fumes into the wine-sharp air. The articulated Scammell wagon-and-drag that housed the waltzer immediately joined in, vibrating with throaty roars. Nell watched with a critical eye as the cavalcade pulled off the field, cheered away by the usual knot of fairground devotees and small boys, before picking her way back round the remaining loads.

Each of the lorries and trucks were liveried in bright blue, with 'Bradleys' Fun Fair On Tour' splashed across them in huge spiky scarlet letters and underlined with a sprinkling of

Day-Glo yellow stars. Her brothers had chosen the primary colour scheme on the retirement of their parents, and Nell, who had objected strongly at the time, still detested it. Outvoted, she'd agreed that it was eye-catching, vivid, up-to-the-minute, but –

It was a big but. Nell, who hankered after the maroon paintwork and romantic gold lettering of the fairgrounds of the past, had dared to say so. Her brothers had been outraged. Old-fashioned, out-of-the-ark, arty-farty to the point of bankruptcy, had been some of their milder comments. Nell had acquiesced with bad grace to Danny and Sam's self-professed superior business acumen, and vowed that one day she'd have an entire procession of wagons, painted in the traditional regalia, with 'Petronella Bradley' picked out in gold leaf.

'Dream on, Nell,' Danny had mocked. 'Those days are long gone. We've got to look to the future and expand. We're way behind the times even with the paratrooper, dodgems and waltzer. We need up-to-the-minute rides that'll bring the punters in in droves. No one wants the old stuff any more.'

But she did, Nell thought, as she checked that every piece of litter had been collected and stacked in sacks for the refuse men to pick up. She always had, she admitted, as she made sure that there were no permanently-rutted wheel tracks or discarded cables to give coronaries to the high-ups on the parish council, and she probably always would. It was a dream that refused to go away.

She straightened up as the Mackenzies, an entire family who ran a juvenile ride, swings and various side stalls and who had travelled with the Bradleys for generations, chugged past her. Nell waved. The older couple were always referred to as Mr and Mrs Mac, and she doubted if even their sons and daughters-in-law and abundant grandchildren were aware of their Christian names.

Satisfied that the ground was exactly as it had been when the fair arrived a week earlier, and would cause no eager cub journalist on the local rag to write headlines about the

6

fairground's desecration of the rural idyll, she headed back towards the remaining vehicles in the gateway.

'Has he gone?' Claudia, Danny's wife, called from the driving seat of her Shogun. 'He's not just parking up the road and coming back to supervise the rest of us with a bullwhip?'

'Not a chance,' Nell said. 'The way he was champing at the bit, he's probably carved up everything on the A34 and is pulling on to the playing fields at Broadridge Green as we speak. Why? Have you got an exciting escapade planned? Are we going to run away and join the circus?'

'Sadly, no.' Claudia flipped down the vanity mirror. 'Just got to see to the priorities. Danny's such an old woman on pull-out mornings. He never understands that it's vital for me to do the full slap before I face the world.'

'Maybe you should get up earlier?'

'That's rich, coming from you.' Claudia paused in applying black mascara to already black lashes. 'There. What do you reckon?'

'Very glam, if a bit OTT for the crack of dawn in Oxfordshire.' Nell and Claudia were far closer than sisters-in-law. Their deep friendship and shared laid-back attitude exasperated the workaholic Danny. 'Still, I'm sure Danny'll appreciate it when you're building up the dodgems.'

Claudia slicked on glossy red lipstick, snapped the mirror back into position, and started the Shogun. 'That's the trouble, Nell, as you know. Danny doesn't appreciate it at all. See ya.'

Nell watched as Claudia negotiated the gate with the Shogun and the long, elaborately-chromed living wagon and gave a sigh. She had a sneaky feeling that her brother's marriage was well into injury time. It was impossible to say anything to Danny, of course, and Claudia would never actually admit it. Nell opened the door of the Volvo. Divorce, or even separation, was very much frowned upon in showmen's families. Their moral code was still deep-rooted in the previous century. You were expected to marry into the business – and stay married.

The Volvo purred into life. Nell wondered what her parents would make of it. Thank goodness their retirement meant they weren't on hand to witness the gradual disintegration. Parental guidance and approval was still much sought after amongst travellers. Patriarchal power reigned supreme. Although in the Bradleys' case it was Adele who called the shots. Not, Nell admitted, that either of the Bradleys had ever been strict parents, but they certainly stuck to the rules – and expected the same behaviour from their offspring.

Adele Bradley made no secret of the fact that she was desperate to become a grandmother. And as neither Nell nor Sam were showing any signs of making a serious commitment, Adele had pinned all her loudly-voiced hopes on Danny and Claudia. Nell winced as the Volvo and living wagon jolted across the field and hoped that the rift would be patched up before her mother got wind of it on the travellers' grapevine. It would not be well received.

'Nell!'

She slammed on the brakes and squinted into the driving mirror. Sam was hurrying along the side of her living wagon. He was five years younger than Danny, and the Bradley tawny hair was their only common feature. Taller and leaner, Sam worked harder than any of them, treated everyone as a friend, and as a result was universally liked. Nell put it down to his being born during the summer of '67. Much of the love and peace mentality had rubbed off on Sam.

'Aren't the taillights working on the trailer?' Nell slid the window down. 'Or have I left Grandma Bradley's prized Minton sitting by the rubbish sacks?'

Sam brushed his hair from his eyes and waved his phone under her nose. 'You've got your mobile switched off. It's Ross.'

Ross Percival. Every girl's dream. Nell's nightmare.

'Oh, sod it! I really don't want to talk to him at the moment. Tell him I've already gone. Tell him I'll call him from Broadridge Green. Tell him I was abducted by aliens last night –'

'I said you were still here. Sorry.'

Nell took the phone from her brother. 'When the hell will you learn to lie through your teeth like the rest of us? Hello, Ross. You're early ... What? Oh, right. Yes. OK. Look we're just pulling out and I've got to go. I'll call you later. Bye.' She handed the phone back to Sam. 'Thanks a bunch. He's going to come over to Broadridge Green this evening.'

'That's not so bad, is it? I mean, everyone expects you to be announcing your engagement before long anyway. Mum and Dad said –'

'Sam, shut up.'

He grinned. 'Right. But you'll have to sort it out, Nell. Especially if Ross is going to become part of our set-up.'

'Over my dead body.' Nell glared at her brother and stamped on the Volvo's accelerator. 'Or at least only after a lot of persuasion and with the aid of a general anaesthetic. If we let Ross into the business we might as well forget Bradleys altogether. We'll be sucked into the Percival empire and everything that it stands for.'

She didn't add that it also meant kissing goodbye to her dream of re-creating a traditional fair.

'Spare me the feminist dirges,' Sam groaned. 'And the preservation of the atavistic traveller spiel as well. It's far too early in the morning. Anyway, you'll probably have to marry him – after all, he's the only eligible showman around who's taller than you are.'

'I might take up starvation diets, recreational drugs and chain-smoking and become a super-model,' Nell said haughtily. 'Tall and slim is still desirable, you know.'

'Tall and slim maybe – gangly, ginger, and covered in freckles is hardly likely to have Naomi and Co. quaking in their shoes.' Sam blew her a brotherly kiss. 'Nah, I reckon Ross Percival is your last resort. Have a safe journey.'

'You too, you hippie pig.'

With a series of rude gestures, Nell steered the Volvo and trailer out through the gap in the Cotswold stone wall and indicated left for Broadridge Green and whatever it might hold. She slotted a Brubeck CD into the player and drummed her accompaniment on the steering wheel. Petronella Bradley was on the road again.

CHAPTER TWO

'Turn your pedals! Press your steering wheels!' Nell clapped her hand over the microphone, then raising her voice above an early Oasis hit, tried again. 'Press your pedals! Turn your steering wheels! All ready for the next ride!'

With a screech of metal on metal and a Grand Prix roar, the dodgem cars spurted into noisy, colourful life. Within seconds three of them were jammed nose-first into the side of the track, rumbling angrily like impotent bees against a shut window. Nell leaned closer to the microphone. 'Terry! Sort them out!'

Terry, who was riding on the back of a car on the far side of the track, explaining the steering to a very pretty girl in a very short skirt, looked up, grinned, and darted between the hurtling dodgems.

Nell leaned back on her seat in the pay-box. Twilight was seeping over Broadridge Green, and the fair, as always on the first night, was packed. The steady thud of the generators made a background bass for the screams and yells of the customers and the splintered rendition of half-a-dozen different pop songs. The hundreds of multicoloured lights had transformed the harshness of the primary paintwork into a kaleidoscopic rainbow. She smiled. It never failed to please her, this ability to bring transient magic into people's lives.

'Sorted.' Terry leapt from the back of a passing car and balanced beside the pay-box with ease. He was a quick learner. 'Here's the dosh.'

Nell took the coins, flicked them expertly into piles, then held out her hand. 'And the fiver.'

'What?' Terry blinked his long eyelashes across dark blue eyes. 'Never had a fiver.'

'The couple over there, the ones pootling cautiously round the outside, gave you a fiver. I saw them. Hand it over.'

'Oh – *that* fiver.' Terry fished the crumpled note out of his jeans. 'You don't miss a trick, do you?'

'Can't afford to.' Nell frowned above the noise of several multiple pile-ups. 'And don't try cheating me or you'll be on your bike. I know exactly how much money we ride with. Every time. I've been doing this all my life.' She grinned at him. He was very good-looking. 'If you want to palm the punters and can get away with it, then that's down to you – but don't expect me to come to your rescue if they suss what you're doing and punch you on the nose.'

'OK.' Terry winked and leapt between the fast-moving cars. 'Oh – an' the sausage sandwiches were great.'

Four fully-packed rides later, Sam swung himself up into the pay-box. 'Go and grab a cuppa. I've got Mick and Alfie covering the paratrooper so I'll take over for a bit.'

Nell stood up and stretched in the cramped space. Things on the fair had changed quite a lot in the two years since Adele and Peter Bradley's retirement, but no one had yet designed pay-boxes that allowed comfort for several people at the same time.

Sam slid into the seat behind the state-of-the-art sound system which Nell had installed as soon as she'd inherited the dodgems. Adele and Peter had played a repetitive stack of Elvis 45s on a turntable. 'Oh, and if you were thinking of making yourself alluring for Ross –'

'Which I wasn't.'

'Well, if you were, I just thought I ought to warn you that you're only second on his agenda for this evening.'

'Oh?' Nell paused on the top step.

Sam switched on the microphone again. 'Two more cars! Two more cars! Hurry along there!' He turned back to Nell. 'Apparently, Danny asked him to come over tonight. It's definitely business – not pleasure.'

Nell groaned. Danny? What the hell for? It was bad enough to think that Ross Percival wanted to travel with them. She hoped that Danny wasn't going to try and coerce her into marrying Ross, yet again, just because he was Clem Percival's son and Danny wanted the kudos of being linked to one of the largest fairs in the London Section of the Showmen's Guild. She'd heard it all before. It made her feel like something mass-produced.

Reading her thoughts, Sam laughed at her expression. 'Are you sure you didn't take Rampant Feminism A-level at that boarding school? Poor old Ross. I think you underestimate him. He doesn't see you as part of the business, even if Danny does. I mean, he must have asked you to marry him three times and –'

'Four,' Nell said, jumping down the steps and treading carefully over the cables creeping from the generator. 'And it might as well be four hundred. My answer will still be the same. Ross is OK. We're good mates – but I don't want to marry him – or anyone.'

The air was fragrant with fried onions and hot diesel. Nell was always surprised that no one ever complained about the smell. The noise, yes, frequently, but never the smell which for ten days each spring obliterated the scent of the blossoms and freshly mown grass of Broadridge Green.

It was a large village, one of the regular ports of call for the fair, and one which the Bradleys considered an easy venue. People spent well and there was never any trouble. Families were out in force in the early evening, teenagers hung on until the bitter end, and everyone enjoyed themselves and disappeared peaceably by eleven o'clock. But Nell was aware that

Danny found these places increasingly dull. Danny, she knew, longed to be running huge gaudy white-knuckle rides on massive fairgrounds that stayed open until the last terrified customer had staggered away. Rides and fairs, she thought as she dodged a knot of children clutching candy-floss, exactly like those of the Percivals.

She sighed. Everyone expected her to marry Ross. That was the problem. She was blocking her brothers' business expansion by her refusal to trip – in her case probably literally, given the length of her legs and her lack of familiarity with frocks that came past the knee – up the aisle.

'Hey!' Claudia called from the hoopla stall. 'Why the thunder face? Are you going to castrate someone we know?'

'Your husband if he's going to do what I think he is.'

'Oh, goody.' Claudia opened her eyes wide. She'd added false eyelashes and another layer of scarlet lipstick. 'Can I watch?'

'Not a chance – but you can get the kettle on if you can find someone to take over in there.'

'No sweat.' Claudia dumped her armful of wooden hoops across the nearest small plinth which held a five-pound note, a plastic watch and a poster of Madonna. Unfastening her money apron, she gesticulated towards the Mackenzie grandchildren who were doing no business now that the Broadridge Green babies had abandoned the swinging boats. 'Here! Rio! Take over for a bit! Ta!' And swinging her legs in the briefest of denim miniskirts and thigh-high boots over the edge of the stall, she caught up with Nell.

For work, Nell stuck to jeans and sweaters with the addition of her long black coat on cold nights and her face-painting stopped at mascara and the inevitable gallon of concealer to hide her freckles. She looked at Claudia in admiration as they instinctively ducked under the para-trooper to avoid the swooping airborne seats and dozens of dangling feet. 'You should be on the cover of a magazine.'

'*Vogue? Harper's?*'

'More top shelf.'

Laughing, they linked arms and headed for Danny and Claudia's trailer. Claudia sighed. 'It's easy for you with those pussycat eyes and those cheek-bones and that glorious colouring. You're drop-dead gorgeous even when you've got your early-morning grouchy face on. I'm not. I have to hide behind the powder and paint to give me confidence.'

'Rubbish.' Nell had to yell as they passed the waltzer with its swirling, screaming, neon-bright cars. Danny ran the ride like a mobile disco with strobe lights and the latest music fads. It was always packed. 'I've got gingery hair and freckles and legs that get in a tangle and I'm as tall as most men. I'll swap you any day. And Danny thinks you're the most beautiful woman in the world.'

'Does he?' Claudia shrugged, unlocking her door. 'I wouldn't know. He never tells me.'

Nell sank into the deeply-cushioned William Morris sofa while Claudia made tea. Danny updated their living wagon every other year. This latest one was American and opulent in the extreme, and was furnished in the traditional showman's manner with rosewood display cabinets for the porcelain and crystal, silk rugs on the polished floor, and velvet swags and tails complementing the Nottingham lace at the windows.

Claudia handed Nell a china mug and curled up on the floor. 'We're slumming it. I get fed up with always having to use the best stuff and getting a thimbleful of tea in eggshell Wedgwood. So – what's Danny done to upset you?'

Nell sipped her tea and watched the crowds through the double-glazed windows. The fair was silent from inside except, of course, for the repetitive muffled thud of the generators. They never quite escaped that. Curious faces, taking a short cut from Broadridge Green's only pub, were attempting to peer in through the windows of the semicircle of living wagons. Quite often, especially in summer, when she trustingly – and much to Danny's fury – always left the top half of her front door open, Nell returned to find a little crowd of people on the top step leaning in. They always seemed riveted and Nell invariably asked them, very politely, if they could return the favour and let her stare into their homes some time.

Once she'd interrupted an excited bunch of old ladies who seemed stunned to see cutlery on the table and had asked if Nell and the other gypsies actually slept in real beds as opposed to makeshift shelters beneath the stars.

Nell had started to explain about gypsies, Romanies, tinkers and other travellers being a different breed altogether, and that showpeople were simply itinerant businessmen, but it had fallen on deaf ears. She'd invited the elderly ladies in to view the decor, the fitted kitchen, the bathroom. They'd sniffed and run fingers along the surfaces and looked disappointed.

'Not what we expected,' one had complained. 'You haven't got no crystal balls.'

'Nor a toilet.' Another had perked up a bit, spotting this omission and being convinced that the operation must surely take place squatting beneath a hedgerow.

Nell had told them that travellers always had their lavatories separate from their living quarters for reasons of hygiene. Either in a separate part of the living wagon or in a detached unit. Far more civilised, she'd added, than the house-dweller's penchant for combined bathrooms, didn't they agree? The old ladies had been most put out, and swarmed down the steps chuntering about folks who didn't know their station.

Wondering again at the fascination her way of life held for people outside it, she turned her attention to her sister-in-law. 'What? Sorry – I was just watching the punters. They always seem so surprised at how we live.'

'Still expect whittled hedgehogs and old crones in black shawls,' Claudia said happily. 'They soon get bored when you tell them we've got satellite telly, central heating, a mobile phone and do our shopping at Tesco. And stop changing the subject or tea-break'll be over, and tell me about Danny.'

Nell didn't particularly want to talk about Danny. At least, not at the moment. The rocky state of her brother's marriage was something she'd deal with later. Just when it had all gone wrong she hadn't noticed. It must have been a gradual decline. She was sure that he and Claudia had been in love when they married. Sadly, she was pretty sure that that love had died some time ago. She was also pretty sure that Danny's sudden passion for acquiring new machines was to replace the lack of it in his marriage. 'He's invited Ross over. Tonight.'

Claudia opened her saucer eyes. 'Is it going to be a "Do the honest thing by my sister, you swine, after all you've been bonking her regularly for the last eight years" speech?'

Nell choked on her tea. 'No, it bloody well isn't. It's to do with the business. Expansion. Buying new rides. Ross Percival joining forces with us.'

'Yeah, I know. It's all Danny talks about. And?'

'And I'm happy with the way things are.' She sighed. When her parents had retired they had left the fair to be run as it had always been run. Not to flog off the waltzer and the dodgems and the paratrooper and buy scary rides that worked on hydraulics and built up and pulled down at the touch of a button and would be obsolete within a year. And could she cope with Ross under her feet every second of the day?

Claudia drained her mug, took Nell's, and scrambled to her feet. 'So? You and Sam own two-thirds of the rides between you. As long as you stick together, Danny can't go over your heads.'

'But Sam wouldn't side with me. He agrees with Danny about modernisation. He's pleased about the possibility of Ross buying a mega-machine and travelling with us.'

Claudia stalked into the kitchen in her high-heeled boots. 'Look, Nell, I honestly don't care either way. I married into the Bradley set-up and I'm supposed to support Danny. I don't have your sense of family tradition. Anyway, modern stuff would bring in more money and need less work, wouldn't it?'

Nell nodded. But she knew that if Ross Percival joined them they'd have to scrap their rides to finance the new ones and lose most of the lads because they would be surplus to requirements. The Mackenzies would definitely decamp because their little bits and pieces wouldn't fit in with the ultra-modern image. And they'd stop visiting all the villagey gaffs that Nell loved – places like Broadridge Green and Haresfoot and Oakton where the fair's arrival was eagerly awaited, marking an anniversary on the calendar as regular and exciting as Christmas.

She stood up. 'It would mean less work, yes – but I like these small places where we can entertain the whole family. There'd be no parents, grandparents and toddlers queuing to get on the Inter-Galactic-Cyber-Hypno-Scramble-Your-Brains-For-A-Fiver, would there?'

Claudia giggled as they jumped down the steps into the darkening evening. 'No, but things change –'

'I don't want them to change. I don't want to be sucked into Clem Percival's "Let's turn every traditional fair into a mobile Alton Towers" mentality. I want our fair to stay the same.'

'And you don't want to marry Ross Percival?'

'Oh, God,' Nell sighed as they reached the hoopla and Claudia swung herself back inside, 'I really don't know.'

'It's starting to tail off now,' Sam said as he handed over the reins of the dodgems. 'Just a few of the larger show-offs and of course the ladies.'

All fairs attracted groupies. Pretty girls with tight jeans and corkscrew curls and Julia Roberts lips. The gaff lads held regular competitions over who could pull the most in a night. Terry seemed to be top of the league.

Within an hour, Broadridge Green had spent up for the evening and was making its way home. Tarpaulins were pulled over the side stalls, lights were switched off, the generators were silenced. Nell, walking back from putting the takings in Sam's trailer ready for his counting and bagging and night-safe depositing, stared up at the dark sky. There was no way on earth she'd give this up. No way that she'd lose sight of her values. The traditions were too deeply rooted. She'd fight her brothers every step.

'Hello, Nell.' The voice sliced through the darkness.

She jumped. 'Oh – er – don't do that, Ross. You frightened the life out of me.'

'You looked as though you were miles away.'

'Not really.' Nell lifted her face for his brief kiss of greeting. 'Just in Oxfordshire and Berkshire villages.'

He walked beside her, not touching. She could smell his cologne. Everything about Ross Percival was expensive. Handmade suits, hand-stitched shoes, salon-layered hair, even his smile cost money. Nell wondered if that was the real reason she didn't want to marry him. Not simply because she wasn't in love with him, but because – despite Sam's assurance that it wasn't so – Ross was so sure that she was just another asset to be acquired; a subsidiary of Bradleys' Mammoth Fun Fair to be taken over with the goods and chattels. Love, as her mother kept telling her, came second to a good and profitable partnership. Love was for films and books and outsiders. That sort of love would grow.

Nell was sure it wouldn't. Nell was convinced that love would one day hit her smack between the eyes with trumpets, fireworks and a deluge of rose petals. She hadn't, of course, shared this with her mother.

The Bradley and Percival families had known each other all their lives, and Nell and Ross had been bracketed together for the last eight years. The entire Showmen's Guild was waiting for the notice in *The World's Fair*, it seemed. 'Mr and Mrs Peter Bradley are delighted to announce the engagement of their only daughter, Petronella, to Ross, only son of Mr and Mrs Clem Percival. Both of the London Section.'

Ross was extremely handsome, extremely rich, well educated, polite, ambitious – Nell sighed. It simply wasn't enough to make her give up everything and become part of the Percival empire. Because that's what it would mean. Not only were showpeople expected to marry into the profession, but women were supposed to throw in their lot with their future husbands. Of course, Nell thought, most women were leaving their parents' fairs and seemed delighted to be striking out on their own. But for her it was different.

The Percivals – Ross, his two sisters and their parents – were as high in the showmen's hierarchy as it was possible to get. Clem Percival, Ross's father, was the Richard Branson of the travelling band. Everything he bought, or into which he invested, returned his money a thousandfold. He was ahead of the trends, rarely made mistakes, was respected, well-liked and, whatever walk of life he had been born into, would have made a fortune.

And, as Adele Bradley never tired of telling Nell, Ross Percival was the catch of the decade. Showmen's daughters across the country were queuing up to leap into her size-eight shoes – and yet her reluctance to marry him only appeared to make him more keen.

'I've got to talk to Danny which shouldn't take long,' Ross said, 'and then I thought we'd go out to eat. I've booked a late table at Ma Belle. As long as we're there before midnight, Antoine'll serve us.'

'Sounds nice – but I really don't think –'

'Why not? No strings tonight, Nell. Honest. I want to eat out and I want some company. I'm not asking you on a date. Just as a friend. OK?'

'OK, then. But if you're talking business to Danny, I want to be there.'

'I'd rather you weren't. You'll argue long and hard and we'll miss the table – and I'm starving. You go and do the necessary and keep out of my way for –' Ross glanced at the Rolex on his wrist, 'ten minutes should do it.'

'Twenty,' Nell said. 'And don't start the wheeler-dealer part without me. I've got some pies and things to heat up for the lads before I even begin to put on the warpaint.'

'Tell 'em to eat at the pub,' Ross said. 'We do.'

'I know. We do things differently on these small fairs, though, remember? The lads work hard for us and we feed them.'

Ross ruffled her hair. Nell wished he wouldn't treat her as though she was pink and fluffy. 'Don't glare at me – I promise I won't get on to the important points on the schedule until you arrive, but try not to be late. I'm fine with your erratic timing – but don't keep Danny waiting.'

She didn't. She fed the lads from the microwave, showered, piled her hair on top of her head, pulled on a Nicole Farhi suit, and was still blotting her lipstick as she opened Danny's door. Claudia had poured huge drinks and Danny, Sam and Ross were all lounging on the William Morris sofa.

'Wow!' Ross patted the seat beside him. 'You look sensational. Come and sit down.'

Declining the chance to be squashed up next to Danny, she perched on the arm of Claudia's chair. 'What have I missed?'

'Nothing except the extremely healthy balance sheet – taxable and declared – of Percival Touring Entertainments.' Claudia, now minus the false eyelashes, and with baggy grey sweat pants replacing the denim skirt and boots, said, 'Oh, and how we can't hope to survive for more than two years if we carry on the way we're going and –'

Nell quickly swallowed her mouthful of gin and tonic. 'Pack it in, Ross. We've heard it all before.'

'Not this bit you haven't.' Ross was leaning back, one elegantly-trousered knee crossed over the other. 'You know we bought the Ice-Breaker last year?'

Nell knew. The Ice-Breaker was the largest touring ride in Britain. Clem Percival had paid an alleged three-quarters of a million for it from a Midlands manufacturer. It had even made national television. She nodded. 'You're not going to tell me that we could have one as a jolly addition to Bradleys' Mammoth Fun Fair, are you? That it would sit nicely beside the swinging boats and the cocount sheet? Or that Danny has already signed the hire purchase agreement? Or –'

Ross uncrossed his legs. 'Dad has just bought the Jesson Company that makes the Ice-Breaker. Which means that Percivals can now supply it – and similar large hydraulic rides – to fairs across the world, and especially in Britain, at far cheaper prices. Danny and Sam agree that something like the Ice-Breaker, maybe on a smaller scale, is exactly what you need to drag you into the next millennium. If you don't, small fairs like this will be a thing of the past.'

Nell put her glass down on the rosewood table. Claudia immediately slipped a coaster underneath it. 'No way. We can't afford it. Not even at your special knock-down rates. We don't want it –'

'*You* don't want it,' Danny said quietly, making Nell look at him. He was deadly when he was quiet. 'Sam and I disagree. And we can afford it if we pool all our money, especially now we're going to join forces with Percivals and –'

Nell glared at him. 'Says who? Bradleys has been a family fair for generations. We're not selling out to Clem Percival – sorry Ross – not ever. You know how I feel.'

Ross smiled his panther smile. 'Yes, I do. And I knew how you'd react. And I'm not asking you to sell your soul. Mergers are happening all the time to keep traditional travelling fairs alive in the face of theme-park opposition. It makes sense. Danny and Sam would get their up-to-the-minute rides and you would keep Bradleys independent.'

Nell was aware of Claudia holding her breath; of Sam and Danny watching her carefully. It did make sense. They all wanted her to say yes; she knew they did.

'How would we be independent with you becoming part of us? We might keep the name but you'd hold the power. No. I'm sorry. I won't agree.'

Claudia sighed. Danny and Sam shook their heads.

Ross glanced again at the Rolex and fished his mobile phone from an inside pocket. 'I'll just ring Ma Belle and tell them we're on our way, shall I?' He laughed at Nell's murderous expression. 'What? It'll be fine – oh, hi. Ma Belle? Ross Percival. I'll be there in half an hour. Tell Antoine . . .' He clicked off the phone and smiled at Nell. 'Why do you always suspect my motives? Sam and Danny are all for it.'

Nell felt her face flame. It was another drawback that went with her colouring. If she agreed to this, she'd never realise her dream. If she didn't, she'd alienate her entire family. And Ross was probably the only man she would marry. But, she groaned inwardly, she didn't love him. Was that something else she was supposed to give up?

'Just don't expect any financial input from me, because you won't be getting it. I won't sign any business cheques and I certainly won't be dipping into my savings.' She shrugged towards her brothers. 'If you can afford to buy in without me, then fine. If you can't, then there's no point in Ross thinking any more about the merger, is there?'

'If you and Ross got married,' Danny clinked the ice in his glass in a very threatening manner, 'none of that would apply.'

Nell felt Claudia wince. She was aware that Sam was watching her.

'Very subtle, Dan.' Ross grinned, then looked at Nell. 'How about it? Marriage first, machines second. Pretty good business proposition all round, I'd say.' He stood up and held out his hand. 'Come on then, Copperknob. Let's talk about it over dinner.'

CHAPTER THREE

Adele Bradley flicked over the potatoes in the roasting pan and wondered if she'd done enough. Nell was bound to be starving. Adele knew, with the universal certainty of mothers, that not only did her daughter not look after herself properly, she also skimped on meals, slept with her make-up on, and never wore a vest.

A good home-cooked Sunday roast, Adele thought as she closed the oven door, was just what Nell needed. Not these convenience things that tasted of cardbord and chemicals and got lasered into life in the microwave. Adele tossed the oven gloves on top of the draining board in disgust. That wasn't how the Bradley women did things. Every Sunday, no matter where they were, she'd produced a full roast meal for her family and the gaff lads – and still had enough for cold cuts and bubble-and-squeak on Monday.

She fanned herself with one of the Sunday supplements. A roast meal, a warm day, and a hot flush did very little for her composure. She reached for the massed ranks of evening primrose capsules and vitamin B, scooped a handful, swallowed them with the remains of a glass of beer, and blew upwards on her damp face. The daytime hot flushes she could just about cope with; the night sweats were quite another matter.

Nell was always banging on about the benefits of HRT, but Adele wasn't sure she'd be happy about filling her body with something extracted from the waste matter of horses. No, she'd cope as her mother had coped, and her mother before her. Women's Troubles, it had been called then. As far as Adele was concerned, it still should be. Along with menstruation and childbirth. She was pretty sure that if the male menopause was physical as well as mental, someone would have done something about it by now. Men had such low tolerance levels. Mind you, it wasn't merely the matter of the discomfort, her entire body seemed to alternate without warning between total exhaustion and firing on overdrive. Adele sighed heavily. This was a twitchy period. She was beginning to get restless again. She needed something to take up the slack of her energy.

It had taken Adele some time to settle down to retirement in Highcliffe. Born in a living wagon in a field outside Banbury, and able to trace her travelling history back through generations, she'd felt nothing but pity for the punters who went home every night to the same house; who looked out each morning on the same view; who knew exactly who they'd see each day. Her life was mobile, ever-changing, and she relished the challenge of pastures new. She would have confidently wagered the family silver on eventually turning up her toes in a layby somewhere off the A420.

When, following Peter's illness, she was suddenly incarcerated in this huge static house with empty rooms – for the first time in her life Adele had to face the challenge of free-standing furniture – and no prospect of going anywhere ever again, she had almost given up. Almost, but not quite. Capitulation was not a Bradley option, but it had been a pretty close thing.

The porcelain and crystal had been bubble-wrapped in packing cases, the Chinese silk rugs still rolled with sheets of tissue, and Adele had, on that first day, sat on the bare boards of the echoing staircase and cried. Then she'd blown her nose, summoned all her resilience, and spent the next few weeks dragging an equally out-of-water Peter round every country-house sale in Hampshire and Dorset. If they were going to have to live in one place for the rest of their lives, then Adele Bradley was determined that they were going to do it in style.

Now, she thought happily, opening the kitchen door and stepping out into the rainbow riot of her garden, there were more than enough advantages to make up for the lack of travelling. Once the house had been furnished and decorated – possibly with a touch too much embossed gold for the more sober Highcliffe residents – Adele, with time on her hands, had discovered Delia Smith and that she had surprisingly green fingers.

Adele's garden now occupied fifth place in her affections, just behind Delia. Elvis Presley was third. There had been quite a hoo-ha in Highcliffe when, merely days after moving in, Adele and Peter had renamed Sunny Gables – over a hundred years old, groaning with wisteria and with a clifftop view of the sea – Graceland. There was even more of a shemozzle when they'd replaced the sweetly-resonant doorbell with a specially commissioned set of chimes which played the first few bars of 'Love Me Tender'.

Joint top of the list was Peter, of course, and her cat Priscilla. Her children, as well as Claudia, were second. Adele and Peter had been married for thirty-eight years – since she was sixteen – and she was simply sure she'd die without him. Priscilla had joined them not long after they'd moved into Graceland – a small scraggy bundle of grey fur mewing pathetically on the drive. Never having had a pet during her travels, Adele had swooped on the kitten and turned it into her surrogate grandchild.

With Priscilla on her knee, she sat amongst the early geraniums which flourished so well in this mild spot, and looked at her watch. Nell had telephoned over an hour ago to say she was just leaving Broadridge Green, so allowing for traffic she should arrive soon. Adele had stressed that Sunday dinner meant just that. There was still some confusion, she thought, especially amongst her new-found Highcliffe friends, over the naming and timing of meals.

On fair days they had had a crack-of-dawn breakfast; lunch, which was elevenses and probably served up somewhere around nine; dinner at midday; tea just before the fair opened for the evening; and supper when it closed. Adele and Peter had turned up at very peculiar times for their first few social invitations in Highcliffe, and still couldn't see why anyone with any inkling of British cultural history could refer to Sunday's midday meal as lunch. Among the upper classes it had always been dinner because it was the only day of the week that the servants had been given the afternoon off and therefore served the main meal before they left. She'd pointed this out at the WI and Cynthia Hart-Radstock had become quite sniffy about Adele's superior knowledge.

'Slacking again?' Peter Bradley clicked in through the wicket gate that led to the clifftop. 'I thought you'd be slaving over a hot Yorkshire pudding or three. Feeling OK?'

'Fine. Cooler now.' Adele moved up on the seat as he sat beside her. 'Nell should be here at any minute.'

'It's a pity they're not all coming.' Peter lifted his face to the sun. 'It's a long time since we were all together.'

'Best they're not this time.' Adele linked her arm through his, delighted at how well he looked after his morning constitutional along the beach. 'I gather from Nell that there are rumblings. She'd never get a chance to say anything if Danny was here – or Ross.'

'I suppose not. She didn't say what exactly?'

'No, she didn't. You know Nell. Prising things out of her is like getting a winkle out of its shell. I will, though. So, when I tip you the nod, you just vanish. OK?'

'OK.' Peter, who had commanded the fair with a loud voice and even louder curses, and who had been mightily feared by his younger employees for his irascible early-morning temper, was only too aware of his parental role. He may well have been in charge of the business, but Adele ruled the family. 'I'll leave it to you.'

They lapsed into silence, enjoying Priscilla's purring and the heat from the late April sun, listening to the screech of the wheeling gulls, and the distant shushing of the sea on the shingle. It was a far, far cry from the cacophony of the generators, the loud music, the shouts and screams, and the chug of diesel engines. When they'd first retired Adele had been convinced that the silence would send her insane. Now she couldn't imagine how she'd spent her life surrounded by so much noise.

After Peter's second heart attack and the bypass surgery, when the surgeons had told her that he would live healthily into a ripe old age only if he stopped work immediately, life had looked very bleak indeed. Most showpeople, when faced with illness, simply took to their living wagons and still travelled with the fair, merely taking on lighter duties. Peter's doctors had said this wasn't an option. Retirement meant just that; a new life with no stress, no involvement, nothing too strenuous.

Adele thought back to those early days with sadness. Terrified that he would die, they'd spoken to the solicitors and accountants, divided up the fair, and taken their living wagon back to their winter quarters in Fox Hollow. Imprisoned in the empty yard, seeing no one, no longer being involved, Peter had fretted and Adele had worried. It had been a sort of living death. It had been Nell who had suggested a complete move away and who had discovered Highcliffe.

Quaintly beautiful, full of retired people, and close enough to the main route to Fox Hollow, it had seemed ideal. There had been teething troubles, of course; but now, Adele thought contentedly, it was the most perfect place on earth. Peter was growing fitter by the day, they had good friends who were fascinated by their previous way of life – and several acquaintances, of course, who weren't – and Graceland. If only Danny and Claudia would produce a grandchild, Sam would marry someone, and Nell – She sighed. If only Nell would marry Ross Percival. A link between the

Bradleys and the Percivals. A real rung up the showmen's society ladder.

Adele shook her head, making her heavy gold earrings chink wildly. If Nell had wanted to marry Ross she'd have done it by now. Young marriages were still fashionable among travellers and Nell was galloping towards thirty. She was going to have to take her children in hand. She brightened. This would be her new campaign. Something to get her confused hormones into.

'Fancy a gin and tonic?' Peter yawned in the late spring sun. 'Or a beer?'

'Beer, please.' Adele hadn't become completely suburbanised. 'And as you're going into the kitchen, just cast an eye on the cooker. If anything is catching, just –'

'Reach for Delia?' Peter stood up. 'Don't fret, it's only Nell. She'll eat everything you put in front of her.'

Adele watched him as he walked back to the house. She loved him with all her heart – but she hadn't at first. At first she'd hardly known him. Their love had grown. She thought how frightened she'd been on her wedding day, how delighted her parents had been with the match, how welcoming Peter's family had been as they whisked her off into their midst. Her own family, with their ancient archery and their coconut shy and a dilapidated ghost train, had been overwhelmed when the eighteen-year-old Peter Bradley – with his family's three large rides and elevated station in the Showmen's Guild – had come a-courting.

Adele's feelings had not really been a consideration. It was a good match, both families approved, and no sooner had her education finished than her marriage had begun. Pregnant at once and a mother at seventeen, Adele had knuckled down to her new life, her new family, and got to know her new husband.

That's how it was then. Not like now. Not like Nell who wanted to fall in love and share her life with a partner and friend as well as a lover. Nell's secret dreams had not escaped Adele. Very little did. Somehow she and Peter had bred a true romantic. Danny was hard-headed and hard-hearted, much as Adele's father had been; Sam was dreamy but still realistic, head in the clouds but feet on the ground, Adele always thought – a good mixture of both his parents; but Nell . . . If Nell didn't face reality she was probably going to be hurt very badly indeed.

She looked up and smiled as Peter returned with the beers. She hadn't shared her doubts about Nell's happiness with him. She didn't want to worry him unduly. She'd move heaven and earth to solve her family's problems without letting him know. She had almost lost him once and she wasn't going to risk it again.

Peter sat beside her and stretched his legs out towards the crazy-paved path. 'You looked deep in thought. Something bothering you?'

Adele took her glass of beer and nodded. 'Yes. I think we should move those lupins into the centre of the perennial border.'

Nell arrived shortly after one o'clock. Adele watched her daughter slide out of the Volvo with a sinking heart. She'd lost weight. The jeans and white silk shirt clung to her slender body and even from behind the dining-room nets, Adele could see the shadows beneath Nell's eyes. Patting her black hair and straightening her pale pink lambswool sweater, she hurried to open Graceland's front door.

'Hello, love.' They didn't kiss. 'I was getting worried.'

'I came through the New Forest.' Nell smiled at her mother. 'It was really pretty – but very slow. Getting through Lyndhurst was a nightmare. How's Dad?'

'Much better. He's joined the bowls club. You'd think he'd been a flatty all his life.'

'Mum!' Nell winced at the fairground slang. 'You don't tell people round here that's what you call them, do you?'

'Course not.' Adele was hurrying into the kitchen. 'They'd probably think it was Romany, anyway. They're pretty vague about travellers. Still, for flatties they're not a bad bunch.'

'And how are you? Started on the HRT yet?'

30

'No need.' Adele indicated the row of bottles. 'I'm coping, love. Honest.'

Nell peered over the pills and a small forest of herbs on the kitchen window-sill. 'Is Dad out there?'

'Doing as he's told. Sitting. Having a beer and trying to stop his stomach rumbling.'

'It smells wonderful. I wish I had time to cook a proper Sunday roast every week.'

'You should do,' Adele frowned. 'What do you give the lads if you don't cook?'

'I do cook,' Nell watched her mother, now perfectly at home in the sunny kitchen. 'I just don't always do a roast.'

'You'll have to when you get married.' Adele started on the gravy, adding cornflour to the meat juices. Nell, who used granules, looked on in envy. Adele continued to stir vigorously. 'I said, when you get married, you'll have to start cooking properly. Not living out of the freezer and slamming everything in the micro.'

'When I get married,' Nell opened the drawer in the pine dresser that had come from a Ringwood farmhouse and gathered the cutlery, 'my husband will make the gravy. In fact, he'll probably cook the meals, clean the living wagon, take the washing to the launderette, bath the babies –'

'Oh, good,' Adele turned from her stirring, 'there are going to be babies then. And is this paragon going to give birth to them as well?'

'If I had my way, definitely.' Nell dealt out three sets of knives, forks and spoons, and lifted the familiar Gypsy Denbyware from its shelf. 'And of course, he'll be running the rides while I lounge around idly, sipping something dry and white and nibbling chocolate.'

'Sounds bloody boring.' Adele poured the gravy into the Denby boat. 'Can't see Ross settling for that.'

'Ten out of ten, Mother.' Nell stuck out her tongue. 'You should be Jeremy Paxman.'

'So? Has he asked you again? Have you said yes? Is that what this visit is about?'

'Yes. No. Yes and no.'

'Too clever by half.' Adele frowned at her daughter. 'I knew we shouldn't have wasted all that money on your education. Go and shout for your father. Tell him I'm dishing up.'

The meal over, the pink flowers of the Denbyware now merely showing scant traces of roast beef followed by apple sponge, and the conversation having flowed non-committally along with the Lambrusco, Adele suggested that Peter should have a nap while she and Nell toured the garden.

Peter, who had spent the best part of his life working flat-out for twenty hours of each day, still found naps fairly self-indulgent, and was only persuaded to retire to the bedroom by Adele's exaggerated stage winks.

'Totally unsubtle.' Nell was helping her mother stack the dishwasher. 'And stop trying to make the garden sound like Sissinghurst. Anyway, I wouldn't have said anything too outrageous in front of Dad, you know that.'

'Like there's no way on God's earth you're going to marry Ross Percival?'

'Not quite that stridently.' Nell grinned. 'But something along those lines, I suppose. I know that everyone else wants us to marry, including Ross, and even I can't really see any reason why I shouldn't – except that I don't think I want to. And I've just refused to purchase his space-age machinery so he might as well forget the merger.' The smile faded. 'Danny and Sam are bursting a gut to be part of Percivals, and Ross says he can be with us at Haresfoot in July – and I don't know what to do! Oh, hell, Mum . . .'

Adele, who had been waiting for this moment, held out her arms. Nell folded herself against the lambswool bosom, just as she had from childhood, and gave a shuddering sigh.

'There, there.' Adele stroked her daughter's hair. 'It can't be that bad.'

It was though, Adele thought afterwards as Nell filled the

kettle for the post-mortem cup of tea. Every bit as bad as she'd feared. Of course, the simple solution would be for Nell to forget all her silly notions and marry Ross – especially now he was offering them such a good deal. How Danny – and to a lesser extent Sam – would love that. And how they would both loathe their sister for evermore if she prevented their opportunity for expansion.

Just where Nell had got this longing to preserve the old ways, Adele didn't know. Both she and Peter would have loved to build up the fair, buy new rides, move into the big-time. It had never been within their scope. But now it was being handed to their children on a gold-leafed Royal Albert platter, and Nell didn't want it. Adele watched her daughter setting the Gypsy cups and saucers on the tray. If Nell had been born a flatty, she thought with some disquiet, she'd be on protest marches, chaining herself to trees, and hurling stones at JCBs. Where on earth had they gone wrong?

'Say something.' Nell was twirling the silver sugar tongs wildly. 'Tell me what you think.'

'What I think,' Adele said carefully, 'will make no difference at all, Nell, and you know it. But for what it's worth – your father and I have no qualms about Bradleys moving into the premier league. Danny's right – the dodgems, paratrooper and waltzer are pretty old hat these days. Oh, I know they give you a more than comfortable living, but you're in business. Think what the new rides would mean. True, you'd probably lose some of the traditional village gaffs, but you must consider the future – the next generation of Bradleys.'

'What?' Nell wrinkled her nose. 'Which new generation? If – and I mean if – I married Ross, our kids would be Percivals. Sam is still playing the field, and Danny and Claudia have been married for nearly ten years, for God's sake!'

Adele, cuddling Priscilla, bit her lip. 'Haven't they gone for any of this test-tube stuff? I've tried asking diplomatically, of course.'

'Mum!' Nell snorted with laughter. 'You're about as diplomatic as Saddam Hussein! I can imagine your diplomatic questions. "Not fallen yet? Is everything all right downstairs? Don't you think you should get yourselves sorted before it's too late?"'

'I'm not that bad.' Adele had the grace to blush. 'And you're changing the subject. OK, maybe there aren't children now, but there will be. And fairs are dying out. We're in competition with every conceivable – if you'll pardon the pun – other leisure organisation now. And housing and industrial estates are swamping traditional fair fields. Things have got to change, Nell, if our business is to survive. Ross Percival is offering you not only the security of marriage, but also the chance to prosper. I think you'd be a fool to turn him down.'

CHAPTER FOUR

It wasn't until she was through Newbury and on the homeward stretch of the A34 that Nell realised that her mother hadn't mentioned the state of Danny and Claudia's marriage. The jungle drums of the Showmen's Guild hadn't reached Highcliffe yet, she thought with some relief. Anyway, she'd given Adele more than enough to chew over. And her own super-king-sized problems far outweighed those of Danny and Claudia.

She'd really thought her parents would have backed her – or at least understood her reasons for not wanting to accept Ross's suggestion. Now, she realised, as she slotted in and out of the two lanes of early-evening traffic, she was entirely on her own. Danny and Sam had leapt at Ross's offer, and expected her to pool her financial resources with theirs to buy into the new ride. They thought Ross Percival and his wealth and his burning ambition – not to mention his hydraulically-operated machine – would be part of the Bradley set-up before the end of the season.

'Which, of course, all makes good sense,' she said to herself and the rear window of a twenty-mile-an-hour Robin Reliant. 'And I suppose I'll just have to toe the party line – whether I like it or not. It would be so much easier if I loathed and detested Ross – but I don't. I can carry on refusing to sign the company cheques, and donate my entire savings to the Cats' Protection League, but I've got a feeling Ross Percival will still find some way round it.' She glanced into the driving mirror. The freckles glanced back. 'Oh, sod it – I think you might just be looking at the next Mrs Percival.'

The Robin Reliant seemed unimpressed with the magnitude of this statement.

As they swept on to one of the downhills of the A34's switchback the three-wheeler reached an unsteady thirty. Indicating to overtake, Nell had notched up a gear and accelerated when her mobile phone burst into a distant and tinny version of 'The Ride of the Valkyries' from the depths of her handbag.

'Oh, brilliant.' She rattled past the Reliant which seemed to have at least six people inside. 'Just hang on.'

Much to the Reliant driver's irritation she pulled in in front of him and then indicated to take the West Ilsley turn. The Robin Reliant flew past her with much light-flashing, horn-blaring, and two-fingered salutes.

Nell pulled into a gateway, scrabbled through her bag, and lodged the phone under her chin. 'This had better be good.'

'My, my, we are grumpy,' Claudia teased. 'What's happened to your body-clock? I thought you were always a sunny bunny by tea-time. Or did Mama Bradley give you a hard time?'

'Claudia!'

'What? Oh, right. Yeah – it's important. Dead important in fact. We've run out of milk.'

Nell glowered into her mobile phone. 'Please tell me that's some sort of code for someone's just nicked the dodgems?'

'Nah. We've really run out of milk. All of us. And you know what Broadridge Green is like on a Sunday – nowhere open. And we're pulling out tomorrow morning and without milk for the Coco-Pops there'll be riots and –'

'Claudia! Get the lads to go and find some. You go and find some. Borrow some from Mr and Mrs Mac. Steal some if you have to. God, the possibilities are endless!'

'The lads are all down the pub, the Macs pulled out half an hour ago because they want to get to Oakton early to see some friends, and I'm,' she sighed, 'unfortunately otherwise engaged.'

'What do you mean otherwise – oh,' Nell blushed. 'Right. So why ring me now?'

'Because Danny phoned Highcliffe and your ma said you'd be nearly home and he thought you could pull into the services.'

'OK.' Nell wanted to end the conversation. If Claudia and Danny were indulging in a bit of afternoon delight – well, early-evening delight – then she wasn't going to be the one to stop them. 'I'll find somewhere. Will six pints be enough?'

But Claudia had already hung up.

Nell sat for a moment, the constant swish of the traffic on the A34 behind her, and the peace and the tranquillity of the downland villages ahead. She hadn't much choice. She started the car and headed off between vivid green and yellow fields just visible through frothy clouds of cow parsley.

Not, she thought, as she edged the Volvo along a high-banked lane, that she was expecting to find a convenient Enid Blyton-type shop, still open on a Sunday evening, staffed by ruddy-cheeked farmers' wives in gingham pinafores, and with the contents of a major Sainsbury's stacked to the low-beamed ceiling. She knew she'd have to backtrack on to the main road eventually, but right now anything was preferable to returning to Broadridge Green, Claudia and Danny's pulled curtains, and Sam looking like a kicked puppy because she didn't want to put her savings into the Ice-Breaker.

The villages with their duck-ponds and rustic benches, their chestnut trees and their thatched pubs, offered very little in the way of milk, but plenty in the way of pleasure. Humming along with something melodic on the radio, Nell began to relax. Therefore when the crossroads appeared with no warning from behind a clump of sycamores, she simply wasn't prepared. Slamming on the brakes to avoid a meandering tractor, and peering in vain for a signpost, Nell realised she was seriously lost. Not that anyone would notice until tomorrow's breakfast, when the lack of milk for the Coco-Pops would probably cause more concern than her absence.

'Backwards, forwards, right or left?' She offered the choice to the honey-voiced radio presenter who ignored her. 'OK, then. Straight ahead. Into the unknown.'

Pretty soon it seemed like left or right or even backwards would have been a preferable option, as the Volvo bumped along a deeply rutted unmade road. Small cottages peeped through willows, and several cows swished lazy tails. Still, Nell thought, cows meant farms, and farms meant people and someone might just be able to tell her where the hell she was.

A crop of outbuildings in the middle of a distant field indicated that there might indeed be human life of some sort close at hand. Nell increased her speed to a reckless twenty, severely tested the Volvo's suspension, and eventually braked to a rather dusty halt.

On closer inspection, the outbuildings were ramshackle to say the least. Condemned was the word that sprang most readily to mind. But the cluster of vehicles parked haphazardly around them pointed to some sort of habitation. It wasn't until she was actually about to haul at the door of the nearest and largest barn that niggling thoughts of ritual sacrifice, witch trials, cock-fighting, and other rural pastimes, surged to the surface. Maybe this wasn't going to be the most brilliant idea she'd ever had. Hesitating for a fraction of a second, Nell opened the door.

At least a dozen men, all with black-smeared faces and wearing gloves, turned to stare at her.

Jesus, Nell thought, it's the hide-out for today's equivalent of the Great Train Robbers. It's drug-running. It's a terrorist cell. It's –

'Bugger off.' The nearest man, who had a woolly hat pulled low over his eyes and a crowbar in his hand, greeted her in a far from genial fashion. 'We've said all there is to say. Now clear off.'

'Er, yes. Right.' Nell fumbled backwards for the door, watching the crowbar. 'Er – um, my mistake.'

Nobody moved but they still continued to stare. The crowbar continued to swing from side to side. Nell continued to back off. Where the hell was the door-catch? Her eyes were becoming more accustomed to the dim light, and forgetting everything she'd seen on *Crimewatch* about getting a good look at ne'er-do-wells so that you'd recognise them later in the queue at Tesco, she peered past the men into the gloom of the massive barn.

With a wave of relief her fingers closed round the rusty door-catch and she tugged it open behind her, allowing a shaft of dusty sunlight to spill across the towering interior. 'So sorry to have disturbed you – I'm really sorry.' She stared, then clapped her hand to her mouth. 'Oh, my God! It's a Savage!'

Twelve pairs of eyes blinked. The crowbar stopped moving.

'You're not Press?' The woolly hat and crowbar sounded a bit disappointed. 'You're not from the Council?'

'Nothing so exciting.' Nell's mouth was dry. 'Is that – um – this – all yours?'

The barn, illuminated orginally only by one fluorescent tube but helped now by the daylight, was stacked from floor to ceiling with machinery. Old machinery. Very old machinery. And most of it steam-driven.

Nell worked some saliva into her mouth. 'Er – what is this, exactly? Some sort of museum?'

'Does it look like a museum, dear?' A thin face had appeared from behind the man with the crowbar. 'We're the Downland Preservation Trust. Or at least, we are until next month.'

Nell's eyes were glued to the almost-complete and half-painted set of gallopers which took up a quarter of the floor space. She would have to pinch herself in a minute. 'It is a Savage, isn't it?'

'Built in King's Lynn around 1907.' A plump man in

greasy overalls seemed eager to show off his knowledge. 'Two careful owners and then total disrepair for the last thirty years. Pity really. It only needs a few more months to be up and running.'

Nell gazed around the barn. There were the skeletons of at least three fairground rides from possibly the 1920s, a small agricultural traction engine in bits, a larger showman's engine minus its wheels, the track of what she was sure was a caterpillar ride, and the cars from a ghost train.

'But where did it all come from?'

'We've bought it over the years.' The man with the crowbar had pushed his hat away from his eyes and now looked almost avuncular. 'The stuff we've already restored we take round steam rallies, you know? These –' he spread his arms wide, 'will never be finished now.'

'Why not?' Nell walked closer to the gallopers. 'I mean, they're amazing. Perfect. Three abreast and all horses – no chariots or cockerels. I've never seen anything so beautiful. So why can't you finish them?'

The thin-faced man shrugged. 'We've been compulsorily purchased. This is smack bang on the route of the new bypass. The farmer took the money and ran weeks ago. We're being evicted at the beginning of June. Real bugger, but there you are. We can't find anywhere else big enough to house it all in the time available, and anyway we can't afford to move it. So we're putting it all up for auction.' His voice was bitter. 'We thought you were from the Press, see. Or the Council. They keep checking up to make sure we're not intending to stay.'

'We've thought about it.' The man with the crowbar had laid it down and was wiping his hands on an oily rag. 'Barricading ourselves in and that. But, what's the point? We've still got some completed pieces to hang on to – and the rest should go to good homes.'

Nell stretched out a hand and touched one of the massive and as yet unpainted galloping horses. The nostrils were flared, the mane streaming. The wood was satin-smooth. 'And if they don't?'

'They'll be scrapped.'

Nell winced at the harshness in his voice. 'But that won't happen, surely? They'll go into preservation?'

'Yes, they'll go into preservation. Probably spend the rest of their days in static splendour in some stately home. We'd always hoped they'd have more of a life than that.'

Nell moved carefully amongst the pots of paint, the jars of linseed oil and varnish, the dozens of brushes. The colours were authentic: golds, rose pinks, turquoises, glossy greens; some of the shields and top centres and rounding boards simply needed renovating, others were being copied religiously from the originals. There were scenes of waterfalls and castles, dragons and damsels, bears, lions and tigers, forests and lakes, fairy queens and lance-bearing knights; each one a perfect miniature masterpiece. Half the horses were finished; the remainder leaned against each other, galloping on the spot, still waiting to be restored to their former glory.

'Did you do all this? This painting?'

'We all do something,' the man offered. 'We've all got skills.'

He introduced his colleagues and reeled off a list of names and professions. There seemed to be Bobs and Jims and Bens, a Jack, a Harry, a Dennis, a Percy and a Fred. There were painters and carpenters, engineers and electricians, skilled and unskilled, all preserving the glories of the past.

'How did you know they were a Savage set?' Dennis, the crowbar and woolly hat, asked. 'Are you a fan?'

Nell nodded. 'Sort of. I'm so sorry that you've got to sell them.'

'Not as sorry as we are. And if you didn't come here deliberately, and you're not a snooper, what exactly did you want?'

Overcome by so much bygone beauty amidst all the dust and decay, Nell couldn't quite remember. 'Oh, right. Yes. I was just going to ask for directions back to the A34.'

'Easy.' The thin-faced man, who was a Jim, smiled and proceeded to tell her. 'OK?'

'Fine. Thanks.' Nell looked around her again. 'I wish there was something I could do.'

'You could nobble next week's lottery for us.' Dennis grinned. 'Other than that, find us one or two preservation-freak millionaires. Simple, really.'

'Is it woodworm-free? Rot-free?' Nell simply couldn't get over the set of gallopers. 'And where on earth did you discover it?'

'It's completely sound now. Both the mechanics and the woodwork. We've treated all the problems. We've even had the rods dipped and re-brassed. It's just cosmetic work left. And the painting, of course. We were tipped off about them by a preservation freak in Cornwall. They'd been lying in someone's smallholding for years.'

'How much did you give for them?'

'Are you sure you're not from the Press?'

'Just curious.' Nell tried to quell the excitement in her voice. Tried to stop the outrageous idea from forming inside her head. 'I – um – wondered how much you were hoping to get at the auction?'

Dennis shrugged. 'Fifty grand – without the organ. Sixty-five with.'

'There's an organ?' Nell exhaled. 'An original? Gavioli? Marenghi? Limonaire?'

'You are definitely a fairground groupie. Want to see?'

She followed him across the barn, still being careful not to knock anything over. The others watched her reaction as he drew back the corner of a towering tarpaulin.

'Bloody hell.' Nell closed her eyes for a second then opened them again, taking in the brilliant colours and the massed ranks of pipes, drums and xylophones. 'It's a Gavioli. It's – it's absolutely stunning.'

Reverently she touched the ornately carved proscenium which housed the organ. It stretched high above them, the painted pillars studded with light bulbs, surrounded by outrageous figures: Harlequins and Columbines, bosomy shepherdesses and moustachioed soldiers, all waiting to leap into life. She hadn't seen anything quite so spectacular for years.

Her voice was little more than a whisper. 'And – um – have you got music?'

Percy bustled across to a tall cupboard and threw the door open with a flourish. It was stacked from floor to ceiling with fat and dusty cardboard music books. He beamed proudly, like the parent of an 'A' student on open evening. 'The originals are mostly Chiappas, of course. We reckon that some of the more recent ones have been cut by Arthur Prinsen. They all play. Would you like to look?'

Nell nodded. Each book, inches-thick concertina'd card-board folds, with the notes for every one of the organ's orchestral instruments cut into them, was heavy in her hands. The tunes ranged from hymns, through dozens of marches, to show-stoppers from Irving Berlin and Gershwin, and even included several modern pieces and overtures. It was like discovering the Holy Grail.

Aware that they were all watching her with growing suspicion, she turned away from the music books. 'My grandparents had gallopers. I loved them. The noise, the colour – well, everything, really. They got rid of them years ago, when I was very young. Scrapped them. Too heavy and cumbersome to build up and pull down, and far too expen-sive to run, apparently. And no one wanted to work on them. They bought an octopus and a set of hurricane jets instead.'

'Hell's teeth,' Dennis said. 'Even they're collector's items these days.'

Percy squinted again. 'So you're a traveller?'

'London Section. We're based in Oxfordshire mostly.' She smiled at him. 'I'm Petronella Bradley. Nell.'

'Ah, right. Bradleys. Nice little outfit. I suppose it would be too much to hope that you're looking for a set of gallopers, a caterpillar and a ghost train to complete your business?'

'If only,' Nell said sadly. 'Unfortunately my partners are intent on looking into the future – not back to the past.'

'Shame,' Dennis said. 'Still, there's no real call for these any more among travellers. Not commercially viable, as you said. The best we can hope for is that they'll fetch a good price at auction and we'll be able to visit them some time.'

Percy was busy tucking the tarpaulin back round the Gavioli organ, shielding the pipes, the gaudy paintwork, the ornate carvings, from the worst of the dust. Nell sighed. 'I hope so too. Thanks for showing me – and for the directions.'

'You're welcome.'

They all waved cheerily as Nell headed for the door. One of the Jims opened it for her. 'Maybe if your partners change their minds, we might see you at the auction.'

'Not much chance of that, I'm afraid. But good luck anyway.'

Following Jim's – or was it Bob's? – directions, Nell found the A34 quite quickly. Darkness was gathering from the high swell of the Downs behind her as she drove back towards Broadridge Green, and a rain-bearing wind buffeted the Volvo. Huge lorries swept past, cars overtook, and reality ceased to exist. The gallopers, as they had been, as they might be again, rose and fell in her mind. The rich orchestral notes from the Gavioli organ struck deeper chords than anything on the radio. She knew she'd dream of them tonight and wake feeling cheated and angry. If only she could persuade Ross to buy the Savage and the Gavioli with the Percival millions, then she might just test her mother's theories on love and marriage and marry him tomorrow. Oh, get real, she told herself. You wouldn't marry Ross Percival if he had a twisted brass rod through his back and played 'Entry of the Gladiators' in ninety-eight keys!

Broadridge Green arrived far too quickly, Nell turned in alongside the red, blue and yellow trucks. They'd pulled down the previous evening ready for Monday morning's move to Oakton. There were no signs of life from any of the living wagons, and the Beast Wagon stood in darkness. They must have all gone to the pub, Nell thought, and knew she wouldn't join them. She didn't want to hear about Ice-

Breakers and Galaxy Invaders, about the Percivals' plans for the future, or even about Claudia's rejuvenated sex-life. She wanted to curl up and remember the Savage and the Gavioli; to imagine what it would be like to own something so beautiful; to see her name picked out in gold leaf . . .

Oh bugger, Nell thought as she locked the Volvo. She'd forgotten to buy the milk.

CHAPTER FIVE

Sex, especially with the wrong person, was seriously overrated, Claudia thought as she watched Danny swagger into the shower. Ages and ages of fumbling and pressing, groping and writhing; and all the way through it you had to look so damn grateful, when a cup of tea and a good book would have been far more enjoyable.

She pushed her tumbled dark hair away from her eyes and slid to the edge of the bed. The early-morning sounds of Oakton were poking inquisitive fingers through the open window, and Claudia wondered if anyone had been outside. She hoped not. Danny's laboured breathing would have left little to the imagination. Fumbling through the drawer in the bedside table she found the packet of pills, popped out Wednesday's, and swallowed it quickly.

Danny, grinning and towelling his hair, appeared in the doorway. 'Nice day. Sun's hot already. Should get a good crowd – especially if we open early this afternoon. Loadsamoney!'

Claudia smiled weakly at the ancient joke and wandered to the window. Still naked, she peered out on Oakton through the gaps in the massed ranks of living vans and lorries, and wished that Danny could have mentioned love or passion or delight or bloody anything other than sodding money. It was always sodding money.

'Come away from the window.' His voice was sharp. 'People can see you.'

'What people? There's no one about. Everyone's still asleep except the Macs. And the work-going Oaktonians aren't going to be interested in my body, are they? They're far too intent on getting to their desks or their shop counters.'

Oakton was not one of the Bradleys' favourite stops. An ugly, sprawling town had been built up around the original village, and the fair site had been squeezed to the edge of a new housing estate on one side and a small and soulless shopping parade on the other. And neither of these neighbours welcomed the visitors with cups of tea and bonhomie. As it was an ancient hiring fair, the Bradleys joined forces with several other showmen, so the dodgems, paratrooper and waltzer were flanked by a twist, a speedway, a helter-skelter, and several smaller rides, while the entire site was ringed with sideshows and food stalls.

The Oaktonians spent well, but the Bradleys had more complaints about noise and mess and environmental pollution here than anywhere else on their travels. The Town Council had been actively trying to have the fair banned for several years, but had been prevented from doing so by the annual production of a charter dating from the 1600s. There were mutterings in *The World's Fair* that Oakton's newly-elected MP was going to raise questions in the House. Already wildly discontented, Claudia absolutely loathed the place.

'This might be it, you never know.' Danny walked up behind her and slid his arms round her waist, his fingers splaying over the flatness of her stomach.

She tried not to jerk away from him. He wasn't going to start again, was he? 'Might be what?'

'Our baby.' Danny's fingers tightened. 'You could be pregnant right now.'

She was glad he couldn't see her face. 'Oh, yeah. That'd be great.'

He moved away again. 'It's what I want more than anything. A son to carry on the business.'

'It might be a girl.'

'Then we'd have to keep trying, wouldn't we?'

'That's very sexist. Look at Nell. She's as involved as you and Sam in the firm. And she works just as hard.'

Danny paused in buttoning his shirt. 'But Nell has no ambition. I mean, she'd like to jog along just as we are – with three standard rides and a lot of past-their-best side stuff. And why?' He pulled a mimicking face. 'Because it's the way it's always been done. Crap. That's the trouble with women – they get all gooey and sentimental.' He patted Claudia's bare bottom on his way out of the bedroom. 'No, I'm going to have to have a son to carry on in the true Bradley tradition. And when Ross Percival comes in with us then it'll be one hell of a business to hand over to my boy, won't it?'

Claudia had long ago stopped feeling guilty. It was her body, after all. Her life. Danny had spent a great deal of time and money on fertility tests – all of which gave them a clean bill of health. Danny couldn't understand why his thrice-weekly performances had not resulted in a son and heir.

Obtaining regular prescribed medication of any sort was not that easy for travellers. All the showmen had private health cover of course, and the gaff lads didn't dare be ill; but apart from being registered with the local GP in Fox Hollow, the Bradleys' winter quarters' village, emergency treatment had to be obtained as and when it could on the road. Claudia always made sure she had a three-month supply of contraceptive pills before the start of each season, and returned for a top-up at least once during the summer.

Once she'd cleaned and tidied the living wagon, the hours until afternoon opening at two o'clock stretched pleasurably ahead. Claudia had perfected the art of deceptive housekeeping by straightening cushions, flicking around the visible surfaces with a perfunctory duster and spraying a good squirt of Mr Sheen into the air five minutes before Danny came in. It gave her tons of free time. The ground rules in their relationship had been set years ago. The living wagon was her domain, the waltzer, his. It suited Claudia nicely. Danny never involved her in testing the rides, cleaning out the waltzer cars, or hosing down the platforms. But then, Danny never involved her in anything.

Claudia pulled on a short black skirt over her bare legs, tucked in a tight scarlet T-shirt, and found her favourite stiletto sandals. As soon as she'd got her face on, she'd go and knock 'em dead in Oakton's precinct. It was a game she played all the time. Painting her face, accentuating her body, knowing that men looked at her and wanted her. It made her feel good. Nell was continually warning her that it was dangerous, but she always knew when to stop. There was no harm in look but don't touch, was there? Not that Nell was likely to say anything today. She'd been distracted ever since she'd come back from Highcliffe. Claudia was in no doubt that Adele had called a three-line whip and instructed her daughter to marry Ross Percival pretty damn quickly.

Anyway, she thought, as she teetered away from the living wagon, carefully avoiding the fairground because Danny would throw a king-sized fit if he saw her, it wasn't her fault that other men fancied her when Danny didn't. Oh, sure, he jumped on her with boring regularity – but only, Claudia knew, because each time he thought he might produce the heir to the Bradley empire.

She'd loved him very much when they'd married but, without nurturing, her love had withered and died. Danny only cared about the rides, about the business, about making more and more money. She was young and attractive and needed to be reassured. And if Danny wouldn't do it, then – she shrugged. It wasn't going to hurt anyone, was it?

Oakton's concrete-and-glass mall offered few amenities. A selection of familiar shops, a very new pub made to look very old, a chip shop and a tea-room tweely called Alice's Pantry. This was Claudia's first port of call. It was a brief stopover.

Settling herself at a window table with a pink cloth and three artificial carnations in a plastic vase, Claudia ordered a cup of black coffee. Alice, who was sixteen stone and had an incipient moustache, served the coffee with a sour glower. Claudia smiled sweetly in return, crossed her legs, leaned back in her bentwood chair and surveyed the top half of Oakton through several yards of chintz.

After five minutes of staring at very little except a faded blue sky above a relentlessly concrete horizon, and becoming less than amused by the disapproving looks from Oakton's twin-setted matrons who obviously resented Alice's Pantry being infiltrated by gypsies, Claudia paid for her coffee, sucked in her cheeks and undulated past the tables of tweed skirts and sturdy brogues.

'Tell yer fortune for a quid, dearie?'

Suddenly the matrons found something very exciting to study on the pink tablecloths. One or two tightened their grips on their handbags.

Giggling, Claudia almost skipped into the precinct. To her joy she had discovered that Oakton had invested in a selection of cheap and cheerful shops, all supplying her favourite skimpy clothes. She enjoyed shopping; enjoyed spending money as much as Danny enjoyed making it. Her credit cards were always right up to the limit. Claudia plunged recklessly in and out of the fitting rooms with a mounting adrenalin rush.

'Fancy a drink?'

She shifted her carrier bags and peered over her shoulder. It wasn't the first time she'd been propositioned in the street. She had a selection of witty put-down lines all ready for such occasions. 'Oh, hell. Hi, Terry. I was just going to say you couldn't afford me.'

Terry widened his choirboy eyes. 'Not on the wages your old man pays I couldn't. So, do you?'

'Why not?'

She followed him to Ye Olde Home From Home and winced at the dark brown paintwork, the dark yellow walls and the preponderance of polystyrene oak beams. There was even, she noticed with some amusement, a plastic spider and web. Gaming machines winked and shuffled in neon brilliance in one gloomy corner, and a rather depressing knot of young men with beer bellies and sleeveless T-shirts seemed to be taking up the bar. They all turned and stared at Claudia, who stared back.

'Go and sit down,' Terry advised. 'They look like they haven't seen a woman in months.'

Claudia sat. Terry was gorgeous; she and Nell had decided when he'd joined them at the beginning of the season that he looked like one of those Australian soap boys. This would do her ego no harm at all. It was only when she watched him walking back, a drink in each hand, that she realised he hadn't even asked her what she wanted.

'Vodka and orange. No ice.'

'How on earth did you know that?' This was very impressive.

'It pays to know how to please your employers.' Terry sat opposite her, crossing lean denim legs. 'I always make a point of doing a bit of research.'

She smiled and sipped her drink. Danny would go ballistic – so, she thought briefly, would Nell and Sam. The gaff lads were not in their class socially. One didn't, ever, mix with them. Claudia smiled to herself. What the hell . . .

'Are you thinking that your old man would string me up if he saw us?' Terry had swallowed half his lager.

'Are you a mind-reader too?'

'Nah,' he grinned and pushed the sun-streaked floppy hair away from his eyes. 'Just used to it. I know my place.'

Claudia sipped the vodka again. It was strong. Probably a double. She was pretty sure that Terry couldn't afford it unless he'd been short-changing the punters. 'Which is?'

'Doing what I'm told, working my balls off for a pittance, being extremely grateful for that bug-infested van we live in, and having more freedom than most guys even dream of.'

They smiled at each other. Claudia looked away first. This was dangerous ground. 'So, where are the others?'

'Testing the rides. Sweeping off the platforms. Washing down the cars.'

'So why aren't you?'

'Because I'm here with you.'

Good God. Panicking slightly, Claudia looked at him again. 'Do you mean you followed me? Deliberately?'

Terry laughed. 'Nah. Don't sweat. Not that it's not a nice idea. Actually, your old man sent me to the post office to pick up the mail.' He patted the back pocket of his jeans. 'I was on my way back when I saw you. Disappointed?'

'Desperately.' Claudia sighed with relief. 'So I suppose you really ought to be getting back?'

'Yeah.' Terry glanced up at the pretend-antique clock on the pretend-nicotine-stained wall. 'Mind, those post office queues can be bastards, can't they? I'm sure we've got time for one more.'

They had two. More than slightly squiffy, Claudia swung the carrier bags with jaunty nonchalance as they drifted back between the looming rides. In an hour's time the fair would burst into sham opulence, with noise and lights and music and excitement; now it was slumbering silently, conserving its energy.

'Claudia!' Danny's roar made everyone stop and stare. 'Where the fuck have you been?'

Claudia wobbled into reverse and tried to clear her fuddled brain. Too much vodka had given her false confidence. Terry bit his lip and looked as if he was going to say something. She shook her head. 'Scarper. It's my problem – not yours.' She smiled at her husband and jauntily waved the carrier bags. 'Just doing a bit of shopping.'

Danny, veins knotted, face crimson, was practically speechless. 'Dressed like that? I've seen tarts with more sophistication than that! You look like a cheap whore!'

'Lay off her.' Terry moved between them. 'She looks great an' she was shopping – like she said.'

Without even changing his expression, Danny swung round and hurled his fist at Terry's nose. Terry, younger and more agile, side-stepped the swipe.

'Don't!' Claudia was instantly sober. 'Danny! For God's sake!'

'Get indoors! Get that muck off your face! Get some decent clothes on!'

Everyone had gathered round. The Macs, Sam, the gaff lads, most of the other showmen, and even several Oaktonians who were drifting about staring at the empty rides. Claudia's teeth were chattering.

Still quivering, Danny pointed a stubby finger at Terry. 'And you can piss off! Go! Now!'

'You've got it all wrong.' Terry's voice was quiet. 'And I'm not going anywhere until I know you won't lay into her the minute you've got her on her own.'

'I don't hit women.' Danny's voice was dangerously level. 'But I'll kill you.'

'Danny!' Claudia brushed away her tears. 'We weren't together. He wasn't – it isn't – Don't sack him.'

'Bollocks!' Danny snarled. 'You think I'm going to keep your toy boy around for you to play with, do you?'

Sam stepped forward and grabbed Terry's shoulder. 'Mick and Alfie need a hand on the dodgems. Two of the cars are knacked. Go on. Now.' He shrugged at Danny. 'We don't sack staff without it being a joint decision – and we don't do anything on the spur of the moment. Stop washing your bloody dirty linen in public, Dan.'

With a last anxious glance at Claudia, Terry headed for the dodgems. The Mackenzies were all shaking their heads. The remaining showmen, most of whom knew about Danny's temper, grinned openly. The Oaktonians, who were pretty sure that the fair was run by tinkers and savages, were delighted to see their theories had been proved correct.

Claudia fled to the sanctuary of her living wagon. Danny was a crass, jealous, short-tempered, evil bastard, she thought savagely, as she ripped off the false eyelashes and wiped away her smeared make-up. He had to spoil everything. She practically fell off the stilt-high sandals, kicking them under the William Morris sofa; then, ripping off the T-shirt and skirt, she wrapped herself in her black-and-scarlet kimono.

'Bugger him,' she muttered belligerently. The vodka and the shouting had made her head ache. 'I'm not bloody going to look like the frump of the year and stand in that damn hoopla all day for him! He'll have to find some other mug to –' She stopped. There was someone at the door. 'Sod off.'

The door opened a crack and Claudia sighed. It was probably Nell being dispatched to read the riot act. 'Go away. You're not exactly lily-white are you? And I wasn't doing anything wrong.'

'I'm sure you weren't.' Sam closed the door behind him. 'But then I'm not your extremely possessive husband, am I? Are you OK?'

Claudia shrugged. Her brother-in-law was invariably the peacemaker in these disputes. 'I thought you were Nell. Yeah, I suppose so. Now clear off.'

'Not yet.' Sam perched on the edge of the sofa. 'Nell's gone into Oxford on business. She didn't tell me why, but I'm hoping she's seen sense and it's something to do with investing in the Ice-Breaker. I thought I'd better check that you weren't contemplating suicide – and don't keep frowning at me like that. Are you sure you're all right?'

Claudia was irritated. 'Sure. Positive. I've been married to him for ten years. I know how his temper works.'

'Then why do you do it? Dress up and flaunt yourself? You know it annoys him.'

'Yes, it does.' Claudia narrowed her eyes. 'But I enjoy it. Both the dressing-up and the annoying.' She paused. 'You're not going to boot Terry out, are you?'

'Would it bother you?'

'Yes, it bloody would. He's a nice lad. He didn't do anything and I'm sick of Danny thinking –'

'That you're having an affair with him?'

'For God's sake!' Claudia plonked down on the sofa. 'Of course I'm not. You know I'm not. Danny always thinks that I'm leaping into bed with every man who looks at me.'

Sam shrugged. 'Well, you do give that sort of impression.'

Claudia wrapped the kimono more tightly round herself. 'I dress up because I want to. For me. Not for anyone else. OK?'

Sam leaned back. 'Have you ever been unfaithful to Danny?'

She gave a self-deprecating laugh. 'Do you think I'd tell you if I had?'

'Probably not.'

'Well, no, then. I haven't.' Claudia scrubbed at the remaining streaks of mascara and took a deep breath. 'Danny is the only man I've ever slept with. That's probably half the trouble.'

Sam didn't say anything. Claudia gave him a sideways glance. He and Danny – the Bradley men – chalk and cheese. She smiled. 'Anyway, we're all a bit unconventional, aren't we? Me and Danny fighting like cat and dog. Nell playing at being the career woman and out-bulling Ross, while we all know she's really hopelessly romantic and dreaming of white satin and orange blossom. And you never seem to keep any woman longer than five minutes. It's hardly the way things are set out in the Showmen's Guild Guide to Relationships, is it?'

'No.' Sam shrugged. 'But I suppose we've all got our reasons.'

They sat in silence, then Claudia said, 'I used to think you were gay.'

'Why the hell did you think that?'

'Dunno.' Claudia wrinkled her nose. 'Oh, you look butch enough, and you're bloody tough when you want to be. I suppose it was just because you never seem to stay very long in a relationship.'

'And that's being gay, is it? That's not being stuffed-full of testosterone and playing the field?'

'I never looked at it that way.' Claudia stretched her long bare legs out in front of her. 'So, if we're having a soul-searching session, how come you've never settled down? You've had masses of girlfriends – and yet you never stick with any of them. Why not?'

55

'You've really no idea?'

Claudia shook her head. 'No. Tell me.'

'Simple really, although I'm not sure that this is the right time to say so.' Sam tucked her curls behind her ears and kissed her cheek gently. 'I'm in love with you.'

CHAPTER SIX

I t had started to rain. Nell groaned, feeling the first heavy
drops as she headed for the dodgems. This was all she
needed to round off a perfectly horrible day; raining at
six o'clock – just when the Oaktonians might realistically be
planning to spend an evening, and their money, at the fair. If
the storm lasted longer than half an hour, Nell knew they
may as well forget it. Televisions and computer screens
would have won the battle.

The trip to the accountants and the bank manager in
Oxford had been less than fruitful. Yes, the Bradleys' joint
business account was extremely healthy, but of course Nell
did understand that she'd have to have the signatures of her
other partners before making any substantial cash with-
drawal? And yes, her own personal account was certainly
buoyant, but the sum she had mentioned would deplete all
her assets and couldn't be gathered together in one day –
wasn't she being just a mite rash? Then, when she'd returned
to Oakton, she'd heard the story of Danny and Claudia's row
from at least five different sources. Each tale had added
embellishments, culminating with Rio Mackenzie who said
she had it on good authority that Claudia was definitely
expecting Terry's baby.

Danny had refused to discuss it with her, Sam was having

mechanical problems with the paratrooper, and Claudia – Nell shook her head as she scrambled up into the pay-box. Claudia had declined to man the hoopla and was wandering about in a hideous blue tracksuit, her hair scraped back in a plastic headband, and her face scrubbed bare of all make-up. And to cap it all, her mother had phoned. '. . . just on the off-chance, love. To see if you've thought any more about Ross's offer . . .'

'Not much going on, tonight.' Terry, the collar of his leather jacket turned up, was leaning against one of the pillars. 'A few mums and dads with kids – and they'll be gone soon if it don't stop raining. Still, I reckon we did all right this afternoon while it was still sunny.'

Nell stared up at the sky. It was ominously grey. The hard Oakton soil would soon become boggy and slippery and they could kiss goodbye to any profits. She almost wished they'd abandoned Oakton this year and gone to Wantage for the Street Fair – but then Clem Percival owned the Showmen's Guild ground rights there and she was damned if she was going to beg him for vacant sites at the last minute. Nor was she entirely happy at the prospect of Danny and Sam spending any more time than was absolutely necessary with the entrepreneurial Percivals and their ever-ready cheque book.

'Sod it. Let's have some action.' She flashed the lights on the dodgem track, turned the sound system up to brain-splitting, and leaning across yelled in Terry's ear, 'This'll fetch 'em away from *Emmerdale* – even if it is only to complain – and don't move. I want to talk to you.'

'No one can talk over that!' Terry mouthed back. 'An' if it's about this morning – don't bother. I've been threatened by Psycho Danny and warned off by Sam. I don't need your lecture as well.'

Nell reduced Meatloaf's volume slightly. 'I wasn't going to lecture you. Just give you a bit of friendly advice. No doubt Sam told you that it's happened before – before you even joined us. Claudia is a flirt and Danny is pathologically

58

jealous. It's not a good combination. So don't even think about getting involved with her. She is definitely off-limits.'

'Christ.' Terry uncurled himself from the pillar. 'I know that. I like this job and I sure as hell don't want to lose it. I've worked for other firms – and this is like five stars in comparison. Claudia's a nice lady – but she's out of my league.' His eyes widened. 'That, though, certainly isn't –'

Nell followed his gaze. A crowd of schoolgirls, all in sprayed-on denim and Lycra and wearing too much make-up, were huddled under the dodgems' multicoloured canopy trying to avoid the drips. Turning up his collar even more and swaggering à la James Dean, Terry went in for the kill. 'Just in time for the next ride, darlings. Would you like some help with the steering?'

The rain continued. However bright the lights, however loud the music, Nell knew that tonight was going to be a failure. The Macs had given up on the swinging boats, and the juvenile ride rotated sadly with just one or two intrepid toddlers driving fire engines or steering buses watched by proudly waving, but very wet, parents.

'Mrs Bradley?'

Nell, miles away – well, halfway down the A34 and dreaming of the gallopers and the Gavioli, jumped as the voice bellowed in her ear.

'Miss.' She leaned across and shifted the volume control so that the Spice Girls sounded almost melodic. 'Can I help you?'

The tall man with rain dripping from the edges of his trilby and trickling down the very shiny shoulders of his quilted brown anorak, shook his head. 'I want to speak to your father.'

'My father lives on the Dorset coast,' Nell said. This was the final straw. A fairground aficionado who probably collected the serial numbers of the dodgems' plates or something equally obscure. 'He retired two years ago.'

'Ah.' The visitor sucked the damp ends of his moustache. 'Your husband, then.'

'Haven't got one,' Nell said cheerfully. 'Can I help you?'

'HSE.' The man produced a wallet and a Health and Safety identity card. 'Spot-check.'

Shit, bugger, damn, Nell thought, smiling angelically. 'You've picked a good night for it. I thought you lot only appeared on sunny days, and then in pairs like Batman and Robin.'

There was no reaction. Nell tried again. 'Is it something specific? Have you had a complaint?'

'There have been several complaints from the new housing estate.' The Health and Safety Inspector looked as though most of them had involved grievous bodily harm. 'Mostly about noise. Sadly, that's out of our environs.'

Oh, goody. 'So? Is there a problem?'

'Not with the dodgems or the waltzer. They were checked at Broadridge Green, I understand. However, I couldn't find anyone in charge of the paratrooper.'

Sod Sam, Nell thought. He must've sloped off and left Barry or Ted in charge. She prayed to every god she could lay her brain on that the technical hitch had been corrected. Still smiling, she shrugged. 'It's not busy. I expect my brother has gone for a cup of tea. Are you going to inspect it now? I mean, all our safety checks and tests are up to date. We've got the certificates.'

'That's as maybe, but you know we have the power, the authority –'

Nell knew very well. Despite stringent safety checks and engineering tests on every fairground ride before a member of the public ever set foot or bottom on it, and rigorous rechecks each time they built up, and again every day before they opened, the fair was still subject to the dreaded HSE spot-checks at any time of the day or night.

'I'll see if I can help you.' She stretched out and bellowed into the microphone, 'Terry! Come up here a minute, please!'

Terry, who was still entertaining the young ladies of Oakton, nipped deftly between the cars and swung himself round the front of the pay-box. 'They've paid every time, Nell. I ain't giving them freebies.'

'What you're giving them isn't my top priority at the moment. Get Mick and that Oakton boy we employed yesterday to collect the money and you take over in here for a sec. You know the ropes. You've watched me enough times.'

'Yeah, sure – but, with the dosh?'

'God, yes.' Pushing past him, Nell almost shoved the damp HSE man out of the pay-box in front of her. 'If there's anything missing I'll know who to blame, won't I?'

The HSE inspector plodded across the wet fairground in Nell's wake. The colours and the lights looked cheap and tawdry, she thought, on dismal nights like this. And the noise wasn't exciting or pulsating, it was reverberating and annoying. The paratrooper was circling on its skyward axis, three-quarters empty. Ted and Barry, the gaff lads who alternated between the paratrooper and the waltzer, were huddled in the pay-box sharing a damp cigarette.

'Where's Sam?'

'Cuppa I think. Problem?'

'HSE.'

The inspector stepped forward. 'Bring the ride to an immediate halt, please.'

Ted did as he was told. Several rather wet teenage boys slid out of the seats as they reached the ground, and grumbled about the brevity of the trip.

'Thank you.' The inspector peered at the car nearest the ground. 'You haven't got a double-safety-release bar on this particular carriage. Are they all the same?'

'Of course they're all the same.' Nell vowed that she'd go straight for Sam's throat if he'd cut corners. 'The cars are standard. They're as supplied – and as your department has checked them.'

'Double-safety-release bars are insisted upon now,' the inspector smirked. 'New legislation. From Brussels.'

'Since when? We haven't seen any new EC stuff recently. I'm sure we've had nothing on the paratrooper this season.'

'No, well, you wouldn't. It's not actually written down yet, but we're taking it upon ourselves to form an advance party.

Counter the problem before it becomes a potential disaster, so to speak.'

Nell glared. 'So we're supposed to be damn psychic, are we? We're supposed to guess the next safety improvisations? Fit them before they've even been invented? God, you lot really want traditional fairs to survive, don't you?' She sighed. 'Just tell us what these bars are, where we get them – and we'll see to it. OK?'

'Not really, Mrs Bradley . . .'

'Miss,' Nell snapped, waving her ring-bare fingers under his nose.

'*Mizz* Bradley. I'm afraid we'll have to close this ride down until the appropriate safety measures have been taken. Er – do you have a more senior partner I could discuss this with?'

'No I don't. My brothers and I are equal owners. However, if you mean is there a man you can impart this to, then yes, I'm sure I can find you one.'

'I'm sure I didn't mean to offend you.'

'And I'm sure you did. And we need to run all our rides all the time to make a living – so just how long is this going to be out of action?'

The HSE inspector sucked his moustache again. 'No time at all. As soon as the double-safety-release bars have been fitted and satisfactorily okayed by my department then you'll be up and running. I'll just wait here while you find someone, shall I?'

Nell stormed past Barry and Ted who were still huddled together keeping out of the worst of the rain. One ride out of action for the rest of the week – especially if it was a wet week – would make a serious dent in the cash flow. The fairground was practically deserted. There were the usual cajoling cries of 'One more car' and 'Get ready for the ride of your life', but very few takers.

Nell dived into the middle of the side stuff. Claudia's customer-free hoopla was staffed by the Mackenzie twins, Nyree-Dawn and Mercedes. She almost grabbed them by their matching PVC shoulders in her agitation. 'Have you seen Sam? And where the hell is Claudia?'

'Claudia says she's on strike and I dunno where Sam is. Try the paratrooper.'

Nell sloshed on. The waltzer was flashing and screaming with Danny still hunched in the fibreglass box in the centre, dee-jaying his heart out to four solitary punters. Of the five of them, Danny looked the most cheerful. Nell's hair was plastered to her face and ice-cold trickles slithered down her neck. Spotting Sam trudging from between the living wagons seconds before he saw her, she broke into a trot. The puddles splashed over the sides of her trainers and saturated her jeans.

'Sam! HSE! Paratrooper! Now!'

'Bloody hell.' Sam pushed his hair away from his face. 'Problems?'

'I'll explain as we go,' Nell said, and did. It was only when she'd finished that she realised that Sam had been coming out of Danny's van, not his own.

'I've never heard of new double-safety-release bars,' Sam groaned. 'And I always check the paperwork. Anyway, the Guild would have told us if they were compulsory, wouldn't they?'

'It's new European stuff – and this bloke is a real jobsworth. Just see what he needs, how much it's going to cost, and how long he wants to close you down for.' She paused between the immobile twist and the empty juvenile. The raindrops were pattering rhythmically on to the leatherette seats. 'I've left Terry in charge so I'd better get back. I think I'll call it a day with the dodgems though. And you haven't got much choice. How's Claudia?'

'What? Oh, Claudia – Miserable. Sulking. Totally furious with Danny. The usual. Why?'

'Because Nyree-Dawn and Mercedes say she's working to rule. And because she was wandering around in her version of sackcloth and ashes earlier. And because you were coming out of her trailer.'

'Oh – right. She – er – made me a coffee. I talked to her this afternoon and I wanted to make sure things hadn't got worse. You know that Danny can be a nasty sod when he wants to, and I reckoned she'd been through enough today. Look – I'd better go and sort this geezer out. I'll see you in a bit.'

Nell retraced her steps to the dodgems. The empty cars were pushed to the sides of the silent track and the music was throbbing softly. A small waterfall of rain cascaded from a dripping corner of the tilt. Terry was leaning out of the pay-box talking to the sole remaining Oakton nymphet.

'Cheers, Terry. Everything OK?'

''Cept for the lack of business, yeah.' Terry nodded. 'An' the money's all there. Honest.'

Nell smiled. 'I was pretty sure it would be. Do you want to scarper now? Go to the pub or something?'

'Great. Yeah.' He fluttered long eyelashes at his latest conquest. 'I'd just asked Karen if she'd like a drink, actually.'

'I'd really, really love a Malibu.' Karen, who was the most over-made-up and tatty-looking of the Oakton bimbos, beamed. 'But I've got to be home before ten, mind, or my dad'll go mad.'

That should give Terry loads of time to initiate the poor child into the ways of the Beast Wagon, Nell thought, as she switched off the electrics and the sound system, gathered the evening's scant takings into a canvas bag, and locked the pay-box. Sam would have an easy time tonight counting the cash. There would probably be so little of it that the regular visit to the night safe could be delayed until the morning. Wherever they were, Sam roared off in his Mazda and banked the money before bedtime. The same battered and double-locked briefcase had carried the Bradley income to the Midland's night safe since Adele and Peter's time, and none of them would have countenanced going to sleep with the day's takings in the living wagon. You never knew who might be wandering around.

With water still slopping in her trainers, and the long black coat clinging damply to the even damper jeans, Nell thought longingly of a scalding shower, a tumbler of whisky and dry ginger, a plate of pasta, and her feet up on the sofa in front of the television.

Sam, the gaff lads and the HSE inspector were still arguing in the middle of the paratrooper as she passed. There was a lot of gesticulating and head-shaking. Nell decided not to get involved. Sam knew where to find her if he needed reinforcements. She ducked beneath the sagging striped tilts of the stalls, where even the most confident pub darts player had long since abandoned the evening's attempt to win a cuddly hippo in pyjamas – this season's most popular piece of swag – for the lady in his life.

Danny remained in the walzer, determined to squeeze every last penny out of the Oaktonians, and as there was no light on in their living wagon Nell guessed that Claudia had already gone to bed. She'd have to talk to her sister-in-law tomorrow, she thought as she unlocked her front door.

The squeal of tyres on wet road made her turn her head. Surely not joy-riders – there had been trouble at several fairgrounds recently. She sighed, recognising the car. Joy-riders probably wouldn't have chosen to nick Ross's red Ferrari – it was a smidge conspicuous.

'Hi,' he smiled and air-kissed her damp cheek. 'I hoped I'd catch you. Guess what I've got?'

'A warm towel, a pair of bedsocks and a hot-water bottle would be top of my list,' Nell said, opening the door and groaning as he followed her inside. 'I simply can't imagine. But no doubt you're going to tell me.'

Ross sat on Nell's curved sofa and dusted away a few stray raindrops. He managed to look merely moist, Nell thought as she dripped into the kitchen. Ross never seemed to get messy or ruffled like other mortals. His suit, shirt and tie were pristine, his shoes showed only small droplets of water on their incredibly shiny toes. 'I decided to pack it in early because of the weather – the gaff lads can run the ride without me. Dad's still going, of course, but then we get a much better turnout at Wantage than you do here. More punters, more money.'

Nell returned to the living room, rubbing her hair. 'We've done OK, thank you. So? What's your surprise? Has Clem bought Drayton Manor Park? Or Chessington? Or are we going to see the Percival logo emblazoned across Blackpool Pleasure Beach?'

'I've managed to get a cancellation at Le Manoir.'

'What?' Nell stopped towelling. This was on a par with mentioning that you'd been invited to Sandringham for Christmas. 'I thought you had to put your name down at conception – like Harrow. How? When?'

'Easy when you know how – or, rather, who. And for tonight. I knew you'd be pleased. We always have such a good time when we're out together, don't we?'

She shrugged. They did. It was pretty annoying, really.

He was still smiling. 'And no one else can turn heads like you can.'

'No one else is nearly six feet tall with hair like a rusty Brillo pad.'

'No one else if half as beautiful. And maybe I was a bit bombastic the other day – about the merger and everything.'

Bombastic, overbearing, choose your own synonym. 'It's a gorgeous idea, Ross, but I've had a lousy day. I'm not sure that I'd be great company. And I haven't changed my mind about anything.'

'I didn't expect you to.' Ross checked his Rolex. 'You've got plenty of time – and wear that green dress. I like people staring.'

Nell, who didn't and was feeling tired and grubby but would have probably accepted an invitation to Le Manoir Aux Quatre Saisons from Dr Crippen, shrugged her shoulders and gave in. 'OK. But I'm wearing black – and don't think supper at Le Manoir, or Ma Belle, or anywhere else, will make me change my mind about the merger – or the Ice-Breaker. Or you joining forces with us.'

Ross leaned back as Nell scuttled round collecting towels and Cacharel toiletries. 'Tonight is strictly for fun. I swear I won't utter one syllable about the rides. I may, of course, ask you to marry me over the champagne – but I'm making no promises. Oh, by the way, wasn't that an HSE guy I spotted with Sam by the paratrooper?'

'Uh-huh,' Nell agreed from the bathroom door. 'How the hell did you know that?'

'Oh, I recognised him.' Ross flicked non-existent specks from his cuffs and didn't meet her eyes. 'He called on us at Wantage yesterday. We were up to date, of course, having European machines, but they're getting very tough on all the older stuff, aren't they? EC policy, no doubt. Still, that'll be one less thing to worry about when Bradleys becomes an offshoot of Percival Touring Entertainments, won't it?'

CHAPTER SEVEN

Adele Bradley had a pretty good idea what was wrong with her children, even though they'd all been non-committal to the point of vagueness during her phone calls to the fairground at Oakton that afternoon. Sam had seemed even more spaced-out than usual, Danny had only just regulated the snarl in his voice, and Nell had sounded thoroughly depressed. Even Claudia, who could usually be relied upon for a good giggle and a bit of gossip, was monosyllabic.

Adele pursed her lips and applied Sugar Babe lipstick in the ornately filigreed mirror. Her hormonal energy was champing at the bit, and she was determined to channel it. When she'd reported on the phone calls to Peter, he'd said 'Best left alone', and 'Least said soonest mended', and other similar trite phrases – which all translated, Adele knew only too well, as 'They're grown-up now, leave them alone and keep your nose out'.

Adele tutted and blotted the second coat of Sugar Babe. Men! What did they know? This needed a mother's touch – and a mother's touch was just what it was going to get.

She patted her hair into place, fixed in her favourite dangly earrings, 22 carat gold and shaped like guitars, and lifted her ocelot coat – imitation, of course, because Nell would have probably fire-bombed Graceland if it had been real – from the cupboard. She wasn't sure that the fur coat was appropriate for a drizzly evening, but it gave her a feeling of gracious elegance as it flapped and swirled and folded around her. And if she was going into battle tonight she was going to need all the allies she could muster.

Peter was at a bowls meeting. This week they'd voted him on to the committee – in preference to Cynthia Hart-Radstock's husband – which was a coup and a half, and he'd taken all his organisational skills along with him. The years of bellowing instructions and chivvying a recalcitrant workforce had stood him in good stead with Highcliffe Bowls Club, and Peter was loving every minute of it. Adele was delighted; not only did it mean that his time was fully occupied, but also he wasn't around this evening to ask her what the hell she thought she was doing.

The idea that had been brewing ever since Nell's weekend visit – and which she'd discussed endlessly with Priscilla – seemed outrageous, even to her. Once she'd decided on it, though, there would be no turning back. Was she deceiving Peter by default? Shouldn't she really be discussing this with him? She shook her head, tangling the golden guitars in her hair. Discussion at this stage was quite out of the question. Peter would say no. She knew he would. All she wanted was to smooth out the wrinkles in the children's lives so that Peter could enjoy the rest of his retirement without worries. No point in increasing his blood pressure. She'd tell him later. Once it was all over.

She had dithered between being completely honest or lying about this evening's foray, and decided to fudge the issue by leaving Peter a note propped against the kettle: 'Gone to visit the Percivals. I'll give them your best. Back before midnight.'

Peter was used to her occasional sorties to fairgrounds. For the majority of the time her new life was completely fulfilling, but sometimes her feet started itching and she needed to scratch. With luck and a following wind, Peter would be so wrapped up in the glories of the bowls club that he wouldn't see through the note's subterfuge until later. She took a further dose of evening primrose, sprayed on a waft of Obsession and went into battle.

Kissing Priscilla goodbye and with her black patent high heels tucked under her arm – Adele always drove in an ancient pair of Gucci loafers – she hurried across Graceland's pink-and-white granite block drive and unlocked the Jag. Seven o'clock and raining. Maybe the ocelot *was* a mistake. It could smell pretty appalling when it was damp. She retraced her steps and replaced the fake fur with a scarlet PVC trenchcoat, covering her abundant hair with a candyfloss-coloured chiffon headscarf. She could be in Wantage by half past eight, spend a couple of hours hammering out the salient points with Clem Percival, then another hour or so to get back home.

She hummed happily to herself as she double-declutched on the drive; she might even return before Peter. Then she'd screw up the note and he need not be any the wiser – at least not until after the deed had been done – by which time it would be too late for him to point out the moral issues. All he'd do then was tell her that she'd been very devious and she'd explain that it was for his sake as well as the children's, and he'd grin and touch her cheek and say how well things had worked out, and everything would be all right.

Adele slotted in her favourite Presley cassette and had eased the Jag up to fifty before she reached the end of the road. After a lifetime spent driving lorries and towing living wagons through the night, getting from Highcliffe to Wantage in the Jag was child's play. She had passed her driving test long before the constrictions of speed limits, drink-driving, or seat belts had been dreamed of. While careful to be sober behind the wheel and always buckling herself solicitously into the car, speed restrictions tended to elude her. Neither Peter nor her children were very relaxed passengers when Adele drove. She could never figure out why.

Singing along with 'Heartbreak Hotel' and 'Jailhouse Rock' – Adele stoutly maintained that Elvis's early hits were the best ones, although Peter favoured the ballads – the journey was over in a flash. Adele parked the Jag behind Wantage market square at just gone quarter to nine, slipped on the high heels, belted the trenchcoat – and prepared to sort out her children's future.

This particular move would affect Nell most, of course, but Nell was a sensible girl. She'd come round. Adele had also made a mental note to discuss fertility treatment with Claudia and Danny later. And then there was Sam. Adele was having some rather worrying thoughts about Sam. Sam might be the most difficult of all to deal with. She'd thought at first it might be drugs – an anathema to her after what had happened to dear Elvis. But, after several whispered conversations at Showmen's Guild Ladies' Nights, she had decided he wasn't showing any of the tell-tale signs. Adele was pretty sure he wasn't gay – he seemed to have cut a swathe through a host of pretty girls despite being a vegetarian – so that left only one thing. A married woman. She blinked rapidly. There had never been a scandal of that nature in Bradleys, and she wasn't going to let it happen now. She'd have to keep a very careful eye on her younger son.

But one step at a time, Adele thought. Danny and Sam's individual problems would have to wait. Tonight she intended to organise the future of all three children, thereby ensuring that Peter had a stress-free retirement. No one could blame her for wanting that.

It was still raining, the street lamps were reflected in the puddles like fallen rainbows, and the noise from the fair was a steady damp thud of excitement. Pausing only to remove the headscarf, belatedly remembering her mother's exhortation that women who wore headscarves or rolled up their sleeves were beyond the pale, Adele headed towards her quarry.

The fair filled the market-place and beyond. Lights swirled across the dark sky, plunging King Alfred's statue in and out of a dazzling coat of many colours so quickly that he looked like a rather confused stripper. Despite the rain, there were crowds of people, jostling, shoving, laughing. Adele's spirits soared at being back amongst the familiarity. It was like looking after other people's children – lovely at the time, but blissful to think it didn't have to be for ever. Raising her hand in greeting and mouthing hellos to various old friends, she threaded her way through the mob.

'Adele!' Clem Percival's East End bark sounded above the cacophony. 'Whatcher, Princess!'

Adele grinned delightedly as he hurried towards her. Clem Percival, big noise in the Showmen's Guild, tall and broad-shouldered, as always wearing a sheepskin jacket and a chequered cap, and with a cigarette dangling from the corner of his mouth, parted the punters as easily as Moses had parted the Red Sea. The Percival children had had their cockney edges smoothed by Millfield. Clem's still bore all the traces of the Elephant and Castle.

'Lovely to see you. You're well missed. Mind, flatty life certainly seems to suit you. You look a million.' He squeezed her hands, practically cutting off the circulation, then gazed over her head. 'Where's the old man, then?'

'Not here.' Adele wriggled her hands free. 'I'm flying solo. Have you got a minute?'

'Yeah. Several for you.' His eyes twinkled. 'Come to see the Ice-Breaker, have you?'

Adele hadn't particularly, but it would be useful, and she knew that to say no would be like telling any proud new mother that her baby wasn't of the slightest interest. She nodded. 'One of the reasons.'

'The other being our bloody kids, eh?' Clem roared above the Bay City Rollers, linking his arm through hers and practically yanking her from her feet. 'Ross ain't here. He hot-footed off to Oakton about an hour since. Taking Nell to some swank gaff for a meal or summat. I told him –' he broke off and shook his fist towards a knot of denim-jacketed youngsters who were tussling against the side of the big wheel. 'Either queue up properly or piss off!' He smiled at Adele again. 'Little bleeders. Sorry. Yeah, I told him that your Nell wasn't one to be swayed by flash restaurants or wads of money. If she ain't going to marry him she ain't, and that's that. Quite a lot of the Emily about that gal, eh?'

'Emily?'

'Pankhurst.' Clem dragged Adele past phalanxes of brightly lit rides. 'Dunno what we can do about them, really. I'd be more'n happy to see them hitched.' He sighed. 'Don't seem to make no difference, though. She's as stubborn as –'

'Her mother?' Adele yelled. 'That's what I'm afraid of.'

'So? Are you on your way to Oakton, then? Going to drop in on them and make sure all's as it should be? Give 'em a bit of the old parental?'

'Not tonight. I've never appeared without giving them warning. It wouldn't be fair.'

The rain had once more softened to a drizzle. 'I hope everything's OK, like. Ross said there was a HSE bloke round here yesterday. Said he'd be going over to Oakton tonight.'

'Rather them than me then – and another good reason to keep away.' Adele wrinkled her nose. 'Honestly, I'm glad to be out of the business. I don't think I could keep up with all the new rules and regulations. Actually, Clem, I wanted to talk something through with you and ask your opinion on – oh, goodness –'

'Yeah,' Clem's eyes and voice softened. 'That's it. The Ice-Breaker.'

Adele gazed in amazement. The Ice-Breaker, a huge circular construction of silvered chrome and electric blue fibreglass, towered into the night. Surrounded by scenes of wildly tossing waves, the cars swirled round in an ellipse, soared thirty feet into the air while tumbling upside down, and plunged immediately into hair's-breadth gaps between massive spiked glaciers and icebergs before starting the journey again. Glass-cold blue and white lights flashed blindingly. Deep bass music thundered. Each car held two frantically screaming passengers securely in place with padded shoulder bars, and the queue waiting to be terrified snaked out of sight.

It was a goldmine. And Clem owned the factory that made them.

'One-fifty a ride,' Clem nodded. 'Three quid a car. Nine cars. One and a half minutes a shot. Six hours a night, six nights a week.'

'Good God –' Adele said faintly, totting this up with the mental agility of all showmen. 'That's –'

'Just under forty grand a week.' Clem sucked on a further cigarette. 'It had paid for itself and made a profit in under ten weeks. And now I've bought Jessons I'm leasing them, and similar rides, all over Europe. No wonder your Danny and Sam want a slice of the pie.'

No wonder indeed, Adele thought dizzily. It relegated the Bradleys' dodgems, waltzer and paratrooper – good earners though they were – into non-league status. No wonder Nell's refusal to join the gravy train was causing ructions.

Realising that someone was waggling bony over-ringed fingers in her direction, Adele gave herself a mental shake and nodded greetings at Clem's austere wife, Marcia, in the Ice-Breaker's pay-box. They were the same age and she wondered fleetingly if Marcia was going through the Change. She doubted it. Perplexed hormones wouldn't dare to rampage around Marcia's rigid body. Whatever other reasons her daughter had for not being sure about marrying Ross, Adele really couldn't blame Nell for not wanting Marcia Percival as a mother-in-law. Marcia made Vlad the Impaler seem like Mary Poppins.

Marcia stretched thin lips over slightly protruding teeth and cackled into the microphone. 'Percival Touring Entertainments proudly introduces the Ice-Breaker! Hurry along there! This is the thrill of a lifetime!'

'Got time for a cuppa, if you want to talk.' Clem grabbed her arm again, tugging her once more through the mêlée. 'Marcia and the kids can do without me for a bit. Come on, Princess. Best foot forward.'

Adele noticed that the Percival daughters and their husbands were all busily employed on the Ice-Breaker and

74

Clem's other big rides. Danny and Sam would be in seventh heaven, she thought, and probably Claudia too. Claudia would have a fortune to spend on clothes and knick-knacks. While Nell – Adele shook her head. Nell's stubbornness would cause more problems in the family than her and Peter's retirement ever had. And she simply couldn't let that happen.

Clem and Marcia's living wagon was like Chatsworth on wheels. Everything was antique, priceless, and gleaming from Marcia's ferocious polishing. Entire rain forests of potted greenery fronded from every surface. Matching oil portraits of Clem and Marcia looking grim hung over the mantelshelf. Perching gingerly on the edge of a plush Queen Anne chair, Adele leaned forward to peer at the array of wedding photographs on the sideboard while Clem made tea.

The two Percival daughters, Melody and Clementine, had made good marriages in recent years to showmen's sons of equal status who had been delighted to join the Percival hierarchy. They'd diligently produced two children each, three boys to carry on the Percival tradition, and a girl who was, according to showland gossip, destined for marriage to one of the Royal princes. As the child in question was still at the Pampers and dribbly rusk stage, Adele felt they might be a little over-optimistic. But the point was that Ross Percival was the only son; the one to carry the family name; the one to pass this revered name on to *his* son; and her damn stubborn daughter simply didn't want to know.

'Thanks.' She accepted the Royal Creamware cup and saucer from Clem as he plonked his bulk opposite her on something in claret and gold with very spindly legs. 'So? What's to do?'

Having removed his cap and sheepskin, and stubbed out the cigarette in a Royal Doulton saucer, Clem sat back and crossed his legs. With his silver hair and handsome florid face he was everybody's idea of a rather dodgy used-car salesman, and would be a wow as a walk-on in *EastEnders*, Adele thought.

'You tell me.' He sipped his tea. 'I know you haven't come belting up here on a piss-poor night just to admire the rides and have a cup of tea. Most of what we've said could be covered on the dog'n'bone. You think Nell and Ross should get married, don't you?'

Adele nodded. Clem had added about six spoonfuls of sugar to the miniature teacup. It was like drinking treacle. She tried not to pull a face. 'They get on well together, they've known each other for years, they're equal in education and intellect – and Ross would provide the security and the means to expand into the future long after Peter and I are pushing up daisies. And yet –'

'Nell don't love him?'

Adele's guitar earrings jangled wildly. 'Love! Bloody foolish notion these youngsters have. Love came second for us. For you and Marcia probably. Maybe even for your daughters. Certainly for Danny – although I think Claudia was always gooey-eyed. It isn't even as though Nell would have to give anything up, is it? Ross is happy enough to join their outfit. And Danny and Sam are all for it.'

Clem rotated the tiny cup on its equally tiny saucer. The porcelain looked strangely out of place in such beefy hands. 'Nell don't want to expand the business neither, does she?'

Adele groaned. 'She's got some half-cooked idea about the good old days. She's about as up-front and astute as it's possible to get and yet she wants love and nostalgia! I could slap her, honestly I could.'

'So?' Clem shrugged. 'As long as Nell digs her toes in, then your two boys don't have any say in the business, is that it?'

'Sadly, yes. It was the way Peter and I arranged things. They each own a ride, but any decisions on buying, selling, merging – anything – have to be unanimous. Not a two-thirds majority. All three signatures on the business cheques.' She gave up on the syrupy tea, and shook her head. 'At the time it seemed the most sensible thing to do. But without Nell's agreement, Sam and Danny won't be able to buy into your machines. And without the machines there's no point in Ross joining forces. So, I've come up with this – um – idea.'

Clem Percival finished his tea and frowned. 'What sort of idea?'

'I'm convinced that if Ross travels with our lot then Nell will change her mind about him. They'd be together all the time then, wouldn't they? And she's dithering, Clem, I know she is.'

Clem lit a cigarette and inhaled luxuriously. 'Yeah, but Ross won't join 'em unless he can get them to go shares in one of our new rides. And you said that had to be a majority decision, and Nell won't agree to the expansion –'

'There'll be expansion, Clem.'

'I'm not sure that I'm following you, Princess.'

'It's simple. But I need to have your backing before I go any further. Do you and Marcia absolutely have no objections to Ross leaving you?'

'None at all.' Clem blew smoke-rings. 'We're all pretty close-knit aren't we? Never far away. I could even put some bigger gaffs their way so's we'd meet up all the time. And me daughters and sons-in-law are blinding workers. No, there'd be no objection this end. But there's really not much point unless your three want the bigger rides. And Nell definitely doesn't. So – no ride, no Ross.'

Now that the moment had come, Adele wasn't sure that she could go through with it. She suddenly felt very hot. Guilt or hormones? She stared at the marble fireplace. The marble fireplace stared back. Get on with it, it commanded in a voice very similar to her mother's, and stop shilly-shallying.

She took a deep breath. 'I want to look at your catalogue – Jessons' catalogue. Now I've seen the Ice-Breaker at first hand, it's even more spectacular than I'd imagined. It'd be too big for the kids though, so what I want is something smaller.'

Clem mulled this over before speaking. 'Let me get this straight, Princess. You're saying that *you* are going to buy a ride? Straight out? And *give* it to your kids?'

Adele nodded. 'Well, it'll be theirs then, won't it? And Nell won't be able to reject it because a third of it will be hers. It won't be a Percival ride. My buying it won't eat into the company money – and it will be the start of the Bradley–Percival union. Nell won't have any grounds for objecting to Ross being with them with a similar ride, because they'll already have one of their own. I think it could sway things.'

'And that's what matters most to you? Ross and Nell getting hitched? More important than the expansion of the business?'

'Absolutely. Although I'm sure that if we can achieve the first, the second will be a piece of cake.'

Clem raised his eyebrows and ambled across the living room, pulled down the flap of a rather gorgeous Davenport, and frisbee'd a glossy booklet across to Adele. 'And how much does Peter know about –?'

'Nothing.' Adele shook her head very quickly, making the golden guitars even more agitated. 'And I'd prefer it stays that way until it's a fait accompli, if you don't mind. I – I just think that he may put a spanner in the works if he gets wind of it early on. He's got some pretty moralistic ideas.' She flipped through the pages. 'I've still got my parents' inheritance money, and a fair bit salted away from over the years.' She bit her lip and looked up at Clem from beneath rock-hard eyelashes. 'The tax man doesn't need to know everything, does he? Ah – now what about this one?'

Clem leaned over her shoulder. 'Nice machine. Good money-maker, the Crash'n'Dash. Very popular in Europe – and of course builds up and pulls down with hydraulics off one trailer. They're in production. We could get one in six weeks or so.'

'As long as it's no longer.'

'You have my word.' Clem swallowed noisily, still looking a bit shell-shocked at the speed of the transaction. 'And how much can I tell Ross about this?'

'Whatever you like – as long as he understands that neither Nell nor Peter must know anything about it. The ride must be delivered before they know what's going on. I think I might let Danny in on the secret. He won't breathe a word.'

'Devious. Very devious, Princess. You're a lady after me own heart. Great idea. What about terms?'

'Cash.' Adele worked some saliva into her mouth and fanned herself with the brochure. 'After Henley Regatta the kids'll be at Haresfoot. That's when Ross was planning to join them. I still want him to.'

'You're on.' Clem rubbed his hands together. 'And no one else will get a sniff of it, I promise you. The Bradleys' very own Crash'n'Dash will be delivered to the fairground at Haresfoot.'

'And Ross?'

'No worries on that score.' Clem stretched out a hand to shake on the deal. 'Ross will be there as well.'

CHAPTER EIGHT

Jack Morland's roar of fury as he scraped the remains of his breakfast cornflakes into the bin echoed round the tidy all-white kitchen. Hurling his Habitat cereal bowl to the floor, he started to scrabble through the bin's debris, discarding herbal tea bags and the remains of the previous evening's pasta in his wake.

'What the hell do you think you're doing?' Fiona's voice stopped him in mid-delve. 'We've got precisely seven minutes before we leave for work – it's hardly time to be indulging in reclamation.'

Jack straightened up amidst the detritus, his hands bunched round several screwed-up pages of newsprint, spaghetti strands dangling from his fingers. He brandished the newspaper in Fiona's direction. 'Did you throw this away?'

'What? Probably – oh, and if you're going to say it should have gone into the recycling box, then I'm sorry but I simply didn't have time.'

'It should,' Jack's voice was dangerously level, 'have been left exactly where it was. I wanted to keep it. You know I wanted to keep it. I do hang on to things for more than thirty seconds, Fiona. Unlike you. This,' he waved the messy pages beneath her nose, 'is important to me.'

'Really?' Fiona's drawl was somewhere above grammar school but not quite St Mary's. 'What is it? Oh, God. It's that awful weekly rag about gypsies that you treat like the Dead Sea Scrolls. There are at least two million of them in the study.'

'*The World's Fair* is not about gypsies. It's a weekly newspaper for travellers. It keeps them in touch, gives them information, lets them know what Guild sites are available for ground lets. All travellers. Showmen. Fairs. Circuses. Preservationists –'

'Gypsies, as I said.' Fiona shrugged. 'They live in caravans and leave a mess.'

'Crap. *The World's Fair* is informative, useful – and mine.' Jack scraped the bolognaise and cornflakes from the newspaper back into the bin. 'After all, I don't bung away back issues of your *Cosmo* or *Marie Claire*, do I?'

'Because there aren't any. I read them, digest them, and dispose of them. Oh, for God's sake, stop glaring – you've found the damn thing, haven't you? If it means so much to you then I'm sorry I chucked it, but just make sure you clear all that mess up – and mind the floor.' Fiona had lost interest and was turning away. 'And we've only got three minutes now.'

'I'm not going in to work this morning.'

Fiona sighed. 'Christ, Jack. You're not serious about this bloody auction, are you?'

'Of course I'm serious. I've spent years with the Downland Trust – I owe it to everyone to be there. I don't expect you to understand how I feel, but a huge part of my life is being taken away on Saturday. I want to be there this morning for the viewing. I'd like to know that the stuff is going to good homes.'

'Oh, pul-ease.' Fiona shook her head. 'Not the personification of a heap of old junk – again. Spare me the sob story. On Saturday I intend to open the Krug and throw a party. Your anorak chums have ruined my social life for as long as I can remember. We've missed weekends away, tennis parties, drinks parties – every sort of bloody party. And when you have made it, you're never on time and never exactly clean, are you? You always have paint somewhere – Jack? Are you listening to me?'

'Yeah,' Jack said, who wasn't. 'Something about your parents' wedding anniversary, wasn't it? Fork supper. Talk of financial bravado and monster takeover coups. "Help yourself to the prawn and avocado, Jack, and try not to drip any on the table. It's genuine Formica."'

'Bastard.' Fiona drifted back across the kitchen and curled herself against his back. 'If you weren't so totally gorgeous and amazing in bed, I'd've left you years ago.'

'I know.' Jack folded the stained and crumpled copy of *The World's Fair* and disentangled himself from Fiona's slender arms. 'And I've got to dash. Call in and tell Dad I'll be in after lunch.'

'I'm coming with you.'

Jack tried not to let his frown show, and failed. 'Why?'

'Because I want to make sure it's really happening. That after Saturday I'll be living with Jack Morland, partner in Morland & Son, builders of exclusive executive homes for the upwardly mobile. Not Jack Morland, frustrated dauber of old trash and would-be gypsy. Anyway, if I come with you I can drive – which means you can leave the other love of your life safely in the garage.' She glanced at the bracelet watch dangling from her wrist. 'I'll wait outside – but not for ever.'

Pausing until the front door had clicked shut, Jack spread the remaining pages of *The World's Fair* open on the pale pine table. The auction had been advertised for three weeks, provoking much interest. The Downland Trust had had several serious enquiries about the collection, especially the gallopers, mostly from places like Beaulieu and Woburn. At least they wouldn't be scrapped – but they'd no longer be his. To him they were real, alive, slumbering; Sleeping Beauty awaiting the Prince's kiss. He grinned to himself. Fiona would have him sectioned if she knew that. The thought of losing the gallopers was intensive and invasive; hurting most when he woke at night, listening to Fiona's contented breathing in the darkness and feeling the oppression closing in.

He flicked through the pages, finding what he sought but not needing to; he could recite the page from memory. *The World's Fair* reported on the itinerary of every fair, every scrap of preservation news. Jack had prayed nightly that someone like John Carter would buy the gallopers. Someone who would give them the resurrection they deserved.

The impatient blast of the Peugeot's horn reminded him that Fiona was waiting. Still. He felt suddenly guilty. She really thought that after today he would return to the suburban fold. She had no idea what he wanted any more. And he'd lost sight of her dreams long ago. They were tugging together but in opposite directions. Sighing, he folded the paper and, with the same feeling he used to have as a child on visits to the dentist, walked out of the kitchen.

The house, neutral and minimalistic, with uncomfortable modern chairs, a futon, and some rather peculiar black ornaments, was Fiona's ideal. Not his. He knew that he should have pulled in the reins a long time ago. But it had been so much easier to let things drift. As long as Fiona was happy turning the house into a slavish shrine to trendiness, she didn't seem to object to his prolonged absences with the Downland Trust. But now the house was furnished and decorated exactly as she'd wanted, Fiona expected him to share it with her. To enjoy it as much as she did. It was a top-of-the-range Morland-built residence, clean, clutter-free, soulless. And Fiona – Fiona was made for the house. Bird-thin, with a blonde no-nonsense bob, severe beige suits, and an overwhelming desire to clamber from her current position of senior sales executive to become a director of her brother's company.

They'd lived together for five years. It seemed much longer.

Jack closed the front door. Both Fiona and the Peugeot were practically quivering with impatience. He had met

Fiona when Morlands had moved the offices for their expanding building company on to a new trading estate on the outskirts of Newbury. Fiona's brother owned the printing firm next door. It was a match enthused over by both families, and one into which they'd drifted happily at first. Jack could never quite remember when the happiness had turned to complacency, and the complacency to vague dissatisfaction and a nagging realisation that he and Fiona were unsuited. Like so many other couples, he guessed, it was easier to put up and shut up, rather than cause a major upheaval.

'I can't give you very long there,' Fiona said, negotiating the car through the rabbit-warren maze of identical houses in identical culs-de-sac. 'I've got appointments in Basingstoke all day. So you'll have about twenty minutes to see who's put their name down for what and work out how much money we're getting.'

'We're not.'

'What?' The Peugeot roared out of the estate in the direction of the A34. 'But you and the anoraks have poured a fortune into that pile of garbage over the years! You must be able to make something from it.'

'We've already agreed we'll take our expenses, but anything else is to go to charity. We never did this as a money-making exercise.'

'Charity, let me remind you,' Fiona muttered darkly, zooming into the two-lane scrum of the A34, 'begins and ends at home.'

The barns looked only slightly less ramshackle in the bright sunlight. The green and golden fields waved happily around them, unaware of the sorrow. A blue haze had settled hopefully over the hills. There were rows of vehicles, people on foot, even someone selling donuts from a mobile kiosk. Jack slid from the Peugeot and felt sick. 'Are you going to wait in the car?'

'No, I'm bloody not.' Fiona was already unbuckling her

seat belt. 'You have no idea how much I've longed for this. I can't wait to see it go.'

The auction-house employees were selling catalogues. Jack waved them away. The Downland Preservation Trust – Jims and Bobs and Bens, Percy and Dennis, Fred and Harry – all greeted him with sad smiles and woebegone faces, like the congregation outside a crematorium.

'They'll all fetch the reserves, I reckon,' Percy said gloomily. 'Do you want to speak to the auctioneer?'

Jack shook his head. 'I'll leave that to Dennis. There'll be plenty of time on Saturday, no doubt.'

'Ah.' Percy nodded. 'Three days away. Then we kiss goodbye to our life.'

Jack patted his shoulder and walked into the barn.

Inside, there was almost a carnival atmosphere; people shoved and shouted; the exhibits, like dogs at Crufts, were being shown to their best advantage, with huge numbered tickets attached; someone was selling coffee. The smell curled into Jack's nostrils, making him feel even more nauseous. He felt empty, bereft. He'd poured all his heart into the years spent here. Far more, he realised ruefully, than he'd poured into either his home or his relationship. He'd have to alter that now. He hadn't been fair to Fiona for a long time. She really deserved better.

The gallopers were Lot 72. The organ was catalogued separately as Lot 84. Both had attracted a large crowd. Jack pushed his way through. The gallopers were simply spectacular. With the barn doors wide open to the strong morning sunlight, Jack's painting gleamed, rich and glossy. Layer upon layer of colour; each layer applied after the previous one had been sandpapered down to a silk-fine finish. It was a job well done. A labour of love. He sighed. The best he could hope for was that whoever bought the gallopers would also love them enough to continue the restoration properly. The lump in his throat grew larger and he turned his head away.

The Gavioli organ, minus its tarpaulin cover, towered in a

corner, looking lost. Without lights and music it was simply an ornately carved monstrous ornament. It needed a massive transfusion of power to roll the drums, crash the cymbals, play the piccolos and the xylophones, and bring the whole gaudy orchestra to life. It needed the gallopers as much as he did.

'Can we go now?' Fiona was gazing at the straw dust on her shoes with horror.' Have you seen enough?'

Jack jerked his arm away from her hand in irritation. 'You go if you want to, I'll get one of the lads to give me a lift.'

'One of the lads.' Fiona snorted in derision. 'Lads! They're all a bunch of pathetic old has-beens. Get a life, Jack.'

He didn't rise to the bait. He was watching the crowd gathering around the gallopers. He couldn't see John Carter, but hopefully he might have sent a Steam Fair representative. 'Now you're here, do you want to have a look? See just what has kept me away from home for so long?'

'Not really. The only thing that interests me is selling the stuff and having you back where you should be.' Fiona glanced at her watch. 'Oh, very well then. If you're quick.'

They paused between the Gavioli and the most recently restored horses. He wanted Fiona to make some comment on his painting, but she said nothing. Her silence caused a physical pain. Did she not understand just how much this meant to him? The crowd were making appreciative noises, but it didn't heal the wound. Jack looked at them all, disliking them intensely.

The clusters of businessmen with briefcases were definitely the stately-home brigade, and the man with the hooked nose and maroon dreadlocks was probably a rock star. The very tall woman with the flame-coloured hair – Jack watched her closely – could she be from Carters? She was studying her catalogue intently. She was wearing jeans and a white T-shirt. There were gold hoops in her ears and a slim gold chain round her neck. Perhaps she was someone's secretary.

'Jack, I said we ought to be going.' Fiona touched his hand. He wasn't listening. One of the briefcase brigade had motioned towards him. 'Damn fine job you've done here. No trouble in selling these. You're the painter, I believe?'

Jack thought he should say guilty as charged or something equally flippant, but there was still a lump in his throat. Percy and Dennis had joined the throng, looking as though they were about to burst into tears.

'Oh, hello.' The red-haired woman lifted her head from the catalogue and smiled at them in recognition. 'I'm so sorry it had to come to this. You must be feeling lousy.'

Dennis and Percy nodded.

Jack wondered how his co-Trust members knew her. He was pretty sure he'd never seen her before. Maybe *she* was from one of the stately homes. Her freckled face had flushed slightly as she tapped her programme and looked anxiously at Percy. 'Do you have a buyer for them?'

'Rumour has it that Lord Montagu is putting in a bid for both the gallopers and the Gavioli – so at least they won't be far away.'

'Beaulieu?' Nell bit her lip. 'Really? Are you sure?'

She wasn't from Beaulieu, then. Maybe Woburn? Jack leaned across to Percy. 'Who is she? A serious buyer or what?'

'Of course, you haven't met have you? This is – Helen, was it? No, sorry. Nell. Nell Bradley. Nell, this is Jack Morland. Our painter. You missed him when you were last here.'

Jack smiled at her. She smiled back. Her eyes, which were on a level with his, were very blue, and had green and hazel mixed in like the glass-blown threads of a marble. 'You've done a wonderful job, Mr Morland. You're very talented. The painting is fantastic.'

Jack, as usual, was embarrassed by praise. 'Er – thank you. Are – are you representing someone? A potential buyer?'

Dennis grinned. 'Nell's from Bradleys. The showmen. She came in here by accident to ask directions, saw the gallopers, and of course found out about the compulsory purchase.' He beamed. 'She knew they were Savages straight away.'

'So you're a connoisseur?'

'Not at all. I just love them. My grandparents had a set.'
She sighed. 'What do you think will happen to them?'

'There are a million stories flying about. Someone said
Richard Branson was going to buy the lot. Someone else told
me that the gallopers were destined for the White House.
There was even mention of –' Jack felt the increased pressure
on his arm and stopped. 'This is Fiona. My partner.' Even as
he spoke he thought the word sounded ridiculous. Very PC,
of course, but it always reminded him of country dancing. He
wished he could introduce Fiona as his lover. It sounded so
much more exciting. 'Fiona, this is – um – Nell Bradley. She
likes the gallopers.'

'I can't understand why. Appalling heap of old junk.'
Fiona shrugged her thin shoulders. 'I shall just be very glad to
see the back of them so that Jack and I can have some time to
ourselves. They've intruded on our relationship for far too
long.' She looked more enthusiastic. 'Are you going to buy
them?'

'I wish I could,' Nell said wistfully. 'They're beautiful.'

'They're awful!' Fiona frowned. 'They belong in a museum
– if not on the scrap heap. I really can't understand the
attraction. Jack's totally besotted. He's wasted years here.'

Nell wrinkled her nose. 'Not wasted, surely? He's a
brilliant painter. Even if you don't like the gallopers, you
must admit that his craftsmanship and skill is incredible.'

'You're obviously an expert in these matters. Anyway, if
you're not a potential buyer, we mustn't keep you. Jack's
keen to talk to people who want to buy. Aren't you, darling?'

'Not necessarily –'

'It's been so nice to meet you.' Nell moved away a little. 'I
do hope you find suitable buyers – especially after all your
hard work.'

Dennis and Percy, Fred and Harry were talking to her now.
Jack wished he could join in. In all the time he'd spent
working on the gallopers he'd met very few genuine showmen. He knew their names of course, from *The World's Fair*,
knew which rides they'd bought and sold, had even seen

them on his frequent visits to fairgrounds. But he'd always been on the periphery. The outsider with his nose pressed up against the window.

And Nell had had a set of gallopers in her family, too. She might even remember the exact shade of the Tudor roses on the original Savage shields, something that had eluded him for months. But it was too late. The stately-home mob had moved in and Nell had disappeared.

'Jack!' Fiona's voice penetrated his thoughts. 'Let's just do what we have to and get out of here. I can hardly breathe.'

'OK. I'll just need to do a final check with Percy and Dennis about serious bidders. Are you sure you wouldn't rather wait in the car?'

'Absolutely. If I leave you here you'll stay for ever and I have to be in Basingstoke before lunch. Oh, hello again.'

'Sorry to interrupt you.' Nell's smile was charming as she indicated Percy and Dennis and the Woburn contingent. 'I just wondered if there was a reserve price on everything – I meant to ask just now, but they seemed so busy.'

Jack's hopes soared. Maybe she *was* serious. 'The auctioneers thought it was best to fix early reserves. They said we can always have another sale if we've set the ceilings too high. Have you changed your mind about bidding?'

'Jack! Really!' Fiona's shrill laugh made several people turn their heads and stare. 'Don't sound so eager to sell. You know nothing about the strategy of marketing, obviously.' She gave Nell a woman-to-woman look. 'Men are so pathetically open, aren't they? Desperation before consideration. I'm sure that's why the top sellers in this country are female. We know how to play our cards close to our Janet Regers.'

Jack looked at Fiona with some surprise. It was the first time for ages he'd heard her make anything near to a joke.

Nell smiled again at the sisterhood reference. 'When I was here previously, I was told fifty thousand for the gallopers and another fifteen thousand for the organ. Does that still stand?'

'We've put a reserve of forty-five thou on the gallopers and twelve on the organ – if they go separately. We'll consider bids of fifty-five upwards for the pair.'

Nell closed her catalogue and tapped it against her teeth. They were very white teeth, Jack noticed, not quite straight. He looked at her hopefully. 'Is Bradleys' Fair looking for a Savage and a Gavioli, then?'

'Quite the opposite, I'm afraid. I was merely curious.' Nell shook her head. There was a galaxy of freckles dusted across her skin, and her wrists were encircled by several thin gold bangles. Old rose gold like the rest of her jewellery. 'I do hope you manage to sell everything to the right people on Saturday, Mr Morland. It's been a pleasure to meet you both.'

'And you,' Jack said.

Fiona was looking perplexed. 'Am I to understand that you're a *fair person*?'

'A traveller,' Nell nodded. 'A showman. Yes.'

'Good Lord. I'm dumbstruck.' Fiona's voice had a trace of reluctant admiration. 'You're so absolutely normal. Oh, well,' she linked her arm through Jack's, 'come on, then. Let's go and see your anorak chums and get out of this dump. Having seen it, I still fail to understand how you find messing around with all this stuff interesting, darling. I simply can't wait for Saturday to come, can you?'

CHAPTER NINE

The weather had been glorious ever since they'd left Oakton. The gaffs at Bicester and Sutton had been packed, the rides full, and now, on the last day at King's Bagley, the scorching spell looked set to continue. Claudia sprawled on the steps of the inert waltzer, nursing a glass of cold lime juice, and lifted her face to the early-morning sun. She adored hot weather. Unlike the tawny-haired and freckled Bradleys, her dark skin tanned easily and she loved the scent of sunshine on her flesh. She rubbed the inside of her arm against her nose, then looked around quickly to make sure no one was watching. Strange, she thought, that she revelled in the senses of smell and sound, of taste and vision, yet would happily pass on touch.

The air was heavy with sweetness. Butterflies, blue and orange, darted amongst the clumps of buttercups and, as if mocking their frenetic activity, small flies hung motionless like notes on a music score. Across the shimmering field the gaff lads, Alfie, Mick, Ted and Barry, were lounging on the grass outside Nell's living wagon. The smell of frying bacon hung on the still air. There was no sign of Terry. He only ever appeared for breakfast on pull-in mornings when he was out of bed by necessity.

Nell appeared, leaping down the steps with the plates,

singing rather discordantly to something by Doris Day, and waved cheerfully to Claudia. Claudia waved back doubtfully. Good God – *Doris Day*? And Nell was bubbly! And it was early in the morning. Claudia wrinkled her nose. Nell had been acting very strangely recently. Smiling a lot and drifting off into silences with a glazed look in her eyes. Even when Claudia had threatened to rip up her entire collection of CK T-shirts if she didn't tell her what was going on, Nell had just beamed and said, 'Yeah, all right, that'd be lovely.'

If she hadn't known better, Claudia could have sworn Nell was in love. But surely not with Ross Percival? Not after all this time?

Love – She wriggled in the sunshine. She had tried really hard to be extra-loving to Danny since Oakton. It hadn't been easy. His temper, already roused to incandescence by the Terry episode, had been explosive after the visit from the HSE inspector. The paratrooper had been out of action for five days while the appropriate safety bars had been fitted, examined, and tested. Sam, poor soul, had come in for the full force of Danny's fury. Claudia smiled to herself and sipped the bittersweet juice, rolling it round her tongue. Sam made everything so much easier.

For the sake of peace she had toned down the make-up and abandoned the tarty clothes, which had delighted Danny. But she'd quickly become bored with baggy sweat pants and T-shirts and, still needing a cloak to hide behind, had reinvented herself again. Her curls were now shaggy and glossy, and she'd rushed off to the nearest Laura Ashley and bought long flowing frocks and floral skirts with broderie anglaise tops. Nell had been pretty scathing and said that Claudia would be back in denim minis and skin-tight Lycra before they reached King's Bagley. So far she'd been wrong.

Claudia felt beautiful now, inside and out. Beautiful – and confident. She stretched her bare legs in the increasing heat, feeling the rough wood of the scarlet-and-pink platform scratching her calves, the grass silky-damp between her bare toes. Sam's declaration had fulfilled all her fantasies. The one man who could never have her, wanted her. Although, she had to admit, the very fact that he loved her changed so many things. It wasn't a fantasy. It was real. And reality had a nasty habit of getting out of hand. She'd have to be very careful to keep the situation under control. Even so, it was lovely to know that there was someone who appreciated her for herself – and not just as the potential mother of his children.

Sam hadn't said it again – just looked at her, smiled at her, laughed at her jokes. He didn't seem embarrassed, Claudia thought, merely relieved that she knew. And, apart from that first rather surprising and gentle kiss on the cheek, they'd had no physical contact even when they were alone together. It suited Claudia admirably. She had always been very fond of Sam. It was the sort of love-affair that every girl should have. At least, every girl who pretended to ooze sexuality when in reality her body cringed at the very thought of love-making.

She squinted through the misty heat haze. King's Bagley was a pretty place. A very small village – practically a hamlet, Sam had said – where the fair was welcomed annually on the green. The green had a stream chattering through it, and was dotted with a church, a pub called the Nutmeg and Spice, and a smattering of cottages, all ringed by trees. Claudia was vague on trees. She guessed they might be beech because they had auburn leaves, but like all travellers, her seasons weren't marked by the emergence of flowers, or the lightness of the evenings.

The start of the season, just before Easter, meant Oldsworth and Swindon, Gloucester and Banbury; spring was the circuit they were on now. Summer meant places like Haresfoot and Witney, fêtes and carnivals, Henley Regatta, Didcot and Faringdon. Then into the back end, autumn, and the huge charter fairs: St Giles' in Oxford, Wallingford, Abingdon and Newbury, before returning to their winter quarters at Fox Hollow.

Still no one moved. A radio murmured through the open windows of Mr and Mrs Mac's living wagon, and she could hear some of the younger Mackenzie grandchildren playing something boisterous with bats and a ball on elastic. Nell was still singing. The gaff lads were scraping their plates and lighting cigarettes. Claudia drained her glass, still thirsty but reluctant to leave her perch. She was enjoying the indolence and the sunshine. And anyway, if she went back to the living wagon Danny might pounce on her.

Saved! She watched as her husband closed their front door and unlocked the Shogun. He was probably going off to meet Ross. The Shogun bumped across the grass and squealed to a halt.

'I'm going to do a bit of business.' Danny looked happy. It had to be something to do with the Percivals, which was bound to upset Nell. 'I'll be gone all day. Back by opening tonight, though. Will you be OK?'

'Fine,' Claudia nodded. 'No sweat. Have a nice time.'

The Shogun roared off across the field. She hadn't asked him what the bit of business was because he probably wouldn't have told her. She didn't really care. He could have his secrets – after all, she'd got hers.

Hearing swishing footsteps through the grass and hoping it was Sam, she leaned forward. Bugger. It was only Terry and that scruffy girl he'd had hanging around yesterday evening. She looked as though she had spent all night in the Beast Wagon. Her dark-rooted blonde hair was in greasy clumps and her make-up was badly smudged.

'You've missed breakfast.'

'Yeah, I know.' Terry pushed his floppy hair away from very slitty eyes and grinned at the girl. 'Still, it was worth it. Can I ask you a favour?'

'If it's a sub then there's no chance. I don't hold the purse-strings.'

'Nah. I'm OK for dosh, ta. Karen wondered if she could have a shower. The Beast Wagon isn't really equipped for that, is it? I mean, I know we've got a sink and hot and cold running – which is more'n most gaffs provide, but Karen'd really love a proper shower.'

'Couldn't she go home and have one?' Claudia looked up

at the rather scrawny Karen. 'You do live in King's Bagley, don't you?'

'Nah.' Karen ran a pink tongue over very bruised lips. Her neck was dotted with love-bites. One good reason, Claudia thought, for not wanting to go home immediately. 'I live in Oakton.'

'Christ! That's miles away. Do you mean you've followed Terry here all the way from Oakton?'

'Not exactly –' Karen stopped.

Realisation dawned. Claudia groaned. 'You mean you've been with us all the time? Since Oakton? God Almighty! How old are you? What about your parents? Jesus, Terry, Danny and Sam'll crucify you.' She sighed and shook her head at the bedraggled girl. 'OK. If you've been in that fleapit since Oakton you probably need hosing down. My trailer's open. It's the one with the walnut and chrome panels over there. Go and use the bathroom – but if you even think about pinching anything I'll break your fingers. Understood?'

'I ain't a thief! I've been brought up proper. An' thanks.' Karen started to skip away, then looked over her bony shoulder. 'You coming, Tel?'

Terry shook his head and subsided on to the waltzer steps beside Claudia.

'Wimp!' Karen poked out her tongue again and skittered away across the grass.

'She'll wear me out,' Terry said happily, lighting a cigarette and offering one to Claudia.

She took it, holding her curls back as Terry flicked the lighter. He was very close. It didn't do anything for her. 'I shouldn't. I gave up last New Year's Eve.' She inhaled and coughed and threw the cigarette on to the grass in disgust. 'That's bloody awful! That's it. I'm a non-smoker. Oh, stamp on it! It could incinerate the whole village – and I've got nothing on my feet.'

'Completely crazy!' Terry laughed as he ground out the glowing cigarette. 'You're ace, Claudia.'

'I'm certifiable. Don't let the others know that Karen's used my trailer, for God's sake. They'll skin me alive. Seriously, Terry, you'll have to get shot of her before we get her parents, or the coppers, or both, on our tail.'

'She's over-age.' Terry looked affronted. 'I ain't that daft.'

'If she's over-age then I'm Methuselah. Oh God, here's Nell now. Don't say a word.'

Terry scrambled to his feet. 'I think I might just go an' keep an eye on her, you know? Make sure she don't nick anything, like.'

'Bollocks,' Claudia said cheerfully. 'Just don't use our bed.'

Nell, looking very swish in the Nicole Farhi suit, was frowning as she approached Claudia. 'You were chirping your little head off just now. What's wrong?' Claudia demanded.

'Nothing.' Nell had wound her hair into a gleaming chignon and looked like a young and flame-haired Joanna Lumley. 'Claudia – are you sure you know what you're doing?'

Claudia felt a momentary jag of panic. Surely Nell didn't know about Sam? How could she? And they hadn't *done* anything, anyway. 'Doing? About what?'

'Him.' Nell motioned towards Terry's departing back. 'I know he's very pretty and all that but, after the shemozzle at Oakton, you and Danny seem to be getting on together. Don't you think –'

'Terry?' Claudia laughed in relief. 'You've got it all wrong, Nell, love. You're way, way off the mark. Terry's amorous intentions are focused in an entirely different direction. An Oakton bimbo, no less. I was merely giving him some big-sisterly advice.'

Nell didn't look convinced, but true to recent form, had suddenly become glassy-eyed. Claudia tucked her hair behind her ears. 'Petronella Bradley, what has happened to you?'

'Uh?'

'Give me strength. You're in a trance most of the time. You're all dolled up and Ross isn't around, so –'

'I'm going into Oxford. To the bank – I thought I ought to look the part.'

'What part?'

'Oh – businesslike, you know?'

'No. Tell me.'

'Not now. Later. Tomorrow – maybe. If Ross is foolish enough to ring, tell him I've been overcome by a surfeit of French cuisine and am gorging myself on fish and chips and don't wish to be disturbed.' Nell's eyes snapped back into focus. 'Christ! Terry's going into your living wagon! Claudia, quick!'

'He's just having a shower. The Beast Wagon is hardly stuffed with mod cons. And Danny's gone off somewhere wheeling and dealing, so what's the harm?'

Nell shook her head. 'I'm not even sure I trust him with the takings on the dodgems – and you let him loose with a vanload of antiques – not to mention Danny's cash drawer! You *are* having a fling with him, aren't you?'

'No.'

'Then why is he wandering into your trailer? Gaff lads don't – under any circumstances, not even life or death – set foot inside –'

Claudia exhaled. 'Nell, I'm not having an affair with Terry. I still feel sorry for what happened at Oakton. He wants a shower and Danny'll never know. I don't think he'll pocket the porcelain or anything, and Danny's money is so well barred and bolted that even I can't get my hands on it. Anyway, to be honest I can't see how we can keep running this feudal system of masters and slaves. He's a good kid. And why are you laughing?'

'You're priceless. Since you've become a Mamas and Papas freak you sound exactly like Sam. Equality for all. Love and peace, man. If you start wearing ethnic beads and not shaving your legs, I'll probably strangle you. I think I preferred you tarty.' Nell shrugged. 'Oh well, it's your funeral. Just don't come screaming to me when Danny finds out about Terry having the run of the trailer.'

'I won't and he won't and aren't you going to be late?'

'God, yes.' Nell glanced at her watch. 'I'll be back this afternoon and we'll talk properly then. And don't do anything stupid. Bye.'

Claudia watched her drift dreamily towards the Volvo. Oxford . . . The bank . . . Again . . . That was it! Nell had fallen in love with the bank manager! Mind you, they must have had a recent change of personnel, because the last time she'd been to the bank with Danny, the manager had been shrivelled and weaselly with tufts of hair sprouting from his ears. She was pretty sure that even Nell's taste couldn't be that bizarre. And the bank manager was a flatty. No showman's daughter – especially not one in Nell's vaunted ride-owning position – would consider becoming involved with a flatty.

'Trying to figure out the theory of relativity?' Sam swung silently from the waltzer platform and dropped on to the grass beside her. 'Or was it something more complex than that?'

'Far more complex. Do you know what Nell's up to?'

'Nope. I know that she's still dithering over Ross, which is pretty short-sighted of her. I know she and he had a flaming row at Le Manoir – no less – and that Danny has gone to meet him and Clem today about a new gaff that Percivals are letting ground on. Apart from that, I haven't got a clue. My guess is that she'll eventually eat humble pie, and we'll be having the wedding of the year before we reach back-end. There – has that solved all your problems?'

'Not really. So Nell's gone off to Oxford and Danny's gone off to the Percivals and –' She faltered. There was no way, despite his lip service to parity, that she could let Sam know about Karen – or Terry – or the use of the trailer. And they could appear at any minute. 'Do you fancy a drink? That is, I'm not inviting you or anything. I mean, the pub's open and –'

'I think I grasp the general concept,' Sam said. 'You've worked out this cunning plan to get me on my own – and you're letting me know that the entire family is out of the way so we can romp happily and –'

'I'm not!' Claudia said in panic. 'I didn't mean – oh!' She realised that he was laughing. 'You bastard!'

'Mum and Dad might argue with you on that point – but yeah, a drink would be great. My thirst is at your disposal, even if you don't want my body.'

Claudia blushed and turned away. Sam caught hold of her arm. 'Hey? What's up?'

'Nothing.' She pulled away from him. She could still feel the pressure of his fingers. 'I just don't want you to talk like that. Not even as a joke.'

He looked at her. 'It's no joke. At least, not to me.'

'Sam!'

But he was already striding off in the direction of the paratrooper, his hands shoved deep in the pockets of his jeans, his shoulders hunched tight beneath his T-shirt.

'Bugger. Shit. Bugger.' Claudia clenched her fists. 'What the hell is wrong with me?'

And sighing heavily, she ran across the bruised grass behind him.

The sun was spiralling, casting short, sharp shadows, and turning the already gaudy colours of the fairground stark and garish. Would Terry and his nymphet have finished – er – frolicking? Would Mr and Mrs Mac spot them sprinting half-naked from the wagon and report back to Danny? Oh, God – Why did life have to be so bloody complicated?

'You didn't have to chase after me.' Sam emerged from the paratrooper's pay-box. 'I would have come back. Sorry about behaving like a prat. Do you still want that drink?'

'Please. And you shouldn't apologise. I was being stupid as well.'

They walked side by side across the bleached grass. It prickled her bare legs. He shrugged. 'No you weren't. I guess you've got every reason to be wary. I should never have told you.'

'I'm glad you did.' Claudia peeped up at him. 'It was nice.'

'Nice?' Sam squinted against the sun. 'You make it sound as exciting as an acceptable pudding. It's been driving me crazy for years – and you think it's nice. Jesus!'

She bit her lip. 'Maybe, not nice, then. Maybe, lovely – oh, I don't know. It was just so unexpected. And well, funny –'

'You certainly have a way with words.' Sam gently pulled her round to face him. 'Before you crush my already fragile ego to dust, perhaps we should just leave it. After all, it's not going to lead anywhere, is it?'

Claudia watched the crane-flies skittering through the shimmering grass and didn't answer. The heat haze throbbed almost as insistently as the generators.

'Is it?' Sam leaned closer.

She shook her head. 'It can't. I mean –'

'You're Danny's wife. My sister-in-law. Strictly a no-go area. I should have told you how I felt years ago before he married you.'

'It still wouldn't have been any good.' Claudia looked at him. She felt like crying. 'I wouldn't have been any good to you. You see, I hate being mauled and touched and groped. I – I don't like sex – I hate it!'

Sam still stared at her. His face didn't move. 'With Danny? Or with anyone?'

'How the hell would I know? I've only ever been with Danny.'

Sam trailed his finger down her flushed cheek. 'Yes, I remember. Poor Claudia.'

'Don't pity me!' She jerked away from him.

'You always say sex. Not making love. Is that the trouble?'

'It's all the same,' Claudia said crossly. 'And don't trot out any old claptrap about sex turning miraculously into making love if you have the right partner because I won't believe you. I've read the magazines. Watched all the bare-your-soul self-analysis shit on the telly. I just don't like it. Any of it.'

'What about cuddles? Or kisses?' Sam had his back to her. 'Don't you like them either?'

'We don't – Danny doesn't – Christ, I shouldn't be saying this.'

'No wonder you don't enjoy it.' Sam turned to look at her. 'What does he do? Roll-on roll-off? The bastard.'

'Stop it!' Claudia blinked back her tears. 'Shut ut, Sam. Just shut up.'

'Do you want me to kiss you?'

She backed off quickly, the panic rising. 'No I don't! Oh –' Across the silent field she saw the door of her living wagon open, and Terry and Karen slip out across the grass, their hair damp, unable to stop touching.

She swallowed the lump in her throat and pushed past Sam in the direction of the Nutmeg and Spice. 'I think we ought to go and have that drink.'

Sam stood aside. 'I want to kiss you. Properly.'

She pretended not to hear. She kept walking. The heat haze continued to shimmer with even more intensity. It was still deserted. No one would see them. But it was wrong. The way Sam made her feel was very, very wrong.

Sam had caught up. 'I said –'

'Maybe we should just forget it.' Claudia jumped as he touched her arm. 'All of it. Danny would kill us both anyway even if we were just having a drink together. Sorry. Sorry. Sorry.'

She ran across the warm grass, cursing, blinking back her tears. Why did he have to spoil it? Why couldn't he just join in with her fantasy? The look but not touch? Why did Sam – who she thought was so different – have to be the bloody same as all the others?

CHAPTER TEN

'And now we come to Lot number sixty-eight. An agricultural hand-plough dating from the end of the last century.' The auctioneer's voice rang fruitily through the dusty rafters.

Nell had folded and unfolded her catalogue so many times that it was as flimsy as tissue paper. She wriggled in the uncomfortable chair. As the sale items were so bulky, the would-be purchasers had been seated in circular tiers facing the walls and the lots were illuminated by spotlights. A viewing area had been cordoned off in front of each exhibit, and some proprietary bidders were still lurking beside whichever items had caught their eye.

Nell glared for the umpteenth time at the small but prosperously dressed knot of people in front of both the Savage and the Gavioli. They looked like they had the full backing of Coutts. She shouldn't have come. It was a Saturday, the busiest day for the fair, and the last day at King's Bagley. There was pull-down tonight so she wouldn't get to bed until at least two. Claudia, Danny and Sam had given her the third-degree and Ross had been so nice to her since the evening at Le Manoir that she was beginning to have serious doubts. Maybe she should just give in gracefully and marry him.

She had seen Percy and Dennis and one of the Jims on her arrival, but none of the other Trust members. The painter – Jack – oh, what was his name? – ah, yes, Morland – wasn't in evidence either. Perhaps he couldn't bear to witness the slaughter. The auctioneer was taking spirited bids for the plough at such speed that Nell wondered how anyone ever purchased anything that they actually wanted. And if they did, how they knew what they'd paid.

She wasn't sure if she'd have the guts to wave her catalogue in the air when the time came. She had already learned that the sardonic lift of an eyebrow, so beloved on celluloid auctions, would get you precisely nowhere. And once she'd leapt to her feet to bid, would the auctioneer even notice her amongst all these professionals? Despite her height, she was pretty sure no one would spot her and she'd be left mouthing helplessly, growing more and more pink-cheeked. Her stomach contracted at the thought of such humiliation.

She'd got the money – just – against the bank manager and the accountant's better judgements, but her high-street draft was going to look pretty small beer beside the massed cheques of the merchant establishments.

Panic kicked in once more. Oh, God. What was she doing?

'Sold to the gentleman in the cap!' the auctioneer called loudly, with a crack of the gavel. 'If you'd see the clerk, sir. And next we have Lot sixty-nine –'

Not remotely interested in a Fordson tractor without wheels, Nell fanned herself with her catalogue. It was stiflingly hot again. Her white silk shirt was already clinging and her leather trousers were the biggest mistake since the poll tax. Her hands were clammy. There were two more lots before the gallopers: a small set of chairoplanes and a barn engine. She wasn't sure that she'd survive the excitement.

'Is that a bid, madam?' The auctioneer nodded in Nell's direction. 'With you for the Fordson at two-fifty?'

'No – er – sorry.' Scarlet-faced, she sat firmly on the catalogue. The bids resumed. Strange what some people would buy, Nell thought. Unless of course, they happened to have a set of Fordson wheels hanging around in their garage, and had been waiting for just such an opportunity.

She wondered what Ross would say if he knew where she was. What she was doing. The evening at Le Manoir had been a disaster. The food, the ambience, the attention had been out of this world. Sadly, Nell's temper-level had been running on a short fuse. Over the melt-in-the-mouth pudding, which had looked far too pretty to eat, Ross, despite his assurances to the contrary, had lit the detonator.

'Danny and Sam still want me to join you at Haresfoot, regardless of your objections.' He'd waved his spoon across the table. 'I'll have to arrive without any rides – mainly because you won't sign the cheques – and wait for you to change your mind. You'll have the pick of Jessons with which to compliment your rather quaint collection. I shall, of course, bring my own living wagon to start with – but I'm hoping that it'll be superfluous by the end of the first week. How does that grab you?'

The auctioneer had sold the Fordson and moved on to the chairoplanes. Nell cringed, recalling the riveted interest of Le Manoir's clientele as she told Ross precisely what he could do with his rides, his wealth, and his living wagon. She'd rounded off the spectacle by hurling down her napkin, asking the rather sweet waiter to ring for a taxi, and telling Ross that she hoped never to see him again – or at least not in this lifetime.

The taxi fare had been astronomical. And when she'd arrived back at Oakton, Ross's Ferrari was already parked outside her living wagon. He'd laughed at her. Laughed! She'd pummelled at him, shouted, and finally pushed him down the steps and locked the door. Any other man on earth, Nell thought, would have taken that as a definite no. Not Ross.

He had sent bouquets of flowers, phoned incessantly, and eventually turned up at King's Bagley, with a shy grin and a bagful of apologies. She had told him coldly and not very politely that the relationship was over. Danny, who had muscled in on the row, had said that it wasn't. Ross had laughed some more, suggested they had a cooling-off period, and said no doubt she'd change her mind when he arrived at Haresfoot after Henley Regatta.

No amount of screaming at Danny or appealing to Sam had made any difference. They were adamant. Ross Percival was going to join them – and she had better get used to the idea and start signing the cheques. In her new hippie mode, Claudia had even had the effrontery to suggest that Nell 'might see things differently then, and wasn't she being just a little bit selfish?'. Nell, feeling venomous towards her entire family, had telephoned her mother.

'Now Lot seventy-one.' The auctioneer had sold the chairoplanes to a pair of old ladies who looked like Hinge and Bracket. 'A Lister barn engine – which can be seen on the stand on the right adjacent wall.'

Heads turned. There were murmurs of appreciation. Failing to see why, Nell drifted back. She'd phoned Adele expecting motherly comforts and received none. Adele had muttered something about not being too hasty and no one knowing what the future might bring – and most surprisingly of all, when Nell had suggested a visit to Highcliffe the following Sunday, her mother had said that actually it wouldn't – um – be all that convenient. Sod the lot of them, then, Nell had thought. She wasn't going to have Ross Percival taking over her life. Not now. Not ever.

The barn engine failed to reach its reserve.

But Ross had changed. Subtly. He telephoned regularly, never mentioning the merger, chatting without threat, even making her laugh on a couple of occasions. Someone who made you laugh, she'd decided, was far more deadly than someone who made you angry. It was really most confusing.

'Lot seventy-two,' the auctioneer's voice had a quiver of excitement. 'A set of Savage Galloping Horses. Built in King's Lynn in 1907, restoration almost completed, and an ownership history available. Who'll start me at thirty?'

Nell felt her stomach contract. Her mouth was dry. Her heart threatened to punch its way through her silk shirt.

A stately-home arm was raised. Another from the rival faction followed suit. Then they were off. The bids rose in thousands, so rapidly that Nell had no idea what was happening.

'Forty-two thousand to you, sir!' the auctioneer bellowed and pointed. 'Do I have forty-three? I have forty-four! Forty-five!'

'I don't think I can stand it.' Jack Morland's voice spoke from the row behind. 'I wasn't going to come.'

Nell turned her head so quickly that their cheeks almost brushed. 'I'm beginning to wish I hadn't. I've only seen the gallopers twice and I feel like I'm abandoning a baby. It must be doubly awful for you. How do you feel?'

Jack squeezed into a vacant seat behind her. 'Almost as bad as the day my dog died.'

'Forty-nine thousand!' The auctioneer was going like the clappers. 'Forty-nine thousand to you, sir! Ah, and fifty!'

Nell staggered to her feet. The leather trousers made it slightly less easy than she'd hoped. The auctioneer paused. 'A bid this time, madam? Is that fifty-one?'

'Er – no. Actually it's sixty if you include the – um – organ. Er – Lot eighty-four as well.'

It was all she had. She couldn't run the risk of entering the bidding at fifty-one thousand only to lose out to the stately homes. Maybe she should have gone in at fifty-five? Hadn't Jack said that was the reserve price? Oh, what the hell – it was too late now.

In the ensuing silence all heads turned to stare at her. She heard Jack murmur something. The bidders from the stately homes muttered between themselves.

The auctioneer raised a quizzical eyebrow in the direction of Percy and Dennis. 'Do you want to take a joint bid, gentlemen? Or would you prefer to sell separately?'

Percy and Dennis looked confused. Jack stood up, the legs of his chair grating across the dusty floorboards. 'The Trust would be more than happy to accept joint bids. I think we said that on the preview day, actually.'

'Possibly. No one tells me anything. I do wish this had been made clear.' The auctioneer, thrown by Nell's interruption, looked hopefully towards the rival bidders. 'Is that what you want to make, sirs? An amalgamated bid?'

They didn't.

'And will the Trust be happy with a starting bid of sixty for both lots?' The auctioneer looked again towards Percy and Dennis who in turn looked at Jack.

'The Trust would be bloody delighted to make that a closing bid.'

'Good-oh. Back to business. Any more bids? No. All done, then? At sixty? Sixty once. Sixty twice. Lots seventy-two and eighty-four sold jointly at sixty thousand pounds to the lady in row three!'

The bang of the gavel rang again through the rafters. Nell, who had sat down again, didn't move. That was every penny in her personal account gone. There was no surer way of preventing Ross joining them. Bradleys could no longer afford him. Danny and Sam would possibly have her excommunicated.

'Christ, I don't believe it.' Jack had leaned forward again, his breath minty and warm against her face. Nell could smell clean skin and soap and something else – petrol? 'You're an absolute angel. Your partners changed their minds, then?'

'My partners know nothing about this.'

'Bloody hell.' Jack blinked. 'You'll be popular. What are you going to do with them? The gallopers, I mean?'

'God knows,' said Nell, who didn't have a clue about either. 'I didn't think I'd have the gumption to bid – let alone be successful.'

'Never mind.' Jack was beaming in delight. 'You did and you have. I can't quite believe it.'

Neither could she. She stared at him over her shoulder. He was wearing black jeans and a vaguely paint-stained cotton sweater with unravelled cuffs. The ornate signet ring on his wedding finger was ingrained with flecks of blue and crimson. She remembered the partner who hadn't seemed to share Jack's interest. 'Isn't – er – Fiona with you?'

'She's at home laying on some hoolie to celebrate my permanent return to suburbia.'

He leaned forward some more. He definitely smelled faintly of petrol – and leather, or was that her? 'I probably reek of bike,' Jack said. 'She's spitting oil at the moment.'

'Bike? You cycle?'

'Christ, no. Motorbike. I've got an old Norton Commando Roadster.'

Knowing nothing about motorcycles, Nell tried to look impressed. 'Is it – um – powerful?'

'Very. Nearly thirty years old. Nine hundred cc – goes like stink.' He smiled happily. 'Fiona detests it.'

Nell felt some sympathy for Fiona's point of view.

'Herumph!' The auctioneer coughed loudly. 'If the young lady who has just purchased Lots seventy-two and eighty-four would like to see the clerk regarding payment and delivery . . .'

God, Nell thought, collecting her scattered wits and unpeeling the leather trousers again. Delivery? To where?

Jack was on his feet and squeezing along his row. He motioned to Nell to follow him. The auctioneer sucked his teeth at the disruption and waited until they'd reached the edge before restarting his spiel.

'Take your cheque to the guy on the desk,' Jack said. 'Then we'll sort out transport.'

Nell nodded and looked at the half-finished Savage and the glorious Gavioli. They were what she'd wanted for as long as she could remember. The enormity of her act hit her with a wave of guilty panic.

She handed over the banker's draft, feeling numb. The clerk stamped it, scribbled out a receipt and handed Nell a sheaf of papers. 'History. Test certificates. Bits and bobs. Let me know when you've organised your designated carrier.'

'Diadem Transport, Upton Poges. I'll get it sorted.' Jack spoke to the clerk over Nell's shoulder, then looked at her. 'They're an excellent firm. They brought the gallopers and organ up here from Cornwall. Once you've decided where they're going I'll make the arrangements. Shall we go and say hello to your children?'

The rival stately-home factions were packing up their briefcases and glowered at Nell with open hostility. Several neutral observers congratulated her. Dennis and Percy beamed. The rest of the Trust were watching the bidding for the showman's traction engine.

Nell simply stared. The noise of the auction and the confines of the barn disappeared. She could see the colours swirl and dance as the gallopers rose and fell in stately waves, circling on green grass, two laughing riders on each horse, their hair flying in the summer breeze, their hands clasped tightly round the barley-sugar twisted rods. She could hear the deep resonance of the Gavioli playing 'Paree'. She could see the ornately carved rounding boards and the words 'Petronella Bradley's Golden Galloping Horses' inscribed in huge gilded letters.

She suppressed a shiver of pleasure. It didn't matter what her family said. What Ross might do. This was what she had always wanted.

'No second thoughts?' Jack was smiling gently, as though he knew.

'None. Absolutely none. God knows what I'm going to do with them – my brothers won't give them houseroom on our gaffs. Still, I'm a Guild member, I can apply for sites. And I'm sure I'll find hundreds of fairground enthusiasts simply dying to play with them.' She knew she was clutching at straws. 'However, that's all in the future. Firstly I've got to find them a home.'

'Your brothers are your partners?' Jack was running his hands along an unpainted mane.

'Yes.'

'So you're not married?'

Nell shook her head. 'Why?'

'It'll just make it simpler if you haven't got your husband's branch of the Showmen's Guild actively opposed to what you're doing.'

Jack's fingers were still stroking the wood lovingly. He was silent for a moment and she watched him, fascinated. She couldn't explain to him. He was a flatty. Flatties always had these romantic notions about travellers. What did he know about the umbilical bonding of the Showmen's Guild, anyway? It was lucky that he wasn't aware of Danny's temper, or Sam's plans for hydraulic rides, or her mother's insistence that their inheritance money should only be spent in dire emergencies. Or Ross Percival. Nell suddenly felt quite queasy.

Jack stopped caressing the horse. 'You must have winter quarters? Why don't you keep them there for the time being?'

Fox Hollow? Why not? There would be plenty of room there, at least until the fair pulled in at back-end. Nell didn't feel quite so sick. 'Actually, that's a pretty good idea. We've got a huge storage shed. And no one will go near them until November – by which time they'll be restored and –'

'So you're going to carry on the restoration, then?'

'No.' She grinned at him. 'You are.' She reached out her hand. 'Welcome to the very early beginnings of Petronella Bradley's Memory Lane Fair.'

CHAPTER ELEVEN

'**D**arling! At last!' Fiona swayed across the miniature patio. 'We'd almost given you up – hadn't we, guys?'

Jack gazed with horror at the half-cut crowd in the garden. Fiona coiled herself unsteadily around him and nuzzled his neck. 'I promised you a party – and here it is. Do stop scowling, sweetheart. Go and get out of that ghastly leather gear and shower off that smell of motorbike. Did you manage to sell all your old junk?'

Jack said nothing. He looked across Fiona's head. They were all there, packed like panatellas in a larchwood fence box. All their neighbours from the Identikit houses: Giles and Caroline, Fergus and Dotty, Adrian and Belinda, Stan and Adam, and that rather peculiar couple, whose names always escaped him, who had stripy hair and nose-rings and rattled on about tantric sex – not to mention several people he'd never seen before. And – oh, God – surely that wasn't his parents crouched over the barbecue? Fiona must have used all her powers of persuasion to drag his father away from work and his mother from her voluntary do-gooding at the local day centre.

'How much have you had to drink? How bloody long have this lot been here?'

'Grouchy! I had to dish out the booze in large quantities, darling, because we've been holding the food until you got back. With some difficulty I may add. Most of them have been here since three. I thought the auction would be over by lunch-time.'

'Well it wasn't. There were a lot of things to sort out afterwards as well. Paperwork, transport, general clearing-up. All I want is a bath and a beer and bed.'

'Sounds great.' Fiona started nibbling his ear. 'I'm sure they won't miss me for an hour or so.'

Jack rubbed his ear in irritation. 'Why the hell are my parents here?'

Fiona pouted at him. Once that pout had seemed little-girlish and appealing and had turned Jack into a protector. Not any more. Nell Bradley wouldn't pout or need protect-ing, he thought. Or maybe she would. What did he know? Fiona was a hard-nosed businesswoman who liked playing at being dithery and sweet when it suited her. Did Nell play those games too. Did all women? He probably understood as little of Fiona's needs as she did of his. Feeling guilty, he didn't push her away.

'I invited your parents because I wanted them to join in the celebration. After all, Eileen and Bill have hated your in-volvement with the anoraks as much as I have. Now go and put on your party face, and come and tell us all about it.'

'There's not much to tell. We sold most of it. We've got until the end of the month to make sure the barns are empty. It went well.' He looked at the crowd. 'And since you've got this lot here I suppose I ought to join in. Give me half an hour to get cleaned up. Tell Dad he can start playing Ainsley Harriot – and keep my mother away from me.'

He barged across the broiling garden. The sun still shim-mered relentlessly in the cloudless early-evening sky. The garden wasn't big enough to liberate half-a-dozen free-range hens in, let alone entertain Newbury's chattering classes to a barbecue. And there was no damn shade. The exact square of the lawn was bordered by orange marigolds, planted six inches apart, with an embryo lavatera in each corner. When they eventually flowered they'd probably be bloody orange, too, Jack thought, baring his teeth at Giles and Belinda or Fergus and Caroline or whatever their damn names were.

'Jack! I say, Jack!'

He groaned. His mother, dressed in her barbecue best – geometric palazzo pants and a voluminous clashing over-shirt – bored her way through the throng. They almost touched cheeks.

'Darling!' Eileen Morland wrinkled her nose in distaste. 'You pong of motorbike! Still, you won't be needing that either now, will you? You can buy a nice roomy Vauxhall and drive around in style.'

'I'm not giving up the bike.'

There was a gust of raucous laughter from the party-goers as someone stumbled into the flower-bed. A lavatera was trampled in the mêlée. Three to go, Jack thought.

'Of course you will,' Eileen insisted, in much the same tone as she had used when he'd said he'd never pass his A-levels. 'You have standards, darling. Standards that have taken a dip in latter years. Anyway, now that all this nonsense is out of your system you can find plenty of things to occupy your time, can't you?'

'Such as?'

'Dad thought about putting you forward for the Rotarians. And the golf club.'

'Over my dead body. I'm not joining anything that in-volves wearing bad-taste jumpers and self-congratulatory pomposity.'

Eileen shrieked. 'Oh, Jack! You're a wicked tease! Your poor father has slaved – yes, slaved – to get where he is today. You're our only son, Jack, and we expect certain things from you. Fiona has put up with your whims and fancies for long enough. Now that you've given up all this fairground tomfoolery, Dad and I are hoping that you'll settle down to a normal life.'

Normal? Jack glowered at the drink-clutching crowd. This was normal? This was what he'd be expected to do for the rest of the summer? Drinks and the latest *Good House-keeping* al fresco meals with the neighbours? And then in the winter – oh God, it would be kitchen suppers and 'just a half of cooking, old boy' in the appallingly modern Turling-ton Arms on the corner. And the only relief would be work, work, and more work. Work that he was increasingly aware he wasn't the slightest bit interested in. If he didn't enjoy living in the Morland houses, why should anyone else? Was this what they expected his life to be from now on?

Well, tough. Someone was going to be bitterly disap-pointed. For the rest of the summer he'd be up to his elbows in turps and linseed oil and paint at Fox Hollow and then, by September, the gallopers would be ready to roll . . .

'. . . and I said, Jack – are you listening to me?'

'What? Yes, of course I am.' Jack was sweltering inside his jacket. He tried very hard to concentrate on his mother's barbecue-flushed face and wondered whether he should tell her she had charcoal smudges on her cheeks. 'That's bril-liant.'

Eileen Morland rocked slightly. 'Brilliant? I'm sure poor Mrs Nettleworth didn't think it was brilliant. Made redun-dant at her age and her husband out of work for months already. There's an awful lot of heartache involved in running the day centre, you know. Do try to concentrate, darling. And go and get spruced up. Fiona's gone to a lot of trouble today, and I for one am absolutely starving.'

Fiona had joined them. She and Eileen shared a pussycat smile.

'Have you told him yet?' Fiona asked artlessly.

Eileen shook her rigid fringe. 'No, not yet. It ought to come from you, anyway. And I really think the poor love ought to go and get into something more suitable. Haven't you got a nice pair of cavalry twills, Jack, and a sports shirt?'

'No I bloody haven't. And what haven't you told me?'

'Nothing. Nothing.' Eileen frowned at Fiona. 'It'll keep – unlike the barbecue. Go on, darling. Get changed. We'll talk later.'

Jack shouldered his way through a giggling Stan and Adam who, arms entwined, were sipping from each other's glasses.

'Excuse me!' Adam flicked white wine from his skin-tight lilac T-shirt. 'Oh, it's you Jack. Hi.'

'Er – hi.' Jack always felt uncomfortable with Stan and Adam. It had nothing to do with their sexuality. It was their happiness that unnerved him. 'Sorry.'

'No probs. You can drench me with wine any time you like.' Adam beamed, then stopped as Stan, who worked in security and had tattoos, glared at him.

Jack was laughing as he barged into the house.

Once he'd showered and changed into clean jeans – Fiona enjoyed ironing and insisted on pressing a neat crease right down the legs of his Levis – and T-shirt, he carefully removed the card with Nell's phone number from his leather jacket. Then he shut himself into the box that Morland Executive Homes claimed to be 'bedroom five with fitted utilities, or a compact study for the home-worker'.

Of course, he thought, as he punched out Diadem Transport's telephone number in Upton Poges, he should really be doing this on his mobile. Not that Fiona ever checked the itemised BT bill, but she might just start. So what? He'd told her he had to arrange transport, hadn't he? He just hadn't been specific. The phone rang and rang. It was probably a stupid time to call. Saturday evening. Diadem Transport had probably packed up and gone home long since.

'Diadem Transport. Good evening. How may I help you?'

'Oh, hello. This is Jack Morland. You made a collection and delivery for me some months ago. Bulk. Fairground stuff. Yes, that's right. From Cornwall. I was wondering if we could transport the same loads – and a few extras . . .'

As he'd expected, Diadem Transport were helpful, efficient and very affordable. Having made the arrangements for Saturday fortnight, Jack replaced the receiver and leaned back in his chair. The mixed scents of charcoal and grilling meat wafted up into the stifling room and he realised he hadn't eaten all day. He was hungry. He wondered if he should ring Nell and tell her he'd sorted out the transport. Maybe she was eating now. No, of course she wasn't. She'd be working. At King's Bagley. Miles away. Another life away.

While Nell had been handing over the cheque for the gallopers and the organ, Jack had confused the auctioneer further by suspending the bidding on the caterpillar and withdrawing the ghost train from the sale.

He'd had hurried conversations with the remainder of the Downland Trust. Yes, he was quite sure he knew what he was doing. No, there wasn't a problem about money; he'd buy them back himself. Yes, they could await collection with the Savage and the Gavioli. Yes, he had plans – but someone had better tell the auctioneer.

Dennis did. After frowning and sighing and sorting out his paperwork, the auctioneer had gathered momentum once more and rattled on to a selection of farm implements. The bidders and watchers had settled back in their uncomfortable tiers and consulted their catalogues, the excitement over.

Jack had found Nell standing beside the Gavioli, still looking stunned.

'What else does Petronella Bradley's Memory Lane Fair need?'

'Need?' She'd looked at him in some confusion. 'I can't afford to buy anything else.'

'No, I realise that. I'm talking hypothetically. Fantasy fairground.'

'Oh, well, in that case, you name it and we'll need it.'

High as a kite, Jack had grinned. 'What about side stalls? And a kid's ride? Pity those old biddies bought the chairoplanes – maybe I could make them an offer they couldn't refuse.'

She'd shaken her head. 'Slow down! I haven't got a clue how I'm going to finance the gallopers – let alone a whole fairground of historic rides.'

'Fantasy historic rides, remember?'

'The gallopers are a reality – and they're going to cost a bomb.' Nell had looked quite worried. 'I really don't see –'

'Simple. The boys'll help with the rest of the restoration. They'll love it. And then once they're ready for the road – well, it'll be like letting children loose in McDonald's. And they'll work for free. Percy and Dennis and the rest of them are raring to go. And don't worry about the practicalities. Things will work out. Now, how about the rest of it?'

'OK, then.' She'd wrinkled her nose, joining in the game. 'A slip – oh, that's helter-skelter to you – being a flatty. And maybe a small big wheel. And a ghost train and a caterpillar would be brilliant. And stalls to you are joints to us. So we'll probably need hooplas, and wheel'em ins, and a roll-up – a really old one like Feed The Ducks would be ideal.' Her eyes had shone with enthusiasm. 'And yes, you're right, a couple of juveniles – rides for the kids in English – and an old-fashioned speedway.' She'd grinned. 'Do I have to explain that?'

'Dodgems without the bite?'

'Dead right. OK then, and a Noah's Ark – because I doubt if I could lay my hands on an autodrome – and –'

'John Carter watch out!'

'I'm hardly likely to be in that league,' she'd said firmly. 'And Jack – I'm very grateful to you and Percy and Dennis and the rest of them.'

They'd grinned at each other, each realising they were within inches of holding on to a dream.

'Er – Jack?'

Catapulted back to the present, Jack swung round on his chair, his body still pounding. His father, red-faced from the barbecue and looking embarrassed, was standing in the doorway.

'Christ. You startled me. Is there a problem? How long have you been there?'

'Quite some time. I wasn't meaning to eavesdrop. I've been dispatched to tell you that the food's ready. Over-ready in fact. Some of it got a bit burnt. Everything all right?'

'Fine. Fine.' Jack knew he might be able to fool his mother. He might be able to conceal things from Fiona. His father was a different matter.

Bill Morland was tall, lean-framed, and had the same dark good-looks as his son. He perched on the edge of the desk. 'I heard some of it. The transport bit. You're not giving it up, are you?'

'No. But if I tell you what's going on I really would appreciate it if you could keep it to yourself. Not a word to Mother or Fiona.'

'We're partners, Jack, as well as father and son. We've kept each other's confidences for some considerable time. But I can't say I approve. You're taking too much time away from the business as it is. Time that should be spent out on the road, negotiating for prime sites. We're up against Barratts and Wimpeys all the time – not to mention the smaller firms coming up on the rails. We've done well – I want to do better.'

So do I, Jack thought, so do I. He sighed. 'You don't give up the Rotarians or playing rounds of golf or –'

'Both ideal for business opportunities,' Bill interrupted. 'Contacts made, deals struck. My interests nurture the firm, whereas yours – well, I won't say they detract, as such, but they certainly don't enhance it, do they? And they certainly don't enhance your relationship with Fiona. She won't be happy about it, Jack.'

'I'm not going to tell her.'

'Good God – you won't have to. Women have built-in radar. Fiona will suss out what's going on very quickly. She's an astute lady. No, I won't say anything – but don't expect me to be happy about it. So, what exactly are your plans?'

Jack told him. Leaving out Nell's involvement entirely, of course. The fewer people who knew about Nell Bradley the better. His parents, like Fiona, were convinced that all showmen were thieves and vagabonds. His father's face grew more stern with each shake of the head. Balls, Jack thought, I'm not a kid any more. I refuse to be intimidated.

He stood up. 'So that's it. And we'd better get downstairs before the vultures have scoffed all of the charred remains. Take it or leave it, Dad. It's my life.'

The barbecue had gone very well. Everyone was so plastered that they ate everything, burnt or not, and trampled the marigolds to a pulp. Stan and Adam had a row, which ended with Adam in tears on the futon being comforted by Fiona and Belinda and Dotty, while the nose-ring couple soothed Stan with details of their three-day sexual marathons.

Eileen and Bill departed at this point. Jack had walked with them to their car, avoiding his father's disappointed eyes. Eileen planted a huge kiss on his cheek. 'It's been lovely, darling. You and Fiona must come to us very soon. Sunday lunch, say in a couple of weeks' time?'

'I'll check with Fiona. I might be busy.'

'I'm sure you won't be,' Bill said shortly. 'Not on a Sunday. Not any more.'

'No.' Eileen squeezed Jack's hand. 'Won't it be lovely? Having your Sundays free now that you don't have to go and paint all that old rubbish?'

'Lovely,' Jack agreed, not looking at them. 'Wasn't there something that you and Fiona wanted to discuss with me? You said earlier –'

Eileen looked coy. 'Fiona will tell you. You'll absolutely love it, darling. I can't imagine why we didn't think of it before. Dear girl, she's put up with such a lot from you – and she loves you very much. It's her way of thanking you for your sacrifice.'

'Sacrifice?'

'In giving up the Downland Preservation Trust. We all know that you've done it for her, darling, whatever you say.'

Christ. Jack held the door open for his mother and closed it behind her. 'Safe journey. See you soon.'

'Very soon, darling. Very soon.'

*

'Oh, wow.' Fiona rolled away from him on the futon, stretching like a cat. 'You are totally wild. Incredible.'

She curled against him again, trapping him beneath one thin naked leg. Jack, lying on his back, watching the night sweep across the ceiling through the straw-coloured vertical blinds, stroked her hair. It was damp from exertion. Eventually Fiona sat up and reached for a cigarette. She kept a packet of Marlboro beside the futon for post-coital enjoyment only. They both realised a packet was lasting longer and longer these days. 'Did you enjoy your party, then?'

Jack murmured his assent. He felt as guilty as sin. Fiona blew a plume of smoke into the warm air and rested her head against his shoulder. Nell would still be working. Or maybe starting pull-down. He was actually involved in business with a real showman; one of the people who had fascinated him all his life. He had always harboured a notion, while at school, of running away and becoming a gaff lad if he failed his A-levels. But he hadn't. And tomorrow morning Bradleys' fair would be in Henley. Tomorrow morning they'd be building-up amongst the traditions of the regatta. Tomorrow morning he'd still be here.

'Did your mother say anything to you?' Fiona stubbed out her cigarette, and ran her fingers across his chest. 'About anything?'

Jack shook his head and stopped Fiona's fingers moving downwards. She laughed softly in the darkness. 'Maybe later?'

'Maybe.' Jack was calmer now. More in control. 'She said you'd got a surprise for me – but I didn't think too much about it. My mother still thinks I'm five years old and should get excited about new socks.'

'Don't be cruel. She's sweet. Anyway, it's tons better than new socks.'

'Oh, good.'

Fiona reached across and switched on one of the very angular black lamps. 'What are you doing the first Saturday in September?'

Oh, God. Not September. The gallopers would be ready. St Giles' Fair in Oxford was the first Monday and Tuesday in September. The gallopers could make their debut. He and Nell and the rest of the Downland Trust would feel like proud parents.

'September isn't good for me, Fiona. It's always busy. You haven't booked a holiday, have you?'

She gurgled with laughter. 'No, darling. I've booked the Register Office. We're getting married.'

CHAPTER TWELVE

Saturday night had become increasingly muggy. Claudia leaned her elbows on the edge of the hoopla stall and watched the King's Bagley stragglers spending their money. The rides were on their last knockings but even the Macs' juvenile still had a few sleepy customers, allowed to stay up long past their bedtime because of the balmy temperature.

Giddy shafts of rainbow light swirled across the sky catching moths and bats transfixed in their beams. The thundering music from the waltzer, dodgems and para-trooper gathered together in distortion and then swooped to freedom among the highest branches of the copper beeches.

'Excuse me. How much a go?'

Claudia unpeeled herself and drifted towards her customer. 'Five rings for a pound.' She indicated the sign swinging above her head. 'Two rings for sixty pence. Or tonight's special offer – ten for one-fifty.'

'Two.'

The exchange was made and Claudia resumed her perch. It was almost too much effort to instruct the eager man with the two small children that leaning over was forbidden. What the heck! The day had drained her. The night was like warm silk. And there was still pull-down to go.

'I got one, Daddy!'

'Me too!'

Claudia looked. Both rings were caught like slipped haloes across the scarlet plinths. She started to shake her head and to go through the routine of all hoops having to fall flat to win a prize, then looked at the beaming faces. Sod it! They were the last punters of the night. Danny'd never know.

'Well done.' She hooked the hoops expertly back on to her arm. 'You've each won a goldfish.' She raised an enquiring eyebrow at the father. 'Is that OK? I can do an alternative prize if you'd rather.'

He shook his head, gawping at the dark glossy curls, the diaphanous floaty dress, the heavy gold earrings. 'We've got a tank at home. Two more will go nicely.'

Claudia preened herself as she dispensed the goldfish into polythene bags, delighted by the attention. The country-gypsy look obviously had its admirers. As the two squirming fish were borne away proudly to their new home, the man turned and waved at her.

She was still smiling when Sam swung himself in beside her. 'We've finished. Nell and Danny are doing last rides. It's so damn hot. I'm going to the pub before they shut – do you fancy it?'

'I fancy a gallon of vodka, an entire iceberg, and a freshly squeezed orange grove.' Claudia started to pull the swag boxes from beneath the hoopla's centre canvas. She and Sam had still not regained their easygoing relationship. 'But not until this lot is done. Anyway, I thought boozing on pull-down night was strictly verboten by Gruppenführer Danny.'

'Try telling that to the gaff lads – especially when they've been paid.'

Claudia emptied the remaining goldfish into their tank ready for the journey and sprinkled ant's eggs liberally across the surface. She watched the hungry mouths plop open and shut. 'Who else is going to the pub?'

Sam was gathering up the plinths. 'The Macs, no doubt. Danny won't, of course, because as you say it's whip-cracking time. And Nell looks pretty sick. No one's got a word out of her all evening. Terry said he gave some punters change for a tenner instead of a fiver and when he confessed his sin she just laughed.'

'Bloody hell. That sounds terminal. I think I'd better talk to her later.' She squinted across the field as the lights started to dim. Nell was outlined in the shadowy pay-box. She fastened a plastic lid on the aquarium. Nell had been gone all day – and no one knew where to.

Claudia could picture the bank manager's red-brick Oxford semi full of sensible furniture and books on wine-making. And Nell, who'd been wearing the leather trousers that Claudia coveted but couldn't wear because of her new milkmaid look, would probably have prepared them a nice little salad and a fruit cup which they'd have had in the garden sitting on plastic chairs from Argos and . . . She realised that Sam was staring at her. 'Er – so it would just be you and me going for a drink?'

'Last orders in a pub full of people is hardly just you and me.'

'Yes it is. So, no thanks. Not a good idea.'

Sam shrugged and started to help with the packing. Claudia watched him in irritation. She didn't need any help. She'd been doing this since she'd been tall enough to see over the side of her parents' stall. 'Sam, go away. Go and have your drink. Leave me alone.'

'I can't.' He straightened up, a clutch of plastic watches in each hand. 'You know I can't.'

'You can.' She snatched the watches from him and dumped them into their box. 'Dead easy. Walk away. Now.'

He laughed. 'I do love you.'

'Bugger off.' Expertly, Claudia rolled up posters of the latest boy band and dragged out swathes of bubble-wrap for the more fragile items of swag. The last bass note of that week's number-one hit single ebbed from the waltzer as the cars rocked to an unsteady halt and the occupants staggered drunkenly down the steps. 'There. Now you'll have to. Danny'll be looking for a spare pair of hands at any second.'

Sam shrugged and swung his legs back over the side of the stall. She watched him stride off into the darkness that gathered in black shadows around the edge of the green, emerging again in the cloudy pool of light round the Nutmeg and Spice. It had probably been called the Red Lion for years, Claudia thought, resuming her haphazard packing. Things changed. But could she? Could she re-educate her body?

'Not a hope.' She stuffed several rather out-of-date posters of Samantha Fox at her most pneumatic into a box. They still went down well with the middle-aged fawn mac brigade. 'Change is one thing – miracles are quite another.'

The work went on, as it always did, in semi-darkness, with good-natured jeering and bad-tempered bawling. The generators, providing light, drummed as rhythmically and un-noticed as a heartbeat while everyone swarmed around, gathering the vital bits and pieces without which the fair wouldn't function. The packing – slabs of wood which slid beneath the rides to make them level – was stacked beside the Foden, along with cable clips and copious reels of masking tape; the rubbish sacks grew fatter; the gaff lads – dragged back from their ice-cold Beck's in the Nutmeg and Spice by Danny – swore mutinously as they undid nuts and bolts, and lifted cars and platforms, steps and rounding boards.

How much easier it would all be, Claudia thought, stepping across the folded bulk of the hoopla's red-and-green-striped canvas tilt and placing the ropes inside with precision so that they were in exactly the right place for building up again, if Ross got his way and Bradleys had hydraulic rides. Imagine the bliss of sitting at a console, pushing a button, and watching everything neatly fold away. Heaven!

The hoopla was flat-packed now and she lifted the brightly painted panels with an ease born of familiarity. Even the Mackenzie grandchildren were loading poles into the swing truck while singing along with their personal stereos. None of them considered it hard work. It was part of their life. If you could walk, you could work. If you couldn't walk, you made tea.

King's Bagley church struck midnight. The audience was smaller. A few King's Bagley residents who were finding it too hot to sleep, and a policeman with a bicycle and constantly buzzing radio, hovered at the edge of the green watching with drowsy interest. The joints were dismantled. The Mackenzies' side stuff, which, including the shelves of prizes, was built into the sides of lorries and folded away neatly, was loaded and locked. The family was now lending its collective muscle to the skeletons of the rides. Several local teenagers, who had been co-opted by Danny, were getting in the way and were being snarled at by the gaff lads.

Claudia closed the tailgate on the smaller of the Foden trucks and shot the bolts into place without chipping her nail varnish. A mechanical roar of protest indicated that one of the lorries was being driven, as usual, in the wrong gear and she side-stepped the Scammell as it reversed at speed between the remnants of the paratrooper and the waltzer. Barry grinned down at her from the cab, his teeth, which were yellow in daylight, looking as brilliant as a toothpaste commercial.

'Nell could do with a hand I reckon,' he shouted above the engine, nodding towards the darkly dismantled dodgems. 'She's a bit off-colour and she's only got Terry with her at the moment. Any chance?'

Claudia gave him a thumbs-up and scrambled across the tow-bar of the pay-box which was standing locked and isolated like an amputated limb, her sandals silent in the grass.

'Jesus!' She blinked in the darkness. 'Nell?'

There was a scrabbling and panting and the sound of zips.

'Piss off. Oh, shit –'

Terry blinked at her with his fallen-angel eyes. Karen, looking more whey-faced than ever in the darkness, seemed to be trying to find her knickers.

The dodgem plates, the floor of the ride, were stacked waiting to be loaded on to the truck. The fibreglass cars were already packed. Claudia glared at Terry. 'Can't you keep it under control for more than ten minutes at a time? And for God's sake get her out of here. Shove her back into the Beast Wagon or something. Danny'll go completely bananas. You're supposed to be bloody working.'

'Yeah, I know. Don't bollock me.' Terry was tucking in his T-shirt. 'I was waiting for Alfie an' Ted to give me a hand with the plates, that's all. Nell's had a really bad headache all night. She went back to her wagon to get some tablets and there wasn't much doing, so –' he looked at Karen and shrugged. 'You know what it's like.'

Claudia couldn't even begin to imagine.

Clutching her skimpy shirt around her, Karen started to skip away across the grass, then turned and gave a smug smile. 'He calls me Martini.'

'Martini?'

Terry winked. 'Any time, any place, anywhere. Oh, balls – Nell's here.'

'Haven't Alfie and Ted started on the plates? Terry? *Terry?* If – you've scarpered I'll –' Nell appeared from between the Scammell and the Seddon-Atkinson and frowned at Terry and Claudia in the shadow of the pay-box. 'Am I interrupting something?'

'Nah.' Terry pushed his hands deep into the pockets of his jeans. 'You missed the best bit. I'll go and give the lads a shout to shift the plates. How's your head?'

'Thumping.'

'Probably the weather.' Terry looked solicitous. 'My mum always used to say that hot weather –'

'Bugger off and get some work done!' Nell growled. 'No work, no food.'

'Slave-driver.' Still grinning, Terry loped off to round up Ted and Alfie.

Nell waited until he'd disappeared behind the Scammell. 'What the hell was that little tête-à-tête all about?'

Claudia shrugged. 'I came over to give you a hand. He said you'd gone to get some paracetamol, that's all. Oh, bloody hell – don't look at me like that. It wasn't a cosy twosome or anything. I'm not stupid.'

'Aren't you?'

'And I'll put that remark down to your headache.'

Nell sighed heavily. 'Sorry. I didn't mean to sound preachy. Just thank your lucky stars it was me and not Danny who caught you and Terry snuggling up in the shadows.'

'We were not snuggling up! Terry has his physical needs catered for by the rather insanitary Karen, believe me. In fact, he was just having them well and truly catered for when I wandered over and spoiled things.'

'Really?' Nell started to grin, then winced as the headache kicked in. 'Ouch. You mean they were actually *doing* it?'

'Up against the pay-box, no less.'

Nell giggled. 'I didn't even know she was still with us. Oakton was weeks ago. D'you reckon she's over-age?'

'I suppose she must be – although she doesn't look it. Still, we haven't had any irate parents screaming about returning their daughter. Anyway, don't accuse me of grappling with the gaff lads again, please. Now, do you want any help or are you going to assassinate my character even further?'

'Help first, character assassination after pull-down – you know the rules.'

'Ah, yes. The rules.' Claudia climbed over the pay-box tow-bar again and hauled on a cable. 'Aren't those the things that say shareholders and business partners shall not abdicate their duties on a Saturday, and shall not disappear all day without saying where they're going?'

'The very same.'

Claudia peered at Nell to see if she was smiling, but it was too dark. She could have stamped with impatience. 'Oh, come on. Stop messing around. Where've you been all day?'

With pull-down nearly completed, lights were flickering on in various living wagons; different late-night television programmes splintered out through open doors; the curses were beginning to lose their edge and the generators beat their perpetual tattoo. Nell picked up a pair of pliers and said nothing.

'Nell! You irritating bitch! Tell me.'

'Not a chance.' Nell poked out her tongue. 'You'd only tell Danny.'

'I wouldn't. Promise. Is it something to do with Ross?'

'No.'

Claudia nodded. It had to be the bank manager. 'What's he like?'

Nell put the pliers carefully on top of the tool-box. 'Who?'

'The man you were with today.' Was she mistaken or did Nell catch her breath? She squeezed her arm. 'Your man in Oxford. Is it really the bank manager, Nell? You can tell me – you know we share everything. I won't breathe a word. Just tell me what you did today.'

'OK.' Nell lowered her voice. 'But you mustn't tell a soul.'

'I won't. I swear.'

'I spent today buying a set of three-abreast gallopers and a Gavioli organ.'

'Oh!' Claudia nearly screamed in exasperation. 'And I thought you were going to tell me the truth. I hate you, Nell Bradley! I really hate you!'

'Get a move on and stop cackling like a pair of kids!' Danny's voice barked through the darkness. 'We're waiting!'

'Wait on, then,' Claudia muttered under her breath, but she moved anyway. It wasn't worth rocking the boat.

She and Nell worked together, coiling cables and storing screws, as the dogems disappeared around them. Eventually it was all done. The paratrooper was loaded; the waltzer folded away on to its truck. Claudia perched on the battered chrome bumper of the Foden and blew a lock of damp hair from her face. 'I need a shower – and you must be baking in those leather trousers. Give me half an hour and come up to the wagon. I'll mix the biggest jug of iced vodka the world has ever seen.'

'Sounds great – and should go extremely well with the handful of paracetamols I've just taken.' Nell looked at her watch. 'It'll be nearly three by then – and I've still got to feed the lads. And don't suggest I give them salad because it's a hot night. If they don't get eggs and bacon in at least half an inch of fat they'll riot.' She stood up. 'But I'll hold you to the drink – even if mine has to be non-alcoholic. And remember – not a word to Danny about the gallopers.'

Claudia sat in the darkness for a moment longer, enjoying the cool breeze wafting round her face, and the chill from the grass between her toes. Moths swooped unseen, their wings beating gently in the soft night. It would soon be light again. And in daylight they'd be on the road to Henley. She enjoyed Henley Regatta with its arcane social traditions, its glamour, its similarity to their own nomadic existence. All those people coming together for a few days each year to do exactly what they'd done for years previously. Why on earth they wanted to row furiously up and down the river completely escaped her, but she was glad they did. She loved the fashions and the haw-haw voices and the enduring quality of it all.

She turned her head and watched Sam jump from his living-wagon steps, look towards her and Danny's van and then cross King's Bagley green towards her. She enjoyed looking at him – even more so now. He was more handsome than Ross Percival and a much nicer person than Danny. She sighed.

'Has Danny dropped his bombshell yet?' Sam squeezed his denim backside on to the bumper, his thigh brushing hers. 'Or is he saving it until we're all together?'

'Which bombshell? I don't think so. Oh, God – what have I done now?'

'Nothing. Don't jump to conclusions. It's nothing to do with you.'

Claudia was ashamed at her relief. She always felt guilty these days. Even the pill packets, secreted behind the veneer in her bedside cabinet drawer, seemed to bleep betrayal. 'Is it to do with Ross and the merger?'

'No.'

'Is it Nell, then? Is it to do with today?'

Sam shook his head. 'Nothing like that either. Do you know where she went?'

'Not a clue. You know what she's like about keeping secrets. Your ma is the only person I know that can wheedle information out of Nell – hey, what are you doing?'

Sam lifted her moist curls away from her face. 'Just looking. I can look, can't I?'

'Stop it.' She jerked away.

Sam kissed her cheek gently. There was no one to see but Claudia felt as though she was illuminated by flashing neon lights. It was nice though. Gentle and loving. What a shame that gentle and loving had to turn into groping and heaving. She turned her head to meet his eyes and felt the slightest tremor deep inside.

Confused, she slid from the bumper. 'I'd better go. I've promised Nell a drink and I need a shower first. And, if Danny is going to make one of his famous Bradley family announcements, I suppose we should be there. Why are you laughing?'

'Because you're beautiful.' Sam stood up beside her. 'And because you didn't smack my face or shudder with revulsion.' He walked away from her, looking over his shoulder. 'Come on then, Mrs Bradley. We'd better not keep your husband waiting.'

'Everyone got a drink?' Danny perched on the arm of the William Morris sofa. 'Good. I've got a bit of news.'

Claudia, showered and wrapped in her silk kimono, sipped her second large vodka. Nell looked as though she was going to drop from tiredness. Sam was leaning back, completely relaxed.

Danny cleared his throat, sounding pompous. 'I've been having recent meetings with Clem Percival – and Ross, of course.'

Claudia glared at Sam. He'd said it wasn't anything to do with the merger. And poor Nell looked as though her headache had returned with a vengeance. Danny was beaming. 'I've acquired some pretty prestigious ground from them.'

Nell stirred in her chair. 'Aren't we supposed to discuss this, Danny? If Percivals are letting sites to us, doesn't it have to be a unanimous decision?'

'Usually, yes, of course. But this was too good to pass up. Clem was going to advertise the space in *The World's Fair*, but he gave me first refusal. I knew you'd all be for it. Apparently, he'd got the ground rights and wanted to take the Ice-Breaker and a couple of his other rides, then discovered they wanted older stuff –'

'Really?' Claudia swirled her slice of orange in her glass, grinning across at Nell. 'One in the eye for Mr Hi-Tech, then. Where is it? And when?'

Danny frowned at the interruption. 'It's a one-off. After Henley and immediately before Haresfoot, so we can fit it in without any trouble. And it's big. Very big. We could take as much there in one night as we have here in a week.'

'Wouldn't be difficult,' Claudia muttered.

Nell shifted in her chair. 'For God's sake get on with it, Danny. I'm dropping here.'

'Blenheim Palace,' Danny said smugly, as though he was on chatty first-name terms with the Marlborough family. 'The South Lawn. They're having a concert – orchestra, champagne picnic, fireworks, fountains – and Bradleys' Mammoth Fun Fair.'

Claudia smiled. No wonder he was looking so pleased with himself. It was quite a coup.

'I take it there are no objections?'

They shook their heads.

'Great.' Danny leaned down from his sofa arm, letting his hand stray along the cushions. 'Now why don't we have one last drink to celebrate and –'

'All be over the limit for the drive to Henley in about four hours,' Claudia said, struggling to her feet to reach for the jug. 'Great idea, Dan.'

She had her back to them. She was aware that they'd

stopped talking. With the jug of vodka and orange still in her hand, she turned round. Nell and Sam looked openly appalled. Danny's face was turning purple. He was dangling something from his fingers.

'These,' he said icily, 'were behind the sofa cushion.'

Claudia swallowed. It was a packet of condoms.

Danny's voice was dangerously level. 'They're certainly not mine, so whose are they, Claudia? Just who have you been entertaining?'

'No one. Don't be silly –'

She looked at Nell. But Nell knew Terry had been in the living wagon at the start of the week at King's Bagley. She had seen him. And Nell had thought that she and Terry had been 'snuggling up' only hours earlier. Claudia thought frantically. Terry must have dropped the condoms when he and Karen had used the shower. They had been hidden for all that time. Oh, holy shit . . .

'They're not mine.' Her hands were shaking. 'I've got no idea how they got there – or who they belong to or –'

Danny's fists were clenched. The veins were standing out on his forehead.

Sam reached out his hand, not looking at Claudia. 'They must be mine. Must have fallen out of my pocket. I was up here earlier, Dan, remember? When you told me about Blenheim? I really ought to be more careful.' He laughed. It sounded wrong. 'Thank God you found them – it could have really fouled up my love-life.'

He took the packet and pushed it into the back pocket of his jeans. Claudia let the jug clatter back on to the tray. She could tell from Nell's eyes that she knew he was lying. And she didn't dare look at Danny. Everyone was standing up now, the refills forgotten.

Claudia rushed to open the door for Sam and Nell, both of whom muttered their goodnights. Closing it behind them, listening to Danny stomping around in the bedroom, Claudia realised with frightening clarity that it was far more important that Sam believed in her innocence than her husband.

CHAPTER THIRTEEN

'And lift – and lower – and rest . . .'

Adele lifted and lowered and panted as she glowered through a veil of perspiration at Emma: blonde, lissom Emma, who looked so young that she was probably bunking-off school. Emma, of Emma's Exercise, who, after her third class of the morning, hadn't even broken into a sweat.

'Well done, ladies.' Emma had the sort of irritating nasal sing-song voice that is compulsory behind cosmetic counters. 'Now, if we can all rest. Rest is vairy, vairy important. Exhale to twenty – vairy slowly, ladies – and then let each muscle unfurl itself. And when we've exhaled and unfurled, vairy slowly of course, we can take our crash mats back to the receptacle, jump on the scales and then avail ourselves of the refreshment facilities.'

Adele always forgot the exhaling and had never unfurled in her life. Now she lay rigidly on her back, her arms clamped to her sides, her eyes seeking guidance from above. The ceiling of the Body Beautiful, tiled in greyish polystyrene, refused to give her any comfort. What she was doing, she thought fixing her attention on a skew-whiff tile in the corner, wasn't that bad, surely? Yes, people might say she was meddling in her family's lives, but it was from a purely selfless motive. In one fell swoop she would solve everyone's problems. Surely that wasn't wrong?

All around her, middle-aged bodies were jerking aching muscles and breathing noisily. It was like being in a labour ward. Since her meeting with Clem at Wantage and her momentous decision to buy the Crash'n'Dash, she'd tried on several occasions to tell Peter. But somehow the words had failed to materialise. It wasn't the money. Peter had enough money, and he never minded how she spent hers. It was the scale of the thing. The whole massive deception. She had never deceived Peter before – and even if this was for the right reasons, she still felt tidal waves of guilt. And Nell? Would Nell ever forgive her for her interference? Adele gulped nervously. Still, there was no going back now. After today, there would be no going back at all.

Scrambling to her feet and tugging her square yard of latex across the Body Beautiful's gymnasium floor she stumbled over Cynthia Hart-Radstock, who was exhaling dutifully.

'Sorry, Cynth. Bit of a rush.'

Cynthia Hart-Radstock opened one perfectly-made-up green eye. 'Are you sure you've unfurled fully?' In her designer yellow Lycra leotard she looked like a slinky Siamese cat. 'You'll knot your muscles, Adele, dear. One needs to cool down, you know – and at your age –'

Adele bumped the mat over two further exhalers. 'No time for any more. I've got an appointment this afternoon.'

'Oh?' Cynthia raised her head. 'Medical? Hair? Facial? Voluntary work?'

'Business.'

'Oh, I see.' Cynthia gave a little smile. Her lipstick was still in place. 'With Peter?'

'Without.' Adele frowned at the immaculate lipstick and wondered why she was the only one who perspired inelegantly throughout Emma's Exercise. Pulling up her leopardskin leggings to meet her tight pink T-shirt, she knew full well that Cynthia Hart-Radstock would translate 'business' into 'affair' and have the whole of the bowls club humming before tea-time.

Well, let her. Peter thinking she was romping with a lover somewhere in a New Forest hotel was probably preferable to him knowing the truth. The truth – along with the hot flushes – kept Adele awake at nights.

'Not taking advantage of the facilities, Mrs Bradley?' Emma enquired as Adele lobbed her mat into the box. 'I understand there is a simply delicious puréed carrot and celery drink available today.' She dragged out the regulation scales – no one was allowed to escape from the Body Beautiful without a weigh-in.

Adele was still not quite sure why she put herself through this weekly torture and public humiliation. During her travelling days, exercise had been part of life, lifting, heaving, constantly working. Her muscles had only started to sag once she'd entered the soft and pampered flatty world. She stepped on to the scales and tried not to look at the flickering digital read-out. Not that it would have been any good. It weighed in kilos. Adele didn't trust kilos. She always felt they were heavier, somehow.

Emma beamed. 'It's a loss. Nearly two hundred and fifty grams, Mrs Bradley. Super.'

Adele practically cartwheeled from the scales. Two hundred and fifty grams! That had to be at least a stone. She could try out that new Delia recipe tonight, the one with the pork and the sautéed onions and the fried potato wedges.

'Try not to be too disappointed.' Emma filled in Adele's card. 'Think of it as a pack of butter.'

Screwing in her earrings, Adele felt her euphoria grind to a halt. A pack of butter? A measly half-pound! She groaned. That was the trouble with this EC stuff – it fooled you every time. Bang goes Delia then, she thought, wondering how Peter would react to a plateful of radishes for supper. She should, she thought, be dishing him up a huge slice of explanation pudding followed by humble pie.

She hurtled into the car park, unlocked the Jag, and slid her feet into the Gucci loafers. It was too late to go back to Graceland to change. She'd just have to hope that the addition of patent stilettos to the leopardskin leggings and the tight T-shirt would make her look a bit like one of the Shangri-Las.

She had to be in the Midlands by two o'clock. To be at Jessons' factory to meet Clem Percival. The Bradleys' Crash'n'Dash was ready for testing. Adele was already in fourth gear as she left the car park.

'Crackin', Princess!' Clem strode to meet her. 'You look a picture. Like one of the Ronettes.'

Close enough, Adele thought, as her hands were crushed. 'Is Ross here, yet?'

'Not yet.' Clem strode across the concrete apron in front of Jessons' factory. 'He shouldn't be too long. Gives us a bit of time to have a quick look-see at the old workings.'

He opened large reinforced glass doors with a swipe card, and ushered the still breathless Adele inside. 'Been to one of these before, Princess?

Adele puffed as she bobbed along behind him that, no she hadn't, but she was really looking forward to it, and was the Crash'n'Dash set-up inside?

'Bless you, no.' Clem wheeled smartly into a factory complex which hummed with fluorescent lights, ranks of computer screens, and some very hi-tech work-benches. 'She's outside. On the test bay. Here we are then. The boys are building three Ice-Breakers at the moment for the Far East, a Crash'n'Dash for Hamburg, and two Moon Missions for Australia. Business is doing nicely.'

Several Percival millions nicely, Adele thought as she nodded at the boys who were wearing corporate coloured overalls and goggles and wouldn't have looked out of place in a Grand Prix pit lane. The boys looked up and nodded back politely over the sound of drills and grinders and Radio One.

Clem walked between the benches and desks pointing out everything in technical terms, referring to structural loads and effects, weight limits and G-forces, while managing to keep up a string of Cockney banter with the boys. Adele could only hope that she was nodding and laughing in the right places. Wasn't Donald Duck rhyming slang for something extremely rude?

Heaps of coloured fibreglass littered the benches, as the computer screens flickered with what must be the up-to-date version of blueprints. Little fire-bursts of welding and soldering lit the darker corners. Adele thought it was very impressive. She was also even more nervous. It was far too late to back out now, she realised that. The machine had been commissioned and built. Soon she would have to tell the rest of the family what she'd done. She hadn't even plucked up the courage yet to mention it to Danny.

'Ready?' Clem was cupping her elbow. 'Best foot forward, Princess – and don't look so worried. It's perfect – and we've got everyone on hand for testing. I'm going to have a go myself. How about you?'

'Good God, no!' Adele's earrings jangled frantically. 'I haven't got a head for heights, Clem. I'm a martyr to anything higher than a four-inch stiletto.'

With the aid of a further swipe card and the punching of a multi-buttoned panel, Clem led Adele out of the factory's back door. Pressed up against his broad back, hardly daring to breathe, she didn't raise her head.

'Whatcher reckon, then?'

Adele took a deep breath and peeped from behind his shoulder. 'Jesus!'

The Crash'n'Dash, all fifty tons of it, loomed into the pellucid sky. Silent, towering, awesome. Adele could feel the adrenalin rush even before the power was switched on. In the catalogue it had looked spectacular. In reality it was mind-blowingly stupendous. Nell would throw a fit.

Constructed in clashing swirls of colour – mauve and orange, red and pink, bright blue and lime green – twin tracks reared upwards. Twelve two-seater cars were suspended from each of the tracks which criss-crossed in four places, and the elliptical design caused all the cars to hang upside down at the highest points, which, Adele calculated giddily, had to be about sixty feet in the air. Huge hydraulic cylinders were poised like rocket launchers at the base, making the Crash'n'Dash look as though it had wandered away from NASA and got lost.

'You'll get a better idea once we start the test.' Clem didn't seem to notice that Adele was still rooted to the spot. 'The main idea is, of course, that the cars travel upwards and outwards on their individual tracks while tumbling and spinning, then hurtle towards each other and look as though they're going to collide at the four crossover points. We reach speeds of seventy miles an hour both on the almost-impact points and on the downward tracks. The ride lasts a minute and a half. It should seem like two hours.'

Adele tried to swallow. 'It's . . . it's quite . . . spectacular.'

'And it's all yours, Princess.' Clem gave her a beefy hug. 'Ah, here come the reinforcements. Now we can really get the show on the road.'

Jessons' rear doors opened and a bevy of people poured into the yard. The overalled boys pushed sack trucks piled high with sandbags, and were followed into the sunshine by two white-coated professorial types and a youngish man with a wispy beard and ripped jeans.

'Test engineers,' Clem whispered, 'and the scruffy hippie is the doctor.'

'Is he expecting accidents?' Adele felt faint.

'God, no!' Clem's roar bounced off the dizzying walls of the Crash'n'Dash as the workforce strapped the sandbags into the seats. 'He works alongside the techno boys at every stage of development, following the international safety codes, and so on. His main purpose is to make sure the acceleration force is enough to give the punters a kick – but not enough to finish 'em off, you know?'

Adele didn't. There had never been this sort of palaver with the dodgems.

The test engineers had settled themselves behind the ranks of buttons in the pay-box and the doctor was supervising the loading of the sandbags into the seats.

'Course,' Clem lit a cigarette, 'it'll all look so much more gutsy in darkness with the lights an' all – but I'm sure you'll get the gist.'

The doctor wandered across and shook Clem and Adele by the hand. 'Magic piece of equipment,' he beamed. 'Can't wait to have a crack at it. Funny to think that something built on the same lines as a heavy industrial crane will bring pleasure to so many people. Fascinates me every time.'

Clem glanced at the doctor and ground his cigarette out with his heel. 'It's all hydraulics, electronics, compressed air and sheer bloody brute force. Push-button stuff. Folds away as neat as ninepence. And the punters can't get enough of it, thank God, eh, Princess?'

Adele felt cold suddenly. The overalled boys were standing clear; the two white-coated engineers had taken up their positions behind the computer panel. The doctor started a countdown.

A galaxy of dazzling white lights appeared as if the North Star had gone in for amoeba-like reproduction; a heavy metal rock anthem echoed from the bowels of the tracks; the hydraulic cylinders quivered and hissed. The twenty-four cars and their sandbag passengers swung gently as the tracks moved on their axis, then slowly began to climb. Adele wiped her palms on the leopardskin leggings. The track speed increased with the bass line of the music, and the lights became more frenzied as the cars started to tumble into the air. The tracks moved suddenly together, swinging half the cars straight towards the other half. She screamed. The miss was merely hair's-breadth.

Clem patted her shoulder, his eyes gleaming. The doctor was muttering in excitement. The tracks swirled, the cars swung and tumbled and the heavy metal music was interspersed with terrifyingly real special-effect screeches of metal-on-metal. It seemed impossible that the cars wouldn't collide as they swung apart at the last possible moment. Through it all, the sandbags stayed motionless.

The minute-and-a-half could have been a lifetime. Adele

was shaking. Bradleys would never be the same again.

'Phew.' The doctor exhaled as the cars rocked back to earth and the tracks glided to a majestic halt. 'That's the best yet, Clem. Totally awesome. Right, then? Who's next for the joy-ride?'

Most of the workforce had removed the sandbags already and were scrambling into the vacant seats. The engineers fastened the padded bars over their shoulders. Clem followed the doctor and grinned at Adele. 'Sure you won't change your mind?'

She shook her head. As soon as the engineers were satisfied that the weight load was evenly balanced, the Crash'n'Dash hissed into life again. It was even more terrifying the second time round, Adele thought, watching the very human legs flailing, the mouths open in silent screams, as the cars plunged together and spun apart high above her. She hoped the doctor had got his sums right.

'Bloody hell!' The exclamation echoed her thoughts.

Adele turned and looked at Ross. Above the roar of the Crash'n'Dash she hadn't heard him approach. She always wanted to greet him with motherly enthusiasm, as she would Danny or Sam. After all, he'd been part of her life for almost as long. Good manners and Nell always prevented her from doing so.

She flashed him a nervous smile, trying to ignore the grinding metallic noises as the Crash'n'Dash started to unwind. 'What do you think? Will it be well accepted?'

'Danny and Sam will think they're in Heaven. Claudia will happily translate it into shock frocks or whatever she's into at the time. Nell,' Ross shook his head slowly, 'Nell will probably never speak to you again.'

'Oh, dear. I was afraid of as much. I just thought –'

'I know.' Ross shrugged. 'I know why you've done it. Dad told me. And it's a brilliant idea – but you know Nell. It isn't what she wants.'

'Maybe not, but it's what she's got.' Adele had stopped feeling quite so queasy. This machine was going to make the children's fortune. This machine would ensure that Peter lived quietly and happily – and yes, proudly – into a healthy old age. 'And it's about time she bucked her ideas up. This will be delivered to Haresfoot with or without her approval. Have you decided how you're going to play it?'

Ross nodded, watching his father, the doctor and the workforce unfasten themselves and totter across the concrete apron. 'Actually, yes. I thought I'd feign huge surprise and amazement along with everyone else – and then suggest that as Bradleys will now be pulling in even more punters, my joining them with my Moon Mission or whatever, and splitting the inflated takings four ways instead of three, would be an opportunity not to be missed and should put us somewhere near the ranks of Wilsons or Irvins.'

'Premier League,' Adele smiled. 'Yes, I like it. A softly-softly approach.'

'But don't you want to make money out of it? Dad said you weren't doing it as an investment, but even so . . .'

Adele took a deep breath. 'I'm doing it for two reasons. First, to get you and our Nell together. If it benefits Danny and Sam and Claudia along the way, then that's all to the good. But I want Nell to marry. And I want her to marry you. And secondly for Peter. I don't want the family bickering over which way Bradleys should go, to cause him any more problems.'

Ross looked less than convinced.

They ran the Crash'n'Dash twice more. The doctor clambered on for each ride and had to be lifted off. The engineers were delighted and kept giving everyone high fives. There were only a few minor adjustments to be made before the final HSE checks the following day. Clem, who for all his bravado had taken at least ten minutes to regain his breath, rubbed his hands delightedly. 'Going to hot-foot off to the regatta and break the happy news to your lot, then?'

'Not yet.' Adele shuddered at the thought. 'Even I think I've done enough driving for one day. No, I'm sticking with my original plan. No one is going to know anything about it until the trucks arrive at Haresfoot. I hope to God it hasn't been leaked to *The World's Fair*.'

'Not by me. They've asked each week for new orders, of course. I didn't name no names. Just what machines had been commissioned, and whether they're for the home market or export. Nothing else. Don't panic, Princess. No one will know until you want them to. Now, if you'll just give me a couple of ticks. One or two minor details –' He bustled away to mull over a few salient points with the engineering boffins.

Ross raised an eyebrow. 'Dad did mention that you were going to tell Danny about your plan. I gather you didn't.'

Adele walked towards the Crash'n'Dash – *her* Crash-'n'Dash – and ran a tentative hand across the multicoloured fibreglass framework. It was warm to the touch and seemed to purr with life. 'I never actually found the right moment. And Danny and Peter are close – I wasn't sure that Danny wouldn't blab before I wanted him to. And recently, Danny has been a bit – well – odd, you know? Very short-tempered. Shorter than usual. And Claudia has been vague – again.' She looked up and intercepted the slightest frown. 'You know what's going on, don't you? Spill the beans, Ross. You owe me that much.'

He grinned at her. It was a very young sort of grin. She really couldn't see why Nell didn't adore him. 'I suppose it's not everyone's future ma-in-law who spends half a million on her daughter's dowry. Look, Nell did say there had been a bit of a to-do on the last night at King's Bagley. Danny seemed to have the idea that Claudia was – well – you know –'

'No. What?'

'Having an affair.' Ross looked extremely embarrassed. 'He sort of found some evidence in the trailer and –'

'What sort of evidence?' Adele's secure world was shifting beneath her feet as though she'd taken part in each of the Crash'n'Dash's test runs. Why hadn't anyone told her about this? 'What, letters, do you mean? That sort of thing?'

Ross shook his head. Adele wasn't going to let him off the hook now. She sighed heavily. 'What sort of things, Ross?'

'Condoms.'

Dear God! Danny and Claudia wouldn't be using *them*, would they? Adele always had trouble with the nonchalant way people said condoms these days. They'd always been referred to euphemistically, if at all, in her youth. But they wouldn't need them if they were trying for a baby, and – oh, God. She tried to look casual. 'In their living wagon? And they weren't Danny's?'

'Definitely not Danny's.' Ross looked as though he wished he'd never started this conversation. 'Nell said that Sam claimed them –'

'Sam! Why would Sam be using condoms in Danny's living wagon?'

'He wasn't. Sam said they fell out of his pocket.'

'Well, so they might have done.' Adele felt the earth start to solidify again. Bloody Danny, making mountains out of molehills.

'Nell said no one believed him. She said it was really obvious that they weren't his, actually. Nell thinks they might belong to one of the gaff lads.'

'One of the *what*? Christ, Ross. You know none of the lads would ever set foot inside a living wagon. They couldn't – wouldn't – Claudia wouldn't – Would she?'

Ross bit his lip and scuffed at something on the ground. Adele, knowing that she wasn't going to learn any more, rubbed her hand wearily across her eyes. Most of her mascara came off on her fingers.

Clem clapped her on the shoulder. 'We're right on course for a Haresfoot delivery. And if you're not going to the regatta, what about the do at Blenheim Palace? I've leased my ground to your lot – did they tell you?'

Adele nodded. Somewhere, long ago, before the reality of the Crash'n'Dash and the news of Claudia and the condoms, she had a vague recollection of Nell telling her something along those lines.

Clem chuckled. 'Should be a mega-do. Posh band, fire-works, that sort of thing. Tell old Peter to put on his best bib and tucker and I'll get Marcia into a swish frock and we'll make a night of it. Ross can come along as well – probably put your Nell in the right frame of mind for a bit of the old romance, huh? OK, Princess? You up for it?' He peered into Adele's glazed eyes. 'Bit too much to take in, the Crash-'n'Dash, was it? Never mind, gel. I'll take that as a definite, then. It'll be nice to see old Peter again and have a bit of a knees-up. All the families together again. Blenheim Palace won't know what's hit it.'

CHAPTER FOURTEEN

There should, Nell thought, trailing her bare toes in the warm shallows of the evening Thames, be a Showmen's Guild law governing occasions like this.

The last day of the regatta had brought Pimms-drinking ladies in Jasper Conran hats and their striped-blazered, boatered escorts, out in droves. The finals had been sculled and won; and now the leisurely Henley river was awash with inebriated varsity boys and celebrating Eights and Pairs, skimming through the water and only narrowly missing being mown down by jolly parties on cruisers or the occasional rubber-necking tourist on a hired Bluebird.

The blue-and-white-striped marquees along the bank had housed the crews, their boats, and their camp followers all week. Tonight this organisation had dissolved into glittering, chattering chaos as the champagne cocktails became larger and the portions of strawberries and cream more massive.

It was, Nell decided, a perfect picture of Old England. As it had always been. As it should always be. The setting sun on the water; the sky changing from the palest blue to lilac and gold; the whispered slap of the tide against the reeds; the laughter; the chink of glasses; the absolute timelessness of it all.

There should definitely be a Guild law passed to say that

the entire entertainment provided for functions of this type should be restricted to fairground rides of a bygone age, she thought. Machines which would, by their very antiquity, serve to enhance the ambience. True, the waltzer, dodgems, paratrooper and assorted paraphernalia had been built up out of sight in one of the far meadows and really couldn't be accused of detracting from the tranquillity, but Nell, in her state of drowsy euphoria, could see Petronella Bradley's Golden Galloping Horses taking pride of place on the bleached bank.

She could visualise the Sloanes in their Laura Ashleys and the Hoorays in their cravats astride the gleaming wooden horses, rising and falling in time to the Gavioli's rich orchestral notes as the 'The Blue Danube' or 'The Carousel Waltz' flooded across the glistening water, looking like the fairground scene from *Half a Sixpence*. The ex-members of the Downland Trust would be moving between the horses, leaning backwards against the motion, taking money, and she'd be in the centre, surrounded by mirrors and shields, feeding the fat cardboard music books into the organ. She felt a shiver of excited anticipation judder inside, as she imagined the whole gorgeous colourful concoction turning in stately circles of reflected glory. It would simply steal the show.

A blast of 'The Ride of the Valkyries' from somewhere under her denim shorts interrupted this reverie. She groaned as the bubble burst, and scrabbled for her mobile.

'Nell Bradley. Oh, hello Jack. I was just thinking about you – well, not you as such – more the gallopers. What? Tomorrow? God . . . Really? Brilliant. Yeah – no problem. We pull down at Henley tonight and we're driving straight to Woodstock for a one-night stand at Blenheim Palace . . . What? Yes, it is, isn't it? No, I'll be free during the day. I can be at Fox Hollow by two and – Jesus!' She stopped abruptly, her mouth falling open.

Claudia had just shimmied along the tow-path away from the fair field. Everyone was staring in suspended animation. Even the rowers had abandoned their oars to get a better look. Champagne glasses were held midway to mouths, conversations halted, strawberries toppled from gilded forks. Claudia had shed another skin.

Nell could hear Jack still speaking, and not taking her eyes from Claudia, lifted the phone. 'No, sorry. It's not you – it's – um – my sister-in-law. What?' She really couldn't stop the gurgle of laughter escaping. 'God, if I told you you probably wouldn't believe me . . . Well, she's wearing Adam Ant make-up and PVC hot pants and a cut-off white vest. Oh God, and she's back in the thigh boots . . . What? Yeah, I bet you would! Fiona probably wouldn't agree with you on that one! Look, I'll have to go before she gets arrested. I'll see you tomorrow . . . Yes – yes, of course. And you . . . Bye.'

She snapped off the mobile and scrambled to her feet. The gallopers and the organ would be at Fox Hollow tomorrow! Nell raced barefooted along the dusty tow-path, hardly able to contain her delight. Her dream had edged one step nearer to reality. Of course there were minor problems to over-come – like telling the rest of the family, but that could be shelved for weeks. No one was going to go near Fox Hollow until back-end anyway, and –

'Claudia!'

She tore through the crowds, wincing as stones nicked at her bare feet. Claudia was still undulating towards the main road. Another few minutes and there'd be a major pile-up.

'Claudia!'

Parties from several of the hired cruisers were standing up and clapping. An entire university boat club was whistling. Everyone else just stared. Sod it, Nell thought, glancing downwards. Her skimpy shorts and red gingham bikini top were hardly *de rigueur* either.

'Claudia!'

Oh, joy. At last! Claudia stopped sashaying and turned her head. Nell panted to a dusty halt. 'What are you doing?'

'Going to see how much money I can earn on street corners – just like your darling brother suggested.'

'You'll probably earn a fortune right here.' Nell pulled a face. 'Come to think of it, I might not do too badly, either. But I thought you and Danny had sorted it out – about – you know?'

Nell really wasn't sure what had happened after the condom incident. Most of her hadn't wanted to know. That the packet hadn't belonged to Sam was painfully obvious; that it might have belonged to Terry didn't bear thinking about. Whatever third-degree had taken place that last night at King's Bagley behind Danny and Claudia's closed door hadn't been for public broadcast. Neither of them had mentioned it again – and until now Claudia had seemed quite happy with her hippie look. It must have been a big row tonight for her to drag out the thigh boots.

The crowd were still watching. Nell linked her arm through Claudia's. 'Come on. It can't be that bad. What happened?'

'My period.'

'What?'

Claudia sighed as they edged through the onlookers and back in the direction of the fair. 'I started my period. You know what Danny's like about wanting a baby? He went ballistic – and started yelling about how I'd never get pregnant if all my lovers used condoms.'

'The insensitive bastard. Anyway, you haven't got any lovers. Oh, shit –' Nell stubbed her toe on a clump of couch grass. 'Have you?'

'Of course not. But Danny won't believe it.'

Nell groaned. The disintegration of their marriage was hurtling ever nearer. 'But, if you haven't got any lovers, and Danny doesn't use a condom, then maybe there is a problem? I mean, I know you've had tests and things and –'

'I'll never get pregnant.'

They'd reached the gate to the fair field. No one was watching the antics on the river. All eyes were focused on them.

'But you don't know that.' Nell trawled round for something to say. 'Maybe you should go back to that doctor in Oxford, at the private clinic, have some more tests done.'

'I won't get pregnant,' Claudia stopped walking again, 'because I don't want to. I don't want to have a baby. I hate the thought of being pregnant, of giving birth, and of being responsible for another human being for the rest of my life!'

Nell swallowed, and was just about to make some soothingly fatuous remark about how all women probably thought like that but once the hormones took over it was sure to be different, when a debonair man stepped forward from the throng.

'Excuse me, ladies.' His accent was cut-glass, his vowels impeccable. 'I wonder if I might have a word.'

'If it's the word I think it is, then no.' Nell frowned, trying to squeeze her denim hips and Claudia's PVC ones through a six-inch gap in the gate. 'I think you've got us muddled with the skiffs and sloops over on the causeway. We're not available for public hire –'

'Aren't you the Bradley girls?'

He made it sound a bit like the Mitford sisters – although they may not have been quite so scantily clad on a Henley tow-path – or as though they should be making regular appearances in Nigel Dempster. Claudia started to giggle. Nell smiled.

'Wonderful! Hold that!'

The flash had blinded them before they realised he was camera-toting.

'Super shot for *The World's Fair*, ladies. Thank you.'

If he'd been wearing a hat he would certainly have doffed it. Nell found it impossible to be angry in the face of such well-spoken chivalry, although if she and Claudia were going to become centrefolds she would have preferred it to be in some publication that didn't drop on to Graceland's doormat each Saturday morning.

He beamed again. 'Probably be in next week's edition – maybe the week after. I'll send you some proofs. Haresfoot next, is it? Post office do you? Right-oh.' He turned away, then looked over his shoulder. 'I've been in and taken shots of your machines. I must say, I thought they were eye-catching – but you two take the biscuit.'

'Bugger,' Nell said half-heartedly. 'Ross'll love that.'

'Danny'll love it even more.' Claudia tried not to smile. 'Hell's teeth, Nell. We've probably just got rid of two of our major problems in one hit.'

Delighted that Claudia's good humour had been restored, Nell thought the next step was to suggest that she took off at least one pair of eyelashes and perhaps the thigh boots, and maybe even covered the PVC shorts with something a little more decorous for the remaining stint on the hoopla. She didn't want to think of anyone's reaction to the photograph – least of all Ross's.

The fairground was heaving with a mix of locals and regatta-goers, the rides were full, the platforms crowded. Nearly all of them had stopped to look.

'Talking of problems,' Claudia motioned towards the cluster of living wagons. 'It looks like we've got visitors.'

Two police cars were pulled up outside Danny and Claudia's front door. Sam swung from the paratrooper pay-box and shouldered his way through the gaping throng. He spoke to Nell although she noticed that his eyes were on Claudia. 'Bit of an emergency. There's a welcome committee in the wagon. Where have you been?'

'I was sitting on the bank watching the river,' Nell said, not wanting to add that she'd been mentally disposing of Bradleys' Mammoth Fun Fair and replacing it with the gallopers. 'Then Claudia came along and –' Maybe mentioning the photographer wasn't a good idea either. She couldn't quite interpret the expression in Sam's eyes.

'We decided to wander back again,' Claudia finished with a sickly smile at Sam. 'So, who's in trouble now? It can't be me this time, surely? Or is there some law about not exposing more than a quarter of an inch of flesh at a time?'

Sam swallowed what sounded like a growl of irritation.

'More to the point, who the hell is minding the stuff?' Nell felt strangely out of kilter. Had she missed something? Claudia and Sam seemed to be doing a lot of silent communication.

'Mick and Alfie are on the dodgems. Barry's on the paratrooper. Ted's on the waltzer with a couple of local casuals and the Mackenzie kids have got the joints.' Sam was still looking at Claudia. 'It's not that sort of problem.'

'Where the hell is Terry, then?' Nell felt a jolt of unease. 'I left him on the dodgems and he promised he wouldn't move –'

'Terry's in the living wagon with Danny.'

Nell felt the warm sandy grass shift beneath her bare feet. So it was *that* sort of problem. No wonder Sam was looking at Claudia with worried eyes. Danny, incensed by Claudia's tarty reincarnation, had decided to lay into the beautiful Terry. Good God – this was just the sort of publicity they could do without. Adele would go bananas.

'Has he hurt him much?'

Sam looked irritated. 'Nobody's hurt anyone, Nell. For God's sake get a grip on your imagination. Terry's in the wagon with Danny because the police have just turned up with Karen's parents.'

Karen who? Did they know a Karen? Nell's cogs turned slowly. Oh – dear God! Karen, the scruffy Oakton nymphet who had been living in the Beast Wagon for weeks! Nell started to run towards the living wagons. Sam and Claudia weren't far behind.

It was like a rather bad party. Every inch of the William Morris was filled. No one moved. No one spoke. The giddy noise from the fair bounced through the swags and tails and, finding itself unwelcome, seemed to sidle out again.

'About bloody time!' Danny got to his feet. He appeared to have been sitting on Terry. 'Tell them –' he indicated towards the three policemen and one woman and a rather pale and wispy couple, 'that we don't know anything about their bloody daughter.'

The policemen seemed riveted by the sight of Nell's long

legs in the cut-offs and her red-gold hair sliding towards the bikini top. The policewoman stared around the sumptuous living wagon, looking as though she was ticking off a lot of *Crimewatch*-reported stately-home robberies.

Nell gave Terry an anguished glance. He looked the picture of sun-tanned, floppy-haired innocence. She couldn't really blame Claudia for fancying him. 'I'm not sure. Of course, the fair always attracts followers – if you get my drift.'

The wispy couple apparently did. They didn't seem to like the inference.

Nell staggered on. 'I mean, we don't check people out, of course. If the lads have girlfriends, well, it's up to them. What exactly does your daughter look like?'

The policewoman thrust a photo forward. Karen on holiday in Benidorm.

'Ah –' Nell looked at Terry again. 'She does look a bit familiar. And, um – how old is she?'

'Fourteen.'

Mother of God! Terry blanched and tried to disappear under a cushion. Nell closed her eyes.

'She was reported missing at Oakton.' The youngest policeman addressed Nell's cleavage. 'No one tied the disappearance in with the fair because she's left home before and been found twice in London and once in Stow-on-the-Wold.'

Why, Nell wondered, would anyone want to run away to Stow-on-the-Wold? Very pretty, of course, but surely not the sort of place for wild teenage excitement?

'One of her friends,' the wispy woman said shakily, 'told us last week that Karen had telephoned her. Said she was getting married.'

Terry whimpered. Nell glared at him.

Karen's father joined in. 'She said that she'd met this boy who looked like the dead spit of someone off the telly. She said he was in show business. Karen doesn't always tell the truth.'

Karen's mother nodded at this understatement. 'We thought then she might have run away with the fair. She was there every night . . . Kept on about it . . . We didn't think at first, you see . . . We tried London and –'

'Stow-on-the-Wold?' Nell looked at their tired, lined faces. She tried to think back to Oakton. What had Karen said that night? 'I'll have to be in by ten or my dad'll kill me'? Something like that. He didn't look capable of killing anyone. He just looked as though he hadn't slept for nights on end. Neither of them looked as though they deserved Karen as a daughter. She took a deep breath. 'I think Terry knows where Karen is, don't you, Terry?'

Danny, who had been simmering during the whole conversation, exploded. 'You mean you've got that slut here? That she's been here all the bloody time?'

No one seemed happy with the word slut. Nell couldn't blame them.

Terry stood up. 'Yeah. She's in the Beast Wagon. Honest to God, she said she was eighteen. She looks eighteen. I didn't ask to see her birth certificate.'

The wispy woman sobbed, whether from relief at having found the errant Karen, or horror at the mental image of her daughter and Terry performing nightly in the Beast Wagon, Nell couldn't tell.

The police got neatly to their feet as if choreographed. 'It would have saved a great deal of time if you'd said that straight away, sir. There may of course be charges, with the young lady being under the age of consent.'

Young lady didn't sound too accurate either, Nell thought, as everyone tried to get out of the door together.

'Quite a bevy of beauties you've got here, sir.' The older policeman saw Claudia and looked as though he wanted to take her in for questioning.

'They're not mine,' Danny growled, condemning both Nell and Claudia with one glower. 'I don't own them.'

'I should think not.' The policewoman seemed quite affronted by this open display of political incorrectness.

'Now, if we could just have a word with Karen and reunite her with her parents, and then –' she glared at Terry, 'I think we'll need to ask you some questions, sir.'

The police presence had attracted a Cup Final crowd. People jostled for a better view. Claudia was watching the proceedings from Sam's side, Nell noticed, looking as if she was going to burst into tears at any moment. Was that guilt or distress? There simply wasn't time to find out as the posse strode forward across the grass. Nell, still barefooted, attempted to keep up.

The removal of Karen from the confines of the Beast Wagon was carried out amazingly swiftly. Glaring at her parents and the police, she hurled herself down the steps and into Terry's arms.

'Bloody Octavia Barrett! I knew she'd snitch! I should never have rung her! Tell them, Tel. Tell them we're getting married.'

'I never said that exactly . . .'

'You did!' Karen wailed as the policewoman prised them apart. 'You promised.'

'And you, sir.' The policeman who had ogled Nell, grabbed Terry by the shoulder. 'Into the car. We'll have to see what charges you face. No, not you, miss –' He had to grapple with Karen who was determined to attach herself to Terry again. 'You go in that one. With your mum and dad.'

The doors slammed shut. Sam looked at Nell worriedly. 'Should one of us go as well, do you think? Terry's our responsibility really. If they charge him he'll need a solicitor, won't he?'

'Might help,' Nell nodded. 'Although I'm not sure that you should suggest he uses the Bradley family one. Mum and Dad'd never forgive you. And we don't want this splashed over the front of the tabloids. We get enough bad publicity as it is. Yeah, go and see what you can do.'

Ross Percival would have a field day over this, Nell knew. And he wouldn't be hotfooting it to the police station to try and bail out one of his miscreant gaff lads. She sighed. She and Ross, so much alike, so far apart.

'Oh, God. Fourteen! Silly little buggers!'

She almost sighed. She was in danger of sounding quite sensible. Sensible Nell Bradley – who had just blued her entire personal savings on a set of gallopers. A set of gallopers, she thought with a quiver of excitement, that would be delivered to Fox Hollow tomorrow. Sensible Nell Bradley – who was dithering over whether or not she should marry one of the most eligible bachelors in the country.

'I think they were in love,' Sam said softly. 'Or at least, they thought they were. After all, it's been ages since Oakton – Terry could have dropped her weeks ago. I'll go down to the station and see what I can do. Take care of Claudia.'

'Claudia? Why? Because of Terry? Christ, Sam – she wasn't – was she?'

'I don't know. Actually, I meant because of Danny – he still looks mad enough to lay into her. Persuade her to wash off that make-up and go back to the limp lace and beaded jackets. Not,' he added quickly, 'that it matters to me – but I think it just might dampen Danny's fuse.'

Nell shrugged. Maybe Sam was right. Oh God, why did life have to be so complicated?

'Where's Sam going?' Claudia asked over her shoulder, watching him reverse his Mazda from between the living wagons.

'Police station. To help Terry. Look, Claudia, don't you think you could cover up a bit? God – now where are you going?'

'With Sam.' Claudia's long, booted legs skimmed across the ground and caught up with the sports car as it reached the waltzer. She yanked the passenger door open and tumbled inside. Leaning from the window she shouted above the cacophony, 'Tell Rio Mackenzie to stay put in the hoopla. And tell Danny what the hell you like! Bye!'

CHAPTER FIFTEEN

S am and Claudia hadn't returned. With Terry also still missing, Danny was tearing out his hair over the staff shortage. Nell, having roped in a dozen or so likely lads from the pubs nearest the river, found that in consequence pull-down was far more good-natured than professional. Several of the regatta-goers had stayed on to watch, and were lounging on the bank with champagne buckets. A full moon illuminated the water and tinged the grass with silver like a hoar-frost. This would have gladdened Nell's romantic soul if only she hadn't been quite so bothered about the absentees, exhausted, and frantic with nerves over the gallopers' arrival at Fox Hollow.

'They left the police station hours ago!' Danny yelled as Nell, helped by Nyree-Dawn, Mercedes, and Rio Mackenzie, loaded the paratrooper cars. 'I've phoned three bloody times! Where the hell can they have got to?'

'I haven't got a clue.' Nell panted to a halt. She'd replaced the shorts and bra top with jeans and a T-shirt and was regretting it. 'What about Terry? Have they let him go?'

'How should I know – oh, bugger me!' Danny dived across the grass swearing violently as one of the Henley locals dropped his end of a waltzer platform. 'I didn't ask about him!'

No, you wouldn't, Nell thought, as rivers of perspiration trickled down her spine. Maybe Claudia had left the police station with Terry. Maybe Sam had driven up to London to see the family solicitor despite her pleas to the contrary. Maybe Karen's parents were charging everyone with abduction . . .

'Christ knows what's got into Claudia.' Danny lifted a pile of paratrooper bars on to his shoulder with ease. 'Belting off like that. Don't know what she thought she'd achieve. Mind, she's always had a soft spot for that Terry, whatever she says.'

'So have I.' Nell pushed her damp hair back into its scrunchie. 'He's a nice kid and a good grafter. It doesn't mean Claudia is having an affair with him, though.' She glared at her brother, trying not to think about Terry being in their living wagon, or the condoms, or of Claudia and Terry in the dark shadows. 'To be honest I think she took the easy option. Rushing off to the police station with Sam was probably preferable to staying here with you. You'd have only gone on about her clothes again, wouldn't you? You're behaving like a pig, Danny – and you know it.'

Danny hurled the heavy bars into the back of the lorry as though they were featherdown. 'She looked like a tart.'

'For God's sake, she looked gorgeous. She always looks gorgeous. And I know why she dressed as she did today – because you'd had a go at her. Again. Anyway, I wasn't dressed so very differently. We were displaying about the same amount of body. You didn't go ballistic about that, did you?'

'Why should I?' Danny kicked a pile of coiled cables into shape. 'That's not my job. That's up to Ross.'

'Christ! No wonder Claudia is rebelling. Where do you get your ideas from? You sound like a Victorian patriarch.' Nell shook her head. 'If you don't lay off Claudia, Dan, she'll leave you.'

'Course she won't. She can't. She's my wife.'

God give me strength, Nell thought, fastening the bolts on the trailer with angry fingers.

The Henleyites' laughter and chatter and chink of glasses echoed through the silvered darkness. The remaining gaff lads had worked hard to make up for Sam, Terry and Claudia; and even the older Mackenzies joined in. By the time everything was loaded, roped and sheeted, and ready to pull out, Nell was growing more concerned. There was no way on earth that Sam and Claudia would miss an entire pull-down unless something awful had happened to them – she'd tried phoning but both mobiles were switched off – and in an hour's time they'd all be on the road for their overnight journey to Woodstock.

She made a quick supper of ham and tomato sandwiches for the subdued Mick, Barry, Ted and Alfie. There was no time for a fry-up tonight, she told them, missing Terry with his compliments and his teasing. She'd make it up to them tomorrow morning when they'd pulled on to Blenheim Palace's South Lawn, she promised. She might even go so far as fried bread.

Speculation was rife. The gaff lads were closely knit, and in an occupation where drifting was the norm, the Bradley workforce had been together longer than most. Terry was like a brother to them. They were tough, hard, unemotional men and Nell found their concern moving.

'We're going to have to do bloody double runs,' Danny fumed at two o'clock when still no one had returned and he realised that they were now three drivers short. 'We'll take the living wagons first, and then see who can couple up to what. This is a fucking nightmare. I'll kill bloody Sam. Why haven't they come back?'

Nell couldn't imagine. Sam, being gentle and peace-loving, may well have taken Claudia for a drink after the day's traumas, but the pubs had shut hours ago. Even the night-clubs would be closed by now.

Danny was pacing up and down. 'How many of the Macs' kids have got licences?'

'The three older girls have passed their tests,' Nell said, out of breath from coupling her living wagon to the Volvo and trying not to think about the gallopers and Fox Hollow. It wasn't tomorrow any more. It was today. In twelve hours' time . . . 'None of them could drive the lorries, although I suppose they could take the living wagons. Oh, hang on.'

A set of halogen headlights were bouncing across the field towards them. Nell willed the lights to belong to Sam's Mazda.

'I heard you were having a spot of bother.' Ross uncurled himself from the depths of the Ferrari. 'We thought we might be able to help.'

He was followed by one of the more Neanderthal Percival gaff lads, who looked as though his knees had been touching his nose for the entire journey. Their faces were ghostly in the moonlight. Nell, who had never been so delighted to see anyone in her life, threw herself into Ross's arms.

'You're a life-saver! How on earth did you know?'

'How does anyone in our business ever know anything?' Ross disentangled himself and dropped a brotherly kiss on the top of her scrunchie. 'Your gaff lads mentioned it in the pub to Pelhams' gaff lads who were going to Shiplake, and it took precisely forty-five minutes to get to our gaff lads thirty miles down the road. So, here we are. Obviously we've missed the hard work – but we can certainly shift some of the loads to Blenheim for you. Shall I go and have a word with Danny?'

Nell shrugged. Instructions must be issued by testosterone, she thought crossly, watching him laughing with Danny – and making Danny laugh back. He obviously didn't see her as much of a lover either if his greeting was anything to go by. God, what did she feel for him? Delighted to see him, of course – but was that really only because he could drive a lorry? Still, between them, he and Danny seemed to have got things under control. Neither of them asked her for any further input so she wandered off towards the quietly lapping river and punched out the number of the police station on her mobile.

After much yawning and paper-rustling, the disinterested

voice on the other end said that Terry had been released. On the understanding that he reported to a local police station every day until such time as they were sure about charges.

'So the Emblings were definitely bringing charges, were they?'

Not allowed to disclose, the disinterested voice told her. And no, he couldn't divulge anything further. No, he didn't know where Terry was. If he didn't report to a police station somewhere in the country by midday tomorrow, though, he'd be arrested.

And what had happened to everyone else?

The voice yawned and stretched. Mr and Mrs and Miss Embling – the parents and the abducted minor – Nell groaned into the phone – had gone home to Oakton to discuss things with the aforementioned minor's social worker. Mr and Mrs Bradley had been extremely helpful – Nell groaned again. How had her parents become involved? Just in time she realised he meant Sam and Claudia. It sounded funny. As if they were a couple.

The policeman sounded as though he was scratching. Mr and Mrs Bradley had stood surety for Mr Freeman – Nell guessed this was Terry. She'd never known his surname – and all three had left together.

When?

Really couldn't say. Some time before midnight.

Nell clicked off the phone. Great. So where were they now?

'Ready?' Ross appeared out of the darkness. 'We've got everything sorted. There are a few dubious three-trailer loads, but the roads should be fairly quiet. We've decided that you can drive the Scammell – and with any luck, we should get it all done in one hit.'

'Thanks. I'm very grateful – we would have been pretty stuck without you.' Nell pushed her phone into her back pocket. 'They've let Terry go.'

'Good riddance. You won't be seeing him again.'

'Of course we will.' She frowned at Ross in the darkness. 'I mean, he didn't know the girl was under age – and he didn't keep her prisoner, did he? I expect she loved every minute of it. It seems mightily unfair to me if they press charges against him.'

'I wouldn't have him back – and I'm sure Danny won't. You don't want that sort of thing going on.'

Nell almost stamped her foot. 'There can't be a gaff lad in the country that hasn't fallen into that trap. And we do have some responsibility for them.'

Ross laughed at her indignation. 'Why? They come and go. He better not show his face round here when I've joined you.' He touched her cheek briefly. 'We mustn't waste any more time anyway. We've got a fairish haul in front of us. We'll talk about it tomorrow night at Blenheim. Did you know that the parents were coming?'

Nell knew. She didn't think it was a particularly great idea. Especially not now. And even more especially if Sam and Claudia and Terry still hadn't made an appearance. Anyway, no doubt Adele and Peter, Clem and Marcia, would be deciding her future. A future that involved Ross, a Percival merger, and a whole shooting match of white-knuckle rides. A future that was completely out of sync with someone who owned a set of gallopers and an eighty-nine-key organ.

She didn't think Ross looked too delighted about the arrangement either. He yawned. 'Oh well, see you at the other end, Freckle Face.'

The first loads jolted away in the moonlight, cheered on by the Henleyites waving their empty bottles and chicken drumsticks. Nell clambered into the cab of the Scammell and started the engine. With a stirring of anger, she noticed Danny and Ross ogling Nyree-Dawn and Mercedes, the eighteen-year-old Mackenzie twins, as they climbed into Claudia's Shogun and her own Volvo. Dressed, as always identically, in frayed white shorts, knotted denim shirts and Doc Martens, they displayed a great deal of sun-bronzed leg and cleavage.

Bloody dual standards, Nell thought, grinding the Scammell's gears. Bloody men!

Nell stood in the middle of the deserted yard at Fox Hollow and felt sick. Nearly quarter past two. She didn't think she'd had any sleep at all. They had managed to arrive at Woodstock and pull into a lay-by for what was left of the night without further incident, and had built up on the splendour of Blenheim Palace's South Lawn as the church bells pealed across Bladon. Ross and the Percival gaff lad had left just before midday. There was still no sign of Claudia, Sam or Terry. The mobiles were switched off. Danny was in a state of white-hot fury, which hadn't been cooled by her own rather garbled excuses as to why she'd be missing for most of the afternoon.

Nell rolled back the doors of the shed. It housed the three Bradley rides over the winter, and was large enough to keep her purchases safe from prying eyes. There were power supplies, excellent lighting, and running water. Jack Morland should be able to get on with his painting without interruption.

At half past two the distant chug of large vehicles in low gear made the hairs stand up on the back of her neck. Her mouth was dry. Her hands shook. This was it.

The convoy of black-and-gold Diadem Transport lorries turned expertly into the yard. Three – no four – artics and a smaller truck. Nell blinked. The Gavioli would be in the small wagon; one lorry for the horses; and one for the platforms and rounding boards and rods. So why –?

The cavalcade hissed to a neat halt, and Jack Morland, beaming from ear to ear, dropped from the cab of the leading lorry. 'Sorry we're late. I thought you might not be here.'

'I nearly wasn't,' Nell swallowed, unable to believe that this was really happening. 'The shed's ready. Do you want a hand with unloading?'

Jack looked quite shocked at this suggestion for a second. 'God, I forgot – you must do this all the time. We've come 'mob-handed, but the more the merrier.' He was still grinning. 'Brilliant, isn't it?'

'Unbelievable,' Nell said faintly, watching Percy, Dennis, Harry, Fred and the assorted Bobs and Jims and Bens of the Downland Trust piling from the vehicles. 'I think I'm going to wake up in a minute.'

'I didn't sleep at all last night,' Jack admitted. 'It was like being a kid on Christmas Eve all over again. OK boys, let's go!'

Diadem Transport's drivers seemed to be keen to help as well. Nell was gratified to notice that two of them were female.

'Georgia and Rory Faulkner,' Jack introduced them briefly. 'Just back from honeymoon, so we're lucky to have them. Oh, and Jed, Barney and Marie.'

Nell shook hands and said congratulations to Georgia and Rory, and thanks to everyone else, and tried to stop her head from spinning as the first parts of the disassembled gallopers were carried into the shed. She lifted with the rest of them, tears of joy prickling her eyelids, simply longing to stroke and touch, stop and admire.

It made sense to have the completed parts stacked at the furthest end, she said, and whatever Jack was still working on nearer all his painting paraphernalia at the front. Yes, and all the rods could be left wrapped in their tarpaulins so that the brass shouldn't tarnish, and the organ? Where should that go?

'By the nearest electricity supply?' Jack suggested. 'It'll run off mains power as well as any other sort. That way we can play it to check that everything's working. If there's any tuning needed, Jim knows the right bloke for the job and we can have it all completed before we build up. I don't think there was any damage in transporting it – we were really careful to bolt everything down, but it'd be as well to make sure.'

The Gavioli was manoeuvred gently into place. Nell twitched up a corner of its cover just to make sure it was really there. A couple of the Bobs and Bens grinned at her with understanding.

It took very little time, considering the delicate nature of the loads. Within an hour the shed was stacked with completed rounding boards, top centres, swifts, shields, folded tilts, rods, platforms, and thirty-six wooden horses, nostrils flaring, manes streaming, still galloping to nowhere.

'I thought,' Jack wiped the grubby sleeve of his cotton sweater across his forehead, 'that we might rename the horses. They had names like Betty and Alice scrolled on their necks, which are traditional, of course, but it wouldn't take me too long to do new ones.'

Nell pondered. They were hers now. She'd like them to be reborn. It was a nice idea. 'I think they should have really old-fashioned, important names. Like Vincent and Jemima, and Lexington and – oh – Cassandra –' She stopped. 'Or possibly not. Maybe shorter ones like Joe and Ned – as you've got to paint them.'

'I've told you, it's a labour of love. You choose whatever you want and let me know.' Jack was looking round the shed. 'We could build up in here, you know. When I've finished painting. A sort of trial run. There's plenty of room. So – what did your brothers think about it in the end?'

'I still haven't told them.' Nell had scoured *The World's Fair* preservation section, petrified that details of the auction would have been printed, but it had been covered in a brief paragraph and no purchasers had been mentioned.

'Where do they think you are today, then?'

'God knows. Well, one of them wasn't around actually.' She smiled at him. 'You know I told you about my sister-in-law last night when you phoned? Well –'

She didn't know why she told him. It was just that he was so easy to talk to, and seemed to find the story interesting and either funny or shocking in all the right places.

'What about you?' she finished. 'What did you tell Fiona about all this? She didn't seem too keen on your hobby.'

'She isn't and I haven't told her anything, either,' Jack

admitted with a cheerful grin. 'She's at my parents' house waiting for me to return from a very pressing Sunday morning at work in time for an extremely late lunch.'

'So we're both being pretty devious about this, aren't we?'

'We are. And before you think that being devious is an integral part of my nature, I think you ought to have a look at something.'

The remainder of the Downland Trust stood back, all wearing huge cheesy grins. Nell wrinkled her nose. What did they know that she didn't? She followed Jack back into the yard, blinking again in the dazzle of the afternoon sun, and round to the rear of the last two Diadem lorries. Rory and Georgia Faulkner had dropped the legs ready for unloading and she peered inside.

'Oh, God!' She swung round on Jack. 'There's been some mistake! I didn't buy them! They're not mine – who on earth do they belong to?'

'I bought them.' Jack indicated to the Downland Trust that they could start unpacking the caterpillar and the ghost train. 'As my contribution to Petronella Bradley's Memory Lane Fair. They're ready to go – they won't need any work. I thought we could just sort of hang on to them until the gallopers were ready and then –'

'Sell our souls for some Guild sites?' It hardly seemed fair to plant obstacles in his path. He looked so delighted. And, of course, two more rides would be wonderful. But he didn't understand. How could he? He was a flatty playing at being a traveller. He had no idea how it worked. You couldn't just buy a ride and park it wherever you wanted. Still, they must have cost him a great deal of money. She certainly wouldn't have been able to afford them for ages. She smiled. 'They're brilliant – and it's a wicked idea. You're very kind to think of it. Thank you.'

'I think I should be thanking you. You were the one who saved my sanity by rescuing the gallopers –'

'Yeah, well, when you've finished with the mutual self-congratulations,' Rory Faulkner interrupted with a grin, 'could you tell us just where these rides are supposed to go?'

Once the two newcomers had been installed in the depths of the shed, and the Diadem drivers had produced very welcome packs of ice-cold drinks, Nell drifted back into the shadows and lifted the tarpaulin that covered the Gavioli. She touched the proscenium. Nothing rocked. It was solidly in place on its temporary wooden pallet home. The cables were neatly rolled behind the drums. There were two heavy-duty ones, originally for the organ's connection to a traction engine, but nowadays to be coupled up to a modern generator; and a single black one complete with plug.

She looked quickly over her shoulder. The Downland boys were sitting in the sun deep in conversation with the Diadem drivers. She knew she should simply thank everyone, close the doors, leave Fox Hollow, and beetle off back to Blenheim. But the temptation was far too strong.

'The music books are in the cupboard,' Jack Morland spoke softly, making her jump. 'It might be a good idea to try her out – just to make sure there's been no damage. And you did say you'd played an organ before, didn't you?'

'Not really. Well, my grandparents' – but that was years ago. I was only a kid.' Nell was tearing off the tarpaulin. 'I've probably lost the knack by now. But there's only one way to find out, isn't there?'

She uncoiled the cable and handed it to Jack to plug in, then, stepping carefully over the hump of tarpaulin, climbed the rickety wooden steps into the back of the organ. It was gloomy and dusty and smelled of sadness. How long had it stood unused and unloved? Nell stroked the unvarnished key frame. Not long now, she promised, and you'll be out on the road again.

'You OK?' Jack's voice echoed up from the front. 'Do you want me to switch the power on yet?'

'I'll shout when I'm ready. I'm just – er – feeling my feet.'

What did she remember? The drums had to be tightened, she knew that. They had wing-nuts that secured the delicate skins and were always loosened during travelling. As a small child, her grandfather had always sent her squirming through the intricate figures to 'fiddle wi' the drums'. She grinned in delight. It was all coming back.

Leaning across the bosomy shepherdess and under the Harlequin's raised arm, she screwed the bass drums and side drums and cymbals as tightly as possible, then slid back to the key frame.

'I didn't know if you had a preference for an opening number.' Jack's face was on a level with her knees. 'I suppose it should really be "Entry of the Gladiators", but I love this one and it was near the front –'

Nell took the cardboard book from him. 'Oh, great. "Sabre Dance". Yeah – that's a real riding tune. Although when we're on the road the first tune we play in public will have to be "Paree". It's traditional.' She grinned. 'OK, then – let's find out the worst. Switch on.'

Jack disappeared again, and after a nail-biting few seconds the organ gave a massive, groaning, wheezing intake of breath as the air swelled into the bellows. The hundreds of lights glowed faintly, then grew in strength, until the darkness of the shed was illuminated like a grotto. Against them, the Gavioli's muted paintwork glowed rich and jewel-bright.

Jack leaned into the back of the organ and gave her a rather shaky thumbs-up. So far, so good. She retaliated with crossed fingers as she placed 'Sabre Dance' on the shelf just below the key frame, lifted the lid, and slid the first perforated page of the cardboard concertina into place.

She understood the basics. Each perforation was a note, the score of the tune, and each perforation corresponded to a key. As the music book was fed automatically through the rubber rollers of the key frame it activated air-blown valves which in turn played the corresponding note. The eighty-nine keys – pipes, flutes, reed, piccolos and drums – could imitate an entire orchestra and, if her memory of her grandparents' organ was reliable, sounded at least twice as loud.

Her hands were clammy. Her mouth was dry. She'd dreamed of this for so long. Maybe it wasn't quite the full culmination – God knows what she'd feel like when the Gavioli was actually playing in the centre of the gallopers – but it was close enough.

Jack smiled up at her encouragingly, his excitement tangible. She closed her eyes, took a deep breath, and snapped the keyboard shut.

Within seconds the shed, the yard, and all of Fox Hollow exploded with the full-toned blast of Khachaturian's masterpiece. Nell, giddy with delight at her success, tapped her foot and felt the tears welling up again as the cardboard folds travelled smoothly beneath the key frame. It was wonderful. Simply wonderful. She didn't dare look at Jack. She'd probably cry.

The three-foot-high figures along the front of the organ crackled with life. The moustachioed soldiers swung their arms with military precision, the shepherdess swayed, and Harlequin and Columbine bowed and curtseyed, as the music soared and roared, with not a note missed, not a flat to be heard. For all its years of inactivity, the Gavioli was perfect.

At last she dared to look down. Jack was shaking his head in silent amazement. The Downland Trust and the Diadem drivers had come in from the yard and were gaping. Nell had never felt such a high; such a surge of pure pleasure.

As the final notes died away everyone was silent. Shaking, she closed the key frame, picked up the music book, almost dropping it, and stumbled down the steps.

'Bloody incredible.' Jack's expression matched her own. 'Totally bloody incredible.'

Percy took 'Sabre Dance' from her clammy fingers, and the other Downland Trusters unplugged, uncoupled, and replaced the tarpaulin. Nell felt as though she was floating. The notes still reverberated inside her head; her body throbbed with the drumbeats.

'I'm really sorry to be a pooper,' Georgia Faulkner

laughed. 'And I must say that that was amazing. Beautiful. It might even persuade me away from Dinah Washington and Ella Fitzgerald and I can't wait until you're actually up and running. But if we don't shift now, Jack will be paying us overtime. And this Sunday work has cost him an arm and a leg already.'

Reluctantly, they checked that everything was secure, switched off, tidy. Nell, left alone, took one last look round in the gloomy darkness before closing the doors. It wasn't sad any longer. It was all merely waiting, as she was, to get out on the road.

The Diadem lorries were revving, eager to make the return journey to Upton Poges. Jack leaned down from his seat in the cab beside Rory Faulkner.

'Enjoy yourself at Blenheim tonight,' he grinned at her. 'I hope your wanderers have returned. And thanks again – what are these?'

'Keys to the yard and the shed.' She handed the bunch up to him. 'You'll be able to let yourself in and out whenever you want to paint. I hope you enjoy the rest of the day with your parents. And I'll come back as soon as I can.'

She stood and watched as the cavalcade reversed and disappeared into Fox Hollow's high-banked lane. It couldn't be soon enough.

CHAPTER SIXTEEN

The fifteen miles between Diadem Transport's yard at Upton Poges and his parents' house simply flew. Jack had never felt so reckless, so completely alive. The Norton Commando Roadster rocketed along the narrow country lanes; the wind was slicing through his thin cotton jersey, and his head was full of the Gavioli's blood-stirring music. Nothing, simply nothing, could put a dampener on his euphoria.

'Where the hell have you been?' Fiona was pacing Bill and Eileen's immaculate drive, and hardly allowed him time to remove his crash helmet. 'Your mother reckoned on you not being here much before three – but it's nearly tea-time. And look at your clothes! She'll have a fit. Couldn't you have gone home and changed first? Honest to God, Jack, do you never think?'

He propped up the Roadster on its rest, and ran his fingers through his hair. 'Hello, darling. Have you missed me?'

'And that won't wash, either.' Fiona avoided his kiss. 'You reek of petrol, you're covered in dust, and your hands are filthy. Why you had to do this corporate spying thing on the day Eileen invited us to lunch, I'll never know. I thought Bill had more sense. I've been sitting here since midday listening to your mother's stories about the day centre and your father's small talk about business. I'm absolutely starving and all I've had is a glass of supermarket sherry and two Ritz crackers and –'

'That's nice,' Jack smiled again and wandered towards the house.

His parents had one of the first Morland Homes. It was much larger than the ones they built these days and had a proper garden, designed prior to the fashion for squeezing a further three blocks of semis on to a telephone-box-sized lawn. There was a smell of overdone chicken wafting from the open kitchen door, mingling with the Jeyes Fluid that his mother used to sluice down every available crevice. It was rather comforting. Like coming home from school for the holidays.

He stepped out into the garden through the patio doors. His father, thankfully, wasn't there.

'Darling!' His mother's eyes were reproachful. 'Where have you been? I told your father he works you too hard – sending you out on scouting missions on a Sunday! And I wish you hadn't brought the motorbike, Jack. The neighbours like to have their forty winks on a Sunday afternoon. Lunch is probably ruined – and we'll have to call it supper now, anyway. Dad's in the study. I'll tell him that you've arrived.' She lumbered to her feet from the vibrantly coloured lounger. 'We're going to eat out here. Pour yourself a sherry.'

'Can I help?' Fiona asked. 'Anything I can do?'

'No, thank you.' Eileen shook her head, disappearing towards the house. 'You and Jack have got plenty to talk about – and you have so little time, don't you? Both working so hard. Sit down and relax, darlings. You deserve it.'

Jack sat on the edge of the vacated lounger, his legs far too long to accomplish this with any degree of comfort. He wasn't hungry, and he certainly didn't want a glass of lukewarm sherry. His entire body ached to be back at Fox Hollow; to start work on the intricate and delicate lettering on the rounding boards; to see the words 'Petronella

Bradley's Golden Galloping Horses' emerge in gilded scrolls from his brush; to start the renaming of the horses –

'– and so I agreed with that. She's arranging something tomorrow. Well, it makes sense, doesn't it? After all, this garden is far larger than ours. What do you think?'

Jack shook himself back to the present. Fiona, in her neat and understated green linen sundress, must have been speaking for ages. He hadn't heard a word.

'Yeah. Great. Sounds brilliant.'

'I knew you'd agree.' She crossed the striped lawn and sat beside him on the lounger. Her hand was on his thigh, circling on the paint-streaked black denim. 'You are a complete bastard, Jack Morland. You don't believe in compromise, do you?'

'No,' said Jack, who didn't. 'Which compromise are we talking about?'

Fiona laughed and snuggled up closer. It was very hot. She kissed his ear. 'Sometimes I don't think you listen to anything I say. You're still off in your own little world. Dreaming. Day-dreaming . . .' She snaked her hand higher.

Eileen came bouncing to the rescue. Bobbing across the lawn carrying a loaded tray, her voice would have out-shrilled the Roadster's exhaust. 'Fiona! If you really would like to lend a hand, could you be an angel and fetch the veggies? They're in the tureens on the breakfast bench. No – Jack – you stay there. I want to have a little word.'

Shit, Jack thought.

Eileen bustled round the canopied wrought-iron table, setting out knives and forks, paper napkins, salt and pepper, plates, and another raft of glasses. Jack stood up to help her, awkward with the trappings of gentility. He wouldn't hurt his mother for the world, but he wished she knew him better. He wished she understood that he'd be perfectly happy with a sandwich and a bottle of Beck's.

'You do look a wreck, darling.' She straightened up and surveyed him. 'Even if you have to wear jeans, why don't you wear those nice ones Fiona got from Marks and Spencer? The ones with the crease? And your sweater – you've got more fray than cuff! And that ring – look at it! Still covered in paint! Still, that'll be different come September when you have your wedding ring, won't it?' She poured a sherry refill and gave a sort of chuckle. 'So, has Fiona told you about the reception?'

He shook his head. Since Fiona had dropped the wedding bombshell he'd avoided all mention of it, hoping that it might just go away. It hadn't occurred to him that the plans were rumbling inexorably onward like tanks invading an unsuspecting and peaceful neighbouring country.

'We're having it here. I'm booking the marquee and the caterer tomorrow because it'll be September in next to no time. Fiona's already arranged the Register Office, of course, and Dad and I will be giving you the honeymoon as our wedding present. Did you have any thoughts on music?'

Oh, God. Music. The Gavioli – 'Paree'? 'Entry of the Gladiators'? 'Sabre Dance'? Jack felt the laughter rising and bit his lips. His mother would never forgive him if he laughed now.

'I wondered about a string quartet.' Eileen squinted at him through the sherry glass. 'Tasteful, I thought. Playing through the afternoon, and then no doubt you youngsters will want a bit of a discotheque for the evening, won't you? Then there's the question of Fiona's parents. With them being divorced and remarried – there must be some sort of protocol relating to second spouses.'

Tell her now, Jack thought. Stop this now before it gets completely out of hand. He'd have to tell Fiona first, of course. He wasn't being fair to any of them. The shackles were being fastened, the noose tightened. It wasn't what he wanted. He had to tell Fiona.

'Ah!' Eileen started to pull out chairs. 'Here come the troops!'

Jack helped Fiona with the tray of vegetable dishes and then lifted the chicken platter from his father.

'We need to talk.' Bill Morland's expression didn't change.

No one but Jack would have known he'd spoken. 'In private.'

'OK. But not now. After we've eaten.'

'Straight after.'

'Isn't this lovely?' Eileen was fussily seating everyone and pouring Liebfraumilch. 'Everyone together! Help yourself to veg, darlings. Bill will do the carving, won't you, sweetheart?'

Bill Morland flourished the carving knife and Jack winced. Holy shit, he thought. He bloody *knows*.

Bill Morland's study was twice the size of Jack's boxroom. The walls were lined with shelves, files were arranged alphabetically, and a fax and computer whirred despite it being Sunday. Morland Executive Homes never slept. Bill sat in his leather boardroom chair with lumbar support and flicked the end of a paper-knife. Jack, leaning against the door, watched this with unease.

'What have you got to say?' Bill's voice wasn't taking prisoners. 'I would appreciate some sort of explanation.'

Horribly reminded of the incident years ago when he'd been fifteen and his parents had found a stack of *Mayfairs* beneath his bed, Jack abandoned any thoughts of bluffing.

'About today, you mean?'

'Of course about today!' Bill swivelled angrily in the chair and faced him. 'I've had to lie through my teeth. Both your mother and Fiona simply couldn't understand why I sent you to recce the new Trencherwood sites on a Sunday. And on your motorbike. You might have had the courtesy to let me know that I was your alibi.'

'Yeah, sorry, I should have done. Thanks for covering, anyway.'

'That's not good enough, Jack. I want you to start playing by the rules. Is it another woman?'

Jack wanted to laugh again. It was far more serious than another woman. It was another life.

Bill tapped the paper-knife against the desk blotter. 'I'll take the silence as an admission, shall I?'

Fuck this, Jack thought, suddenly angry. I'm not a kid any more. 'OK. I shouldn't have buggered off without telling you. I shouldn't have assumed that you'd back me – but it was the easy option. I always take those. No one gets hurt that way. No, it isn't another woman. It's the Downland Trust.'

'Christ! I thought you'd finished with that. Oh, I know that you were arranging to have stuff moved – I heard you. I know you said that you hadn't completely abandoned the preservation thing, but as you hadn't mentioned it again, I hoped you'd had second thoughts. Do you mean that you've simply shifted the machinery to a different site? Do you mean that you still have every intention of playing at being a traveller and *painting*? And that you still haven't told Fiona?'

'More or less. Fiona wouldn't understand. I hoped you might.'

He didn't though, Jack realised, watching his father's face. They'd had the conversation after the auction, but Bill Morland hadn't realised its significance. His parents thought he should be happy with his executive position, his house, Fiona, and his life. Their dreams were the acceptable dreams of the middle classes. Never stepping out of line. Conforming. Being normal.

Bill put down the paper-knife. 'So, where does that leave us? I warned you before that Fiona would discover what you're doing, so don't you think you should tell her? Because, if you don't, then I will. You're a couple of months away from being married. You do want to marry her, I take it?'

Jack exhaled. He was very tired of all this. Of the confines. The restrictions. The having to explain his every move. It would be bad enough if he merely had to explain to Fiona – but he had to justify himself to his parents, too. Overwhelmed by the urge to tell his father to stuff his job, his executive homes, and his string quartet and marquee, he turned to leave the room.

'Jack!'

'I'm thirty-two, Dad. I'm old enough to run my own life. To make my own decisions and my own mistakes. Yes, I shall tell Fiona. But in my own time. And I won't be using you as an alibi any more. I'm sorry if I've embarrassed you. I just happen to think that there are more important things in life than working twenty hours a day and acquiring things that you're too bloody knackered to enjoy. Death doesn't go away. It creeps closer and closer. I want to have a bit of life first. My life. And if that's selfish then so be it.'

Hell, he thought as he thundered down the grey carpeted stairs, now we won't be speaking civilly again for ages. It was almost impossible to work together and not speak. Still, it should speed up boardroom agendas. Bill snarling and him responding with shakes or nods of the head. It was like being back at school and falling out with your best friend.

Fiona and his mother were still in the garden, sitting on the loungers with identical cups of tea. They'd be discussing the wedding, he knew they would. He wandered towards the greenhouse and fiddled with the heads of some richly coloured flowers. Which should he tackle first? The truth about the gallopers or his feelings about the wedding? Either was going to cause major problems. Both would hurt Fiona – but any delay would hurt her even more. He'd tell her tonight.

The decision made, he headed towards the loungers. His mother was flushed, but Fiona still looked ice-cool. He looked down on her, realising again how little he knew her. They never really shared anything; never talked unless it was about work. She rarely joked, rarely showed enthusiasm, never displayed vulnerability. How wrong he'd been to jog along with her for all these years. How cruel to want to stop jogging now.

'Jack – come and sit down.' Eileen patted a third lounger. 'You and Dad have a nice chat? I still think he's an old meanie to make you work on a Sunday. Surely he could have said whatever needed to be said tomorrow?'

Jack sat awkwardly again. He wanted to leave. Now. He wanted to go home and talk things over quietly with Fiona. 'We probably wouldn't have time to talk tomorrow. Best to get everything out in the open.' He raised his eyebrows in Fiona's direction. 'Are you ready to go?'

'Oh, not just yet!' Eileen looked woebegone. 'I never have you all to myself these days. And I wanted to show you this outfit.' She delved into a pile of magazines under a deck-chair. 'I thought I'd get one for the wedding – possibly in lilac. Although I'll have to make sure that I don't clash with Fiona's mother – or her stepmother for that matter! Goodness, isn't this going to be exciting?'

They spent another hour looking at suits and dresses, refilling the teacups, planning the wedding. His father remained upstairs in the study. Jack, trying to shut his ears to the gushes and exclamations and the rustling of glossy pages, stretched out on the lounger and attempted to sleep. It wasn't easy. The lights and colours of the Gavioli played behind his eyes, the growing crescendo of the 'Sabre Dance' roared inside his head. He almost whistled the tune. He could see the gallopers now, completed, painted, revolving in gaudy magnificence.

He was aware of feeling uncomfortably hot and sticky, and opened his eyes straight into the low rays of the evening sun. Fiona was standing over him.

'I'm off now. I need to go through my appointments for tomorrow.'

Jack sat up groggily, feeling sweaty and off-balance. 'Where's Mum?'

'Packing us up a food parcel of cold chicken. She's sure I don't feed you properly.'

Jack uncurled himself and stood up. He had to look down at Fiona. He suddenly thought of Nell Bradley. Her eyes were on the same level as his. Her freckles all smudged together to form a splodge across the bridge of her nose. He'd talked to Nell Bradley with the same unconscious ease as he did to his friends. Why couldn't all women be so uncomplicated?

'You go on, then, if you've got work to do. I'll wait for the food parcel. The Roadster will probably beat you anyway.' He kissed her briefly. 'See you at home.'

It was nearly midnight before they went to bed. Fiona had worked diligently in the study, checking her filofax against her laptop, telephoning, printing, sending faxes. She hadn't wanted to talk to him.

'Later, darling. When we're in bed. When I've had a shower, washed my hair, and generally pampered myself. You know I like to plan my week on Sunday evening. We'll talk in bed. Why don't you go to the pub? Fergus and Stan and Adam are bound to be there.'

Restless and completely at a loss, Jack wandered down to the Turlington Arms. The pub had been built at the same time as the estate, on what the architect fondly imagined was the nouveau equivalent of a village square. There were cobbles and plastic terracotta pots jammed with clashing busy lizzies. The Turlington Arms was brick red and pristine and looked suffocatingly hot. Buying a bottle of Beck's, Jack sat in the beer garden, which was, if anything, even hotter than inside and made desultory conversation with the neighbours. Children squawked and screamed as they swarmed over multicoloured climbing frames, while their parents ignored them and drank massive gins.

'Another?' Adam, who was wearing a rather daring cutaway singlet, batted his eyelashes at Jack. 'I do like a man who drinks straight from the bottle.'

Stan obviously didn't, by the way he frowned. God, Jack thought, am I watched here too? He hadn't realised that everyone else had glasses.

'No more, thanks.' He stood up. 'I've had a heavy day.'

They chorused their goodnights. He had nothing in common with them either, he thought as he walked slowly back through the culs-de-sac. He wondered what they would have said if he'd told them about the gallopers and the Gavioli, about Fox Hollow and Nell Bradley. They would probably have laughed at the vividness of his imagination. They'd never been really sure about his involvement with the Downland Trust. After all, they spent their Sundays washing the car, lunch-time drinking, sleeping with the colour supplements on their Texas garden furniture, another visit to the pub, a quick glimpse at the late tele-vision news, and then bed. And then Monday morning. And then death . . .

Jack laughed as he unlocked the front door. He really was becoming very cynical about life and death and the mean-ingful use of one before the other. He hoped Fiona would understand.

The radio alarm glowed at eleven forty-six. Fiona was already curled on the futon in the darkness, the moonlight casting white pools across her naked body. Jack padded from the bathroom and dropped his towelling robe on the floor. She didn't tell him to pick it up as she usually did, and he thought she must be asleep. He eased himself on to the bed beside her, listening to her breathing, wondering if he could turn on the light and read. It was still so hot.

Fiona moved her legs. 'I'm not asleep. No, leave the light. Do you want to talk?'

'If you're not too tired. It'll keep if you are.' Coward! he yelled at himself. 'Do you want to go to sleep?'

Fiona didn't answer. He wondered how much she knew. She was ferociously intelligent. He never underestimated her ability to read between the lines of his silence.

'I don't want you to talk.' She rolled towards him, propping herself on one elbow and looking at him with unblinking eyes. 'I want you to listen. I want you to answer my questions. Just yes or no will do.'

Jack sighed, understanding now what she was doing.

'You are so horny.' She stroked his body with her left hand, trailing her fingers across his chest. 'You're so bloody beautiful, Jack. You annoy me, exasperate me, with your laid-back attitudes and your refusal to conform. I hate you sometimes. Then I look at you, at your face, at your body, and I never want to let you go.'

She was still stroking. He tried to join in but she pushed his hand away. She often did this. She enjoyed the dominance. Jack thought that making love should be a joint participation, and never enjoyed these sessions as much as she did. He felt strangely disadvantaged and used, as if it didn't need to be him. It could have been anybody.

Fiona wound her slim body around him, still stroking, still trapping his hands so he couldn't touch her. 'You still get that stupid gypsy paper, don't you?'

'Yes.' It was part of the game. He knew the rules.

'You're still playing with your anorak chums, aren't you?'

Oh, God. 'Yes.'

'And you're not going to give it up?'

'No.' At least this way was easier.

'And is that where you were today?'

'Well, sort of – I mean –'

'Yes or no.' She nipped at his neck with her teeth, then kissed it better. 'Yes or no?'

Bloody hell. 'Yes.'

She seemed to be excited by this. Still stroking, using her fingers and her tongue to arouse him, she climbed on top of him. Her face was angular, pointed, almost vicious in the moonlight.

'Do you want to get married?' She was rocking backwards and forwards quickly now, her head thrown back. Her voice was jerky. 'I said – do you – want to – get married?'

He couldn't speak. Not now. Neither could she. Fiona eventually shuddered and collapsed on top of him. He lay there, not touching her, feeling exploited.

'I knew.' She climbed off him and sat cross-legged on the futon, still staring at him with glittering eyes. She was breathing heavily. 'About the fairground stuff. I knew you wouldn't give it up. I wish you'd told me.'

'I just did.' He wished he could have one of her bedside Marlboros. He'd given up smoking five years earlier. Right now seemed a damned good time to start again. 'Do you object very strongly?'

'I've got other things to worry about.' She leaned across and lit the obligatory cigarette. He inhaled the smoke greedily. 'You didn't answer me about the wedding.'

'It would take more than a yes or no answer.'

Fiona nodded and waved the glowing red tip of the Marlboro closer. 'Then shall I make it easier for you? You like things simple, Jack, don't you? Well, they don't come much more simple than this. I'm pregnant.'

CHAPTER SEVENTEEN

Sam's Mazda crunched across Blenheim Palace's gravelled courtyard at just gone three o'clock on Sunday afternoon. Early picnickers were already arriving, struggling from the car parks with rugs and hampers.

'Henley yesterday, Blenheim today,' Claudia said cheerfully, peering out through the windscreen. 'How the other half lives, eh?'

'Living may not be a luxury we'll enjoy for much longer,' Sam said, squealing the tyres on a tight bend, ricocheting gravel, and narrowly missing a verdigris'd statuette. 'Not if Danny has his way. We should have phoned and told him what was happening.'

'No we shouldn't.' Claudia waved regally at a couple in evening dress. 'He'd have told us to come back. Demanded. Ordered. Just stick to the story of the batteries being dead.'

'On both mobiles? And we didn't have access to a payphone?' The Mazda jolted across the South Lawn and into the fairground. 'And we missed pulling-down and building-up? People have been slung out of the Guild for less. Still, they seem to have managed very nicely without us. But he'll know we could have phoned this morning to let him know we were OK. He must have been worried sick about you.'

'Get real. He would only have missed three pairs of hands at pull-down. This is Danny we're talking about. I think you might be mistaking him for a husband who cares.'

Sam winced as he pulled to a halt on the shingle strip in front of the cluster of living wagons. There was no sign of life from any of them. Nell's Volvo was missing. 'Do you want me to face Danny with you?'

'Definitely not.' Claudia, still in the PVC hot pants, vest and boots but minus most of the make-up, got out of the car. Several middle-aged men stopped abruptly. 'We've done what we thought was right. Humanitarian. What anyone would have done under the circumstances. Anyway, as you say, he'll probably be so delighted to see me back that we'll be all lovey-dovey before the first firework. See you later.'

She waited until Sam's car had disappeared out of sight behind his living wagon and then pulled an agonised face. Danny, she knew, was going to go totally ape-shit. No question. She'd never been away all night before without him knowing exactly where she'd been. She took a deep breath and opened the front door.

Danny was asleep on the sofa, stripped to the waist, wearing only crumpled black cords. Claudia looked at him with deep sorrow. He had a lovely body, but his face, even in sleep, was angry. Was that her fault, too? She wished she still loved him. The television was chattering to itself but as he had the remote in his hand she decided against even attempting to switch it off. Tiptoeing through into the bedroom, she closed the door quietly behind her and sank down on the bed.

Within minutes she'd wiped away the smeared make-up, replacing the mascara because she'd always vowed she'd go to her coffin wearing mascara and a pale pink lipstick; whipped off the fantasy island clothes, pulled on a rather pretty sleeveless Monsoon frock, and tamed her corkscrew curls into tousled and shaggy.

'There,' she addressed herself in the mirror. 'Mrs Daniel Bradley is ready to face her public.'

It was a pity that Mrs Daniel Bradley wasn't quite so ready

to face her husband. It was also a pity that she couldn't have a shower, but the noise of the water was bound to wake Danny and the longer he slept the better. So she compensated with an extra-lengthy squirt of Arpège and counted to twenty with a Mum roll-on. Flapping her arms above her head as an aid to quick-drying, she leaned from the bedroom window.

Blenheim looked gorgeous beneath the cloudless blue sky, its honey-coloured buildings and perfectly manicured grounds everything that a stately home should be. At the front of the picnic area the bandstand was being erected. With a pleated white silk canopy, it looked like something from the Arabian Nights. The cordoned-off section past the fairground at the top of the lawn must be for the fireworks display, she decided; and in the background the fountains sparkled and danced in the sunshine, spilling their perpetual shower in a million crystal droplets.

It was all very different to last night. Claudia shuddered at the memory of the police station: hot and stuffy and with a definite smell of fear.

Terry had been hustled off into an interview room, as had Karen and her parents. She and Sam had sat rather awkwardly on spindly chairs and waited. It seemed like for ever. Sam had wanted to ring Danny and let him know that they were staying until things had been sorted out. Claudia had persuaded him not to.

Danny wouldn't have understood how guilty she felt. Terry had been her friend, and she'd encouraged Karen to stay with them really. Made it easy for her to remain in the Beast Wagon. And she had, hand on heart, always known that Karen was probably under age. But they had seemed so happy. And Terry was a nice kid.

Of course, as Sam had said, with hindsight it was pretty obvious that Karen's parents were frantic back at home. She simply hadn't thought about it.

That is why, when the policewoman emerged and asked if they were prepared to stand surety for Terry because there were some discrepancies between his story and Karen's and no one seemed too keen to press charges, they agreed and Sam had written the cheque.

Terry had appeared, looking shocked and scruffy, and tried to say thank-you, which was when Sam had said he'd stop the money from his wages. Claudia smiled, remembering Terry's grin.

'You mean you're not going to sack me?'

'Can't do that, can we?' Sam had shrugged. 'We don't officially employ you, remember? When did you give us your P45 and your National Insurance number?'

And they'd all laughed, and then stopped just as abruptly when the Duty Officer had said Terry must report to a police station every day until such time as they'd sorted out charges. If he didn't, he'd be arrested. Understood?

That, Claudia thought, watching the music stands and golden chairs being set in semicircles on the bandstand, was when the night had become rather strange. Up to that point, it had been fairly straightforward. Unpleasant, of course, but straightforward.

Then Karen and her parents had staggered out of their interview room, all looking very pale and shaken. Karen had immediately broken away and thrown herself at Terry. Neither her parents nor the police seemed to have the heart to separate them.

'Seems to me,' Karen's father had said, 'that there's more to all this than meets the eye. I think we could all do with a nice cup of tea.'

'Brilliant,' Claudia, who was dying for one, had agreed. 'There's a fairly good all-nighter just up the road.'

'Oh, I don't think so.' Karen's mother looked as though she was about to throw her petticoat over her face in horror. 'There's nothing like a good brew in your own home, that's what I always say.'

'Quite right, Mother. So I vote we all pootle off home and enjoy the cup that cheers,' Karen's father had looked almost perky. 'We might even be in time for Horlicks.'

Karen had shaken her head violently. 'I ain't going without Tel.'

Karen's parents, much to Claudia's surprise, seemed to have known she wouldn't. 'No, that's all right. You bring the lad along with you. We need to talk this through.'

Sam had looked at her with horror. 'That means we'll have to go as well. He's got a thousand quid of my money riding on him. Where do they live? Outer Mongolia?'

'Oakton,' Claudia had said faintly. 'Bloody miles. We'll never get back in time for pull-down.'

They had driven off in convoy, Sam keeping to a sedate forty-five miles an hour behind Karen's father's oatmeal Fiesta. It had taken well over an hour, and Karen and Terry had scrambled from the back seat of the car with far more love-bites than when they got in.

The house in Oakton was fairly oatmeal too, Claudia had noticed, with touches of salmon pink and mushroom. It had been a pretty bizarre tea party. The Emblings, Karen's parents, who called each other Mother and Dad, had confided that Terry seemed such a nice boy and they didn't want any trouble, you know. And Karen and Terry had sat side by side on the sofa and held hands. Karen had apparently sworn to every police officer who questioned her that she'd left home of her own accord because 'she wann'ed to do summat diff'rent with 'er life'. No, Terry had never laid a finger on her; he'd looked after her like a brother; they'd had separate beds. Sam and Claudia had practically choked on their very weak Tesco ground-leaf.

Karen, the Emblings said, had been – er – active for some time. Too many hormones, they explained. Advanced for her age. And she'd be fifteen next week – and everyone in their family got married at sixteen and eight months' pregnant. Sam and Claudia had murmured and felt very old. So, the Emblings had continued, if Karen was serious about Terry, wouldn't it be nice to announce their engagement on her birthday – and plan the wedding for next year? Terry, at this point, had tried to slide beneath the sofa. Sam had kicked him.

'What a lovely idea!' Claudia had smiled radiantly at everyone. 'I haven't been to a wedding for ages!'

So, as the dawn was breaking through the Emblings' mushroom curtains, it was agreed that Terry should stay in Oakton and accompany Karen and her father to the police station, where the misunderstandings could be sorted out once and for all. When everyone was satisfied that no offence had been committed, Terry would rejoin the fair, and Karen would return to school, and they'd see each other as and when. Then Mr Embling had excitedly made Horlicks and the four of them had trooped off upstairs to bed, leaving Sam and Claudia facing each other on rather hard-stuffed oatmeal fireside chairs.

'I think they think we're a couple,' Claudia had grumbled, easing off her boots.

Sam had punched his salmon-pink cushion. 'Suits me. Wake me up in an hour and we'll drive home.'

They'd woken at lunch-time.

The bedroom door opened and a bleary-eyed Danny staggered in, heading for the en suite. He didn't seem to see Claudia at first. She held her breath. It wouldn't take long.

It didn't.

'Where the fuck have you been?' Danny squinted at Claudia's new look rather doubtfully. 'And when the fuck did you get back?'

'Ages ago.' Claudia chewed the inside of her cheeks to stop her teeth from chattering. 'We tried to ring. Um – you managed OK without us, then?'

Ignoring this, Danny thrust his head forward. The veins were enlarged; the muscle in his cheek was twitching. Claudia felt very, very alone. His eyes were bleary. 'Where have you been?'

'Sorting things out with Terry.' She tried walking backwards but came up against the wall. She changed tack and started sliding sideways. He'd never hit her – yet. 'It took ages. Sam will explain.'

'Ter-ry!' Danny's tone was sing-song mocking. 'Darling Ter-ry! And where is the bastard now?'

'I don't know. Oakton, I think. It's all OK. I'm sorry we didn't ring –'

'You will be.'

'Don't threaten me, Danny. I haven't done anything wrong. I'm sorry I didn't let you know where I was – but you knew I was with Sam. You knew I was safe. You knew –'

'I knew –' Danny grabbed her shoulder, 'that you were with that pretty boy! How many condoms did you get through, eh? D'you really think I'm that bloody thick? Did you really think I believed they were Sam's? I *knew* who they belonged to – I just wanted you to tell me! And now you have!'

She squirmed under the pressure of his gripping fingers. 'Listen to yourself for once. Think, Danny. Why did we have yesterday's row? Because I'd started my period. Because I wasn't pregnant. I've never, ever been unfaithful to you.' The words tumbled over each other in indignation. 'I'm sorry I didn't ring you, I'm sorry I'm not pregnant – and I'm really, really sorry that I don't love you any more!'

Claudia wrenched herself away from him. Gathering the Monsoon frock up round her knees, she leapt across the bed and out of the bedroom, then belted across the sitting room towards the front door.

'Shit!' She landed barefooted on the strip of shingle. Oh, God. Why had she told him that? What on earth would happen now? She flew across the grass between the living wagons and pounded on Nell's door.

'She's gone out,' Rio Mackenzie, who was sunbathing in a brief bikini, informed her. 'Ages ago. Dunno where to. What happened last night?'

'Tell you later,' Claudia muttered, leaping over Nyree-Dawn and Mercedes whose bikinis were even scantier. 'If Danny comes looking for me, you haven't seen me, right?'

'Right,' the twins chorused in unison, replacing their Ray-Bans and rubbing each other with Ambre Solaire. 'No sweat.'

The picnickers seemed to be fairly unconcerned about where they sat. A whole host of them were spreading tablecloths on the grass between the Scammell and the Foden, right next to the generators. They'd be covered from head to foot in diesel spray the minute the rides started, Claudia thought, wondering if she should tell them. Probably not, she decided, stepping over unevenly-hewn hunks of gala pie and rather flaccid sausage rolls. If they couldn't make more effort than that for Blenheim Palace they deserved to get dieselled.

The concert wasn't due to start until eight o'clock, with the fireworks at ten. The fair should open at seven. Claudia saw no reason why she shouldn't man the hoopla as normal. Still, it was going to be tricky for a while. She stood forlornly amongst the living wagons. Oh, sod Nell. Why couldn't she be in? No doubt she'd gone rushing off to spend an illicit afternoon with her bank manager lover, not giving a thought for anyone else.

Sam, also stripped to the waist and wearing faded Levis, pulled open his door and anchored it back against the side of the living wagon. He grinned across at her. 'You look pretty swish. Quite a transformation, in fact. What's the matter? Decided that I'm not so unbearable after all, have you? Can't keep away – oh, Christ.' He leapt down the steps and gathered her in his arms. 'What's he done to you? Come on, sweetheart. Come on.'

She sat in Sam's living wagon – its dark wood and scarlet furnishings as familiar to her as her own home – and poured it all out. 'And I told him I don't love him any more,' she sniffed into a handful of kitchen roll. 'I shouldn't have done that.'

'Is it true?' Sam handed her a brandy.

'Course it's true.' Claudia drank the brandy as if it had been lemonade. 'You know it's true. Everyone knows it's bloody true. I just shouldn't have said it.'

Sam shrugged and sat beside her. 'Maybe it wasn't quite the right time, but I guess Danny knows it's true as well. I don't think it matters too much to him, honestly. Love isn't top of his agenda.'

'Not like Nell's – or yours, you mean?'

'Something like that.' Sam pulled her head down on to his shoulder. She didn't pull it away. He spoke into her hair. She wished she'd washed it. 'I actually quite enjoyed last night. We had a nice time together, didn't we?'

'We always do,' she mumbled into his bare shoulder. He'd showered and smelled of citrus and soap. 'I like it when we're friends.'

'So do I. Do you want me to go and talk to Danny?'

She shook her head. She liked the comfort, the security, of Sam's arms around her. Of not having to apologise. Of not fighting. Danny was best left to simmer for a while. It'd all blow over, probably. It usually did.

'Those condoms – in the van – at King's Bagley. They were Terry's. Oh, no – not like that. I let him and Karen use the living wagon, and he must have left them in there. You were very kind to say they were yours.'

'I was bloody angry to know they weren't.' Sam's voice sounded relieved, as if it was smiling. 'And Danny would have divorced you if he'd known you'd let a gaff lad into the trailer. You're really daft sometimes.'

Claudia sighed. She knew. 'Most times, actually.'

She moved her head, turning to face him. His eyes were watching her face. His lips were parted. She moved her head a little bit more, tentatively brushing her mouth against his, feeling the muscles contract in his shoulder. Slowly, very slowly, she kissed him.

Sam's eyes were still open, wide, surprised. Then they closed. He returned the kiss with gentle passion and Claudia's world simply tumbled upside down.

It wasn't, she thought dreamily, leaning on the edge of the hoopla and watching the crowds in their finery drift through the fair, as if she'd done anything wrong. Wrong, she reasoned, was merely the way other people saw things. Right and wrong was a matter for your own conscience. She'd kissed Sam. And enjoyed it. And he'd kissed her, a lot, and it had got quite serious as kissing went. She smiled to herself, reliving the sensation – the way her body felt as though it was melting. Quite a revelation. Not threatening or frightening – just thoroughly delightful. It was, she was sure, because Sam didn't act as though he possessed her – or even wanted to – he merely gave her pleasure and received it in return.

Maybe, she thought, as she sold a whole armful of hoops to a man in a tuxedo, that was what everyone went on about. What she'd been missing. If it was, then she had no intention of missing it any longer.

The sky was still cloudless; there was no wind. The picnic parties covered the South Lawn like racegoers on Derby Day. The fair was in full swing, and they had agreed to lower the volume of their music when the concert started. Claudia was determined to abandon the hoopla to Rio and watch the entire concert from the lawn. Danny had stormed past the hoopla without looking at her and immediately blasted aggressive strains of The Buzzcocks and Generation X from the waltzer. She really didn't care.

She sneaked a look at Sam who was in the pay-box of the dodgems covering for Nell, who had been late getting back. Claudia was absolutely itching to talk to her. He saw her looking and winked. She bit back a giggle and was pretty sure she was blushing. Crazy!

She was very busy for the next ten minutes, and watched with amusement as people with haw-haw voices took careful aim and became ecstatic over winning a naff digital watch or a tiny, lopsided teddy bear. The rides were full – even the swinging boats – and the punters were spending well tonight. She presumed that if they could afford tickets to a Blenheim concert they'd probably got oodles of small change. And the middle classes, she'd discovered, were stalwart supporters of fairs at gaffs such as this. They'd probably never set foot in a street fair or visit a village green, but give them a fair at a stately home or a venue like Henley or Epsom, and they were in their element. Almost as though the whole rather grubby and doubtful travelling process had been sanitised especially for their benefit.

She looked across at Sam again. He was busy now, not looking at her. It made it easier to stare. She had known him for so long and never really thought of him as anything other than her brother-in-law. Now – she sighed. Now it was completely different. Sex, of course, was out of the question. She didn't like it – and anyway, she was married. Shame really. She thought Sam might be quite good at sex. He was certainly bloody brilliant at kissing.

'Can't stop.' Nell leaned into the hoopla and touched her arm. 'I – er – got delayed earlier so I'm ages late.' She didn't look as though she cared too much, actually. 'I'm supposed to be on the dodgems, and with Terry absent, we're short-handed. Sam's been brilliant – he told me what happened last night – and about Danny – poor you. Look, when the concert starts we'll grab a bottle of champagne and talk, OK?'

'OK.' Claudia peered warily at Nell. She looked sensational in a long strapless dark blue dress; but it was more than that. Everything glowed: her skin, her eyes, her hair. It was as if someone had turned on a light inside her. 'You're not going to work dressed like that?'

'Too right. Look at you, Lady Muck! Anyway, Ross is coming over with the family. I thought I ought to make an effort. See you later.'

Claudia nodded. Nell might well have been making an effort, but she'd lay a pound to a penny it wasn't for Ross Percival's benefit; and she'd bet even more that it wasn't Ross who had made her sparkle like that.

'Snap!' She beamed at a rather suprised woman in faux pearls. 'The Bradley girls do it again!'

CHAPTER EIGHTEEN

The pair of high-heeled golden mules was possibly not the most sensible footwear for trekking over Blenheim's South Lawn, Adele conceded as she wobbled in Peter's wake. In fact, she thought, tonight might turn out to be a bit of a disaster all round.

They'd booked into the Bear at Woodstock, along with Clem and Marcia. It was truly sumptuous and Adele adored the elegance. She didn't, however, adore Marcia's constant company.

Neither was she really looking forward to meeting Nell. It had been easy to talk on the phone, but face to face was an entirely different matter. The purchase of the Crash'n'Dash still gave Adele nightmares – and its delivery to Haresfoot was looming ever closer. And she'd never been any good at lying. Nell was so astute, she would sense something was up straight away, she just knew it. And then what was she supposed to say? Admit that she'd just spent a terrifyingly large amount of money on a ride that at least one of her children didn't want, and none of them – or, even worse, Peter – knew about?

No one knew about the Crash'n'Dash – except Clem and Ross, of course – and, should such momentous news break tonight, it wouldn't do Peter's heart any good at all. Adele had confided in Priscilla during a hot flush, and Priscilla had responded with a disdainful stare and stalked dismissively away, her tail ramrod straight. Adele was beginning to wonder whether she might not have made the biggest mistake of all time.

Her hormones had started playing up as soon as they reached the Bear, egged on, she had no doubt, by nerves and guilt, which was when she'd discovered that she'd left her supply of evening primrose at Highcliffe. Peter, bless him, had volunteered to go into Woodstock for fresh supplies. In the middle of a real drencher he'd returned with Yeast-Vite. And, to cap it all, there was this hoo-ha about Claudia and Sam and one of the gaff lads. Ross had made some pretty scurrilous allegations and Marcia's eyes had flickered with predatory pleasure as she recounted them.

'Poor Adele.' She had oozed saccharine sympathy. 'Your children are such a worry, aren't they? Thank goodness mine are no trouble. No trouble at all. Never have been. Still, once your Nell has married Ross he'll soon bring her to heel, you mark my words.'

Adele had thought she'd like to see him try, and experienced the first flicker of doubt over the suitability of the match. Oh God – it was too late now. She'd bought the Crash'n'Dash – Ross Percival would be only hours behind it.

Then tonight, when she'd come downstairs at the hotel still fastening her rather outrageous Isle of Bute topaz earrings, Marcia had clasped her claws together and shrieked. 'Oh, I say! What an unusual frock! Is it British Home Stores?'

Adele, who had lost over half a stone at the Body Beautiful, and had been very proud of the fifties-style gold lamé creation which clung and moulded and which, she thought, made her look like Mitzi Gaynor, wanted to rip it off and change into something sharp and understated. Something like Marcia's stark black-and-white Chanel which might have been a small size eight and screamed 'cost a fortune'. It didn't matter that Peter had told her that she looked wonderful, or that Clem's eyes had lit up when she walked into the bar. She felt like a turkey basted and wrapped in tin foil.

'Here should do us nicely, ladies.' Puffing slightly after the climb to the South Lawn's best vantage point, Clem eased himself between two picnicking groups and shook out a massive tartan rug. 'Good view of the bandstand and the fireworks. And you can just see the fair from here. So, Princess – ' he gave Adele a very theatrical wink, 'do you want to go and speak to your offspring now or later?'

'Later.' Adele sat down, carefully avoiding his eyes. She didn't want any references to her duplicity, however veiled. 'Is Ross joining us? Will he know where to find us?'

'With you in that dress, Adele dear,' Marcia arranged her greyhound legs, 'he should have absolutely no trouble at all. Come along, Peter, let's be at the bubbly.'

Peter unpacked the Fortnum & Mason hamper which Marcia had insisted on, despite them having had a four-course dinner at the Bear. Adele knew Emma at the Body Beautiful would throw up her hands in horror at the sight of so many calories all in one place. There was pâté and salmon and various roast meats and cream sauces and Belgian chocolates and a gateau that looked like it had been designed by Gertrude Schilling. Four bottles of Krug nestled among a lot of shredded green paper and Adele thought secretly that if they managed a quarter of it between them, then someone would have to carry them back to the hotel.

'Here comes the band!' Clem roared, as the Oxfordshire Philharmonic climbed on the dais. 'Give 'em a cheer.'

'I think it's an orchestra, actually,' Marcia said, her buck teeth resting on the rim of her champagne flute. She had once been to the Last Night of the Proms. 'Band conjures up an image of something altogether different.'

'Like the Grimethorpe Colliery – or Bob Dylan,' Peter said. He'd already knocked back a fair bit of champagne. Adele was slightly concerned as to how it would react with his

Warfarin. 'Bob Dylan's backing band was called The Band,' he explained to Marcia. 'Showed a total lack of imagination, if you ask me. Should have been called Under Milk Wood – or was that someone else?'

'Dylan Thomas,' Adele hissed, trying to recork the Krug.

'Ah, right,' Peter nodded happily. 'Thomas Dylan. Welsh bloke. Any more champagne going?'

The music was wonderful. Dvořák, Rachmaninov and Mozart played against Holst, Britten and Dankworth, and at half-time it was a well-deserved score draw.

'Wasn't that brilliant?' Ross picked his way through the rapt groups, and squatted beside his parents. 'Sorry I didn't get up here in time for the first half but I was talking to Nell. Or at least trying to.'

Ross looked altogether grand, Adele thought, in his navy canvas trousers and his very expensive blue lawn shirt, with his hair and shoes gleaming and his very white teeth. He looked, she decided, the way 'preppy' boys did when she was a fifties bobby-soxer. Physically, financially, Nell couldn't do better. But she wouldn't settle for that, would she? She wanted to be in love – and for some unfathomable reason she didn't love Ross Percival. Adele wished she had some of the love-dust which was being sprinkled around in the performance of *A Midsummer Night's Dream* that she and Peter had seen at Stratford last year. It would solve an awful lot of problems.

'Where is Nell?' Adele looked quickly over her shoulder. 'On her way up?'

'No. Still in the pay-box. The dodgems are packed. Everything's riding full. They should make a bomb tonight. Nell's a bit – well – strange, actually.'

'Not well, you mean?' Adele was scrambling to her feet. 'Is she still upset about last night, do you think?'

'Hard to tell – is this a quail's egg, Mother? – I couldn't get a word of sense out of her, to be honest. She looks totally divine, though. And when I told her she just started humming something.'

Peter nodded. 'Probably one of the tunes from just now. "Figaro" or "Jerusalem", maybe?'

'We haven't had "Jerusalem", yet.' Marcia was pecking at a peach. 'That was "Jupiter".'

'I think I'll just pop down now and see her during the interval.' Adele decided to take the bull by the horns. At least if Nell was in the pay-box they could get this initial meeting over without an audience. She just hoped she wouldn't give the game away. 'No, you all stay here. I'll be back in next to no time.'

She tottered slightly on the mules as she started to make the downward descent. Peter had already seized the opportunity and another bottle of Krug. She heard Ross laugh and then say, 'Do you know, I think the tune Nell was humming was "Sabre Dance". God knows why. They didn't play that one, did they? Does anyone want that last truffle?'

Having reduced the volume to accommodate the concert, the fair ground sounded strangely muffled. There was nothing strange about the punters, though. Adele nodded with professional pleasure, watching the elegantly dressed throng clambering on and off the three Bradley rides, crowding round the joints; spending, spending, spending.

Maybe the Crash'n'Dash was going to be a good idea after all, she thought hopefully, then remembered that it was because Clem Percival had modern machines that he'd had to lease this gaff to Nell and the boys. Places like this would always want traditional accompaniments. The Crash'n'Dash would be like a big, brash kid in torn Levis gate-crashing a black-tie supper. Adele's fragile moment of hope crumbled.

She exchanged greetings with the Macs, marvelling at how the three older girls had grown. Rio was really very pretty and the twins – well! In their matching Lycra dresses they looked like pop stars, she thought. Surely they'd just been schoolgirls when she and Peter had retired? How time flew.

They were three-deep round the hoopla but she just caught a glimpse of Claudia in something floaty and pink and looking gorgeous. She'd talk to her later. Have a bit of a laugh. Whatever unhappiness Nell was suffering, or whatever temper Danny was in, or whatever problems Sam was having with the never-smooth-running paratrooper, Adele knew she'd get a giggle out of her daughter-in-law.

She elbowed her way through the droves and fetched up beside the pay-box of the dodgems. Nell, taking money from one of the gaff lads, hadn't seen her. Good Lord! Ross had been right. The dodgems were packed, with crowds waiting. And Nell looked simply out of this world. Her hair tumbled like a red-gold river over her creamy shoulders, and the blue evening frock made her eyes look turquoise. She smiled to herself, noticing that despite the heat, Nell had covered her face with a veneer of foundation. She was still trying to obliterate the freckles.

Negotiating the pay-box steps – a tricky manoeuvre in mules – Adele eased herself in beside her daughter.

'Oh – you made me jump!' Nell's starburst smile of welcome wasn't lost on Adele. 'How long have you been here? Where's Dad? Wasn't the concert lovely? I'm going to get out of here for the second half. Gosh, your dress is great, Mum. Hang on. All ready for the next ride? Press your pedals! Turn your steering wheels! There – isn't this wonderful?'

Drugs, Adele thought, or a man. It had to be one or the other. Nell was positively buzzing. Please God let it be Ross. Let her daughter have seen the light. Let the Crash'n'Dash not tear the Bradley family asunder.

Nell sat back, still beaming, swinging one of her sandals from the end of her bare foot in time with the music. But not the track playing on the dodgems, Adele thought. Nell's foot was beating to an entirely different rhythm.

She pushed her hair behind her ears and leaned towards her mother. 'I've nicked Barry from the paratrooper to sit in the pay-box for the second half of the concert. We can't talk properly in here. Give me five minutes.'

Waiting until the cars had crashed their way round the track twice more, and Barry had been given his pay-box instructions, Adele followed Nell down the steps. Nell, she noticed, had stopped the perpetual stooping which she'd adopted since puberty to try and disguise her height. Her shoulders were back and her head was high. It was almost as though tonight she was delighted to be nearly six feet tall.

'That's better. I can hear now. Where are you all sitting?'

'Clem took the high ground,' Adele said. 'Ross is already up there. There's loads of food left.'

'I'm not hungry.' Nell's eyes were focused on something in the distance. 'I'm not really in any rush to see Ross again, either, come to that. Or mardy Marcia. No doubt Ross has told everyone about last night? Made a big fuss out of nothing, of course. Still, he was a great help when Sam and Claudia didn't come back. I suppose we couldn't have managed without him – much as it galls me to have to say it. He's so smug about things like that. Did you get the whole story?'

'In fine detail,' Adele agreed, being knocked sideways by a group of teenagers in hired evening dress. 'Although I feel I might have missed out on some of the salient points.'

Maybe that was just as well, her daughter thought, under the circumstances.

Nell was still humming, with a faint smile on her lips. 'I'll fill you in on the gory bits later. But a word of warning, Mum. Danny and Claudia have had a real humdinger over it – so it might be as well not to say anything to either of them, OK?'

Adele nodded, trotting now to keep up with Nell's long stride. Blast! Whatever had made Nell this high had nothing to do with Ross. And now Danny and Claudia were daggers drawn – and it was ten to one on that there would be some problem with Sam.

They scrambled up the hill, stumbling over discarded wine bottles and chicken-bones, and reached the tartan rug just as the orchestra retook the stand. Nell hugged Peter, smiled at Clem and Marcia, and then plonked herself down on the farthest corner away from Ross. Adele wondered, as she tugged the gold lamé neatly behind her knees, whether she could move everyone round a bit, the way she used to when the children had birthday parties and best friends were sharing jelly and ice-cream with sworn enemies. She had a feeling that Nell might object fairly strongly.

'Oh, goody.' Marcia had abandoned the Krug in favour of little bottles of Bacardi pinched from the hotel's mini-bar and was consulting the programme. 'It's Rimsky-Korsakov and Tchaikovsky and Elgar next.' She shot a beady look across the rug towards Nell. 'What's that you're singing, dear? Is it Bartók?'

'Probably something from one of Elvis's early films.' Ross grinned. 'After all that's what she was brought up on, wasn't it, Adele? "Blue Hawaii"? "Jailhouse Rock"?'

Adele was aware of the stiffening of Nell's shoulders even though her expression didn't change. Things were definitely not right between them. Not right at all.

The evening sky had darkened without anyone noticing. As the orchestra swelled into *Romeo and Juliet*, the fountains below in the butterscotch courtyard turned into pastel rainbows, rising and falling with the beat of the music. Adele felt the lump in her throat grow larger and moved her hand across the rug to find Peter's. It was so perfect. So incredibly romantic. Marcia and Clem were conducting with their champagne flutes. Ross was idly eating black grapes, watching his parents with fond indulgence.

With tears of emotion blurring her eyes, Adele sneaked a look at Nell, willing her to wriggle across the rug to Ross's side. Nell, however, was gazing at the beauty of the fountains, still smiling, still miles away.

'It's the sing-along, next.' Clem was delving into the hamper for leftovers. 'Where are you off to, Princess?'

'I must find a loo.' Adele had scrambled to her feet. 'Too much champagne, I'm afraid. No, no, I'll be back in plenty of time for the finale. There shouldn't be a queue – not while the concert's on.'

'Mum!' Nell was laughing. 'You don't have to use the public ones. Use my living wagon. The door's unlocked.'

The Percivals drew in a joint breath of indignation. Adele winced. She really couldn't listen to Marcia crowing about how things like that would have to be tightened up when Ross and Nell finally tied the knot. She couldn't stay there and watch the Percivals snuff out the light in Nell's eyes.

It had taken longer than she'd anticipated to negotiate the thousands of people, both on the South Lawn and through the fairground, and the first part of the Elgar section had already kicked off as she left Nell's living wagon and skirted the hoopla stall. All three Mackenzie girls were in there, she noticed, attracting the boys from the minor public schools like magnets. Claudia must be listening to the concert, too. Adele hoped that she was listening to it with Danny.

'Hell,' she muttered, as she reached the waltzer. Danny was still sitting in the pay-box, alone, blasting out punk with a face like thunder.

He saw her and raised his hand in greeting. Adele's heart went out to him. He was loud-mouthed and aggressive and his own worst enemy but he was still her child. She wished she and Peter could have been more generous when it came to the distribution of their sons' genes.

'Hi.' Danny darted between the wildly swinging waltzer cars and dropped from the steps with expertise. 'Where's Dad?'

'Enjoying the concert with the Percivals. Nell's up there too. Coming to join us?'

'Not my sort of thing.' Danny looked over his shoulder. 'Oy! Alfie! Get in the pay-box!' He turned back to Adele. 'It's been a right bugger, this business with that bastard Terry. Being one lad down, I mean. We've taken on a couple of locals but – well, you know what it's like.'

Adele gave a non-committal nod. There was no way she was going to ask Danny about his row with Claudia. There had always been rows between them, and she had no reason to think this one would be any different.

'Takings good?' At least this was safe territory.

'Great.' Danny frowned. 'Be even better if we had a decent ride. Oh, don't get me wrong – it's not that I'm ungrateful or anything – but Ross spent last night with us and he was telling us about the stuff Jessons are putting out at the moment. Bloody incredible! What I wouldn't give for something like that. Christ, I wish Nell would stop pussyfooting around and marry the bloke! What's she waiting for? If Ross was in with us we could have machines like the Ice-Breaker. We'd be big-time then.'

She almost told him. So help me God, she thought, I could put the smile back on his face with half-a-dozen words. 'Is that all that's bothering you? Not having the latest rides?'

Danny nodded. 'Yeah. That and not having kids. You know how much I want kids, Ma. I want sons to carry on after I'm gone.'

'I'm sure Claudia feels the same. I mean, it isn't her fault –'

Danny laughed. It was harsh and made Adele flinch. 'Claudia! What use is Claudia to any man? She says she wants to have a baby but every month when she's not pregnant she doesn't care! She doesn't bloody care! And she's got the nerve to tell me I want a baby for the wrong reasons! Silly cow!' Danny jerked round angrily. 'Oy! Alfie! What the hell do you think you're doing? Not like that! Jesus!' And he vaulted back over the merry red-and-yellow rails of the waltzer.

As the sea shanties came to an end the first firework exploded in the sky. There was a mass gasp, and the crowds pointed upwards. Another and another burst in screaming multicoloured profusion, skittering and shrieking across the sky. The orchestra was playing 'Rule, Britannia' and everyone was singing at the tops of their voices.

Adele joined in as she pushed through the throng. She knew she wouldn't make it back to the tartan rug in time so she leaned against one of the mellow honey brick walls and tried to let the rousing music and the spectacular aerial display take the pain out of Danny's outburst. Poor Danny.

Poor Claudia. She had listened on Guild Ladies' Nights to other mothers with similar stories and always felt complacent. It could never happen to her family.

The fireworks exploded like rainbow stars, forming huge cushions of colour that overlapped and hung suspended in the sky before scattering into a million fragments. Over and over again, red and blue, gold and silver, green and yellow, growing, glowing, disintegrating. And then the orchestra burst into 'Jerusalem' and the South Lawn went crazy.

Adele clung on to her safe stone pillar and sang along, wondering if Peter was getting the words right. Lasers sliced across the darkness and huge fountains of fireworks sizzled into infinity. The laughing, singing crowd parted for a moment and on the other side of the courtyard Adele could see Sam. His head was back, watching the sky, and he seemed to be singing and laughing at the same time. Her heart skipped a beat. At least one of them seemed happy. She'd wait until the last notes had died away, the last sparks had disappeared, then she'd go over and talk to him. Sam, more than anyone, should be able to help Danny.

They were on the final chorus now, the massed voices, the emotion, awe-inspiring. Adele looked across to Sam again. He was still laughing. Laughing down at Claudia who was leaning against him, one hand on his waist. Sam's hand was behind her neck, beneath the cloud of her curls. As Adele watched in disbelief, he leaned down and kissed his sister-in-law.

CHAPTER NINETEEN

The photograph made the front page of *The World's Fair* two weeks later. Nell collected her copy of the paper from W. H. Smith in Haresfoot, unfolded it in the pedestrianised shopping precinct and screamed with laughter. She and Claudia, all legs and chests, were squeezed together in the gateway at Henley, looking like total bimbos.

The caption read: 'Bradley Beauties Revel at Regatta', and the article, apart from getting their ages wrong, went on to give the fair some excellent coverage.

'Nice one of you.' Claudia, who had been window-shopping in Oasis, peered over her shoulder. 'Twenty-five? You wish! God! Look at my make-up! I'm surprised they didn't lock me up that night. We look a bit "tarts on tour" though, don't we? Danny'll love it.'

Nell pulled a face. The situation between Danny and Claudia had deteriorated rapidly since Blenheim. There had been a blazing and very unpleasant row after the concert, which was witnessed by the entire Percival clan. Nell, who had wandered down from the picnic as the last strains of 'Jerusalem' died away, clutching a bottle of Krug and seeking out Claudia for their promised chat, found her mother in the middle of a surprisingly ferocious argument with Sam. Claudia and Danny were having their own slanging match beside the waltzer, which, of course, reached its crescendo just as the rest of the party arrived.

Danny had said some unforgivable things. Adele, Peter and Ross had whisked him off out of the way to calm him down, while Clem and a very smug Marcia teetered back to the Bear. Exasperated by the whole business, Nell had suggested to Sam that they should act as mediators in the marriage. Sam had refused point-blank. Nell could only assume that this was what her mother had been suggesting earlier and, as no one seemed to need her input, she'd taken the Krug and her 'Sabre Dance' dreams back to the living wagon.

Claudia had spent the night with Nell, sharing the champagne but refusing to say what had sparked this particular explosion. She'd returned home the next morning and what she and Danny were like in private was left to speculation. In public they hardly spoke. Claudia seemed to be handling it with her usual equanimity, and Danny – well, Danny was coping by drinking heavily and spending a lot of time with Ross.

Nell worried about both of them. Divorce, as far as she could see, simply wasn't an option. They were stamped right through with the travelling tradition like the lettering in a stick of rock. Part of her wished they'd just try and patch things up; the other part, the part that felt that being bound by the rigid confines of showland convention should no longer be a threat to civil liberties, desperately wanted to see them free and happy. After all, there *were* divorces among travellers – and remarriages too – however rare, and they'd stopped burning people at the stake for heresy years ago.

She, however, was still on cloud nine, having been back to Fox Hollow twice to play the organ and admire Jack's handiwork. Although he'd not been there on either occasion, he must have spent a lot of time working: at least half of the horses were completed now, and he'd made a start on the gilded background of the rounding boards. Nell thought he must have a very tolerant employer.

He'd left her a note the previous week.

'Nell – I've christened Jemima, Vincent, Lexington and Cassandra – and taken the liberty of throwing in some of my own. Please say if you have any objections – or further preferences. We've still got loads to go. It's hell being parents in a multiple birth, isn't it? Love, Jack.'

His writing was thick, black and bold. She'd smiled over his selection of names. They matched really well with hers. He'd chosen Jonquil, Zachary, Merlin, Giselle and Guinevere, and they were painted in glorious scrolled colours along each glossy neck.

She'd written back:

'Dear Jack – Thank you. I love them. They must have taken hours – you're very clever. How about Valentine, Lucian, Theodore, Florence and Dominic? And if you're going to be Arthurian, don't forget Lancelot. Beat that if you can! Maybe we'll actually meet again one day! Love, Nell.'

She was going to Fox Hollow that afternoon. The stay at Haresfoot was a long one – one of the longest of the season – and she was already impatient for the gallopers to be completed and built up. The fact that when they were, she might have to confess to owning them, was a bit of a worm in the apple, but she was sure she could handle it.

She had no idea whether she could handle Ross, though. He was going to be joining them at the end of the week, just before they left for the street fair at Marsh Minster. Confessing that she'd spent all her personal fortune on the Savage and the Gavioli was going to be a darned sight easier than accepting Ross Percival as a permanent part of her life.

She looked at the photograph again. God knows what Adele and Peter would make of it. They were worried enough about Danny and Claudia without this. However, she grinned to herself, it wasn't all bad: Ross would be outraged.

'Are you going to have it framed for Ross's Christmas present?' Claudia asked as they crossed the main road and headed back to the fair with carrier bags of boring food-shopping. After all, it's probably the most he's going to see of your body.'

'Are you a mind-reader?'

'Palms be me speciality, dearie.' Claudia broke into a wheezing cackle. 'Cross the gypsy's palm with an Amex Gold and hear exactly what you want to hear. Holy cow! What's going on over there?'

Nell peered in the direction of a yelling, giggling crowd of girls outside the Virgin megastore. 'Must be one of those boy bands doing a personal appearance. Heel! Stay! You're far too old! Thirty-two according to *The World's Fair*.' Laughing, she grabbed Claudia. 'Good God! It's Terry!'

They watched in amazement as Terry, golden, floppy-haired, and as beautiful as ever in his sprayed-on jeans and black T-shirt, autographed scraps of paper, legs, arms, and other proffered bits of anatomy.

'Has he signed a record contract or what?' Claudia nudged Nell. 'He's only been gone a couple of weeks.'

Nell shook her head. Maybe the pale and wispy Emblings had been friends with Richard Branson and pulled off some super-deal that would keep their Karen in clover and out of harm's way. Terry looked up from signing the thigh of a pretty girl with cropped hair and a ring in her navel, and grinned broadly. Shoving his way through his admirers, he loped towards Nell and Claudia.

'What are you doing?' Nell was aware that the girls were staring enviously. 'Have we missed something? Last I heard you were being groomed for marriage or locked up for life and not necessarily in that order.'

'I'm coming back. I hitched a lift into Oxford, then thumbed it down the A34. I knew you'd still be at Haresfoot.' He surveyed them proudly. 'You both look great – not as good as that photo in *The World's Fair*, though. Have you seen it? It's –'

'We've seen it, thanks. I'm really pleased that you're coming back – the dodgems haven't been the same without you and the other lads have missed you – but what was all that about? And what's happened to Karen?'

'Karen is now wearing my engagement ring and going back to school in September to study for her exams. I'm a reformed character – honest. The police have decided that there are no charges to answer. Not even abduction. Ma and Pa Embling were pretty neat about it all, actually. And with Karen's track record for bolting, the police were just glad to close the book, I reckon. And those girls – well,' he shrugged. 'They were staring at me, so I said I was Rudy Yarrow.'

'Who the hell is Rudy Yarrow?'

'Sexy little boy from that teenage soap thing on Channel Five,' Claudia said with authority. 'Hottest thing in faded denim this year. Actually, you do look a lot like him. Honest, Nell, don't you know nothing?'

'Obviously not. So, will Sam get his surety cheque back now?'

'He's already got it,' Claudia said happily. 'Last week. Didn't he tell you?'

Returning to the fairground, they received a mixed reception. Haresfoot was a large affair with half-a-dozen showmen's families combining their machines. They had all without exception got a copy of *The World's Fair*. The majority seemed to find the photograph either amusing or titillating or both, and good-naturedly whistled and cat-called their approval.

Danny, of course, didn't. Breaking off from tinkering with the underside of one of the waltzer cars, he glared at them. 'Don't know how you two have got the nerve to show your faces round here. What did you think you were up to – posing like that? I've had people taking the piss all bloody morning! Christ! You looked like complete scrubbers!' He blinked in disbelief. 'And what the fuck is he doing here?'

Nell patted Terry on the shoulder. 'Ignore him. You work for me. Go and find yourself a space in the Beast Wagon.' She grinned at Claudia and handed her the Sainsbury bags.

'You're on your own with this one. I'm – er – going out. Think you can handle it?'

'No problem at all.' Claudia was already walking away from her husband. 'Piece of cake. Oh, and Nell –'

'What?'

'Give my love to the bank manager.'

Jack's motorbike was parked outside the shed when Nell arrived. She locked the Volvo and looked furtively over her shoulder, making sure that her arrival hadn't been noticed. Not that it would have mattered even if she had been spotted by the Fox Hollow locals, she told herself, hauling open the sliding doors. Everyone knew it was the Bradleys' winter quarters, but no one knew what the shed currently contained. It was only her sense of guilt which convinced her that the words Savage and Gavioli were printed in indelible ink across her forehead.

The lights were on and the air smelled warm and stuffy and mysterious. Nell had never smelled paint and linseed oil and white spirit in such vast quantities before. It was illicit and exciting, like a heavy waft of civet-based scent. If the summer was going to continue being so hot, she must remember to bring an electric fan otherwise Jack would be asphyxiated before he was finished.

He didn't hear her walk across the shed. Didn't hear her stop behind him. A portable wireless was playing brash music. He was busy painting the name on one of the horses, and she watched, fascinated. Totally immersed, he used the brush like an extension of his fingers, each tiny movement flowing and controlled. The hairs on the brush were needle-fine; each letter, each inlaid colour, took time and patience. Nell enjoyed looking at him. His shoulders were hunched under the thin cotton sweater, the black jeans smeared as always with rich colours. His hair was dark and thick and looked blue under the harsh lights.

'Hello, Nell.' He stopped painting and looked up at her over his shoulder.

'Hi. Sorry – you haven't smudged it or anything, have you? I tried not to make a noise.'

'You didn't.' He dropped the paintbrush into a cloudy jar. 'I could smell you.'

'Sorry?'

'Your scent.' He stood up, smiling, and switched off the wireless. 'It's light, flowery, beautiful. All I could smell before was paint, then suddenly I knew you were there.'

He looked tired, Nell thought. Older, somehow. There were shadows beneath his eyes and he'd lost weight. Was he having problems, too? It seemed strange that they shared this huge secret and yet knew so little about each other. She looked at the horse he was working on. The name-scroll against the golden neck was outlined in black, royal blue and crimson; the lettering was black and gold.

'Miranda? An ex-girlfriend?'

'Sadly, no.' Jack indicated the neighbouring two horses. 'Unless I also went out with Prospero and Caliban. I took you up on the Lancelot suggestion, and then I wondered why we were letting Tennyson have it all his own way, so I've started on Shakespeare. I gather you studied English literature?'

'Only to A-level.' Nell ran her fingers over the herd of completed but as yet unnamed horses. 'Was that a friendly enquiry, or were you sussing out whether I'd been educated at all?'

'There was never any doubt about that. I just didn't want you to think I was a complete philistine so I went to the literature section of the library. My education took in maths and science. I'd thought of Pythagorus and Archimedes . . .'

'The stuff of my nightmares!' Nell grinned at him. 'We had a cow of a maths teacher – and our physics teacher wasn't much better. Anyway, I would have thought you'd have named them after artists. You must have been to art school, I mean, with all this.'

'Self-taught.' Jack dipped the tip of his brush in a miniature pot of vermilion. It looked like blood. 'Art was not something my father encouraged. Sissy stuff, he always said. I never had art lessons – it was just there and my secret.'

Nell watched him working. He was obviously good at keeping secrets. 'So when other boys were kicking each other to death on the football field you were daubing in the attic?'

'God, no. I also used to be the Vinnie Jones of our school eleven.' He looked up at her again. 'So you'd be happy with artists then? As names for our horses, I mean? We've already got your Vincent, so why not Leonardo, Pablo, Pierre Auguste, and Camille?'

'Stop trying to blind me with science – or art. Da Vinci and Picasso I recognise – who the heck are the other two?'

He placed the brush in a jar of white spirit and started swirling it round. 'Renoir and Pissarro, of course. What sort of naff education did you have?'

Nell poked her tongue out at him and leaned against Caliban, simply enjoying watching him work. So many flatties thought that showmen's children didn't go to school at all. She and Danny and Sam had attended school in Fox Hollow in the winter, and had travelling tutors in the summer. At eleven they'd been sent as boarders to a fairly exclusive educational establishment in Hampshire.

'Well, I chose not to go to university – so did Danny, my older brother. Sam went though. He got a 2.1 in History. Really handy that, on the paratrooper.'

'I can see that it would be.'

She stroked Caliban's stiff, varnished mane. 'A lot of the younger generation of travellers never go back to the fair after college, which is a great pity I think. I've got cousins who are lawyers and accountants and one – who we never talk about – who practises private medicine.'

'The black sheep of the family?'

'Definitely. His parents are still waiting for him to come back and take over the big wheel.'

She wandered into the far recesses of the shed behind the Gavioli. There wouldn't be time to play it today. Maybe next week, when they'd built up at Marsh Minster. She was getting as bad as her mother with her Delia treats. The stacked ghost train and caterpillar loomed towards the rafters. The light was dimmer here and she flicked on one of the overhead fluorescents. She blinked in disbelief.

'Oh! wow! Oh, my God!'

'I hoped you'd think that.' Jack was still standing among the horses. 'Is it what you wanted?'

What she wanted? What she'd dreamed and schemed and prayed for. The rounding boards had been painted, the lettering ornately filigreed in jewel-bright colours on the gilded background, and the sections laid out to dry. When the gallopers were built up the boards would revolve round beneath the tilt and proclaim to the world: 'Petronella Bradley's Golden Galloping Horses' and then, after a gap, 'The Memory Lane Fair'.

The words blurred and she rubbed quickly at her eyes. She'd never, ever be able to thank him enough. 'I – I don't know what to say. It's incredible – oh, God.'

'That's OK,' he said gruffly, squatting down again and concentrating on Miranda. 'Just as long as you're pleased.'

Pleased? There wasn't a word that would begin to describe how she felt. It was real, now. Not a dream. Reality. Frightening and exciting reality. 'I'm really going to have to pay you for this. You must be taking so much time away from work. Using up your holidays. And I had no idea just how talented you were. If I'd hired someone I'd have had to pay a fortune. Can you do me invoices, or something? Please?'

Jack was putting the finishing touches to Miranda's name. He didn't look up. 'Not a chance. You've given me more than money. And I work for myself, anyway. I don't have to beg for time off.' He executed a curlicue with a confident flourish. 'There is one thing you could do, though.'

Anything, Nell thought, realising again that she knew nothing about him. He'd revealed more in today's few sentences than at any of their previous meetings. 'Name it.'

'I've got to be back in Newbury this afternoon. I'll have to pack up in a minute – but it's so hot and I'm gagging for a drink. Would you – er – come with me?'

'Love to. Did you have anywhere in mind?'

Jack shook his head. 'This is your neck of the woods. Your choice – my shout.'

'No, then.' She smiled. 'The least I can do is buy you a drink for this. Anyway, you've got that monstrosity outside so I guess you won't be able to handle anything more than a very weak shandy. It seems a fairly reasonable price to pay for a dream.'

She watched him cleaning brushes, folding things away carefully in a leather artist's pouch. He shouldn't do anything else, she thought. This was as natural to him as breathing.

Jack locked the doors and pocketed the keys. The sun spiralled on the dusty yard. 'Where are you taking me, then?'

'The Maybush, at Newbridge. You must have passed it when you came. There are two pubs on either side of the bridge. The Rose Revived is bigger, but I thought the Maybush would be more us.'

'Yeah, I know where they are. Jump aboard then.' Jack indicated the Roadster. 'It'll only take five minutes.'

'What? I can't – not on that! I mean I haven't got a crash helmet or anything. No, look I'll drive and meet you there.'

'You either ride pillion or the deal's off,' Jack said cheerfully, dumping his own crash helmet on the Volvo's bonnet. 'There. Now we can break the law together.' He swung one leg over the black leather saddle and kick-started the Norton, yelling above the feral roar, 'Come on, then. You'll love it.'

I've got to be crazy, Nell thought, climbing unsteadily behind him, and tucking her long legs out of the way. Completely crazy. I've got to twenty-nine and I've never ridden pillion before. This is absolutely no time to start.

'Put your arms round my waist, keep your legs away from the exhaust pipe, hang on, and enjoy it.'

The motorbike throbbed and growled, wobbled unsteadily for a second and then flew out of the yard. It was the most giddy, mad, adrenalin rush Nell had ever experienced. The power from the engine pulsed through her body, the wind was a punching scream in her ears, and her hair tangled behind her like a maenad. She clung to Jack's waist like a drowning man clutching a solitary rock. His body under the thin sweater was firm and warm beneath her fingers, and as she swooped from side to side it was her only bit of stability. She hoped she wasn't holding too tight but there was no way on earth she was going to let go. The wind sliced through her T-shirt with icy blades. Jack's hair streaked into her mouth and once she'd got used to the motion, the exhilaration set in. It was like flying: freedom personified; wild, reckless, and disturbingly exciting.

Everything went by in a mangled blur of noise and colour. There were no roads or hedges, no pavements or buildings. There was only the overwhelming thunder of the engine, the speed, and the spiralling intensity of sensation.

As they plunged into the Maybush's car park, scattering gravel, Nell felt a thud of disappointment. She wanted it to go on for ever. Even after Jack had brought the bike to a halt, she could still hear the roar in her ears, still feel the throb inside her body. Her legs had turned to jelly.

'Simple, huh?' He grinned at her, swinging his legs to the ground, and running his fingers through his hair. 'Do you want any help?'

'I think I can cope, thanks.' Nell slithered over the pillion, then staggered backwards. Her face had frozen into a stiff mask while the remainder of her body had liquefied. 'Ooops. I don't seem to have quite got my sea legs yet. God, that was brilliant. Can we do it again?'

'We're going to have to if you want to get back to your car.' He watched her trying to sort out the tangles in her hair. 'I wouldn't bother. It looks great – and it'll only get all messed up again on the return journey. OK? Through here?'

Nell bought two ice-cold shandies with trembling fingers, delighted to notice that the lunch-time office escapees were eyeing Jack with open lust. He was stunning, she admitted, in a dark and dangerous sort of way. A complete contrast to Ross's glowing golden good-looks. And the secretaries weren't to know he didn't belong to her, were they? She basked in the borrowing.

They found a table outside on the white-railed deck that overhung the river. It was warmed by the sun and refreshed by the breeze rippling through the overhanging trees.

'My hands are shaking – but I think there's still some left in the glass.' Nell plonked the shandies on to the wooden table. 'You're totally crazy.'

Jack downed half his pint in one go. 'That's the best way to ride. It becomes far more sensible when you have crash hats and leathers. We'll probably get arrested on the way back.'

They talked, small talk, desultory conversation, at first; touching on the gallopers and how no one else at Bradleys had been told anything about them, the Downland Trust, the fair and the recent gaffs. Nell told him the latest about Claudia and Danny, about Terry and Karen, about the concert at Blenheim. Jack spoke of his job, his parents, and how Fiona didn't seem to mind too much about his continuing with the restoration of the gallopers.

'Does she know I bought them?'

Jack shook his head. 'She didn't ask. I didn't bother to enlighten her. I don't think the ownership mattered to her, anyway. What about you? Surely there's someone in your life who ought to know?'

She shrugged and told him about Ross. All about Ross. He was so easy to talk to. He listened so well.

'And will you marry him?'

'God knows. We don't go in for a lot of living together – not like flatties. It's marriage or nothing. I'd rather it was nothing. But I've got a feeling that everyone else thinks otherwise. It's such a bloody mess, to be honest.'

'Fiona wants to get married.' Jack swirled the remainder of his shandy in the bottom of his glass, staring at the swans in their stately glide beneath them. 'In fact Fiona has booked the Register Office and my mother has booked the caterer and the entertainment.'

'And you – you're not – um – keen?'

'It shows, does it?' Jack drained his glass and stood up. 'I'll get the next ones – no, I mean it. Same again?'

'Yes, please. As long as it's very weak. Thanks.'

As he walked back into the Maybush the secretaries once again devoured him with their eyes. So – he was going to marry Fiona. She thought it over. Did it bother her? Should it bother her? She came up with yes and no, and felt confused.

He returned with the drinks and they sipped the second one more leisurely. 'We've got a lot in common really, haven't we? Considering that we're poles apart?'

'I suppose we have.' Nell looked at him across the table. 'Both being honour bound to carry on our parents' business. Both being headily in love with the past – and the gallopers. Both about to marry when we're not really sure that it's the right thing to do.'

'I have to – do the right thing, I mean.' Jack stared away across the river where a single gaily coloured cabin cruiser was causing a tidal wave in its wake and the moorhens were bouncing on the crest. 'Fiona's pregnant.'

Nell watched the boat and the moorhens. She drank her shandy. Some of the secretaries got up with a clatter and brushed past their table, very close, leaving a waft of Poison behind them.

'Congratulations.'

'Thanks. I haven't got my head round it at all yet, to be honest. I'd never thought about children. It – er – wasn't planned. I'm surprised that Fiona . . . oh, well.' He smiled at her. 'It's my problem.'

'Shouldn't you be at home now, then? Planning the wedding? Being supportive.' God! Nell thought, shocked. She hadn't meant it to sound that barbed. 'I mean, if you're going to get married soon there must be loads to do. Will you still have time for the painting?'

'It'd take Armageddon to stop me working on the gallopers. But yeah, I suppose there must be plans and lists and things. Fiona and my mother seem to have it all organised though. No one's actually asked me for any ideas. Anyway,

Fiona's working in London this week. She's trying to increase her sales portfolio. She's very ambitious.'

'So she won't be giving up her job?'

'Fiona will never give up anything,' Jack said bitterly.

CHAPTER TWENTY

'For goodness sake!' Nell drummed impatiently on the Volvo's steering wheel. 'What on earth is going on?'

There was a tailback on the Haresfoot road coiling into the far distance. Turning down the perennial Brubeck tape, Nell leaned forward and peered through the windscreen. There must have been an accident ahead; there could be no other explanation for jams like this on a mid-week afternoon. The cars in front started to move forward slowly and Nell eased the Volvo up into second. She was already late. She hadn't left Fox Hollow until after three and knew that Danny would have the fair open by five. It was too much to hope for that the tailback was caused by eager punters.

Eventually turning off the High Street and moving towards the Common, she'd almost reached twenty miles an hour before the traffic ground to a halt once more. A very young policeman, on point duty for possibly the first time, bit his lip and waved his hands in a gesture of despair. Nell leaned from the window. 'Has there been an accident?'

The policeman looked at her, perked up considerably, and shook his head. 'Large load through the town centre earlier. Jammed up everything for a while. Sorted now though, miss. You should soon be on your way.'

Oh, goody, Nell thought, cursing lorry drivers who chose to ignore the bypass. She'd hoped her absence wouldn't have been noticed. She didn't want to have to answer too many questions.

She needn't have worried. No one on the fairground took the slightest notice of her arrival simply because there was nobody around. The Common looked like the *Marie Celeste*. Leaving the Volvo alongside her living wagon, she hurried through the deserted rides.

Where the hell was everyone? Even Mr and Mrs Mac, who always sat outside their living wagon in deck-chairs to watch the world go by when they weren't working, were missing. She reached Danny's walnut-and-chrome wagon. The door was open. God! Danny never went anywhere without double-padlocking everything. This had to be serious. Nell had horrific visions of splintered furniture and overturned vehicles. She turned the corner.

'Holy hell!'

It was more serious than she'd even imagined. Ross Percival's Ferrari and forty-two-foot Sipson living wagon, with its Italian marble and granite work surfaces, bath, and pearlised leather bloody upholstery, was pulled into place as though it had every damn right to be there!

It was too soon. Far too soon. Nell tore round the side of Teddy Pratley's Skid and slithered to a halt. Things simply got worse.

'Jesus! What on earth is that?'

She blinked at the enormous articulated lorry pulling into place at the end of the row of machines. They hadn't extended the ground, had they? No one had mentioned being joined by anyone else. It wasn't the way things were done. The lessee of the fair, in this case Art Maycroft, advertised any spare ground to let weeks in advance. Vacant sites on Haresfoot Common were like gold-dust.

As far as Nell was aware, all the ground was taken by the usual families, as it always was. Year after year. Ground passed down from father to son; ground, in the Showmen's

Guild, being far more valuable even than the machines. No one parted with it unless they had to. Fairs didn't, unlike the common flatty misconception, drive aimlessly round the countryside in convoy looking for a nice place to stop. It was a precisely planned and intricate business operation. There were pages of *The World's Fair* devoted to the transfer of Guild Rights and sub-letting. It was easier to get into a sealed Masonic lodge. And it would be rarer than snow in August for the council to allow another big machine on to the Common at this late stage. There had to be some mistake.

Everyone was watching the lorry's manoeuvre. Nell, thanking the Lord for once that she was taller than most, could see easily over their heads. Satisfied that everything was in place, the driver jumped from the cab and disappeared round the back of the massive trailer. The crowd moved closer. There was a hiss of hydraulics as the ride started to unfold. The lorry was a brand-new Foden, sparkling with fresh paint – brilliant blue paint with spiky red letters underlined with a lot of very yellow stars . . .

She felt a stab of foreboding and stared more closely. Bloody hell! The spiky red letters spelled out 'Crash'n'Dash' on one side and 'Bradleys' Fun Fair On Tour' on the other.

Lean and debonair and with sons at Eton, Art Maycroft was leaning against the trailer of Burton's Toy-Set watching with everyone else. He winked as Nell elbowed her way towards him. 'Great picture of you and Claudia in the paper this morning. Dead sexy. I got three copies.'

But Nell didn't have time for niceties. 'What is that?'

'Crash'n'Dash. Straight from Jessons. Smashing, eh?'

'Why?' Nell asked slowly, 'does it have our name on it and what is it doing here? There's got to be some mistake.'

'No mistake, Nell. It's all yours. Well – and Danny's and Sam's, of course. You kept it very quiet – not that I blame you. Bradleys must be doing even better than I thought.'

'It's not ours,' Nell insisted. 'Honestly. We only rented space for three machines – *our* three machines –'

'The ground was organised some time ago – I did a deal with Clem Percival, although I didn't know what machine we were getting. I must say this is a mega-bonus. We'll have 'em in in droves with this. Thank God I'll be with you lot at Marsh Minster, too. This'll line a lot of pockets.'

'But –' Nell felt she was drowning in treacle. 'It isn't ours. Really. We haven't bought anything like this. I don't know anything about it.'

She stopped. Clem Percival . . . Clem owned Jessons. Ross had always intended joining them at Haresfoot whatever she said. Ross, the conniving bastard, had bought the ride, had it liveried to Bradleys, and thought that he'd get away with it!

Ignoring Art's murmur of appreciation as the spectacular Crash'n'Dash was borne aloft from its tri-axle trailer, Nell thrust her way through the mob. The air was electric with excitement. Danny was up there with the driver, she could see the flash of his tawny hair – and Sam – the two-faced quisling! And, yes – as she'd suspected – Ross bloody Percival!

She charged towards them. A ride like this must have cost millions – well hundreds of thousands at least – and Ross had thought that was what it would take to get her. And she'd been simple enough to believe that once she'd spent her money on the gallopers and refused to sign business cheques, Bradleys would be safe from his financial fiddling! She'd kill him!

The Crash'n'Dash was already half erected, its dual tracks curving into the air. The murmurs of appreciation had grown into a simultaneous intake of breath. Nell, blinking in disbelief, looked at the machine in horror. She thrust aside the open-mouthed Mackenzie twins, and grabbed Ross's arm just as the cars started to climb.

'We need to talk.'

Ross's eyes were diamond bright. 'Sure. Later. I'm a bit busy right now. If it's about the photograph, I thought it was excellent. I've ordered an enlargement of the original.'

'It's nothing to do with the photograph. I want to talk to you. About this. Now!' Nell tried not to look at the vibrant paintwork, the huge garish paintings of high-speed two-wheel chases and tumbling cars, the towering tracks. 'Now, Ross.'

Danny and Sam were swarming over the damn thing like children in an adventure playground, with Mick and Alfie, Ted and Barry not far behind. Terry wasn't there. At least one of the gaff lads was showing some solidarity. But then – neither was Claudia. Oh, let them get on with it. She had more urgent problems to deal with.

'Take it away.' She glared at Ross. 'Take it back to your father and tell him thanks but no thanks. We don't want it – we can't afford it – we will not be running it –'

'It's nothing to do with me.' Ross was grinning in the most irritating manner. 'Honestly, Nell. Nothing to do with me at all. It is exactly what it says – Bradleys' Crash'n'Dash. Ordered from Jessons, yes. But not by me.'

Nell sighed heavily, her patience sorely tried. 'OK. Let's try again. You were joining us at Haresfoot; your father owns Jessons; Danny and Sam wanted a hydraulic ride. Right so far?'

Ross nodded, still grinning. Fighting the urge to slap him, Nell continued. 'And here we are – at Haresfoot. Your living wagon is parked next to Danny's. And what else do we have? Surprise, surprise! A bloody Jessons machine. Come on, Ross. Don't treat me like a fool.'

'I never have.' He seemed eager to get away from her all of a sudden. 'Look, Nell. Believe me. I didn't put a penny into this. I didn't order it, commission it – nothing. We'll talk later. Danny and Sam'll need a hand. I'm here to run it, yes. But it's not my machine. It's yours.' He moved away. 'Oh, by the way, I love the new hair-do. Very wild. Did you have it done in Haresfoot?'

She glared at him. 'No. Actually it got like this because I was tearing about the countryside on the back of a powerful motorbike without a crash helmet. The motorbike was driven by a gloriously sexy artist who's just about to marry his pregnant girlfriend but wanted to take me out for a drink. OK?'

'Sounds great,' Ross nodded. 'Glad you had a nice time. Look, sweetheart, don't you want to come and look at your new toy?'

'Ross! You must know who paid for it! Who?'

'Of course I know, but my lips are sealed. I've been sworn to secrecy. But I swear it wasn't me. Now, I've got work to do – and so have you. We'll have a drink later. In my living wagon. OK?'

Nell groaned with fury as he strolled back towards the now almost completed Crash'n'Dash. It was, as they'd all said, child's play to build up. And Ross was a permanent fixture. They'd said that too – and she hadn't believed them. And he expected her to shimmy up to his granite and leather and marble palace for cocoa. Tonight and every night for the rest of her life. Self-satisfied bastard. Complete and utter pig!

But actually, much though she didn't want to, she believed him about the Crash'n'Dash. She'd known Ross for ever. She knew when he was lying; he went all bombastic and bristly. So, if he hadn't bought it, then just who had? Danny? It had to be Danny. But where would Danny have raised the cash? Even if he and Sam clubbed together they would have still needed her signature. Or maybe they wouldn't. She'd bought the Savage and the Gavioli without anyone finding out, hadn't she? Were they all being equally devious?

'Pretty cool, isn't it?' Claudia, in another Monsoon dress and looking very perky, was standing beside her. 'Bit of a surprise, though.'

'Is it?' Nell peered at her sister-in-law. 'And where were you just now? Your wagon door was open and you weren't around. You weren't with Terry, were you?'

'No. Why? Oh, God – not that again. I was having a nose round Ross's van, if you must know. While he was otherwise engaged. Pretty hedonistic, Nell, isn't it? God, the place is made for orgies!'

'I really wouldn't know. So, how much did you know about – this?' Nell jabbed her finger towards the Crash-'n'Dash. 'How much did Danny tell you?'

'I didn't know anything about it until it arrived. It was as much a shock to me as it was to everyone else. Danny is over the moon, though.'

'Well, he would be, wouldn't he? He's obviously bought it.'

'Dream on! We don't have that sort of money. It would have to be a three-way thing, and you and Sam didn't – I mean, well, I assume you and Sam didn't –'

'I certainly did not! Ross says it was nothing to do with him – and strange as it may seem, I believe him.'

Claudia grinned. 'Yeah, well, you know him better than most. Did you know he'd got satin sheets and a goatskin rug in front of the hearth?'

Nell did. She didn't want to talk about it.

Claudia changed tack. 'I like your hair. Did you have it done in Oxford?'

'I wasn't in Oxford. What on earth makes you think I was in Oxford?'

'Dunno. The bank manager, I suppose.'

'Why do you keep on about bank managers? Oh, hell – what's happening now?'

'HSE and Jessons' engineers,' Art Maycroft informed them, nudging his way through the throng. 'They're going to do the installation and safety checks and a trial run. Any volunteers?'

The crowd surged forward, eager to be first on as soon as the all-clear was given. Nell, shaking her head, turned away. It had to be Danny. It simply had to be. But whoever it was, it would toll the death knell for Bradleys as she'd known it. They were moving up into the Percival league. And Ross Percial was here. Complete with sybaritic living wagon. She'd really be expected to marry him now. Even more so now that Bradleys owned four rides – and one of them was the Crash'n'Dash. She was no longer a poor relation. Her dowry was at last acceptable. What on earth, she wondered, would her parents think? They'd probably be pleased. They'd see it as a pathway to the future.

Feeling exhausted, Nell turned away from the feverish excitement and headed for her living wagon.

An hour later, after a shower and having washed the tangles out of her hair, she leaned from the window and watched the Crash'n'Dash's first trial run. It was scaringly spectacular, she had to admit, even in daylight when the lights weren't shown to their best advantage. At night it would certainly pull people in from miles around. Which was exactly what they were supposed to do. They were in business, mobile business, to do just that, weren't they?

There was a tight knot of pain in her chest as she watched. The pulsing heavy metal music drowned everything else; the car-crash sound effects were terrifyingly realistic. It didn't matter what she thought about it. Ross and Danny, Nyree-Dawn and Mercedes Mackenzie and all the gaff lads, including Terry – the turncoat – were already clambering into the seats. The Crash'n'Dash and Ross were here to stay.

Sam and Claudia must have missed the inaugural flight because she couldn't see them as the cars swooped up into the sky; she could see everyone else, though. Intending to be completely detached, she watched as the tracks revolved faster and faster, and the cars swung, climbed and fell. At the point where the tracks first moved together and the cars were on a breakneck collision course, she caught her breath.

'Sod it,' she muttered, 'it's brilliantly designed. It looks like a dream – and it'll outshine everything else at any gaff we go to. It'll make our fortune and I hate it!'

She watched two further test runs, and then when the HSEs and the Jessons engineers were satisfied, the machine was opened to the public. Word had spread rapidly and soon massive queues wound through the fair almost as far as the living wagons. Nell couldn't help working out the takings. They were phenomenal. It didn't matter. She still hated it.

Turning away from the window, she dried her hair, pulled on a pair of tailored shorts and a silk shirt and went to work.

The dodgems were packed all night. Word of the Crash'n'Dash must have spread to three counties and the crowds were shoving and laughing, waiting for their turn to be terrified, and riding on everything else in the meantime.

'Great to be back.' Terry swung up to the edge of the pay-box and handed Nell the takings. 'I always knew I had excellent timing. Bloody brilliant machine that Crash-'n'Dash. We're making a fortune. I might even ask for a pay-rise.'

She watched him leap from car to car, and was only faintly surprised to see that the girl with the cropped hair and the navel ring whose thigh he'd autographed earlier, was entwined sinuously round one of the pillars. He had probably told her that Rudy Yarrow was on location, or that he was getting background for his next role. Either way she felt a pang of sympathy for Karen.

Sam was elated on the paratrooper; even Danny was grinning and playing the Beach Boys on the waltzer. Claudia, with her hair gathered up into a trailing silk scarf and looking wildly gypsyish, had got all three Mackenzie girls working with her and had men hurling hoops like there was no tomorrow. Everyone, Nell thought, was overjoyed. It was like winning the lottery. A huge unexpected bonus. Was she being churlish not to share in their pleasure? She could see the plus points, of course she could. Even her fears that the gaff lads would be out of work were groundless. With Ross in the Crash'n'Dash's pay-box they'd probably need more staff – not less. And whoever had put up the money had done it for the benefit of the whole family. She groaned. She was tied to this arrangement now as surely as if someone had welded her bracelets to the Crash'n'Dash's rocket-like hydraulics.

They closed very late. Nell had carried a tray of bacon sandwiches and mugs of tea over to the Beast Wagon, and passed Art Maycroft counting his takings.

'Better'n Nottingham Goose Fair,' he grinned at her. 'I'm reckoning on putting up the rents at the next gaff. Great night, Nell. And a great step forward for Bradleys. I've had Meridian telly on the blower. They're going to come to Marsh Minster and do a feature. Brilliant stuff, huh?'

Ross was waiting for her in the darkness outside his living wagon, looking elated. He'd changed from his working jeans and T-shirt into the navy trousers and shirt from the Blenheim concert. Nell hoped he wasn't going into seduction mode. She simply wasn't in the mood.

'I've poured you a drink – tons of ice, and I've made some food.' He climbed the steps and opened the door for her. 'And don't frown. I'm not going to pounce on you the minute you walk in. You said you needed to talk – I just thought we'd do it in comfort.'

She smiled. He was OK. He *was*, she told herself firmly. He was just ambitious. But she still didn't love him. The large Martinis stood on an ebony tray, and he'd made open sandwiches with prawns and iceberg lettuce and thin slivers of tomato. The lights were dim and Oscar Peterson spilled softly from somewhere unseen and flowed across the marble and pearlised leather. I am such a fool, she told herself, perching on the edge of one of the huge chairs and feeling the rough hair of the goatskin rug tickle her toes: he's rich, he's got style, he's handsome, and he wants to marry me. Why, oh why, isn't it enough? Why can't it be what I *want*?

Ross handed her her drink, a plate of sandwiches, and a napkin. God, Nell thought, he even uses linen napkins – not bits of kitchen roll like she did. He sat opposite her. 'I've dreamed about this. Being here like this. Breaking away from my parents at last. Gaining my independence.'

She balanced the prawns precariously, glad that he hadn't thrown her in there as a bonus. Maybe he was just glad to escape from Clem and Marcia. She'd give him the benefit of the doubt. 'And glad to have the Crash'n'Dash?'

'It isn't mine.' He managed to bite into his sandwich without dropping any of it. 'But yes, for the time being. Once we've drawn up new agreements, then I'd like to add another Jessons ride, maybe a Moon Mission. We'd be well on the way to the big time then. Danny could run the Crash'n'Dash and put Claudia up in the waltzer. We'd take on a few more lads. And –' he leaned forward, 'I've applied for ground rights at Wallingford, Abingdon and Newbury in the autumn. With Dad's Guild influence it shouldn't be a problem. We should even be able to let some ground out. Strike out on our own. Be like Dad or Art Maycroft – or even Irvins or Collins.'

'Or Wilsons or Mellors or –' Nell gave up trying to eat graciously and picked the prawns up in her fingers. It was, as she'd feared, all slipping away from her. She'd never be able to amalgamate the Memory Lane Fair with the ranks of hi-tech white-knuckle rides now. The Savage and the Gavioli would never sail round in stately splendour on village greens. The ghost train and the caterpillar would remain in the shed at Fox Hollow. Jack and the Downland Trust would have to find a new home – again.

She thought fleetingly about Jack, and how very different it had been with him at lunch-time. How relaxed; without threat. The wild bike ride, the laughing, the whole friendliness of it all. She wondered if he was sitting at home with Fiona, planning his wedding, choosing names for their baby, dreaming of the gallopers. But Fiona was away in London being businesslike, wasn't she? Still, she was sure of one thing: he wouldn't be thinking about her. Jack had his future organised while hers just flapped lamely like a broken branch in the wind, being pulled in all directions at once.

She realised that all the time she'd sat with him at the Maybush, on the bank of the river, in the sun, she hadn't worried about her freckles. Not once.

Ross was still talking. She scooped up strands of lettuce. 'Oh – sorry? I – er – didn't catch that last bit.'

'I said it's symbiotic.' Ross sipped his Martini. 'Everyone benefits. Fairs change. I mean, it's not that long ago – certainly within the last forty years – that crowds flocked to fairs to ogle malformed animals. And God forbid, even people. Siamese twins in preserving fluid – three-legged sheep – freak shows, for Christ's sake. Thankfully we've moved on since then. That's what we do. What all businesses do. Move. Forwards.'

Nell still wanted to move backwards. Not to the freak shows; of course not. But to the days when things were calmer and gentler and you didn't pay to be frightened out of your wits. She knew he wouldn't understand so she stayed silent.

Ross was well into his stride. 'Of course there will be places we can't take the new machines, but I don't see that posing a problem. Quite the reverse. You and Sam can take the dodgems and paratrooper to one gaff while Danny and I take the hydraulic rides and the waltzer to another. Diversification. Expansion. All to the good, Nell. Where on earth is the problem in that?'

She didn't know. She couldn't see one. It just wasn't what she wanted.

She put her empty plate back on the ebony tray and took a mouthful of Martini. It was perfect. Ross even knew how to mix Martinis. 'Just tell me one thing. I do know it wasn't you who bought the Crash'n'Dash. I happen to believe you. So, how did Danny manage to pull this one off?'

Ross slid from his chair and sat on the goatskin rug at her feet. He ran his hand up her bare leg to the bottom of her shorts and stroked her knee. She wished he wouldn't. He took her free hand and kissed it. 'Oh, well, you're bound to know sooner or later, Freckle Face. I don't suppose it matters any more. It wasn't Danny. He knew nothing about it. It was your mother.'

Nell sat in stunned silence. Adele? What the hell had she bought it for? And where had she got the money? She shook her head violently. 'You're wrong, Ross. I don't know who told you – but they're pulling your leg. Mum wouldn't –'

'She would and she did.' Ross eased himself on to the arm of her chair and slid his hand beneath her hair. 'I was there at

Jessons when she came up for the first test. I saw her write the cheque. It was supposed to be our secret. She didn't want you to know.'

Nell's world was slowly falling apart. 'And Dad? Was he in on this, too?'

'He still doesn't know anything as far as I'm aware. Your mother swore me and Dad to secrecy until – well – until today. She'll probably tell Peter tonight – before someone else does.'

And give him another heart attack, Nell thought bitterly. Poor Dad. Poor her.

She swallowed the rest of the Martini without tasting it. Her mother! The one person she really believed in. The one person she thought she could trust. And all that time at Blenheim – and all the phone calls – and she hadn't breathed a bloody word!

'But what did she think she was doing?'

'Moving Bradleys forward – because you wouldn't.' Ross stroked her cheek. 'She did it for you, sweetheart. For your dad's peace of mind. And for us.'

Oh, holy shit, Nell thought. Adele might as well have forced the wedding ring on to her finger. Adele might as well have consigned the gallopers to the scrap heap. Adele had just destroyed her dreams.

CHAPTER TWENTY-ONE

News of the Crash'n'Dash seemed to have spread pretty rapidly. Not only were Meridian television due to send cameras and a reporter to Marsh Minster when the fair opened later that afternoon, but Central had also got wind of it and were billing the Bradleys as 'our local travelling family'.

Claudia simply couldn't decide what to wear.

Discarding anything in leather or PVC as too hot for the sultry afternoon and anyway bound to inflame Danny – and really not wanting to resort to Monsoon or Laura Ashley because they were Sam's favourites – she thought she might just have to go shopping.

Danny would have no objection to a spending spree – the Crash'n'Dash had made a fortune in its first week. In fact, at the moment he would have agreed to anything. Maybe she could encourage Nell to come with her. Nell had been thoroughly depressed ever since Haresfoot and could do with cheering up, although for the life of her Claudia couldn't see why.

So what, if Adele had paid for the Crash'n'Dash? It meant they didn't have to, didn't it? And Danny had assured her that no, according to the arrangement with Clem Percival, his mother didn't want reimbursing – nor did she want a cut of the profits. She'd simply done it, Danny said, to help the family move forward and to make Peter's retirement re-cuperation that much easier. Claudia knew differently. Claudia knew that while that may well have been Adele's second and third motives, the primary one had been to get Ross and Nell together.

And, she thought, pulling on a pair of wide-legged cotton trousers, it had worked. Maybe Nell didn't want to go to bed with Ross – she couldn't blame her if she didn't fancy the sex side, after all – but there were compensations. Ross wasn't a bad-tempered pig like Danny; he was attractive and generous. And the Sipson living wagon was a total dream. Even she had been in and begged the use of the shell-shaped bath, which was bliss after months of showers. She had already made up her mind to ask Danny to get a similar bath when he changed their van next year. God – what more did Nell want? Well, apart from love, of course, and some sort of traditional fairground. But, she reflected, slipping into a white shirt and knotting it under her rib-cage, you just couldn't have everything you wanted, could you?

Claudia had tried really hard to make a go of things with Danny since the row at Blenheim. Now that she knew – thanks to Sam's expert tuition – how delightful kissing could be, she'd tried initiating her husband. It hadn't been an unmitigated success. Danny wasn't into preliminaries. It really was roll-on roll-off, as Sam had correctly surmised, and he'd pushed her irritably away when she'd tried to kiss and cuddle first.

Then of course there had been that embarrassing episode during the Blenheim concert when Adele had seen her and Sam together. It had taken all Sam's powers of charm and persuasion to convince his mother that she'd witnessed nothing inflammatory; that all she'd caught had been an innocuous kiss between brother and sister-in-law during a moment of inebriated emotion over the music and the fireworks. Adele had eventually believed him. Adele would never know that they'd been stone-cold sober and deadly serious.

They had decided then to cool things down. Not, Claudia thought, sliding her feet into a pair of strappy Portuguese sandals, that things had reached boiling point. At least, not for her. But they were beginning to simmer nicely. And so, irritatingly, was her conscience. She was beginning to have really deep feelings for Sam. Her heart stirred when he smiled at her, and she shivered when he touched her. Worst of all, she really enjoyed just being with him – that was the scary part. And as for the kissing – well, the kissing sometimes made sleeping difficult, especially when Danny had just performed one of his loveless and rather brutal manoeuvres. But she was married. And she was going to have to stay married because she didn't have any choice. And cheating – she flinched at the word – was something she read about in the *News of the World*. Other people cheated. She didn't. Kissing, she was still convinced, didn't count. Cheating began below the waist.

She checked that she had a full house of credit cards, picked up her bag and headed for the door.

Nell was sitting on the steps of her living wagon, looking very slinky in a blue denim mini-dress, and reading the latest Jilly Cooper with some ghastly music playing in the background.

'What the hell is that?'

Nell peered over her sunglasses. 'Poet and Peasant Overture. Played on a ninety-eight-key Limonaire organ. It's a tape I bought yesterday in that shop just past Woolworths. Why? Do you want to borrow it?'

Claudia grinned. 'Not really my style, thanks. And I wouldn't have thought it was yours either, quite honestly. It hardly goes well with Motorhead and Iron Butterfly on the Crash'n'Dash, does it?'

'The Brain-Scrambler is nothing to do with me.' Nell removed the sunglasses completely and turned down the page of her book. 'And when I run my bloody mother to ground I shall tell her so.'

Claudia laughed. When they'd found out from Ross that Adele was the mystery benefactor, Nell, Sam and Danny had all wanted to talk to her, although their reasons for doing so varied from outrage on Nell's part to delight on Danny's. Sam, she'd noticed, had been far more ambivalent. But Adele had proved elusive.

They had all simply got the answerphone at Graceland; the mobiles were switched off and no one, not even Clem and Marcia Percival, had a clue where they were. Nell had borrowed Sam's Mazda – Ross had offered the Ferrari but she'd refused it – and belted down to Highcliffe in a white-hot fury. She'd been practically volcanic when she'd returned.

The Hart-Radstocks – who were keeping an eye on Graceland – had told her that Adele and Peter were on holiday. On the Elvis Presley Memorial Tour. Yes, that's right, dear – in America. Probably for about two weeks. Adele had been rather vague about the itinerary. It had all been arranged at the eleventh hour.

They still weren't back.

'I wondered if you fancied spending some dosh.' Claudia thought it would be a good idea to steer Nell away from the subject of Adele. 'Unless, of course, you were going to have another clandestine meeting with the bank manager?'

'I hadn't planned one until later in the week. And yes, why not?' Nell switched off her ghetto-blaster, and hurled her book and sunglasses on to the sofa inside the wagon. 'Although I want it put on record that any dosh I spend today is strictly my share of the takings from our rides – not anything to do with the Brain-Scrambler.'

Claudia knew. Ross had told them all that Nell was adamant that she was not going to be taking a penny from the Crash'n'Dash's quite considerable earnings. Claudia secretly thought such high ideals were seriously misplaced when it came to money. But then again, Nell had the bank manager. He probably had a nice little nest egg tucked away somewhere in PEPs or whatever it was Danny was always rattling on about.

Nell locked her front door. 'And is there any particular reason for this sudden urge to spend money?'

'Not really. Oh well, yes, actually. Because the telly people are coming – and I can't decide which image to go for. I thought of trying something grown-up like Next or Benetton.'

'Pretty drastic for you. If it's grown-up you want, maybe you should be looking in that nice little shop behind Art Maycroft's machines.' Nell was grinning. 'They do pleated skirts and Tricel blouses. Just up Danny's street. But, if it's a change of image you're after, I've got an even better idea.'

Claudia was feeling pretty sceptical as they headed for the town centre through the ranks of closed-down rides and joints. Marsh Minster was a large street fair, and seemed to be welcomed by shopkeepers and residents alike. There had been all sorts of problems in the past when all the shops bordered the road and customers from the town defected in droves for the week, but since the Minster Mall – all chrome and glass and fountains – had been constructed, everyone seemed happy.

'OK.' Nell stopped in front of a pink-and-lilac shopfront with huge windows swathed in miles of lace. 'Yeah, I know it looks like a knocking-shop in a Humphrey Bogart movie – but it's actually really nice. I – um – popped in yesterday to suss it out. Are you up for this?'

Claudia felt doubtful. Top-to-Toe sounded a bit radical when she only wanted to buy a new dress. 'Won't we have to have appointments?'

'For some of it, no doubt.' Nell was already pinging her way in through the frilly-knickered door, 'but when I asked yesterday they said they always try and squeeze people in. They do hair and facials, and waxing and manicures, and pedicures and body-wraps, and exfoliating and – Oh, hi, you two.'

Claudia smiled warily at the Mackenzie twins who were just paying at the pink desk. They didn't look any more or less glamorous than before; just glowingly young in their skimpy white shorts and vest tops. Claudia suddenly felt ancient.

'Just had our bikini-lines waxed,' Nyree-Dawn informed them.

Mercedes grinned. 'You know – just in case we get lucky.'

'Are they old enough to *know* about bikini-lines?' Claudia stared after the twins as they drifted outside. 'I never even showed mine to anyone until my wedding night.'

Nell was leafing through a pile of glossy brochures and asking questions of the woman behind the desk who had the very surprised look of the recent face-lift. She turned to Claudia, the light of fanaticism in her eyes. 'We can have facials and make-overs and hair-dos today, now – without appointments. Manicures and body-wraps will have to be booked. What do you reckon?'

Claudia reckoned that a nice frock from Next and a new pair of earrings would probably go down a treat on Meridian telly, but as Nell looked so enthusiastic and this was supposed to be a sort of Samaritan expedition she nodded. 'Facials, then –'

'Oh, come on.' Nell was already heading through a mass of pink voile curtaining. 'A change of image you said. Don't be such a wimp. Let's go the whole hog.'

Two hours later, Claudia blinked in amazement at herself in the mirror. Oh my God! Danny would go neutron.

'It's super, dear! Simply super. You won't know yourself.' The Top-to-Toe assistants crowded round in their little pink-and-lilac overalls and clasped their silver fingernails in delight. 'Quite a transformation!'

Was that her? Was that really her without the ten years of shaggy curls and the black eye-liner and the false eyelashes? Had she always had those cheek-bones hidden away? And her lips! They looked like they'd just had intravenous collagen! Could that have been achieved with merely a different shade of lipstick? And had her eyes always been that huge?

'You were wearing very heavy make-up, dear,' the woman whose breast-pocket announced that she was called Kizzy, said happily. 'Totally unnecessary with your gorgeous features. And as for your hair – well, Jennifer has transformed you.'

Jennifer has probably ended my marriage, Claudia thought, looking again at the inch-long, multi-layered spiky crop that framed her face and made her look younger than the Mackenzie twins. Danny had always said that women should have long hair. He liked women with long hair. He especially liked Claudia with long hair.

'It's incredible!' Claudia bounced out of the chair, struggling to free herself from the rather unpleasant lilac coverall. 'I love it! Where's Nell? I can't wait to see – oh!'

Nell emerged from the next-door cubicle and screamed in simultaneous delight at Claudia.

Nell's long red-gold hair had been trimmed to one length, falling just below her shoulders in a heavy, glossy curtain exactly, Claudia thought, like one of those shampoo adverts on the television. It moved and shone as she moved, lit with fire. The Top-to-Toe hairdresser had cut a heavy fringe that now framed the slanting sleepy-cat eyes. And those eyes! Claudia shook her head. Nell's long eyelashes, naturally pale, had been dyed jet black. The rest of the make-up was understated so that the eyes and the hair said everything. She looked stunning.

'Christ!' Claudia eventually managed to whisper. 'Ross and Danny will think they've got new women.'

'I just wish Ross would hurry up and get his.' Nell beamed happily, already writing the cheque. 'I asked them to bleach out my freckles but Charmian said they enhanced my colouring. That you shouldn't argue with nature. And that a lot of people find freckles attractive.'

'I don't think anyone will actually be looking at your freckles.' Claudia reached the desk and handed over one of her cards to the woman with the startled expression. 'How do you feel?'

'Ten feet tall,' Nell beamed in delight. 'And ready to take on the world.'

Claudia couldn't decide whether she was referring to Ross, Adele, the Brain-Scrambler – or even the bank manager. Still, it didn't really matter. Nell was smiling again – and that had been the whole point of the exercise.

In an aura of mutual appreciation, they stepped outside into the Minster Mall. Heads turned almost immediately, Claudia noticed with satisfaction, without needing to resort to leather or PVC or anything. She hugged Nell. 'You're brilliant! I can't wait to see Danny's face.'

Deciding that the new looks deserved new clothes, they found a small shop specialising in one-offs in jewel-bright colours. Discarding the skirt suits as too hot, the neat and smart little shifts as too grown-up, they pounced on silk shorts with cropped-off matching jackets. Nell's was emerald and Claudia's, ruby. A bit like the Mackenzie twins, Claudia thought, as they stalked in front of the boutique's bevelled mirrors, only far more attractive.

'No, don't bother wrapping them,' Nell was saying to the boutique owner. 'We'll wear them.'

The suits had even more effect, Claudia thought gaily, as they left the Minster Mall and headed back to the fair-strewn High Street, combined with the makeovers. Drivers of cars which had been diverted and had been sitting in sweltering tailbacks round the town, suddenly looked far more jaunty and leaned from windows shouting their approval. Nell, who had strong feminist tendencies, pretended to be offended, but Claudia was pretty sure that by the way she was stalking on those legs, she was enjoying every minute of it. As she was. It was a novel experience, attracting attention without even trying.

'Christ!' Art Maycroft blinked as they strode through the rides. 'You'll knock 'em for six! You'd better hurry though. I reckon Nyree-Dawn and Mercedes have stolen a bit of a march on you two.'

Claudia frowned. 'What? What march? Where?'

'The Crash'n'Dash,' Art said, jogging along beside them. 'Meridian and Central telly have arrived early and they want to start filming. They were looking for a couple of pretty girls to sit on the seats and look gorgeous for the cameras and –'

Claudia grabbed hold of Nell's arm and belted towards the top end of the fair. Ignoring Nell's yelps of protest they arrived at the pay-box just as the Mackenzie twins in their white cut-offs were sashaying towards the ride.

'I don't think so,' Claudia said firmly, elbowing her way in front of them and smiling at the men with the cameras poised on their shoulders. 'So sorry we're late. We were just getting ready. We're Bradleys –' she increased the smile. 'We own the ride. Now, where do you want us?'

The cameramen muttered something salacious and Claudia had to tighten her pressure on Nell's arm to prevent her from running away. 'We're only going to sit on it, for God's sake! It's ours after all – so why should those Mackenzies muscle in? Just smile at the cameras and think of the bank manager.'

She almost had to drag Nell into the padded seat on the far side of the Crash'n'Dash where apparently the light was better. A crowd had gathered. Nyree-Dawn and Mercedes were glowering. Andy Craig and Wesley Smith from the rival television companies were talking to Art Maycroft, then moved towards the ride, microphones bristling.

The questions were chatty and informal. Claudia answered most of them. The cameramen seemed intent on getting shots from every angle.

'And are we going to see this amazing contraption actually in action?' Andy Craig asked the camera.

'Indeed we are,' Wesley Smith informed his videoman. 'At any moment. Stand by for blast-off!'

Claudia clenched her fingers into Nell's thigh. 'You can't get off now. They won't really run it. There's no one in the pay-box. They'll just pretend. They can do anything with special effects – oh, bugger!'

Dragged from their afternoon siesta, and completely un-prepared for the media invasion which had been scheduled for five o'clock, Danny and Ross were standing behind the cameramen, nodding. Obviously agreeing to be filmed in the pay-box, they squeezed in behind the computerised console and began chatting animatedly into Andy and Wesley's microphones.

Danny, unfortunately, saw them first. His eyes were riveted on the top of Claudia's shorn head. His jaw dropped. 'What the fuck – ?'

There was a lot of tutting and covering-up of the sound equipment. Claudia leaned forward and yelled at Ross, 'Push the bloody button! He's going to kill me!'

'So am I,' Nell hissed, 'if this thing moves as much as an inch – oh!'

It was the most terrifying minute-and-a-half of Claudia's life. Surrounded by white lights, ear-splitting music, the horrifying feeling that she was about to be smashed to pulp at any second and complete disorientation, she clung to her shoulder supports in relief as the Crash'n'Dash glided to a halt. Still, it was probably preferable than facing her hus-band.

'Am I dead?' Her head was spinning. Her tongue seemed to be glued to her teeth. 'What happened? Nell? Are you OK?'

'I think so.' Nell tried a tentative smile. 'Actually, that was pretty exciting. Shall we do it again?'

Claudia was fumbling to undo her padded bars. 'Not on your life. Never, ever –' She smiled in gratitude as a strong pair of hands helped her with the catches.

'Get out,' Danny snarled. 'Out! Now!'

Wesley and Andy were interviewing Ross. The cameramen seemed delighted with the footage. And Nell was smiling her 'I'm-dreaming-of-the-bank-manager' smile.

'Not now, Danny.' Claudia's legs buckled as she put her feet to the floor. 'Not in front of all these people.'

'You've really done it this time, haven't you? You know how I feel about long hair. Women have long hair, Claudia.

You didn't even tell me what you were going to do, did you? I don't like that. I don't like it at all.'

He had one arm under her elbow. Meridian and Central were packing up. Claudia looked at Danny's furious face. She couldn't go on like this. She was frightened of him. More and more frightened. No one else seemed to have noticed that his fingers were leaving white marks on her arm, or that his mouth was snarling, not smiling.

'Bloody hell!' Sam appeared from the crowd. 'Have I missed all the excitement? I was just hosing down the paratrooper when Rio Mackenzie said the television crews had arrived early.' He smiled at Claudia. 'Wow! I love your hair! Don't you, Danny? A real improvement – very pretty. Actually,' he spread his hands in a gesture of helplessness and looked at his brother, 'I've got a real bugger of a problem with the balance on the centre truck. Can you give me a hand, Dan, or I won't be able to open tonight.'

Danny sighed and slowly, very slowly, released his grip on Claudia's arm. 'Christ! I suppose so. You ought to get rid of that heap of junk, though. Come on then – let's have a look. I've got other things to do.' He glared at Claudia. 'And other things to see to. Don't go too far away.'

Claudia watched as he barged his way through the crowd towards the paratrooper. Her eyes were stinging with tears. 'Thanks.'

'It's OK.' Sam stroked the marks on her arm which were now turning a livid red. 'Now go back to your living wagon, get what you need, and for God's sake leave him.'

'I can't. How can I? I've got nowhere to go.'

'Yes you have,' Sam said quietly. 'You know you have.'

CHAPTER TWENTY-TWO

Fiona was due home that evening. She'd telephoned from her car just after seven in the morning while Jack was still in bed, and said no, she wouldn't be stopping over the weekend in London with her mother and stepfather as originally planned. She'd followed up all her contacts of the previous week and firmed-up her client portfolio. She had a couple of appointments that day with customers she'd been courting, then she'd come home and work on the quotes. Yes, she was feeling fine. Why shouldn't she be? No, she thought she'd be too tired to eat out. Maybe Jack could cook some pasta when she got back?

She hadn't, Jack thought as he drizzled the marinade over sliced courgettes and tomatoes and slid the dish into the refrigerator ready for this evening's meal, said that she'd missed him. But then he hadn't said that he'd missed her either. In fact he was getting quite used to these breaks. Fiona was spending more and more time on the road. It suited him well. He'd been spending more and more time at Fox Hollow. Percy and Dennis, Harry and Fred, had joined him on the last two occasions, and all were sure that the gallopers would be completed by September. Just in time for his wedding.

Nell's visits hadn't coincided with his since that crazy day they'd ridden to the Maybush. He knew she'd been there – she was still leaving notes. He'd kept them. Just as he'd kept the photograph from *The World's Fair*. He wasn't sure why.

In one of her notes Nell had asked how he knew about the Crash'n'Dash – she'd referred to it as the Brain-Scrambler – and mentioned Ross Percival's arrival at Haresfoot; the appearance of all three on Meridian News had come as something of a shock.

Jack had been perched on the edge of the rigid sofa with his without-Fiona dinner of two cans of Beck's and a Chinese take-away. They had played into the news item with a blast of organ music, the way all television companies seemed to announce fairground coverage, and he'd raised his head from the sports pages of the local paper. Seeing Nell, with her hair gleaming like copper in the sun and her long legs in ⸫right green shorts, being strapped into the confines of the Crash-'n'Dash, had made him choke on his noodles. They'd interviewed Claudia mostly, but he could see Nell in the off-focus background looking distinctly unhappy. Her freckles – God, he loved women with freckles – were practically glowing with indignation. Poor Nell, he'd thought, knowing how much she hated the intrusion into her life; guessing how much its arrival threatened her dreams – his dreams too, come to that.

They had cut to the Crash'n'Dash in action and he'd sat, chow mein suspended in midair, literally holding his breath. Christ – she must have nerves of steel. That must have been hairier than the pillion ride on the Roadster. Nell appeared surprisingly calm afterwards, although he thought Claudia looked a bit queasy. Nell had had her hair cut. He liked the way the long fringe drew attention to her eyes. She was really stunning. No wonder the television cameras were lingering so long.

They eventually panned away and Andy Craig was talking to – he'd squinted at the byline on the screen – Danny Bradley. That must be the older brother – the one who was so unpleasant to the attractive Claudia. And – Ross Percival.

Jack had bitten quite angrily into a piece of chicken. He knew of the Percivals – anyone with any knowledge of the fairground fraternity knew of the Percivals – but he hadn't expected to see Ross looming large in his living room. So this was the man who was responsible for buying the Crash-'n'Dash and who wanted to marry Nell. Not that he blamed him for the latter, of course. He'd stopped for a moment. Christ! Did he really think that? It had disturbed him considerably to find that he did.

He added some black pepper to the chopped onions, covered them with clingfilm and put them in the fridge with the courgettes and tomatoes. There'd be no need to pan-fry the chicken breasts until Fiona got back. He'd do some rice in the microwave while she was having a shower and he'd buy a bottle of Chardonnay on the way home. He was going to make the best of this. He had no other choice. Not now.

The Roadster looked quite out of place in the Morland & Son executive car park – especially next to his father's BMW. Jack removed his crash helmet, straightened his hair and was fastening his tie as he galloped up the stairs. He'd hoped his father would be out.

'Morning, Jack.' Margaret, their middle-aged and motherly secretary, beamed at him. 'Coffee?'

'Please. If it's not too much trouble.'

'No trouble. I've just put a brew on for your dad. He's having a meeting.'

Oh God, Jack thought, he bloody would be. He pushed open the office door. His father looked up from his desk. He didn't smile. Neither did the suited and tied and heavy-jowled men sitting opposite him.

'Sit down, Jack. I believe you know Steve Reynolds and Phil Smith? They're site managers at Fairy Dell,' Bill Morland said.

Jack tried very hard to look serious. It wasn't easy. The more bleak and ugly the housing development, the more whimsical the name of the estate. He had long since learned that Kingfisher Lakeside and Willow Fronds meant ten thousand identical houses, in identical roads, with minuscule gardens, with no view except of other houses and an industrial estate, and probably a six-lane bypass on the doorstep.

'You know Phil and Steve, don't you?' Bill had picked up the letter-opener. Jack winced. Not a good sign. He knew them vaguely by sight, of course. They were regular contacts for Morlands. Bill dealt with them. Jack usually spoke to them on the phone. He couldn't remember meeting them recently.

'Yes, of course.'

'But not quite as well as you should do,' his father full-beamed straight into his eyes now, 'considering that you spent a whole day with them last Monday. At Fairy Dell. Discussing our tender.'

Oh, shit. Jack had spent last Monday at Fox Hollow.

'Steve and Phil have just called in to tell me that they did in fact leave a couple of messages on your answerphone as you seemed unable to make the meeting. You didn't get back to them. They couldn't, naturally, contact me as I was involved with that green-belt meeting in Bournemouth. They've also, because they're old friends, called in to tell me that we're too late to tender and the deal has gone elsewhere.'

Double shit.

Bill Morland hadn't finished. He was flicking through the computer screen with one hand and a pile of papers with the other. 'As has the potential tender for Merrymead, and the unnamed complex at Didcot, and the very prestigious new marina flats on Folly Bridge in Oxford.' He stabbed the paper-knife into the desk. 'I trust you have an excellent explanation for this?'

The door opened and Margaret bustled in with the tray. Thank God, Jack thought. His mouth had dried up.

'Not now, Margaret!' Bill barked. 'I'll ring when – if – I'm ready!'

Margaret, much to Jack's dismay, backed out again.

There were two options: neither of them particularly pleasant. The truth or lying. Jack had never really been in favour of telling lies. It made life far too complicated. Withholding some of the truth at times was a different matter. But this, he felt, was a time for utmost honesty.

'No explanations. No excuses. I didn't go.'

'I know you didn't bloody go!' His father banged so hard on the desk that Steve and Phil jumped. 'I want to know bloody why!'

Not a moment for complete truth here, Jack reckoned quickly. A bit of fudging might help. 'Actually, I think I got the dates muddled. I think I put them in my organiser for next month. All four of them. I thought they were in August.'

'I have access to your organiser on my network. The dates are all here. Very clearly. For July. Not good enough, Jack. Try again.'

Steve and Phil shifted in their seats. Jack sucked in his breath. 'OK. I apologise to Mr Reynolds and Mr Smith for wasting their time. I apologise to you for missing out on this and the other three deals – and I'd rather like to conduct the rest of this conversation in private.'

Phil and Steve, who were looking increasingly uncomfortable, rose as one with relieved and embarrassed smiles.

'Sit down, gentlemen!' Bill Morland's voice would have halted a whirling dervish. They sat. 'This won't take long. No, Jack, there are things that must be said – and I'd prefer to have witnesses. Especially witnesses of the calibre of these two colleagues who have been true and trusted friends of mine through many years of business. I certainly wouldn't want them to leave here with the impression that Morlands don't work ethically, or are in any way unreliable. Any impression of that kind, passed on in the field, could bankrupt our company. Understood? Good. One missed appointment I could forgive – we all have delays and slip-ups – but *four* – and without notifying anyone of your absence. Sit down!'

Jack shook his head. 'I'm not some kid at school being ticked off by the headmaster. I am your son – yes – but I'm not ten years old. Nor am I some incompetent who can't get the stationery order correct. I'm a partner in this business – or at least I was. Now you've got your witnesses, Dad, they can witness this. I resign. Now. Immediately. Goodbye.'

He turned and stalked to the door, yanking it open so hard that Margaret nearly tumbled through it. Stepping into her office he closed the door behind him and bit his lip. 'You heard?'

'Course I heard.' Her eyes were glistening. 'I wouldn't know anything that went on here if I didn't listen in, would I? Don't go, Jack. I couldn't bear working here without you. Don't –'

The connecting door flew open and Bill, red-faced and barely containing his temper, seemed to swell in the opening. 'Jack! We haven't finished!'

'We have. I mean it. I'm sorry, Dad, really I am – but my heart hasn't been in it for months. You'll find someone else to take over. Someone who feels the same way about the company as you do. I've tried for so long – but it's never felt right. I only stayed as long as I did because I didn't want to let you down. I do appreciate that you've made life easy for me, and I'm grateful, but I don't enjoy it. I need to do something on my own, make my own mistakes, have my own successes, without them being a pale reflection of yours. I didn't go to those appointments because I simply forgot. I had my mind on other things.'

'Such as?'

Oh, hell. Fact or fiction? It might score him Brownie points if he laid the blame squarely at the door of the wedding and the impending baby – but Fiona hadn't wanted him to tell his parents of the pregnancy until after they were married.

'The Downland Trust. The gallopers.'

'Fucking hell! You'll throw away an executive career, a vast salary, security, prospects, everything that I've fought tooth and nail for, for a heap of old fairground junk? Jesus, boy! You need certifying!'

I probably do, Jack thought. But now that he had actually said what he felt, actually resigned, he had never felt better in his life. OK, there'd be problems. Massive problems. Money for one and Fiona for about three hundred. But she'd calm down eventually. She wanted to carry on clambering up her career ladder, didn't she? He'd stay at home and look after the baby. Be a house-husband and paint . . .

'You're fucking insane!'

Margaret bristled behind the computer. 'Excuse me, Bill, but if you use that word again, then I'll resign too. I do have my principles, you know.'

'Fucking! Fucking! Fucking!' Bill roared across the office. 'Fuck—'

'That's it.' Margaret gathered up her cardigan and her handbag. 'I don't need this. I've been head-hunted by the customer service section of Chaseys Biscuits, you know.' And she slammed out of the office.

'Now see what you've done!' Bill howled. 'You and your fucking stupid ideas! Go and get her back!'

Jack shook his head. It wasn't his problem any longer. This wasn't his office any longer. He'd just joined the ranks of the unemployed.

He thought afterwards, as he swerved the Roadster into the cul-de-sac, that this must be how people who suddenly lose a limb felt; numb with shock and disbelief, so that you have no awareness of the horror. He was quite sure that by this evening, when he'd told Fiona about it, and his mother had squawked down the telephone for hours, he'd feel every grinding, biting inch of the pain.

Right now however, he thought, leaping from the Road-ster and nearly tearing off his tie and suit jacket as he fumbled for the front-door key, he felt as high as a March hare on an amphetamine overdose.

'Cooee! Jack!' Adam, wearing a tight pink T-shirt, was leaning from his upstairs window across the road. 'If you're at home today, I've just made some rather nice drop scones for Stan – but I'm sure he wouldn't miss a couple. I've only got the bedroom to polish round. Shall I pop over in – say – twenty minutes for a coffee and a chat?'

'Sorry, no.' Jack at last got the key in the lock. 'I'd love to, really. But I've only come home to change and then I'm off out again. Maybe some other time.'

But Adam had slammed shut the window with a crash and flounced away.

Fox Hollow was deserted. The Downland Trusters had obviously been there since his last visit. The galloper platforms had been laid out round the centre truck in the middle of the shed. Someone had manhandled the striped tilt down from its shelf and propped it against the wall. The swifts had been sorted into numerical order. Jack walked round them. In a very short time they'd be able to build up for the trial run – and then what? Now he had all the time in the world to indulge his obsession – and Nell had none.

He sighed. She would marry Ross Percival and become so involved with the new rides that she'd have no time for the gallopers. There was no way that Ross Percival – or that aggressive brother of hers – would give the gallopers gaff-room. Nell might, he thought with a pang of anguish, even decide to sell them on. Oh, shit. Why did life never run in concentric circles? Why did someone always have to put a U-turn in the way of happiness?

He painted for three hours. It was very therapeutic. Today he didn't even switch on the radio. He just let his mind drift along with the colours and the textures. The horses were all completed now, as were the rounding boards and the platforms. He had a few finishing touches to do to the shields and the top centres, but they were small fiddly jobs that needed every ounce of his concentration. He sat back on his haunches, relaxed his aching shoulder muscles, and surveyed his morning's work. It was a million times more important to him than selling red-brick boxes to avaricious building-site owners.

The centre drum panels, which would surround the organ on three sides, were lavishly carved and he was enjoying painting the gilded scrolls against the crimson background. They looked rich and gorgeous. He wished Nell could be there to see them. It might just persuade her not to let go of her dream.

'They're beautiful.'

'Christ!' He jumped and looked up at her. 'It must be thought transference. I didn't hear you come in.'

'I didn't think you needed to. I thought you could sniff me out.'

'All my senses are a bit slow today.' He could smell the scent now. He ought to ask her what it was. He'd buy some for Fiona. 'I like your hair.'

'Thanks.' Nell squatted down beside him. 'It's nearly ready, then?'

He wanted to laugh. The dream that had kept him going was almost over. He could practically hear her saying the words. Every sentence would begin with 'Ross thinks that . . .'

She studied his painting without speaking, occasionally closing her eyes as if visualising the whole. Then she stood up and walked across the shed to the laid-out platforms. She still said nothing. She was wearing jeans again, and a pale blue angora cardigan. Her name on the rounding boards seemed to hypnotise her. It was almost as though she was weighing everything up. He prayed that she wasn't going to ask him to paint out her name ready for a new purchaser.

Now she was looking at the horses. He washed his brushes vigorously, holding his breath.

'Oh, my God! You didn't tell me!'

He wiped the brushes deliberately slowly. 'I didn't know if you'd be happy with it.'

'Happy with a horse called Petronella? I'm ecstatic! Oh, God – it's immortality! You are brilliant!'

Her delight was infectious but the anaesthetic of shock was already wearing off and the reality was already creeping in.

He felt his face grinning back although his heart was crying.

Nell stopped smiling. 'Jack? What's the matter? You look awful. Well, no, I mean you don't – that is – Are you all right?'

'Not really.' He shrugged. 'I don't suppose you fancy another trip on the Roadster, a pint in the Maybush, and an incredibly soggy shoulder?'

He insisted that she wore the crash helmet this time even though she laughingly protested that it would ruin her new hair-do. He thought, as they powered towards Newbridge, that he should invest in a second crash helmet, just for moments such as these. It really wouldn't do, on top of everything else, to have a criminal record – however minor the offence. Still, if Nell was about to become a Percival, there probably wouldn't be too many more Roadster rides to share.

He enjoyed her hands gripping his waist – he could actually see the freckles on her wrists – and the waft of that evocative floral scent that every so often filtered through the cold spiciness of the wind and the heat of the petrol.

'Do you always drive so fast?' Nell was smiling as she unfastened the skid-lid and freed her hair in the Maybush's car park. 'Or was that a catharsis?'

She seemed less shaken by the journey this time – but then she'd just experienced the Crash'n'Dash.

They walked into the cool interior of the pub and she headed straight for the bar. 'Shandies again? I know they're probably not good for soul-baring sessions, but anything stronger would probably have us both in tears.'

'I'll pay.'

She shook her head. 'You get the next round. I – I want this to be the same as last time.'

So did he, but he had a feeling it was going to be very different. He noted with pleasure that all the businessmen, in the pub for their lunch-time ploughman's and lager, were gazing at Nell with admiration. Probably beautiful women who were nearly six feet tall with a waterfall of red-gold hair were a rarity round here. Or maybe they'd seen her on the television news and were trying to place her. Either way, their interest was tangible. Fiona, he realised with a jab of guilt, never turned heads. And Nell wasn't *with* him, as such. Still, no one knew that, did they? He experienced a glow of pride as the office eyes continued to follow them as they walked outside.

They sat at the same table. It wasn't quite so hot, and today a breeze rippled through the overhanging trees and stirred the surface of the river. High-piled clouds hovered on the horizon. He thought, inconsequentially, that it might rain and wondered if it would put the punters off the Crash-'n'Dash.

'You first then,' Nell said over her glass. 'But don't think this is going to be one-way traffic. I've got a few minor problems of my own.'

They talked. They had two drinks but the conversation well outlasted them. When he told her about his resignation she nodded enthusiastically.

'Good for you. I mean it must have taken some guts to do it. But now it's over. It can't get worse. And I've always said you'd make a fortune as a painter – you could advertise in *The World's Fair* and have people snapping your hand off.' She laughed. 'Which would, of course, defeat the object a bit, I admit. Anyway, I told you I'd pay you for the work you've already done. I could start right away. I owe you so much.'

'You haven't got any money,' he reminded her gently. 'You spent it all on the gallopers and the Gavioli.'

Nell shrugged happily. 'I can start taking my share from the Brain-Scrambler. I don't see why that shouldn't subsidise you for a bit.'

'No way! That'd be like prostitution. But you really don't think I'm mad? Giving up my career? Walking out?'

'Completely crazy.' She sat back in her seat. 'I only wish more people were as mad as you. So, what does Fiona think?'

They'd gone on eventually to discuss the Crash'n'Dash –

and her mother's involvement and convenient disappearance – and Ross Percival. Jack had a thousand questions bubbling in his head. He wasn't sure that he wanted to hear the answers.

'So, what happens now?'

'God knows.' Nell was fiddling with the flaking wood on the table-top. The sun glinted on the old rose gold of her bracelets. The freckles on her fingers fascinated him. 'He's playing it very cagily. Not pressurising me or anything – and I must admit I was wrong about the Brain-Scrambler. Oh, I still hate it, but it hasn't *changed* things the way I thought it would. I mean, we're doing even better than before and we've taken on a couple of extra lads. I just get the feeling that Ross is biding his time. I think he'll let me get used to the idea of the Crash'n'Dash – and then suddenly produce a whole fleet of Jessons' rides before back-end.'

Jack took a deep breath. 'And if he does? Will you sell the gallopers?'

'What?' Her shout of disbelief made people turn and stare. He didn't care. 'Why on earth should I want to sell them? What gave you that idea? No way. Not a chance. In fact, ever since the Brain-Scrambler arrived, Ross and Danny have been banging on about diversification – splitting the fair for various gaffs – and I've been thinking along very similar lines.' She was almost glowing again now. 'I think that it's high time I applied to the Guild for my own sites. I also think that it's high time that I came clean about the gallopers – and the ghost train and the caterpillar. I think the Memory Lane Fair should clamber from the closet.'

Jack wanted to kiss her. He compromised by nodding enthusiastically. They made a pact that he would tell Fiona and she would tell Ross. Nell, of course, would have the added hurdle of approaching Clem Percival over Guild Rights for ground – but she was a member. There shouldn't be a problem.

Jack felt elated. Everything was going to be all right. Or almost everything. 'What about when you and Ross get married?'

She flickered a frown. 'I don't see what difference that would make, honestly. I'd still be running the Memory Lane Fair, while Ross and Danny – and I guess Sam – will be splitting with the bigger rides. It'll be a further expansion of the business – and none of them will complain about that. We'll do some places separately and others together. Bradleys and Percivals amalgamating to become big-time. I suppose,' she stared out across the river, 'that this was what my mother had planned all along.'

He nodded. He didn't – really didn't – want her to marry Ross Percival, not even for business reasons. It was entirely unreasonable, he knew, as he would be marrying Fiona in a few weeks' time. It just wasn't the same, somehow.

They talked round in circles, covering the same ground, convincing each other that things would be just fine. They agreed that he would contact all the Downland Trust members and fix a date for their first build-up of the gallopers in the yard at Fox Hollow. They might even invite Ross and Fiona . . .

They were, Jack knew, encouraging each other to take drastic and irrevocable steps.

The chicken was sizzling in the pan when Fiona walked into the kitchen. Jack scooped the vegetables from their marinade and stirred vigorously. 'Good journey? You look tired. There's a bottle of wine in the fridge. Pour a couple of glasses. Supper won't be too long.'

Fiona dropped her briefcase on the table. 'I don't want anything to eat. You shouldn't have bothered. I had something before I left London.'

Jack was starving. He felt like switching off the cooker and storming down to the Turlington Arms for a pie and a pint. He counted to ten and continued stirring. 'You might change your mind when it's ready.' He leaned across to kiss her cheek. She was already opening her briefcase, flicking through papers. 'Leave that for a moment. Come and sit down. I want to talk to you.'

'OK, but not for long, Jack. I've got tons to do.' She tucked her hair behind her ears. 'I've got this brilliant proposal lined up that you can help me with, actually. I think I may just have captured the Wiseman market.' She sighed at his non-comprehension. 'For God's sake! They produce brochures for new housing developments. All those misty soft-focus shots of lavish houses in tree-lined avenues. They were very impressed with our laminate prices. I'm practically sure we've got them in the bag. If you could persuade all your potential sites to go to Wisemans for their brochures, and I could let them know of the increased business, I'm pretty sure I could swing this one before the end of the week.'

Jack exhaled. The chicken was beginning to catch. He had to do it. Now. He'd promised Nell. Nell was probably confessing all about the gallopers to Ross Percival at that very minute. He opened the fridge, took out the Chardonnay, and poured two careful glasses.

'Actually, that might be a bit tricky. You see, I'm not working with Dad any more.' Oh, Christ. There was no easy way to do this. 'I resigned from Morlands this morning.'

To his amazement, Fiona laughed. 'Don't be silly, Jack! You can't resign! You're a partner!'

He hitched his hip against the kitchen table, and told her all about it. Not about the gallopers, of course. One step at a time. He even threw in the bit about being a house-husband, looking after the baby, working from home . . .

'At what?'

'Well, painting and restoration and stuff.'

'Don't be so bloody stupid!' Fiona drained her glass and refilled it. 'I'm not prepared to support you while you *daub*, for Christ's sake! You get on the telephone and apologise to Bill this minute! Tell him you're sorry – things said in the heat of the moment and all that – and tell him that you'll be back in the office tomorrow morning, OK? I'm going to have a shower – and switch that bloody stuff off. The smell's making me feel sick.'

CHAPTER TWENTY-THREE

After all the media interest, the following days at Marsh Minster seemed very flat. Apart from the time spent at Fox Hollow with Jack, the only excitement in Nell's life was finding different excuses not to sleep with Ross. Her ingenuity was being tried to its limits.

She was also disgruntled by the continued absence of her parents on their conveniently-timed holiday. How on earth was she ever going to hammer things out with her mother if she insisted on trekking round America on the Elvis Presley Memorial Trail? Despite her assurances to Jack, she didn't want to mention the purchase of the gallopers to Ross until she'd sorted out the business implications with Adele. The Crash'n'Dash of course continued to pull in the crowds – takings were doubled – and everyone was delighted. It was all extremely frustrating.

Claudia had been seriously subdued since the day of the makeover and the filming. No one was sure which had screwed Danny up most, and he'd spent two days grizzling about women with short hair being halfway to dungarees and testosterone implants. Nell was beginning to agree with Sam that Claudia and Danny really should separate. Claudia, however, hung on with dogged determination.

'Fancy escaping for the evening?' Nell paused beside the

hoopla on her way to the dodgems. 'We haven't had a break for ages. We used to have fun on our girls' nights out, didn't we? You could get Rio or the twins to take over in here, and Terry's ace on the dodgems now that he's turned respectable. Why don't we –'

'Danny wouldn't agree.' Claudia, who was wearing very drab jeans and a black T-shirt, didn't look at Nell, but handed two hoops to a child of indeterminate sex which was far too small to see where it was throwing.

'I wasn't thinking of including Danny in the invitation.'

The child had hurled both hoops into the side of the stall. Its mother rapped smartly on the scarlet panels. 'Excuse me! I think this is unfair!'

'So do I,' Claudia muttered, leaning over to retrieve the rings and displaying a fist-sized bruise just below her rib-cage. 'Have a free go on me. Have several free goes on me.'

She handed half an armful of hoops to the mother who yanked the child on to her hip and started raining them against the plinths.

'Claudia!'

'What? She probably won't win anything and anyway, I'm feeling generous.'

'Not the freebie,' Nell said quickly. 'The bruise. On your side.'

'Is it?' Claudia sounded bitter. 'It must be the only one who is, then.'

Nell leaned across, and grabbing at Claudia's T-shirt pulled it away from her waist. There were several red marks as well as the bruise. 'Jesus! When did he do this?'

'Who do what? Oh, that? It wasn't Danny. Well, it was – but not in anger. I mean, we got sort of passionate and –'

Nell shook her head. She didn't believe a word. Some-one had to do something. The mother squawked excitedly as she lobbed one of the hoops around an unpleasantly-coloured plastic Teletubby and Claudia drifted across the stall.

'So you don't want to come out tonight?'

Claudia shook her head. 'No thanks. You go. Have a nice time.'

Nell wandered along the pavement between the back of the joints and the now empty High Street shops, stepping over cables and being deafened by the massed ranks of generators reverberating from the lichened walls. Who could she talk to about this? Danny was the obvious choice but he and Claudia had clearly worked out their story, and it would probably do more harm than good. She didn't want to risk Claudia gathering more bruises. Sam? Sam was likely to tell her to leave things alone; much as he was into love and peace and thought they should split up, he wouldn't actively interfere. Ross? Ross and Danny were currently joined at the hip. And Ross might frown on physical violence but he'd believe the moment-of-passion story because he'd want to. And even if Adele and Peter were in the country, she wouldn't tell them.

She reached the dodgems. It was early evening and the riders were all safe drivers: fathers with small children, and chubby pre-pubescents kitted out in the latest glittery fashions and their first lipstick.

'Nice and steady.' Terry indicated the piles of notes and coins in the cash drawer. 'Nothing spectacular, but no doubt it'll hot up when the Crash'n'Dash starts.'

No doubt. She watched him leap back across the track from car to car. She was able to rely on him completely these days. He was a good kid with a pretty astute head on his shoulders. It would be a shame to lose him. It would be a shame to lose any of them. And she would have to leave them all behind, she was sure, when the Memory Lane Fair made its breakaway. They wouldn't be remotely interested in a gaff full of nostalgia.

'All ready for the next ride!' She spoke mechanically into the microphone. 'Pay in the car!'

Thinking of the Memory Lane Fair led to thoughts of Jack. Of course, she'd be able to talk to Jack about Claudia and Danny. She could talk to Jack about anything. It was a pity that she didn't know when she'd see him again. The pull to go to Fox Hollow was increasingly insistent. Idly watching the cars skitter round the track, she wondered how he'd got on with telling Fiona about his plans for the future. Better than her non-attempt with Ross, she was sure. Fiona would probably have been pleased that he'd made the break from a job he hated and would be able to spend more time at home once they were married and had the baby. Nell had tried not to think too much about either of those things.

'Press your pedals! Turn your steering wheels!'

She turned up a revamped Deep Purple CD to full volume and knew that she was bored. This wasn't what she wanted. There were no highs and lows in the business any more. Not since the Crash'n'Dash's arrival. It had changed things – not necessarily in the way she'd feared, but changed them none the less. There wasn't the speculation of turning up at gaffs and wondering if they'd make enough money to buy diesel and food. There was no more peering out of the pay-box and wondering if anyone was going to stagger out from in front of their television screens to ride on anything.

Danny and Ross had been right. The punters wanted machines like the Brain-Scrambler to bring them back to fairgrounds. Ross would now add a Moon Mission – and who knows, they could have their own Ice-Breaker before back-end. They'd been right – and she'd been wrong. Of course, Nell thought, anyone else would relish this sort of secure expansion – but she didn't. From now on it was just going to be bland. And to Nell, bland was about as exciting as death.

That was why she fancied a night out, she told herself, taking a further pile of coins from Terry, just to break the monotony. She'd never felt dissatisfied with her life before. She had changed since the arrival of the Brain-Scrambler and Ross. Or had she? No – it was before then. The dissatisfaction had started to creep in since she'd met the Downland Trust and found the gallopers and Jack Morland.

A starburst of lights and a thunder roll of metallic screaming indicated that the Crash'n'Dash was on its first run of the night. Nell turned up Deep Purple and practically shattered her eardrums.

'Christ!' Ross had to shout as he climbed up into the pay-box. 'What the hell are you doing?'

'Attracting the punters,' she yelled back. 'And why aren't you on the Brain-Scrambler?'

'Danny is. He insisted that Claudia be removed from the hoopla and put on the waltzer. Promotion or what? She didn't seem particularly overjoyed, actually. Anyway, I haven't come to talk about them – I've come to talk about us. And can't you turn that thing down?'

'No. What about us?'

Ross leaned over and slid the volume control down to merely deafening. 'Dad's just phoned. They're at Hampton Court. He wanted to come and give the Crash'n'Dash the once-over tonight, so I've invited him for a meal.'

'I don't want to go out.'

But Ross was on fast forward. 'I've managed to get a table at the Swan. I'll do the business with Dad, then bring him across, shall I? Meet you about half-eight?'

She supposed she could get Terry to take over again. Sometimes that was safer – from a moralistic point of view. He found it difficult to seduce anyone in the pay-box and Nell still felt a little responsible for Karen at home in Oakton.

Anyway, if she went for a meal, she'd be able to sound out Clem on sites for the gallopers and the other Memory Lane stuff. As a Guild member she had a right to apply for sites, but Clem being such a big noise would be able to pull a few strings, grease palms, oil ropes. No, oiling ropes didn't sound quite right. Maybe it was cogs . . . Of course, it would probably mean letting Ross know what she'd done – but it was expansion; he couldn't really object. And after all, Jack had had to tell Fiona far, far worse news. The thought of Jack made her smile.

Ross interpreted the smile as acquiescence. 'Great. I'll see you there – and wear something glamorous.'

Nell nodded, not listening. It would be one step forward for the Memory Lane Fair.

The Swan was the oldest pub in Marsh Minster, dating back to the fifteenth century, with a great deal of brass, and beams that looked as though they might have come from Shakespeare's time rather than the local branch of Wickes. Ordering a gin and tonic, Nell perched on a bar stool to wait for the Percivals, and wondered if they would have to remove the Gavioli from its proscenium before they put it into the centre of the gallopers. She wished Claudia was with her. She'd looked very miserable in the waltzer pay-box, and was playing suicide music by The Christians.

'Beautiful.' Ross kissed her cheek ten minutes later and approved the Fluide dress with his eyes. 'Didn't I tell you she looked great, Dad?'

'She always does.' Clem, not to be outdone, kissed her on both cheeks. 'Takes after her mother.'

Christ, Nell thought, I sincerely hope not.

She also thought, rather sadly, how much nicer it had been at the Maybush, sitting on the terrace with Jack, laughing and looking out over the river. Being casual. Being friends.

Ross and Clem made a big show of ordering further drinks, talking about the Brain-Scrambler in glowing terms and studying the menu. Nell wondered about the gallopers' centre truck. Had anyone checked the tyres? She certainly hadn't. And she ought to unroll the tilts next time and make sure they were waterproof. And then there was transport. No one had considered the logistics of how they were actually going to move the gallopers from one gaff to another, had they?

They'd need a truck for the horses, as well as the Gavioli, and the centre of course, and the platforms and rounding boards, not to mention all the other paraphernalia. Once they were on the road it would take a three-truck-drag to cope with the loads and then – she shook her head and swallowed the rest of the gin and tonic – there was the ghost train and the caterpillar too. Neither she nor Jack had given a thought to actually *moving*. They'd been so wrapped up in just *having*. She held an HGV licence – but did Jack? Did any of the Downland Trusters? And even if they did, how were they going to finance the purchase of so many specialist vehicles?

'Jesus!'

Clem and Ross looked up from the vellum-bound menus. 'Found something you like, Princess?'

Confused, Nell jabbed a finger halfway down her menu. Ross peered at the same place on his own. 'Not very exciting, sweetheart. Risotto. Still, if that's what you want. Everyone decided? Great. Let's freshen up the drinks then, and go through.'

Ross had ordered hors d'oeuvres for everyone, and as they sat back in the velvet chairs waiting for the main course, Nell's head was swimming. She had hardly any money left in her personal account. It was gradually building up again, of course, but there was nowhere near enough for a small van, let alone a virtual fleet of lorries. She thought briefly of a bank loan. But banks were reluctant to finance fairs at the best of times and the Memory Lane Fair with no track record and minimal assets was going to be a non-starter. Borrowing privately? Well, Adele had cleared out the family coffers by paying cash for the Brain-Scrambler. And Ross? Not a chance. Even if he was willing to lend her the money she didn't want him to have a finger in the Memory Lane pie. He was up to his damned elbows in everything else.

She forked up her rice. Maybe Jack would have some money . . . God no, of course he wouldn't. He'd just chucked in his job. And then there was Fiona and the wedding and the pregnancy to finance. She forked up more risotto, looking down at her plate for the first time. A baby squid, minus one small tentacle, looked reproachfully back at her.

She swallowed another mouthful, feeling sick. Ross and

Clem were dealing out verbal balance sheets across heaped plates of lamb cutlets. She covered up the accusing *calamari* eyes with a mound of rice and pushed her dish away.

'Not hungry, sweetheart?' Ross paused in the middle of his duchesse potatoes. 'Would you like something else?'

Nell shook her head. She'd still got some rice to swallow. She may well have got bits of squid in there too. She took a huge gulp of Shiraz, fighting the urge to swill it round her mouth to make sure everything had gone, and wished she'd read the menu.

Clem scraped his plate enthusiastically and mopped up his redcurrant jelly with a slice of bread. 'So, Princess? How's the world treating you?'

'Er – fine.' Nell draped her napkin over her plate. She could still see those eyes. 'Very well. The Brain-Scrambler – I mean – Crash'n'Dash, is doing better than anyone expected.'

'Not better than I expected! Nor your ma. Good head on her shoulders, Adele. Did it mainly for your dad's sake, you know. Take away the worries for the future. Lessen the strain on his old ticker. But of course she did have another motive.'

Ross began to shift uncomfortably in his seat. 'I don't think that Nell wants to hear about that, actually –'

'Yes, I do,' Nell nodded. 'What other motive?'

'Getting you two together, of course!' Clem roared, splashing Shiraz into all three glasses and waving at the wine waiter for fresh supplies. 'And it's worked really well, bless her. I mean – you two were shilly-shallying around – and you, young lady, kept making all sorts of objections to Ross joining you. Now you can't deny that, can you?'

She couldn't, Nell agreed, wanting to kill her mother. It was bad enough to think that she'd bought the Brain-Scrambler knowing that Nell didn't want it – but to buy bloody Ross as a son-in-law as well! It was far too high a price to pay, even for Peter's peace of mind.

'So,' Clem tipped the wine waiter twenty pounds and carried on. 'Is this what tonight's all about? You two making your announcement?'

Nell stared across the table at Ross. He was smiling sheepishly, the bastard, and looking pretty shifty. But if he was going to do that, he'd have asked her first, wouldn't he? And insisted that Vlad-the-Impaler Marcia was also in on the act?

'Not as far as I'm aware,' she said coldly, wondering whether, if she had the Victorian trifle – which she absolutely loved – for pudding, the memory of the squid's doleful expression would spoil it for her. 'In fact, since Ross has joined us we haven't mentioned getting married. Have we?'

'I don't think we have actually, no.' Ross was studying the pudding menu with an air of feigned innocence. 'I suppose I just took it for granted that we would, you know . . .'

Nell took a deep breath. 'At the moment, I'm happy being single. I've seen enough of other people's children to put me off motherhood. And I've never felt the need for a wedding ring!' She bit her lip – now or never. 'Anyway, just supposing that Ross and I did marry, what sort of deal would you throw in?'

Both pairs of Percival eyebrows climbed. Clem's lowered first. 'Deal? What deal, Princess?'

'Well, my mother must have got a job lot with the Brain-Scrambler. How would it be if you chucked in a couple of permanent sites with the wedding-present cheque?' A cheque, she thought, of such magnitude that it would buy lorries and trucks.

Ross, who had his finger on Strawberries Romanov, swallowed. 'We'll have all the sites we want, Nell. Even if we add a Moon Mission and eventually an Ice-Breaker. And we've already talked about splitting to two separate gaffs. Not a problem.'

'What about splitting to three separate gaffs? What about ground for a set of gallopers – and, say, a ghost train and a caterpillar?'

The Percivals seemed to find this as screamingly funny as the *Fools and Horses Christmas Special*.

'Come on, sweetheart.' Ross clicked his fingers – rather

rudely, Nell thought – towards the waiter. 'We don't want any of that sort of thing. We're going forward – and it's proved to be a success. We don't want to be taking backward steps now, do we?'

'I've already taken one.' Nell smiled sweetly at the waiter. 'I'll have the Victorian trifle please and –' she looked expectantly at the Percivals who didn't answer. 'Make that three trifles then. Oh, yes – thank you.' The squid was borne mercifully away.

Obviously miffed at not getting the strawberries, Ross scowled. 'What have you done, Nell? You haven't seen some decrepit heap of junk advertised and got some airy-fairy idea about renovation, have you?'

She shook her head. There was a joint Percival exhalation.

'I've already bought it. Or rather, them.'

She couldn't have had more effect than if she'd leapt on to the table, shimmied out of her Fluide frock, and started dancing the cancan in her La Perla knickers.

Deciding to capitalise on the moment of silence, she carried on. 'So, in true Bradley tradition – and just like my mother – I'm prepared to do a deal. I'll marry Ross if I can be guaranteed sites for my rides. And a cheque big enough to cover transportation.'

'Over my dead body!' Ross snatched his trifle from the waiter. 'What the hell possessed you to do that? What have you bought? And where did you get the money? And, if you've bought all this crap, where the hell is it now?'

Clem took the other two bowls of trifle and held them aloft.

'The money was from my personal account – which is now virtually empty – and the rides are –' She thought maybe this wasn't such a good idea. 'They're – sort of – being looked after by a friend until such time as we can get on the road.'

'God Almighty!' Clem stopped balancing the trifles and slammed them down on to the table. 'That's pretty devious, Princess.'

Devious for her, good business sense for her mother, Nell thought icily.

'And who else knows about this?' Ross stabbed at his mountain of cream.

'No one. Well, the people who are helping me with the restoration, of course. But no one in the family. I wasn't going to say anything until we were up and running but,' she smiled across the table, 'as we're talking dowries –'

'We're not!' Ross got to his feet. 'And there's no way that I'll have anything to do with this nonsense at all. Percivals don't want to be involved with this sort of thing!' He made it sound on a par with drug-pushing. 'Neither will Dad, will you?'

Clem didn't look quite so sure. 'Sit down, Ross. Come on – I'm sure we can talk this through. Surely if you and Nell get married, then she can run her side of the business – and there's good money to be made from nostalgia, you know, look at John Carter – while you run yours?'

'Not a chance!' Ross was still standing. 'I don't want any part of this.'

Nell watched him stalk out of the dining room and carried on eating her pudding.

'He'll calm down.' Clem scraped Ross's trifle into his own bowl. 'He just likes to get his own way. I'll talk him round. So – is that your price, Princess? You'll marry Ross and make over your Bradley shares to him in return for regular Guild sites for your gallopers and other machines, and some new trucks?'

Nell thought it over. She wished she could ring Jack and ask him what he thought. Would he consider she was selling her soul? Still, he'd probably sell his for the Savage too.

'Yes,' she said quietly. 'That's my price.'

CHAPTER TWENTY-FOUR

The soft drizzle slanted across the slat-blinded windows of the kitchen and gathered in dusty pools on the window-ledge. Jack looked up from the Sits Vac pages of the *Independent* and watched the day closing in.

'Just what we could do with,' Margaret, his ex-secretary said cheerfully, placing a cup of instant and two Chaseys bourbon biscuits in front of him. 'A nice drop of rain. Always so handy when it rains during the evening, dear, don't you think? Makes the following morning so fresh.'

She'd popped round on her way home from her new job – 'ever such nice people, Jack, but not chummy like we used to be' – to make sure he was OK, to share her first Chaseys staff perk – six packets of bourbons and two of custard creams – and to discuss a wedding present. She didn't seem wholly at ease with Fiona's all-white minimalism.

'Your Fiona doesn't do much cooking, does she? Not a lot of call for a set of Pyrex bowls, then?'

'None.' Jack closed the Sits Vac pages. He was only going through the motions anyway. He had no intention of applying for any of the posts advertised. He'd escaped from one death sentence – he certainly didn't want to walk into another. He wondered just what sort of job would offer 'in excess of £120K for the right team player' and who would ever be bumptious enough to admit to fitting the criterion: 'must be a people person'. 'I do all the cooking.'

'Lucky Fiona. A handsome man who can cook. I wish I'd found one of those when I was younger. And how are all your other plans going?'

Jack, whose plans had been drifting along somewhere between Fox Hollow and the Maybush, was instantly wary. 'Other plans? How did you know about them? Who told you?'

Margaret adjusted her bifocals. 'Crikey! You sound just like Magnus Magnusson used to. *Your* plans Jack. I mean, even though we don't work together any more, I still thought I'd be coming . . . We're such chums, dear – and I don't have to speak to your father all day, do I? I've bought a new two-piece, and a hat.'

What on earth for? Jack wondered. Why would Margaret be remotely interested in the gallopers première? His father was hardly likely to be there. And why would she want a hat?

'I took the liberty of telephoning your Fiona last weekend – did she tell you, dear? – and she says you've got the wedding list at Ikea. Available on the Internet. As I'm not au fait with that, I wondered if you wanted a toaster?'

Jack smiled affectionately. 'I'm sure Fiona would love a toaster. Love it. It's very kind of you. Thanks.'

Fiona, who still thought that his resignation was a family squabble which would be resolved eventually with a manly handshake, seemed to have rather lost interest in everything except her client portfolio. The wedding had hardly been mentioned since he left Morlands. One more toaster was neither here nor there.

His mother, on the other hand, had taken the news of the family split predictably badly. After she'd screamed and pleaded, cried and cajoled, she had finally taken to her bed with a bottle of sal volatile and several back issues of *Woman's Weekly*. He had heard nothing from his father.

He and Margaret managed to demolish most of the biscuits and half a jar of Nescafé. It would do nicely, Jack thought, in place of an evening meal. Fiona had been away for two days and was due to return at about eight. He wasn't going to make the mistake of having a meal ready again. If she was hungry they'd eat out.

He saw Margaret off with a kiss on the cheek and watched fondly as she pedalled away down the cul-de-sac wearing the gabardine mackintosh she'd had as long as he'd known her. His father was a fool to have lost her. He'd heard on the grapevine that she'd been replaced by a curvy blonde with minimal keyboard experience and forever legs. He'd also heard that his father had been sending out scouting parties to other building companies, looking for a junior partner to buy into the business. Bill Morland, at least, knew that Jack would not be returning.

Jack closed the door on the damp evening and wondered if Nell had told Ross about the gallopers. He sincerely hoped she hadn't revealed their location. Anyone with Ross's clout in the Guild could probably have them blackballed and removed. He missed talking to Nell, and on several occasions had got as far as punching out the first three digits of her telephone number. He had stopped each time, in case she was busy, or with Ross, or any of the million other unknown things that occupied her time away from Fox Hollow.

He knew from *The World's Fair* that the Bradley–Percival amalgamation had left Marsh Minster and moved on to a small site in one of the Oxford suburbs. No doubt the Brain-Scrambler would be dragging them in despite the weather. Maybe he'd ring her in the morning and find out when she was next planning to visit the gallopers. She knew more about him – the real him – than anyone else.

Wandering into the living room he gazed at the severe surroundings with mounting gloom. It would be so nice on a dank and grey night to have a cosy chair and a couple of mellow table lamps beside a proper fireplace. It would be great to have some sort of warmth and colour, some fluidity of feature, rather than all these monochrome angles. He and Fiona had never discussed it. It hadn't seemed important.

Still, he thought, perching on the edge of the sofa and flicking through the television channels, when the baby arrived, Fiona would probably let the rigidity drop. There would have to be softness and cushions and things, surely, for a baby? Jack was fairly vague about babies. He had never known any. It was quite exciting though, the thought of *his* baby. He tended to skip over its formative years in his imagination, and settled on it being about six when he could introduce it to the joint joys of painting and preservation.

It would be a friend, he thought; a confidante; an ally. Someone to pull faces at when Fiona got into one of her strops. The prospect was really quite pleasant. One thing he was absolutely sure about was that this child – male or female – would be given total freedom of choice in its life. If it loathed fairgrounds and art, then so be it. Whether this child wanted to study astrophysics or be an eco-warrior, it would have his support. He would never shackle it with the bonds of filial duty that he'd had to suffer.

He heard Fiona's key in the lock just as the *Nine O'clock News* began. She walked past the living-room door and straight into the kitchen. Tough, Jack thought, if you're expecting a meal. He heard her sighing over the coffee cups and biscuit crumbs, heard her walking back along the hall.

He looked up. 'Hi – you're a bit late. Bad journey?'

Fiona sat on the edge of the oatmeal director's chair furthest away from the television and eased off her shoes. 'Not really. Who've you had in for coffee?'

'Margaret.' Jack knew Fiona didn't like Margaret. Fiona thought that motherly, chatty secretaries were anachronisms. She would also be very rude about the toaster. 'She came to tell me about her new job.'

Fiona wasn't interested. 'What about *your* new job? Or your old one? Any progress?'

She knew there hadn't been. She knew that he would have told her.

'I'm not going back to work with Dad. He's already head-hunting my replacement. And I'm still hopeful of making something of the painting. I've drafted an advertisement.'

She watched the news. She didn't want to know. Jack tried again. 'There are plenty of people who want coachwork jobs, liveries, traditional skills. It's what I want to do. Maybe it's not what you want from a husband, and there'll be a drop in income, but –'

'I've been made a director.' She still looked at the television. 'They confirmed it yesterday, although I more or less knew last week.'

'Brilliant! Congratulations.' He was genuinely pleased for her. It was what she'd always wanted. He stood up. 'Come on then, let's go and celebrate. It'll have to be the Turlington Arms so that we can walk and both have a drink – but so what? We can brag to all the neighbours. It won't take me long to get ready.' He stopped by the director's chair – how appropriate! – and dropped a kiss on the top of her neat, blonde head. 'So, now you'll be bringing home the bacon and I'll be the penniless artist. Look, Fi, it'll work really well, won't it? You can devote yourself to your career and I can do what I said – painting, take over running the house, looking after the baby . . .'

Fiona stared at the screen. It was an item on some particularly violent uprising. 'There isn't going to be a baby.'

Her words didn't filter through straight away. They were lost in a hail of gunfire and a lot of screaming. She turned her head, her eyes challenging him. 'Did you hear what I said?'

He didn't understand. 'Have you lost it? Was it a false alarm? Oh, darling – you must feel awful. Why on earth didn't you tell me?' He slid his arms round her thin shoulders. She didn't move towards him. She must feel appalling, he thought. He felt pretty terrible himself. 'Are you – um – all right?' He was very hazy on this sort of thing. 'Shouldn't you be in bed? Shall I call the doctor?'

Fiona shrugged him away. The news had moved on to the humorous item at the end. 'I've seen a doctor. I've been in bed.' She stared at him. 'I had the pregnancy terminated. Yesterday.'

Jack froze. He still had his arms towards her and dropped them by his side. She'd killed his child. No – his dream. Oh, God. He'd always had liberal views on abortion; always felt that it was absolutely a woman's right to choose what to do with her body. He'd never understood how so many men could appear on anti-abortion rallies; what did men know about an unwanted pregnancy? What did men know about how a woman felt? He just hadn't expected to feel such pain.

'Why?'

'I didn't want it. I never really wanted it.' She didn't look upset, or even angry. 'I would have had to give up everything, while you – you haven't given up a thing, have you? You're still playing with the anoraks, still following your stupid dreams. Therefore, when I knew about the director-ship being practically in the bag –'

She'd disposed of the baby for her bloody career! And she knew he would have looked after it, cared for it . . .

'Why didn't you talk to me about it?'

'There would have been no point.' She shook her head, but it was more a gesture of irritation than sorrow. 'You're so full of woolly idealism, Jack. You see everything through rose-coloured glasses. You think life can be like a bloody happy families cornflake advert! I didn't plan to become pregnant. I didn't plan to be a mother. And the more I thought about it, the more I realised it was wrong. I didn't want the responsibility.'

Jack knew he should be comforting her. Supporting her. Saying that it didn't matter; that if it was right for her, then of course he agreed with her decision. But he couldn't. Maybe if she'd discussed it with him, told him how she felt, maybe then he would have agreed. But she just – did it. As if he were of no consequence. No importance. It had been his child, too – however unplanned and ill-timed.

She snapped off the television as the weather forecaster was predicting a return of the heat wave. 'So, are we still on for this celebration drink?'

'No, we're fucking not!' Jesus! A quick trip down to the Turlington Arms to celebrate the directorship with Fergus and Caroline and Belinda and Adam and whatever their bloody names were. And then a quick, 'Oh, by the way, we're also celebrating Fiona no longer being pregnant.' He stared at her with something like revulsion.

'I'll take that as a no, then.' She stood up. 'Suits me. I'm knackered. Anyway, there'll be plenty of time for planned babies when we've been married for a few years. When you've got this fairground crap out of your system and made it up with your father, and when I'm more settled in the directorship. When we can afford a nanny. The time simply wasn't right. And it wasn't as if we'd decided to get married because of the baby or anything gruesomely old-fashioned, was it? We'd already planned the wedding before either of us knew that I was pregnant.'

'You and my mother planned the wedding.' There was a drumming in his ears. He had never felt so angry. So hurt. 'I didn't have any say in that either. I can't imagine why you ever wanted to marry me.' He walked past her, his nostrils filled with her sharp scent. Not floral and floaty; spiky and aggressive.

'Where are you going?'

'Upstairs to grab some clothes and the very few things that are mine.'

'Why?'

'Because,' he clenched the Roadster's keys very tightly in his hand as if trying to transfer the pain, 'I don't want to live with you any more. I certainly don't want to marry you. You can have the house. I'll keep up my share of the mortgage or I'll arrange for you to buy me out if that's what you want. You can have what's left in the joint account. You can have your directorship and your business colleagues and your greedy, grasping, ladder-climbing existence.'

'You're leaving because of the abortion?' She didn't look upset. Just surprised. 'Because of something that wasn't even a baby – just a cluster of cells?'

'I'm leaving because I can't love you.'

Jack drove for hours, the night and the rain closing in in a shroud of grey. He pushed the Roadster to its limits, hoping that the swooping, roaring, rushing power would salve his pain. Would produce answers. It did neither. It made his head ache. He wished he could cry. He wished his father hadn't instilled in him from such an early age that crying was for girls.

He slewed the bike to a halt on one of the A34 crossovers, looking down at the constant swish of night-time traffic. Were all the drivers going home to somewhere? To someone? For the first time in his life he had nowhere to go.

His hands were frozen by the continual fret of rain and the frantic way he'd clasped the handlebars, but he managed to wrench the signet ring from his finger. He looked at it for a moment, illuminated only by the garish orange lights. Had it ever meant that much to him? The flakes of paint – crimson and royal blue – meant more.

He hurled the ring into the night sky and watched as the light caught it fleetingly in its arc before it disappeared for ever.

Kicking the Roadster into life again, he roared away.

His mother, in a quilted dressing gown, opened the front door the merest crack. She'd left the chain on. 'Yes?'

'It's me. Jack.'

He heard the chain rattling and the door opening. The light from the hall dazzled him. The smell of supper and disinfectant made tears well in his throat. His mother looked pleased to see him. 'Come on in. Dad's working upstairs. I'll call him. It's not too late, Jack. I know it isn't. Go and sit down. Cup of tea?'

'I haven't come for my job back. And, yes, I'd love a cup of tea. Don't call Dad yet, please.'

Eileen looked at him for a moment, seemed to be about to speak, then thinking better of it, bustled off into the kitchen.

Jack leaned back in the comfort of the Parker-Knoll recliner and knew he didn't belong.

His mother hustled back with a tray. The cups and saucers were flowery and she'd added digestive biscuits on a matching plate. There were three cups but she hadn't called his father down. Jack watched her as she poured the tea, not needing to ask how he liked it or whether he wanted sugar.

'Thanks. No, no biscuits.'

She sipped her tea and munched a digestive, being careful to flick the crumbs from the corners of her mouth. 'Have you and Fiona had words?'

Words! Whole bloody sentences! 'Sort of . . .'

Eileen nodded. 'It's pre-wedding nerves. You're bound to be on edge. Both of you – especially with this silly hoo-ha with your father. I told him that's what it was. Nerves. Stage-fright. You'll get over it –'

'I've left her.'

The words hung in the air. He wasn't sure that she'd heard him so he said it again. Eileen bit her lip. Her teacup rattled slightly against the saucer. By the time she looked at him, she was in control. She still said nothing. The silence was more accusing than a ricochet of reproaches.

'I'm not going to marry Fiona.'

'Of course you're going to marry her.' The cup and saucer rattled a bit more. 'Get a grip, Jack. You can't just walk away from everything. Your job, your marriage, your home. People have to do things they don't want to do, live lives they don't particularly enjoy because that's how it is. You make the best of things. You have to. Just because you and Fiona have had some silly quarrel is no reason to walk out. And as for not getting married! Everything's organised. Whatever has got into you?'

Eileen, without her make-up, looked old and tired. There were lines and pouches that seemed to have crept up from nowhere. He needed someone to comfort him – but neither his mother nor Fiona had ever been any good at that. He drank his tea and wondered if he should go. But where? It hadn't occurred to him that his parents might not want him to stop, at least for tonight.

'It's not a silly quarrel. It was deadly serious. And I'm not going back. I'll make all the necessary arrangements in the morning. She can have the house and everything. I'll sort all that out. I do need a bed for tonight, though.'

'You've got a bed. Your own bed.' His mother put the cup and saucer back on the tray and stood up, drawing her quilted dressing gown more tightly round her. 'You're not staying here.'

Shit. 'Then can you call Dad down? I'd like to speak to you together before I leave.'

Bill Morland must have been listening. He was in the room far too quickly to have been in the study, and he certainly didn't need a précis. His scowl said that he'd heard it all.

Jack told them. They seemed unaware of his pain. Maybe because they hadn't known of the pregnancy, its non-existence now wasn't a problem to them. They couldn't seem to accept that it was a good enough reason to walk out, to cancel the wedding, to leave home. They even looked quite happy when he told them that Fiona had been made a director. It shocked him to realise that perhaps they thought her decision had been the right one.

'At least one of you will have a decent job.' His father was staring at the wall over the fireplace. 'Can't blame the girl for doing it. Someone had to bring a crust into the house. And there'll be other children.'

'It was my baby too.' Jack wanted to shake them. 'She didn't discuss it with me. She just did it. Anyway, it's not just the abortion – it's everything.'

Bill snorted derisively. 'To be frank, I can't see why someone like Fiona, with a good head on her shoulders, wanted to marry you in the first place. You walk out on me – you walk out on her – it's hardly the stuff good husbands and fathers are made of, is it?'

'And you'd know all about that, would you? You being expert at both? Goodbye.'

He crashed towards the front door. Eileen, looking tearful, hurried after him. He longed to hug her but he'd never been encouraged to, and it was far too late to start now.

'Jack! Wait!'

'I'll be in touch. I'll let you know where I am. Don't worry . . .'

'I'm not worried.' Eileen's eyes flashed. 'I just want to know what to tell the caterers and the string quartet.'

Jack rubbed his hand wearily across his face. 'Tell them that the wedding is cancelled due to lack of interest. But knowing Fiona, she may well capture another far more suitable bridegroom before September, so it won't all have been wasted, will it?'

As he kick-started the Roadster, he could see the twitch of net curtains and one or two bedside lights flickering on. The neighbours would be forming their own opinions and gossiping across their herbaceous borders in the morning. Speculating. And Eileen and Bill would tell them the whole sad story and get the sympathy vote.

Sod them, Jack thought, roaring away. Sod the lot of them.

This time he really didn't have anywhere to go. His friends would probably welcome him in, but wouldn't be able to let him stay for ever. Not that he'd want to. Nor did he want pity – he wasn't sure any more if he'd even get it. Was he wrong? Was it all his fault? Not all, he admitted, as the blackness and the roaring wind punched his face, but enough. He should have left long ago. He'd let Fiona believe that her plans were the same as his because it was the easy option. Not any more. There were no easy options left to take.

It had stopped raining. He skidded the Roadster into the yard at Fox Hollow and pulled it out of sight. Unlocking the door and switching on the first set of lights he immediately felt better. Not great, but relaxed. He could hole up here for a while. No one except Nell and the Downland Trusters would disturb him here – and certainly not tonight. Tonight he just had to get his head sorted out. He needed time alone to think

– and to mourn. It surprised him that he felt grief. Grief for the child who would have come here to Fox Hollow, or somewhere similar, and shared in the painting and the machines and been his friend. Grief for what might have been. Grief for the child who would never see any of this now.

Jack undid the leather artist's roll, took out a handful of brushes, and began to paint through his tears.

CHAPTER TWENTY-FIVE

Perhaps, Adele thought as she hauled armfuls of crumpled holiday clothes from the last of the suitcases and stuffed the first lot into the washing machine, she would tell him tonight.

In fact, she decided, as she returned the passports to their cubby-hole in the dresser, coming clean with Peter this evening would leave the way clear to visiting the fairground at Oxford tomorrow. She bent down and picked up Priscilla, taking deep steadying breaths in the silky grey fur. She wasn't sure which was going to be worse. Peter's discovery of her chicanery, or having to face Nell's accusations of major meddling. Nell's answerphone messages – immediately erased last night in case Peter played them – had been scalding.

While they were revelling in the glories of Memphis, Adele had almost convinced herself that the fuss would have died down by the time they got back. She had known that the Crash'n'Dash would be *in situ*; that Ross would have moved smoothly into his partnership with Danny and Sam; and had hoped that Nell – once she'd recovered from her initial shock – would have accepted the Crash'n'Dash – and started to accept Ross too. It didn't seem to have happened exactly as she'd planned if Nell's threats on the answerphone were anything to go by.

The minute they'd scrambled out of the taxi Adele had had to hide all the accumulated *World's Fairs* from Peter, and blamed their non-delivery on the cross-eyed paper-boy. Peter had been pretty shirty with Mr Grewal, the newsagent, on the phone this morning.

She knew that she'd have to pick her moment with Peter. Knew that to prevent him blowing his top and risking further palpitations, she'd have to tell him before anyone else did. Tucking Priscilla under her arm she flicked open Delia's *Summer Collection*. If she offered to cook Peter an extra-special supper the day after returning from the States and while still jet-lagged, would it raise his suspicions? Probably. However, she knew she would have to soften him up before breaking the news of the Crash'n'Dash's arrival. One of his favourite meals – a good old down-to-earth *English* meal – might just make things easier.

The enormity of the deception had almost ruined her holiday. Adele had woken in various vast American hotel rooms, feeling the drowsy euphoria of early morning; thinking of the joys of the day ahead; lovingly watching Peter still sleeping; and then the realisation and the guilt had kicked in with twin stiletto stabs.

Each morning she'd groaned and promised herself that this would be the day she'd come clean and confess her sins. But of course, she hadn't. Like Scarlett O'Hara, a confession tomorrow had seemed preferable to a confrontation today.

And now, back in England, and with the showman's grapevine tingling with gossip, she knew it would only be a matter of time before Peter found out, and then all hell would break loose. Why she hadn't been up-front straight away, she couldn't imagine. Now, she'd have to admit to *weeks* of deception.

Then there were Claudia and Danny. That row at Blenheim had been appalling. And Claudia and Sam. She still wasn't convinced that that little episode was as innocent as they'd made out. No, she thought, poring once more over Delia's tempting pages, the thought of whisking up a confessional supper for Peter would be a piece of cake compared with having to deal with the rest of her family.

'Look what I've got!' Peter swung jauntily into the kitchen. 'Mr Grewal had a couple of back issues! Lucky, eh?'

Adele put Priscilla down and stared at the *World's Fairs* in horror. Short of wrenching them from his grasp and ripping them to pieces there was very little she could do. 'How kind of him – especially after what you said about his paper-boy.'

Peter was leafing through the pages. 'I know. I gave the lad some dollar bills to make up. Mr Grewal said he couldn't imagine what had happened because, although we'd cancelled all the other papers, Dick Hart-Radstock said he'd quite like a glimpse through *The World's Fair* when he and Cynthia came in to feed the cat, so I didn't cancel it and – Would you believe it!'

Adele gulped and clutched Delia to her bosom. 'How do you fancy some good home cooking tonight? I thought that we'd go for something really nostalgic –'

Peter tightened his grip on *The World's Fair*. 'Good God!'

'Delia says here that –'

'No! This can't be right!' The pages crackled in indignation.

'– its really quite fashionable again now to have prawn cocktail and steak and kidney pudding and even –'

Peter shook his head. 'Bugger me!'

' – Black Forest Gateau. So, I thought that rather than being clever with sun-dried tomatoes and lime marinade and corn-fed chicken, if I use low-fat substitutes because of your cholesterol level, we –'

'Adele!' Peter glared at her over the newsprint. 'You'll never guess what it says here!'

Adele closed her eyes and took a deep breath. 'What?'

'The Council powers-that-be in Thame are still insisting that there should be no big rides alongside the Town Hall now that it's been tarted up! Thame street fair's a bloody Charter! Been a bloody Charter since Norman times! And now they've put in prissy paving blocks and tubs of flowers and say there's no place for the fair! And the townspeople *want* the fair, for God's sake! And – they're meeting the Guild to discuss it! Discuss! If I were Clem I'd tell 'em –'

Adele exhaled with relief. She had every sympathy with the showmen who visited Thame; every sympathy with the townspeople who wanted their traditional fair and not a cobbled precinct – but she thanked God that they had stolen the headlines.

'Shame . . . I hope they sort it out. Now, about tonight's dinner . . .'

Adele looked round her kitchen and beamed. There had been nothing incriminating in the back issues of *The World's Fair*. The washing machine was humming gently with the last load of holiday clothes. Delia had come up trumps and the scents wafting through Graceland's panelled rooms would have tempted even the most ardent weight-watcher. Peter was wrestling with the corkscrew. Everything was going to be all right.

Tomorrow, when she'd done the deed and Peter knew about the Crash'n'Dash, they'd drive up to Oxford and he could see it in all its glory. She'd be able to face Nell then, too. And she'd brought presents back from America – three the same, as she always did so that none of the children felt more or less favoured. She was sure that they'd be delighted with the Elvis and Priscilla commemorative wedding dolls that she'd found in that little chapel in Las Vegas. With Elvis in his GI uniform and Priscilla in a swathe of white net and a bouffant hair-do, they lit up when activated by sound waves and broke into a rather nasal version of 'Suspicious Minds'. Adele couldn't help thinking that maybe the manufacturers might have been a touch more sensitive with the choice of tune.

'Smells grand.' Peter eased the cork from the Rioja. 'Nothing beats a bit of steak and kidney pud. And you,' he beamed across the kitchen, 'look wonderful. That outfit suits you a treat.'

Adele had bought her gold Capri pants and fringed tunic in

Tennessee and hoped they didn't seem a little *beachish* for English evening wear. She hugged him. 'Come on then – into the dining room – and keep your eyes closed. No, no peeking. It's a secret. You gave me that lovely holiday, and this is my way of saying thank-you.'

Peter closed his eyes obediently. He'd been wine-tasting for most of the afternoon, and with his heart pills plus something a boy with dreadlocks had given him at the airport to counteract the jet lag, had become increasingly laid-back.

'Promise to keep your eyes shut.' Adele linked her arm through Peter's and led him across the hall. 'There! Now you can look!'

Peter gazed open-mouthed at the dining table. Adele had bought an entire Presley dinner service in Memphis, and some tiny gold goblets engraved with the words of all the greatest hits in the Graceland Gift Shop. The napkins – linen and showing dear Elvis in the latter stages of his life, white jump suit, rhinestones and more than a hint of corpulence – had come from Nashville. She'd even put Elvis candles in the silver candelabra, although she wasn't too sure that these were going to be a success. They seemed to have burned right down to his sideboards in a matter of minutes.

'What do you think?'

Peter looked at her with the sleepy eyes that were so like Nell's. 'I think you're a star.'

It was all going very well. Adele hadn't served prawn cocktails since she'd discovered deep-fried brie, and the steak and kidney had tasted every bit as good as it smelt. Peter had lurched his way into the kitchen for the pudding. She still hadn't found exactly the right moment to mention the Crash'n'Dash.

'Wow!' Peter wobbled back with the gateau: layer upon layer of Delia's finest sponge soaked in kirsch, oozing with luscious black cherries and awash with cream. 'This is some pud! We didn't have anything like this while we were away. It's great to be home.'

Adele dished up across Elvis's guttering-wax remains and

the re-mix version of 'King Creole'. 'Extra cream? It's only single . . . should be OK for the arteries. Peter, there's something I've got to tell you –'

A blast of 'Love Me Tender' from the doorbell clashed unpleasantly with the opening bars of 'All Shook Up'. Adele closed her eyes. Not now, please. Not when she was just about to grasp the nettle.

'Probably someone complaining about the noise.' Peter dropped his cake fork with a clatter and pushed back his chair. 'I bet the Finbows never did much entertaining when this was Sunny Gables. Of course, they couldn't, not with Mr Finbow's trouble. I'll tell 'em we're sorry. Won't be long.' He managed to exit the dining room without falling over anything.

Adele refilled the goblets and rehearsed her confession. Priscilla had taken advantage of the open door and was weaving sinuously around the table-legs. Not strangers then, Adele thought. Maybe it was the Hart-Radstocks. She hoped they wouldn't stay long.

'We've got visitors!' Peter shouted from the hall. 'I've told 'em that they've missed the best bit – but we've still got some pudding left.'

He ushered Nell and Ross into the dining room.

Completely wrong-footed, Adele dived beneath the damask and grabbed Priscilla. 'Oh – er – hello, you two. Um – if you'll just excuse me . . .' She glared at the purring Priscilla. 'Naughty cat! Not in the dining room! Come along!' She hurtled towards the doorway. 'Lovely to see you both. Dad'll pour you a drink and I – um – won't be a moment.'

She bolted across the hall, Priscilla struggling beneath her armpit, into the kitchen. 'Oh, my God!'

She hadn't heard Nell following her.

'Exactly, Mother.' Nell closed the kitchen door behind her. 'I think you and I need to have a little talk, don't you?'

It was, Adele thought afterwards, one of the most embarrassing half-hours of her life. Nell gave no quarter. Priscilla, ever the opportunist, leapt on to the Saxon Granite work surface and ate the leftovers.

'He still doesn't know, does he?' Nell had calmed down a bit. 'Poor Dad. Still, Ross has possibly saved you the bother of an explanation by now.'

Adele shuddered. Would that be good or bad?

'What exactly did you intend to tell him?' Nell drummed her fingers on the table. 'About the finance in particular – and the whole thing in general?'

'As little as possible,' Adele was grateful that Nell could at least see the Crash'n'Dash's benefits. 'But I suppose now it'll have to be the whole truth.'

'Which is?'

'That I bought the Crash'n'Dash to further the family business, to make your father's retirement a long and peaceful one, and to help your partnership – both professional and personal – with Ross Percival.'

Nell shook her head but she was, Adele noticed with some relief, smiling. A proper smile that reached her eyes. Nell looked beautiful again tonight. There wasn't quite the inner glow that she'd noticed at Blenheim, but she'd done something to her eyes – more mascara or was it dye? – and her hair looked stunning. And she was with Ross. Adele allowed herself a sneak at her daughter's fingers. Damn it. They were still ringless. She had hoped that Nell would be wearing a gull's-egg diamond by now.

Nell stopped drumming and leaned against the table. 'And the money? Were you going to tell him how you paid for it?'

'Only if I had to. You know – just my little nest egg. Clever investments. Fudge a bit . . .'

Adele had never been so relieved as when separate taxation was introduced. True, she'd never declared all her savings, but it had been extremely difficult not to let Peter know just how much she had salted away for the children's future. Once she'd been responsible for her own tax returns, the accountant had been a gem. She was pretty sure Peter wouldn't ask too many probing questions about the money, anyway. He had some pretty hefty fiscal secrets of his own.

'And – um – everything else?' Adele thought she ought to

make coffee and reached for the percolator. 'You and Ross? Being together? Is that OK?'

Nell didn't answer immediately. She was rummaging through the dresser for the coffee set. 'Yes, I suppose so. I cursed you to hell to start with, Mum. I swore I'd never forgive you.' She placed the pile of tiny cups and saucers on the table and sighed. 'As it is, you've indirectly helped me out.'

Thank God she had done something right, Adele thought, decanting the demerara. She would have to observe them together, of course, to see if things had improved since Blenheim. But maybe just being in close proximity had made them realise what she'd known all along – that they were a match made in Heaven. She felt fairly jaunty as the percolator glugged and wondered if it would be too soon to get together with Marcia Percival over the wedding outfits.

But all was not well in the dining room. As Adele wheeled in the trolley, Ross was leafing through the photographs they'd taken in Kentucky and Peter was snapping his fingers in time with 'The Girl of My Best Friend'.

Adele glanced at her husband. Still calm. Maybe, she thought, knowing him so well, dangerously so?

Nell and Ross exchanged some intricate eye-talk across the table, Adele noticed. Not all of it friendly. She clattered out the cups and made a big show of cream and sugar.

Peter still sat quietly, apparently stone-cold sober, then leaned forward. 'So you've got something to tell me?'

'Later,' Adele said.

'Ross has obviously already done it.' Nell spoke at the same time.

Peter poured rather shaky coffee for everyone. 'It seems as though my womenfolk are out to corner the travelling market without the courtesy of informing me.' He looked from Adele to Nell. 'Here's to the two best-kept secrets in the Showmen's Guild. You were, I suppose, going to break it to me some time?'

Adele could sense undercurrents. Naturally, she had expected Peter to be shocked, but there was real bitterness in his voice. Not too clever considering his heart condition. And *two* secrets? What had she forgotten?

'Peter, look, I wanted to tell you –'

'It just slipped your mind, did it? Acquiring a Jessons Super-Ride without my knowledge? And I suppose you also knew that Nell has purchased a set of gallopers and some other preservation machines –'

Adele blinked in disbelief. 'Nell?'

Nell was fidgeting and didn't look at her parents. She did, however, hurl a 'I'm going to kill you' glare at Ross.

'Gallopers?' Adele raised her voice above 'Old Shep'. She usually fast-forwarded that one because it made her cry. 'You mean, while I was trying to push Bradleys into the next century, Nell has dragged them back into the last?'

'That about sums it up, yes.' Ross was unwrapping After Eights at the speed of light. 'She's also bought a ghost train and a caterpillar.'

'What for? What with?' Adele's words tumbled together in indignation. 'Did Danny and Sam –'

'They knew nothing about it. It came as a bit of a shock to them, too.' Ross started to build little houses with the chocolates. 'I'm sure, now that everything is out in the open, that Nell won't mind me telling you that she has used all her personal savings to buy them –'

Nell seemed to mind very much indeed. Adele blinked furiously. She and Nell – playing the same game. Secretly spending their entire fortunes, and going in completely opposite directions. She was fairly confident that Peter would eventually accept the addition of the Crash'n'Dash – however devious its purchase – but what on earth did Nell want with a set of gallopers?

'Ross and I will be getting married.' Nell looked mutinously from Adele to Peter. 'At the end of the season. The Bradley–Percival partnership which you so carefully manoeuvred, Mother, will be able to travel in two or three directions. You'll have achieved your aims. All of them. Dad's happy and stress-free retirement. Bradleys' expansion and profitability – not to mention a wedding. I hope you're happy?'

Adele opened her mouth to issue congratulations, then looked at the expressions of the participants. Ross demolished his After Eight skyscraper in a squish of peppermint cream. For someone who had been pursuing Nell for years, he certainly didn't seem too overjoyed. Nell looked as though she had just had root canal treatment.

Adele, who had been waiting for this news for as long as she could remember, suddenly felt deflated. Something wasn't right. Maybe she was still fuddled after the flight. Everything would be clearer in the morning.

She stretched her smile to a hundred watts and leaned towards Ross. 'So you don't mind this daugther of mine carrying on with her notion of old-fashioned rides?'

'Why should I? Nell will do whatever she wants. Anyway, the gallopers are nothing at all to do with me. You'd better speak to my father if you want any further information. He and Nell have come to an arrangement.'

Adele shook her head. What arrangement? Clem Percival surely wouldn't want to be involved with old machines, would he? Not now he owned Jessons? Peter, who was still looking extremely angry and would – Adele knew – be blasting her ears off the minute the visitors had gone, splashed the remains of several wine bottles into the goblets. Elvis seemed to have got stuck on 'Crying in the Chapel'.

Why wasn't anyone smiling? Adele sat down again. This wasn't how she'd planned Nell and Ross's engagement. There should be group hugs and Krug corks and laughter.

Nell's hands were shaking as she lifted her goblet. She raised it towards her parents in a gesture of defiance. 'I think we can still have a toast, don't you? After all, if it hadn't been for Mum none of this would have happened. What shall we drink to? Your happy retirement? My engagement? The overnight trebling of Bradleys?' She looked across the table at Ross. 'Or can you think of anything else?'

Ross shook his head. 'I can't think of anything else at all.'

CHAPTER TWENTY-SIX

The Bradley–Percival amalgamation moved on to Monkton Regis three days after the Graceland invasion. Anything that happened now, after the Highcliffe débâcle, Nell thought as she scrubbed vigorously at a stubborn wodge of chewing gum barnacled to the dodgems' pay-box, could only be an improvement. In retrospect, the astounded expressions, the stuttered excuses, the revealed double-dealings, had been quite amusing. Of course, it had been unfortunate that she and Ross had gatecrashed one of her mother's Guild-famous buttering-up sessions, but maybe now that there were no more skeletons to clatter from the closet, life might just settle down.

Ross had been reluctant to go to Highcliffe that night, but she'd insisted that he had to; that they had to bring everything out into the open. Her parents were back in the country and there could be no more secrets. She grinned to herself. Even Ross – who had been uncharacteristically po-faced throughout the whole affair – had to admit, as they whizzed back to Oxford in the Ferrari, that it had been surreal. Nell reckoned it had been far more than that. The evening had quite quickly disintegrated into farce: it would only have taken the four of them to go crashing in and out of Graceland's multitude of oak-panelled doors to have put it right up there with Brian Rix's best. And the memory of the expression on Ross's face when Adele handed him the Elvis wedding dolls would lift her depression for years.

And, she thought, gouging at the welded lump with no regard at all for her nail varnish, everyone had calmed down in the end. Once he'd recovered from the shock of Bradleys' sudden expansion, her father sounded quite excited, especially when Ross started to explain the cash benefits of both the new acquisitions and the proposed split.

No doubt her mother and father would have had some harsh words over the deceit of it all, but she knew from years of experience that in any parental row her mother would emerge victorious. And as for her mother – well, to be honest, Adele had played a clever hand, Nell thought with grudging admiration. She'd diffused the situation by disappearing to America and letting the Brain-Scrambler speak for itself. Her own initial fury had somewhat diminished by the time they'd had the confrontation, which was probably what her mother had hoped for all along.

The sun was filtering through misty grey clouds, promising an end to the last few days of wet weather. They were making more money than ever before; Ross had stopped trying to lure her into his marble and pearl leather palace – saying that he was more than happy to wait until after the wedding – and Claudia and Danny seeemed to be making a real go of their marriage. Well, Claudia didn't seem to have any more bruises; there had been no late-night shouting matches; Danny had stopped criticising her short hair, and she'd started wearing mascara again. It might not be Happy Ever After, but at least it wasn't Imminent Divorce.

There were only a couple of things that marred Nell's total happiness – and one of them she could do nothing about. OK, so she still wasn't delirious with the towering presence of the Crash'n'Dash, but as everyone else was jubilant it would probably be churlish to keep saying so. And once the restoration was finished she'd be travelling on her own with the gallopers a lot of the time, with the aid of the Downland

Trusters, of course, so she wouldn't have to put up with it for much longer.

Clem Percival had been an angel over potential steam-fair sites for her nostalgia machines. And, true to his word, he'd got straight on to his friendly truck dealership to organise transport for the gallopers. Three Seddon-Atkinson lorries were being fitted out by Eckstrucs as specialist wagons. He'd even gone to auction and bought a couple of second-hand Fodens and a Scammell for the ghost train and caterpillar, and was having the whole lot liveried in maroon and gold with the legend 'The Memory Lane Fair'. These were to be his and Marcia's main wedding gift, and his only stipulation was that if she refused to have Percival emblazoned across them, he wouldn't pay for Bradley. They'd settled on the trucks staying nameless, and Nell, who had no intention of dropping her maiden name once she and Ross were married, had reckoned she could bribe Jack to add 'Petronella Bradley' at some later date.

Nell dislodged the chewing gum at last and straightened up. Of course, to accomplish all this she had to marry Ross. So? She'd achieved more or less everything else that she wanted, hadn't she? She couldn't have it all. She would play her part, she told herself every night, and make Ross a good wife and an excellent business partner. She would really try to be pleasant first thing in the morning. She might even, one day, love him.

Fortunately, after his temper tantrum in the Swan, Ross hadn't seemed remotely interested in her machines, so she hadn't needed to tell him where they were being stored. It wasn't that she didn't trust him, of course. She still hadn't actually told anyone. Foolish as it may seem, she smiled self-indulgently as she wiped away greasy smears from the dodgems' red and yellow pillars with a J-cloth, Fox Hollow didn't seem to have anything to do with this life. It belonged to the other Nell Bradley – and to Jack. To talking and listening and sharing dreams. To mad dashes through the countryside on the back of the Roadster. To laughing and to drinks beside the river at the Maybush.

She climbed on to the dodgem track, checking every inch, making sure it was free of debris. Terry and Mick were testing the cars. Terry, who still had his Rudy Yarrow fan club from Haresfoot turning up sporadically, received a letter from Karen every day. He rushed off to the post office each morning and disappeared into the Beast Wagon to read them. Claudia and Nell had looked at each other and felt positively ancient.

The fair had moved from Oxford the previous day and they weren't due to open until this evening. Ross was off somewhere with Danny – and she was going to Fox Hollow this afternoon. She hoped Jack would be there. She wanted to know how his search for restoration painting work was going – and she couldn't wait to tell him about Clem's gift of the transport. She didn't, she realised with a sharp solar-plexus punch, want to hear anything about Fiona, the wedding, or the baby. Which was pretty silly when she'd be marrying Ross merely months after Jack and Fiona's nuptials. When she was old, she decided, and Petronella Bradley's Memory Lane Fair had gone down in the annals of showland history, she'd bore her grandchildren rigid with the story.

Grandchildren? To have grandchildren she'd have to be a mother first. Motherhood, as she'd told Clem, had never figured highly on her list of must-dos. Ross, of course, would expect her to produce at least one heir to the Percival dynasty. Nell wrinkled her nose and tried to stop her thoughts wandering along that path. Babies, she liked. Children – when they were yours – were probably a whole lot more acceptable than the squabbling, squalling, badly be-haved brats she watched every hour of her working day. Creating a baby with the right man was possibly the most wondrously happy thing any woman could do. It was just a shame that Ross wasn't the right man . . .

The yard at Fox Hollow looked like Asda's car park on a busy Friday evening. There were vehicles of all descriptions pulled skew-whiff up against the hedges. The organ had been wheeled out and was standing, still sadly truncated, alone in a corner. A set of ramps had been constructed, and the centre truck was anchored in place. Jack's intricately decorated rounding boards, the long yellow-and-red lighting spars, and the scarlet swifts that supported the tilt, were stacked outside the double doors. The twisted brass rods, throwing off prisms, were leaning like giant sticks of barley sugar against the beautifully painted, gilded and Tudor-rosed platforms. And the horses, with Petronella leading the battle charge, were galloping on the spot in a riot of glossy colour.

The Downland Trusters had finished their restoration.

With a surge of joy, Nell tore inside. The Jims, Bobs and Bens were all busily carrrying things from the back of the shed out into the sunshine – looking like the Munchkin workforce in the Emerald City, Nell thought, only much larger, of course – and greeted her with smiles of welcome. Percy and Dennis were having a deep discussion in front of the music-book cupboard. She couldn't see Harry or Fred. And there was no sign of Jack. Had the Roadster been outside? Nell hadn't noticed it in the scrum of cars. Surely he'd be here? It was obviously an auspicious day. Her euphoria was diluted by a splash of disappointment.

Percy spotted her, raised his hand in greeting, and bustled across. 'You must be on radar, my dear. We were going to give you a bell to see if you could make it. We're timing ourselves for a build-up.'

'And,' Dennis had joined him, 'we're going to need another strong pair of arms. How fit are you feeling? OK for lifting the platforms?'

'Not even a hoof.' Nell teased. 'I'll just stand on the sidelines, be helpless and feminine, and flutter at your manly strength. Anyway I'm hardly dressed for work, am I?' She'd worn the emerald green silk shorts suit that she had bought in Marsh Minster because – well, because it was a nice day and because she knew it looked good. Those, she told herself firmly, were the only reasons. 'If I'd known you were going to have me grafting I'd have stuck to jeans.'

'We're bloody glad you didn't,' Percy winked. 'You look good enough to eat. Don't she, Den?'

Den affirmed this statement with a sort of guttural 'Ar'. Nell blushed. She didn't want to ask them about Jack. 'It's just a dry-run build-up, is it? Not the organ or a generator or anything?'

They shook their heads. Nell was relieved. There was no way she'd allow them to have a full run-through if Jack wasn't there. He'd done more than any of them. Far more than she had. And they'd promised themselves, hadn't they, that they'd play 'Paree' together on that first occasion.

She was itching to tell them of her deal with Clem Percival, to let them know that they'd soon be on the road – with authorised gaffs – and some really swish transport courtesy of Eckstrucs. But again, she wanted to tell Jack first. Funny, fanciful ideas were sneaking into her head and she pushed them out. Quickly.

'Seriously, is there anything I can do?'

'Hold the stopwatch,' Dennis grinned. 'We've been to Pinkneys Green and timed John Carter's lot. We're aiming to beat 'em.'

'And I'm sure you will. So, I suppose I'm relegated to tea boy, am I?'

'Some tea boy!' Dennis and Percy were still looking at her as though they'd just realised that she was a woman. Perhaps the shorts suit was a little blatant for Fox Hollow and the Downland Trusters. They nodded in unison. 'You've been bloody brilliant, Nell. Bloody brilliant. We couldn't have done any of this without you. And yeah, tea would be grand. Are you up to making twenty-odd cups?'

'Easy peasy,' Nell said, heading towards the small kitchen which her grandfather had built in a corner of the shed to prevent his wintering gaff lads escaping into town for tea breaks. 'Twenty cups of tea I can do standing on my head – not that I'm going to, so don't hold your breath. After feeding my family and the gaff lads at three in the morning for most of my life, a tea urn holds no threats.'

She was still grinning as she pushed her way into the kitchen and manhandled the water heater which looked as though George Stephenson had used it as a prototype from the stone sink to the bench. There was a cupboard full of mismatched mugs, several trays nicked from pub beer gardens, a collection of tarnished spoons, and her mother's appallingly plum-coloured Tupperware which contained sugar, tea and coffee.

'Bugger.' Nell pulled open the fridge. There wouldn't be any milk. They'd have to drink it black. 'Jesus!'

The fridge was stocked, not only with milk, but with orange juice, eggs, bacon, butter, a mass of salad and cold meats, half a trifle, and at least two dozen bottles of Beck's. The Downland Trusters had obviously made themselves at home.

Having made the tea and loaded milk and sugar on to the trays, she carried them into the shed. Everyone was outside now, heaving and sweating the numbered swifts into place from the top of the centre, swarming up and down ladders, shouting, thoroughly enjoying themselves.

'Tea's up!'

Two dozen faces grinned cheerfully at her and she felt a shiver of exhilaration. If only this was what it could always be like. Out on the road, building up the gallopers – not simply because it was a business, but because everyone loved it just as much as she did.

'We're not going to be fixing the lights or anything,' Dennis told her, wiping a grimy hand across his sweating face. 'Just making sure that everything is as it should be. Any idea when we'll be making our debut?'

'September, definitely.' Nell knew she was searching the faces for Jack and stopped. There were several end-of-season steam rallies, Clem had said, who would welcome her with open arms once he'd approached the lessees. But Jack was getting married in September. 'I'm not sure when exactly. But will you all be able to make it? I mean, the pay will be minimal to start with no doubt and –'

'We don't want paying.' Dennis had been joined by some of the other Trusters, all reaching out grateful oily hands for the steaming mugs. 'We'll do it for nothing. That's like saying we should be paid for breathing. Anyway, you'll have to fork out a fair bit for the sites, then there's transport and –'

'I'll still pay you. You'll get travelling expenses and we'll just divvy-up the takings,' Nell interrupted him. She didn't want to discuss any of this. Not yet. 'I won't be able to take you on as proper gaff lads anyway, because you all have your own lives to lead – but we'll have to come to some arrangement.'

They grinned happily and still clutching their mugs, swarmed back to work.

Deciding that the temptation of an ice-cold Beck's was far more alluring than strong tea from a chipped mug, Nell headed back to the kitchen. She opened the bottle and looked around for a glass. Stupid. The Trusters wouldn't bother with glasses – and there was no one to watch her swigging from the bottle, was there? Ross would have had a fit. He had some really red-necked notions sometimes.

Enjoying the coolness of the beer on her dry throat, she walked to the back of the shed to make sure that the ghost train and caterpillar were still anchored securely. They'd been practically hidden beneath the gallopers ever since their arrival, and she'd hate to see them damaged at this late stage in the Memory Lane Fair's development. She needn't have worried, of course. The Trusters had secured them back against the wall. She was dealing with professionals in love here, she told herself, and any qualms she might have were totally unnecessary. There was some packing or something that seemed to have worked loose. She bent down to have a closer look.

'What the – ?'

She peered at the odd assortment of clothes and blankets piled in the musty darkness between the two rides. Had they got a tramp at Fox Hollow? They quite often did during the winter, and she and Claudia and Mrs Mac always made sure that they had at least one hot meal a day and access to the shed's kitchen and outside lavatory – but they'd never had any in the summer before.

'Good God!'

If it was a tramp it was a pretty stylish one. As well as a duvet and pillows, there was a collapsible bed, a razor and a whole heap of Yves St Laurent toiletries. Nell peered more closely. Three pairs of black jeans were folded on top of several T-shirts, and a bundle of recently washed and very expensive black jersey underpants and black silk socks lay in a tangle of clean towels. She could smell the faint linseed oil, the cologne, the petrol . . .

'Dennis said you were in here – it's going well, isn't it?'

'Oh – er – hi.' She spun round to see Jack pulling off his crash helmet, shaking his black hair free. In some confusion, she waved the Beck's bottle towards the bedding. 'This is definitely above and beyond the call of duty. Still, you'll be able to go home now you've finished, won't you? Yes, the gallopers look incredible – you've worked so hard. I'm really glad you're here – I've got so much to tell you.'

'Obviously.' He smiled. 'Tell you what. I'll get a bottle and join you. Do you want another?'

'No. I'm driving. Shouldn't we be outside, building up, timing them?'

'Probably.' Jack shrugged out of the leather jacket and dropped it beside the crash helmet on the makeshift bed. 'But it's only a dry run. I'd've phoned you if I thought it was going to be the real thing. It wouldn't have been right without you. You look great, by the way – although it's hardly suitable for the Roadster. I loved that outfit the last time I saw it.'

She watched him walk into the kitchen. When on earth had he seen it?

'You wore it on television,' Jack returned, interpreting her puzzled frown and taking a much-needed swig of beer. 'I thought you and Claudia looked incredible. I ogled you unashamedly. Didn't listen to a word Andy Craig was saying. 'So,' he sank down on the edge of the bed and patted the duvet, 'sit down and tell me your news.'

Nell eyed both Jack and the bed with some suspicion. She didn't think she really wanted to perch chummily on it, beside him, and chatter like friends. Not any more. God – this was ridiculous!

She sat as far away from him as possible, trying and failing miserably to arrange her legs with some degree of decency. He laughed at her attempts. 'No point, I've seen most of them already. And why you'd want to try and hide them is totally beyond me.'

'I hate them,' she said. 'I hate being so tall – and I hate every one of my damn freckles. I'd love to be small and cute and blonde.'

Jack didn't speak. Just smiled. It was far more disturbing than words.

Outside, through the open doors, she could see the Downland Trusters still heaving the platforms across the yard. Percy and Dennis, having assumed their natural roles as foremen, were barking orders as expertly as any traveller. This life – this one – was the real one. And before long it would be the only one. Except, of course, that the Trusters, and Jack, were only playing. They were still flatties enjoying a fantasy. She would be married to Ross, and Jack would be married to Fiona and be a father before long. He'd have found a proper job and have responsibilities. He wouldn't be able to devote all his time to the gallopers . . .

'So,' he sliced into her thoughts, 'what's your news?'

She told him about the promised gaffs, about the Eckstrucs wagons, about the livery, her words tumbling over each other in her excitement. 'And if you could just pass your Class I before we hit the road, it'd be great.' She placed her empty Beck's bottle on the dusty floor. 'What do you reckon? Could you do it?'

'Why not?' Jack squinted at her through the green glass of his bottle. 'I haven't got anything else to do now that the painting's finished. I can actually drive a small lorry – I got a Class II four years ago when Dad thought it might be useful on the sites. So, one step up shouldn't be that difficult. How long does the course take?'

'About five days, I think. We put the gaff lads through because Mum and Dad always had. I mean, in our game, the more people who can drive a lorry, the better. But – would you? I mean, Fiona wouldn't mind you taking time out?'

'Not at all.' He put his bottle on the floor beside hers. 'The only problem I've got at the moment is ready cash. No doubt it would be expensive and –'

'I'd pay. It's the least the Brain-Scrambler can do.' She looked at him in delight. 'I'll ring Big Wheelers when I get back to Monkton Regis and book you in. It's going to be fantastic, isn't it?'

He nodded. 'As long as you let me pay you back. I'm still unemployed and impoverished at the moment. But I will pay you back, I promise.'

'OK. Five pence a week.'

They grinned at each other. The dream was growing again. Spiralling.

Jack stretched and stood up. 'I suppose we ought to go and show our faces. After all, this is supposed to be a co-operative.' He reached out to help her. 'Do you need any assistance in untangling your legs?'

She shook her head and ignoring his hand, scrambled to her feet.

Jack laughed at her as she tried to pull the shorts into some semblance of modesty. 'Waste of time, I've told you. So – what made Percival the Elder have this massive change of heart? What part of your soul did you sell to secure us gaffs and wagons?'

'It wasn't my soul.' She didn't look at him. 'It was my body. Oh, no – not like that. I wouldn't go to bed with Clem Percival even for the gallopers! It's my wedding present. I – um – agreed to marry Ross – at last.' She was walking ahead of him. 'Still, it was always on the cards, and at least this way we get everything we need to get the show on the road. You don't think it was wrong of me, do you?'

'No.'

'Oh, great. Only I did have a few pangs of conscience about it. Not that I needed to. Ross is a businessman – and showmen always see their offspring all right with either cheques or machines as wedding presents. It's traditional.' They'd almost reached the doors. The sunlight was spilling over the floor. 'I think Clem was just a bit surprised at what I needed the wagons for, but Ross thinks a three-way split with the fair is a great idea.'

'Yes, I suppose he would.'

'So, I'll be teetering up the aisle just after you. You'll be able to give me some tips. Unless, of course, it's when the baby arrives and then –' She looked over her shoulder. 'God Almighty, Jack. What's wrong?'

Nell, embarrassed at having been so garrulous, embarrassed at not sensing his unease, stared at him in horror. Why hadn't she noticed how thin he'd become? Why hadn't she noticed the dark shadows bruising his eyes?

'Jack? Oh, shit. Do you feel ill? Why didn't you tell me to shut up? What is it?'

'There isn't going to be a baby any more.'

'Oh . . . oh, poor Fiona. Poor you. Miscarriages must be devastating.'

'She had an abortion.'

Nell closed her eyes. Strongly pro-abortion, she'd never given much thought to the practicalities. She'd never really considered how it affected the man. Like everything, it was so easy to hold an opinion that you'd hopefully never have to put into practice.

'Why?'

He told her, quietly. All of it. 'I think she made the right decision, to be honest. It was just that I was beginning to quite like the idea of fatherhood. It was a hell of a shock.'

'It must have been. I'm so sorry.' She moved towards him, instinctively, wanting to offer comfort and not knowing how. 'Maybe later, when the time is right, there'll be another baby. When she's more settled in her new position –'

'Not for me and Fiona, there won't. I've left her. And before you say it – not just because of the termination. I would have left her anyway. I've made a clean break with my old life.'

The fridge . . . the bed . . . the clothes . . . 'You're living here?'

'For the time being. You don't mind?'

She shook her head. Of course she didn't mind. How else was he going to find the solitude he needed to grieve for his child? She touched his arm. 'Jack, I really am sorry.'

He looked down at her fingers and then up into her eyes. 'Thanks.'

'C'mon you two!' Percy shouted from his perch at the top of the ladder. 'Stop slacking and get some work done. It's taken us an hour and thirty-seven minutes so far! We're beating John Carter's lot by three minutes!'

CHAPTER TWENTY-SEVEN

Turning the packets of pills over and over in her hands, Claudia knew what she had to do. This was it. She had to make the decision. She loved Sam, really loved him, but there was no question of them ever having a future. Her future was with Danny – and if they were to have this future, then she'd have to have a baby. She could work at it, she guessed. She'd loved him once. It surely wouldn't be hard to do it again. If only he didn't frighten her so much.

She looked out of the bedroom window. The fair was just easing itself into its first night at Monkton Regis, the punters were the usual early-evening families and young teenagers, the lights were dimmed by the evening sun, and the music was its customary tinny cacophony of a dozen different tunes.

Everything was the same. Only after tonight, everything would be different. After tonight she'd be a proper wife. She repressed the shudder of revulsion. Danny would have to calm down. She couldn't go through that again. Still, she'd face that hurdle later. It was best not to think about it now.

'Claudia! Are you in there?' Nell yelled from the living room, sounding fairly frantic. 'Are you decent?'

'No, never.' Claudia said cheerfully, thrusting the four-month supply of pills back into her bedside cabinet. She'd flush them down the loo later. 'What's the matter?'

'Everything.' Nell, who was wearing the green shorts suit and had been away from the fairground for hours again, looked pretty distraught. 'Absolutely bloody everything.'

She hurled herself down on the white-and-gold flounced counterpane and pushed her hair away from her face. The bank manager, Claudia decided. Obviously married. His wife had found out . . .

'It can't be that bad.' Claudia was faintly disappointed with Nell. The story about the gallopers and the Gavioli had been true, for God's sake. All that intrigue and subterfuge over a prehistoric ride. She'd heard Ross and Danny discussing its financial possibilities. It all sounded pretty boring to her. Claudia had been far happier when she'd imagined that Nell was harbouring a secret of mammoth sexual proportions. She wasn't even sure if the bank manager existed any more. 'Is it – um – Ross?'

'No – well, yes. Sort of.'

Claudia tugged off her kimono and pulled on the baggy grey sweat pants and huge black T-shirt behind the wardrobe door. She didn't want Nell to start screaming about the bruises again. Mind, looking at Nell, she probably wouldn't have noticed if Claudia's limbs had been hanging off by bloodied threads.

She emerged fully covered and tried a different approach. 'Have you been playing with the gallopers this afternoon?'

Nell still stared at the deep-piled white carpet. 'Why?'

'Just wondered. Danny was saying earlier that he and Ross ought to go and check them out. He asked me if I knew where they were kept. He's going to ask you –'

'And I won't be telling him.' Nell sounded as though she was going to cry. 'They're nothing to do with him. Oh, shit. Have you ever felt that you have completely and irrevocably screwed up your life?'

'Frequently.'

Claudia wondered if Nell was going to say anything at all that made sense. She really should be getting changed into something more suitable and hauling herself into the dodgems' pay-box. Surely a set of gallopers – especially now that everyone knew about them and approved – couldn't cause this sort of despair? She drew kohl lines round her eyes and added mascara. Maybe, she thought, she'd be able to go back to false eyelashes and that brilliant stay-forever purple lipstick once she'd sorted things out with Danny. Maybe she could even wear the PVC shorts and the wonder-bra leather top. On second thoughts, things would never be *that* good.

'Nell, sweetie – are you going to tell me or not? Because if you're not, then you really ought to be shifting your bum and going to work. We don't just have Danny screaming these days, remember? We also have your future husband – holy shit! Now what have I said?'

'Nothing.' Nell clambered from the flounces and headed towards the door again. 'You wouldn't understand. No one would understand . . .'

Bloody hell, Claudia thought, running styling wax through the short spiky layers of her hair, and I thought I was over-emotional.

The evening blossomed into one of those rare fragrant-after-the-rain ones, and as usual since the arrival of the Crash'n'Dash, the fair was filled with excited crowds. Ross was in the Brain-Scrambler's pay-box tonight, which meant Danny had the waltzer and she'd been demoted once more to the side stuff. Claudia was glad. She enjoyed running the hoopla on first nights; it gave her the chance to stare at the crowds, to look beyond them at new scenery, to dream.

So, everything was working out nicely. Well, fairly OK, then. Nell was marrying Ross, the Crash'n'Dash was making them a fortune and Danny had ordered a Moon Mission, Nell's gallopers would be able to go to country-park dos and stately homes and places where they couldn't, and Sam . . .

Claudia looked across to the paratrooper. Sam was loading and unloading the cars. She did love him so very much. She loved his kindness and his friendship. She loved the way he looked and the way he kissed her. And after tonight she would have to forget him.

She sold hoops and dished out the occasional prize as darkness fell. She wanted the evening to last for ever. She didn't want to have to go to bed with Danny and try to get pregnant.

'I'll take over,' Mercedes Mackenzie yelled across from her own stall, 'if you want a break. I'm not doing much here, and Nyree-Dawn and Rio can cope.'

'Cheers.' Claudia vaulted across the side. 'I'll go and grab a drink.'

Mercedes, who was wearing the ubiquitous white cut-offs and a midriff-baring orange top, swung her legs into the hoopla and reached for the money apron. 'Things going OK with you and Danny now?'

'What?' Claudia blinked. 'How do you mean?'

Mercedes shrugged her well-oiled shoulders. 'Come off it. Everyone knows. We're not deaf – or blind. You've been having some purlers. You shouldn't wind him up so much –'

'And you should mind your own bloody business! Who the hell do you think you are? You wait until you're married – it isn't all hearts and flowers, you know.'

Mercedes tossed the corkscrew curls. 'I'm sure it isn't. Trouble with you – and Nell too, when she marries Ross – is that you're too set in your ways. You don't like changes. Danny and Ross want to move forward. And you and Nell – well, God you're nearly *thirty*. Nell's playing at being an old codger with a set of bloody gallopers, and you –'

'Yes?' Claudia laid her palms on the hoopla's counter. 'And I'm what exactly?'

'God, Claudia, we're mates, but you've got to admit you don't have a clue how to handle Danny. If he was my husband –'

'Yeah?' Claudia drummed her nails on the flaking paint-work. 'If he was your husband you'd what?'

'Keep hold of him.' Mercedes shrugged. 'Especially now he's going to be loaded. He's wicked.'

'Wicked? Too right he's wicked. He's downright bloody evil at times. That's not what you mean though, is it? You mean –'

But Mercedes was wiggling away towards a bunch of punters. 'Ten rings, sir? Of course. Would you like me to show you how to do it?'

Tart! Claudia fumed, turning away. Is that what everyone was saying? Well, the Mackenzie girls, anyway? That she and Nell were dinosaurs? That they didn't know how to handle the men in their lives? What the hell did Mercedes and Nyree-Dawn know about it? They were only kids, after all.

Nell might well have notions about old-fashioned rides, but she was pretty sparky in all other areas. And what had Mercedes been hinting at about *her*? She was twenty-seven – not ninety-seven! Life hadn't even started yet! Oh, God – yes, it had, she thought, side-winding to avoid a bunch of teenagers carrying toffee apples and candyfloss. And tonight it would probably end.

'Looking for me?' Sam yelled over a blast of Nirvana as she passed the paratrooper.

'No.'

'Thanks. That's what I like. A woman who knows her mind. Where are you going?'

'Mad. Coming?'

'Went ages ago.' He grinned suddenly. 'Didn't like it much so I came back.' He jerked his head towards Alfie to take over and shoved his way through the crowds beside her. 'Has Danny upset you again?'

'Mercedes Mackenzie thinks I'm past it. And don't laugh. She thinks Nell and I are in our bloody dotage!'

'The Mackenzie girls are teenagers.' Sam ducked beneath the bobbing onslaught of a black girl selling helium balloons. 'They think everyone over twenty is geriatric.'

'She also thinks Danny is wicked – as in superlatively OK, you know? Silly cow. She doesn't think I handle him right. And she said that Nell wasn't right for Ross! Jesus!'

Sam, shoving between the crowds of punters, grinned. 'The Mackenzie girls have just had the advantage of A-level psychology. They probably studied marriage as part of their course work. You and Danny probably featured in their final theses, which must have given the examiner heart failure. Am I being invited in for coffee?'

'No.'

'Great. I'll have mine black and with two sugars – just in case you'd forgotten.' He stopped at the bottom of the living-wagon steps. 'I want to talk to you anyway, but not in here. I don't want Danny bursting in.'

Neither did she. And they needed to talk. If she was going to dump the pills, stay with Danny, have a baby – then she owed it to Sam to tell him.

'OK. Your place, then. But you make the coffee – and don't mention bloody Mercedes.'

He didn't. He made coffee, while Claudia sat on the scarlet-cushioned window seat and watched the lights. The generators thumped their continual life-beat as a bass line to the music. The screams from the Crash'n'Dash's victims were mercifully muffled by the double-glazing. Claudia gazed at it all and thought about motherhood. Showmen's babies slept through all this, she thought. Showmen's babies, born and raised into this noisy, nomadic existence, thrived and prospered.

She could have a baby. Women had babies all the time. Pregnancy couldn't be that bad otherwise people wouldn't keep on doing it. Giving birth must be fairly forgettable too – at least after a while – otherwise there'd be far more only children. All she needed to do now was convince herself that the conception part would be a magical experience too, and she'd have performed the greatest bit of self-brainwashing since Houdini promised to return from the grave.

Taking the red-and-gold mug as Sam sat beside her, she sighed. 'Do you want to talk first, or shall I get my bit over?'

'Ladies first.'

Sam's arm was along the back of the window seat and she

leaned against it without thinking. 'I'm not going to leave him. I'm going to make a go of it. I do love you. No, please don't say anything. Not yet. Let me tell you what I'm doing and why I'm doing it –'

Sam listened. She wasn't watching him but she knew that he heard every word. The muscles in his arm tightened every so often, and his breathing pattern changed, but he didn't interrupt her.

When she'd finished, he didn't speak for ages. 'So you think that having a baby will solve all the problems, do you?'

'No. But it's what Danny wants more than anything. I'm married to him, for God's sake. For ever.'

'And do you want a baby?'

She shook her head. She didn't. She never had.

'And what makes you think that you'll be able to produce this child for Danny now? After all, you've been married for ten years.'

'I've been on the pill for ten years.'

'Fucking hell!' Sam grinned. 'And he didn't know? Didn't suspect? All those tests? All that money on infertility treatment. God, Claudia, you are amazing. Bloody incredible. You devious little –'

'Not devious.' She put her empty mug on the window-sill. 'Simply a case of self-preservation. Look, Nell's made compromises, hasn't she? She's going to marry Ross and we both know that she doesn't love him. But she's going to do it all the same. I'm sure that Danny and I can –'

'Nell and Ross are completely different. He's hardly likely to scream and threaten and scare her half out of her wits, is he? Anyway, I'm not sure –'

'What?'

'Nothing. It doesn't matter. We're not talking about them. So, you're prepared to sleep with Danny, live with him, love him –'

'Not love.' She shook her head. 'I don't. He knows I don't. I love you.'

Sam's fingers stroked the back of her neck. 'Can I talk now? I'm not going to state the obvious – you know I want you to leave him. To live with me. I'd leave all this for you.'

Claudia laughed. 'You'd have to. We'd never be accepted as a couple here, would we? We'd be bloody outcasts. Drifting from crust to crust. Starving, penniless . . .'

'Hardly. We'd have the paratrooper and the hoopla. We could travel with other showmen. Marriages do break up, Claudia. Other travellers make the best of it. Move on with new partners.'

'Not with their brothers-in-law, though.'

Sam sighed and continued the stroking. It was lovely – sensuous without being invasive – not threatening. Gentle. If only love could be like this. If only sex didn't have to equate with pain and humiliation and fear. Claudia moved her head against his hand. 'Anything else you want to say – apart from don't do it?'

'Plenty. But you wouldn't listen. If – just if – it all works out, who will you be? You know, which identity will you adopt to be the doting Mrs Danny Bradley – epitome of the perfect wife and mother? Sackcloth with ashes earrings? Downtrodden shoes? Hangdog jumpers? Tell me, honestly, about the dressing-up. Which one is the real you?'

'All of them.' She curled her feet up on the window seat, her head sliding on to Sam's shoulder. It felt good. No one could see them. It would never happen again. She'd remember this for ever. 'I dress for the way I feel at the time. Why?'

'Because that's what I'd want you to do. Wear the sexy stuff, if you wanted to, or the pretty floaty things on your romantic days, or smart suits – or whatever you bloody wanted. I want you to be you. To be happy. Not to wear things that you hate – like this,' he flicked at the black T-shirt. 'You hate this, don't you? What's the matter?'

She wriggled away from him, gritting her teeth, her eyes watering. Last night's bruises were still angry. Sam leaned over and lifted the T-shirt, and gazed with incredulity at her ribs.

'Jesus! I thought you said he never hit you. The bastard. I'll kill him – I'll –'.

'He didn't hit me. He doesn't.' She stared at him with defiance. 'It wasn't like that. He –' Her eyes filled with tears and she dashed them away, angry with herself at letting him know too much. Angry at having revealed this awful, shameful secret. 'He just wants a baby so much – you know . . .'

Sam stared at her in horrified disbelief.

She closed her eyes. 'It's my fault. I deserve this. If I hadn't been taking the pill I'd have got pregnant years ago and it would be all right. It's my fault . . .'

'He raped you?' Sam was on his feet. There was no sign of love and peace in his eyes. Just anger. 'He bloody raped you?'

'No. Of course he didn't. We're married. It's my fault that I don't want to – Sam! Sam! Don't!'

She flew to the door of the living wagon but Sam had gone, punching his way through the crowds, his tawny hair fleetingly visible in the swooping, gaily coloured lights. Claudia wiped her hand across her eyes and jumped down the steps after him. It *was* her fault. Danny kept saying so. If she was normal – if she enjoyed sex – if she could have a baby . . . She'd short-changed him. He expected more from his wife. It was all her fault.

Claudia cannoned into people. Someone trod on her toes. Elbows gouged into her painful ribs, making her catch her breath. She thrust her way through the Crash'n'Dash's snaking queue. She had to stop him. Stop them. Stop Danny finding out. Stop Sam getting hurt. Yes, that most of all. Danny would kill him, brother or no brother. She hurled herself towards the waltzer.

Barry and Ted, the gaff lads, were riding on the backs of cars, swinging them round beneath the starburst spars of light. The track undulated in time to throaty jungle music. Eager punters hung from the pillars and crowded two-deep on the platforms waiting for the next ride. Through it all she could see Danny in the centre pay-box, his shoulders hunched, counting the money.

Then she could see Sam, leaping on to the moving machine, weaving his way through the swirling blur of the cars with ease. He'd done it all his life. Claudia stuffed her fist into her mouth as he kicked his way into the pay-box and Danny, thinking he was being mugged, jumped to his feet. After that it was all in slow motion. Claudia watched helplessly, the tears sliding down her cheeks.

Danny's face relaxed when he saw Sam, then looked surprised, then faintly contorted as Sam grabbed him and pulled him off his seat. The jungle music screeched and died. The gaff lads turned their heads to see what was happening, and immediately leapt from the cars into the centre. They stood there, rooted to the spot, not understanding. Not knowing what they should do. Sam, hauling Danny after him, still managed to avoid being hit by the cars on the return journey and they tumbled from the waltzer platform, locked together, amidst the yelling, cheering punters.

The crowds parted, making way for them, standing back like the bit-parters in an old-fashioned Western saloon brawl. Sam had Danny's throat in a stranglehold, and he scrambled upright, dragging his brother with him.

'Sam!' Claudia fought her way through the excited audience. 'For God's sake!'

Danny was retaliating now, punching and kicking; the movements jerky and furious. Everyone gave them a wide berth as Sam bounced Danny away from the waltzer and towards the stalls.

People were running – some to see what was happening, others to get out of the way. There were screams – but these were lost in the yells from the rides. Claudia pushed her way behind them, searching frantically for Ross or Nell or Terry – for anyone who had seen what was going on and could stop them.

It was all her fault. Every bit of it. She collided with families hurrying in the opposite direction; parents trying to protect their children from the violence. Violence – the word echoed in her head. She'd been on the receiving end of quite a bit of it.

'What's going on?' one of the Mackenzie twins screamed in her ear as she followed Sam and Danny's erratic progress through the joints. 'What the hell is happening?'

'Family squabble,' Claudia yelled back. 'Just a bit of fun.'

Sam was hauling Danny up the steps of her living wagon now, stumbling, white-faced with fury. She fled after them, kicking her way in as Sam slammed the door and locked it behind them.

'Please,' she wiped her eyes with her fist. 'Please don't –'

Sam threw Danny on to the William Morris sofa and stood over him, shaking with anger. He didn't look at her. 'Claudia – get out. Go. Now.'

She shook her head. She couldn't let them do this. She didn't want to see Sam reduced to Danny's level because of her.

'What – the fuck – is – going on?' Danny was breathing with short, sharp, punchy inhalations. He rubbed his throat and tried to stand up. Sam pushed him down again. He squinted at them both. 'Have you gone fucking mad?'

Sam still said nothing. Claudia, scrubbing at her eyes, pushed her way between them and lifted her T-shirt. 'This, Danny. He found out about this.'

Danny almost laughed. He shook his head. 'What? So fucking what? What's that to do with anyone else – especially him? How did he see them, anyway? I told you to keep them covered up – or were you wearing one of your slapper outfits again, huh?'

Claudia didn't answer him. She didn't want him to know. She didn't want any of this to be happening. Someone thundered on the door. They ignored it. She could hear Ross's voice – and Nell's? High-pitched. Concerned. She looked at Sam and Danny and hurried across the living room.

She unlocked the door and opened it slightly. Their faces were shocked. Terry was behind them, and several of the

Macs. She tried to smile. 'It's OK. I'm all right. Honest. There's no problem. Just a bit of a disagreement. Please go away. Please. I'll be out in a minute.'

She closed the door and locked it again but she knew they were still there.

Like all travellers, Danny was physically fit. He'd quickly regained some of his breath and was squinting up at Sam with a belligerent smirk. 'You want to beat the crap out of me because she says I belted her – is that right?'

Sam let his hands fall to his sides. The muscles in his shoulders were still bunched. Still on full alert. 'I don't think with my fists. I've never believed that violence is the answer to anything. And no, Claudia didn't say you hit her. She didn't say anything. But I know that you raped her.'

'I did *what*?' Danny smiled in pure disbelief. 'Rape? Jesus, where have you just beamed down from? You can't rape your own wife!'

'You can and you did. And I reckon you've been doing it for quite some time – and making her feel guilty about it. No, don't move. Sit there. Shut up. And listen. She didn't tell me any of this – I've watched you for a long time. I know what you're like, Danny. She's scared stiff of you. All she bloody wants is to be happy. She's tried so hard to please you. For years. That's all she's done. And you raped her . . .'

'Bollocks.' Danny started to stand up again, lunging towards Claudia. 'Tell him. Christ, woman, so what if I get a bit rough? If you weren't so fucking useless I wouldn't have to! If you'd just show some sort of interest and not lie there rigid and with your eyes closed I might not need to get aggressive. You're frigid and I want a baby. You're my wife for God's sake! I can do what I like with you! Tell him.'

Claudia's sob caught in her throat. This was appalling. And it had been going on for so long. So many years.

'I'll tell you, Danny. Oh, I'll tell you.' She gulped back the tears and crashed through into the bedroom. She practically ripped the cabinet from its moorings, wrenching at the drawer, grabbing the pills.

314

She stood still for one moment looking at the bedroom. She hated it. The white-and-gold flounces and the deep white carpet had witnessed some of the most terrifying moments of her life. And she'd never told anyone. Never.

Sam shook his head warningly as she stumbled back into the living room, but she ignored him and flourished the packets under Danny's nose. 'Look! Go on! Bloody look! This is why I've never become pregnant! This is why I haven't given you a son!'

Danny peered at the packets. They meant nothing to him. Claudia opened them with fumbling fingers, spilling out the little bubble-marked monthly sachets all over the pattern of the sofa.

Furious realisation flickered in Danny's eyes. His mouth dropped open. 'You cheating little whore! I'll –'

But Danny got no further. Sam bunched his fist and punched him, just once, on the jaw. Danny, still open-mouthed, still looking amazed, slid soundlessly from the William Morris sofa into a graceful heap on the carpet.

Sam took Claudia's hand very gently and led her towards the door. 'Come on, sweetheart. Out. Now. I'll sort everything else out. Just wait for me.'

He opened the door and pushed Claudia into Nell's arms. 'Take care of her for me, please. Always.'

CHAPTER TWENTY-EIGHT

'This, Princess, has got to be sorted. Right now.' Clem Percival glared at Adele over Ross's marble-topped kitchen table. 'You damn well started it – now it's down to you to stop it. A scandal like this is the last thing we need. And it's certainly not the sort of thing I want to have the Percival name mixed up in. We've always been squeaky clean. Understood? You've got to do something about it.'

'Me?' Adele, who'd been crying on and off since she and Peter had arrived at Monkton Regis, looked very tired. The golden guitars, however, jangled with an inner indignation. 'Why me?'

'They're your bloody children,' Clem roared, looking less than avuncular. 'Bring 'em into line. You were the one who gave 'em ideas above their station –'

Adele wiped her eyes. 'What's that supposed to mean?'

Nell, who hadn't slept and who could have done without this family inquest, stood up. 'I think what Clem is so delicately hinting, is that if you hadn't interfered by buying the Crash'n'Dash and changing our lives, none of this would have happened. Which,' she glared at them both, 'is a complete load of rubbish. Much as I'd like to blame the Brain-Scrambler for every malady known to man, I really think this one is down to Danny!'

She pulled open Ross's front door and jumped down the steps. There was a gap in the row of living wagons like a pulled tooth. Sam's van had gone, along with Claudia's Shogun. The Mazda was still parked alongside the empty space. Sam's 'always' had lasted less than an hour. He'd collected Claudia from Nell's living wagon, and leading her gently by the hand had disappeared into the darkness. Nell, desolate, shocked, and completely helpless, had heard the Shogun start, had heard the living wagon pull away.

Earlier, Claudia, rocking in Nell's arms, had blurted out all of it. Nell had wanted to rush over to the living wagon and add her own punches to Sam's. Danny was a complete bastard. Claudia kept repeating how it was all her fault, how she deserved it, until Nell wanted to scream. Claudia – bright, brave Claudia – had been reduced to this – by her brother. For the first time in her life she was ashamed to be a Bradley. She and Claudia had drunk and spilled brandies and said the same things again and again and cried some more. Then Sam had arrived, kissed Nell's cheek, promised to be in touch, and taken Claudia away.

Nell had paced her living wagon all night, unable to sleep, unable to forget.

Now it was a glorious morning. Silent and scented, with the heat being dragged from the earth by a spiralling sun. Nell, barefooted on the warm, damp grass, simply couldn't believe that any of it had happened. That she hadn't *known*. Of course she knew – as everyone knew – that there were problems; but she'd never guessed at the brutality or the humiliation. Poor Claudia. Why hadn't she confided in anyone? Why hadn't she told her what was going on? They'd talked so many times – and Claudia always *joked* about it. Always went back to Danny. Always tried so hard. Because she thought that was the right thing to do. Nell, feeling that she should have been able to do something to prevent it, wanted to cry. So much was clear now. It had been a nightmare of a night.

Ross had forced his way into Danny's trailer immediately

Claudia was out of the way, and had stayed in there. He was still there as far as Nell knew. Peter had joined them this morning as soon as the elder Bradleys had arrived from Highcliffe. They were probably holding a male-bonding session or a post-mortem or both. Nell didn't care.

And Sam? She still wasn't sure about Sam's involvement – although she knew that he'd always been fond of Claudia. But was it something more? Or had he just been defending his sister-in-law as he would have defended anyone? Claudia hadn't mentioned Sam – and Nell hadn't asked.

Naturally, the whole fairground had been buzzing with the scandal since last night. Nell heard nothing but whispers. There were dozens of permutations of the same few questions. Had Danny really treated Claudia like that? Why had she put up with it? How long had it been going on? Sam and Claudia – were they having an affair? Sam hitting Danny? It was unheard-of! Sam didn't even have a temper – did he? Where had Claudia and Sam gone? Where could they go – they'd left everything behind them, hadn't they?

Loyalties were divided. No one, it seemed, was neutral. The Mackenzie twins were firmly in Danny's camp, saying loudly – although they shut up the minute they knew Nell was listening – that if Claudia and Sam were having an affair then Danny had every right to exert his authority. Nell had silenced them with a few sharply chosen words. Most people seemed to be on Claudia's side, if, as was rumoured, Danny had beaten her up.

Everyone seemed to think that Claudia and Sam would hole up for a few days until the hoo-ha died down and then come back and carry on as normal. Nell knew they wouldn't. They would never be able to. She wondered if they might have started to travel up north to Claudia's family, but thought it unlikely. Claudia had very little to do with them. And no showland family was going to welcome a scandal of this sort on their doorstep. She'd tried ringing them but both mobiles were switched off.

Nell didn't know who had telephoned Adele and Peter, and Clem Percival. She assumed it was Ross, although what for was anyone's guess. All they were doing was making matters worse by speculation and accusation; neither of which would bring Claudia back.

'Oh, bugger.' She dashed away her tears. Life without Sam and Claudia would be unbearable. Travelling with the unspeakable Danny, married to Ross . . .

'Any chance of some breakfast?' On cue Ross opened the door of Danny's living wagon and called across to her. 'We're starving.'

'Tough. Get it yourselves.' Nell scowled. The nerve of the man. She'd cooked for the gaff lads hours ago. She sure as hell wasn't going to be playing waitress to bloody Danny.

'Have a heart.' Ross, grey-faced, bleary-eyed and unshaven, walked towards her. 'It's been hell in here all night. The poor guy's distraught –'

'Distraught?' Nell knew the tiredness was making her screech. 'What would he know about distraught? I should think Claudia was fairly intimate with distraught, wouldn't you?'

Ross rubbed his eyes. 'Hardly. She seems to have been keeping her intimacy very nicely in the family.'

'And what if she has? I don't blame her. Sam is worth a million of Danny.'

'Nell!' Ross looked horrified. 'You don't mean that. You're tired. You're upset –'

'I'm feeling bloody guilty! We should all be feeling bloody guilty. We stood by and let it happen! We should have stopped him ages ago!'

'How could we? It's private – between husband and wife. If Claudia didn't complain too much about it, I'd say that she made up the abuse stories to cover up her little fling with Sam, wouldn't you?'

'No, I wouldn't. And you're a fool, Ross, if you believe that. You've obviously been subjected to far too much of Danny's brainwashing. All I can say is that if he can still spout so much crap, then Sam didn't hit him half hard enough.'

The Mackenzie family were listening. Clem and Adele appeared from Ross's trailer at the sound of raised voices.

Peter, looking every one of his fifty-seven years and a few more, peered through Danny's window. Nell felt so sorry for him. He'd be very torn between his sons – and none of this would do his heart condition any good at all. She wished he hadn't come. She wished her mother had made him stay at home in Highcliffe. She smiled at her father, hoping he understood. Luckily Danny stayed inside the living wagon, nursing his bruised jaw or his bruised pride, whichever was currently giving him most pain.

Nell looked at them all. 'Well, its true. And if any of you – any one of you – take Danny's side against Claudia or Sam, then I'll never, ever, speak to you again.'

'Nell!' Ross was moving even closer. 'Come on, sweetheart. Calm down. Look, I know you and Claudia were close, but you're Danny's family, for Christ's sake. And families stick together . . .'

'You stick with him if you want to. I'll never have anything to do with him again!'

She tore along the venue of deserted stalls, the flinty path making her stumble, the sharp stones like needles in her bare feet. She was desperately tired – but the show must go on, she thought hysterically. In a few hours it would be all lights and music and jollity. The rides and the joints closed in around her. It was stifling. Her tiny world was suffocating her.

'Nell,' Terry swung down from the Beast Wagon. 'Is there anything I can do?'

She stopped between the sheeted-up darts stall and the mobile canteen with its incongruously cheerful adverts for hot dogs and burgers, candyfloss and toffee apples. 'I don't think so, thanks. I know all the lads were up in arms this morning – but half of them work for Danny. They'll have to keep their mouths shut if they want to keep their jobs.'

'Alfie and Mike were worried about the paratrooper. Like, with Sam gone, and now that Danny's got Barry and Ted on the waltzer, they wondered –'

'I'm sure the paratrooper will be open tonight. Ross and Danny will make sure of that – and it they don't then I will.

Alfie and Mike can run it themselves. They know the ropes. Just tell them not to worry.'

'OK. But you will tell me if you hear from them, won't you? They were great to me – Sam and Claudia – that night at the police station and afterwards. I'd like to kill fucking Danny. He always treated her like dirt.'

'I know.' Nell felt the tears welling up in the back of her throat again. 'Look, as soon as I hear, I'll let you know. But honestly, in the meantime, just keep out of Danny's way.'

She drifted through the remainder of the side stuff and sat on the steps of the dodgems' pay-box. Birds were singing in the high trees and the air fluttered with butterflies. It must be the same as this when someone died, Nell thought, scrubbing at the ground with her toes. Everything going on as normal when you think it should stop. Life outside being the same when inside you're screaming.

Logistically, the loss of Sam and Claudia wouldn't cause problems for very long. The gaff lads could work the paratrooper; Mercedes and Nyree-Dawn would be delighted to be elevated to the hoopla; spare pairs of hands would be co-opted in from the Percival minions before they left Monkton Regis. The show, she thought bitterly, would definitely go on . . .

'Nell, love,' Adele sat wearily beside her. 'Oh, Nell – what a balls-up.'

Despite her misery, Nell smiled. 'That about sums it up. What are you going to do?'

'Nothing.' Adele jiggled the golden guitars. 'There's nothing we can do. I knew – I knew about Claudia –'

'What? And you didn't say anything? For God's sake –'

'Oh, no. Not the bedroom stuff.' Adele looked embarrassed. 'God, no. I'd have stepped in long ago if I'd known about that. I mean Claudia and Sam – I saw them together at Blenheim. They were kissing. I knew then . . .'

'Christ! I didn't even suspect.' Nell shook her head. 'And does Dad know?'

'No. Best not worry him with that as well, I thought.

Anyway, I could have been mistaken – I spoke to them about it – they said they were messing around. And I wanted to believe them. I love them both. Claudia has always been like a second daughter.' Adele sighed heavily. 'After all, we had the Crash'n'Dash and the gallopers to throw at your father – and they were realities. I thought anything else might be a bit too much. Anyway –'

Nell's phone burst into its 'Ride of the Valkyries' and they looked at each other. Claudia and Sam? Nell snatched at the aerial, yanking it up eagerly, her words spilling over themselves. The answering voice didn't belong to anyone she knew. For a second her tired brain couldn't quite assimilate the words. Five-day course . . . paperwork OK . . . start Monday . . . nine o'clock . . . OK?

God! Big Wheelers. Jack's HGV course! Was it less than twenty-four hours ago that she'd telephoned to book it? Less than twenty-four hours ago that she and Jack and the Downland Trusters had beaten John Carter's build-up time – admittedly without the organ, the lighting and the horses, all of which would have been far too heavy to have been included in that first build-up – by ten minutes? They'd toasted themselves in freezing Beck's, and she'd gazed at the rounding boards and wanted to cry. She'd done a lot of crying since. It seemed like a lifetime ago.

Adele was watching and listening intently as Nell confirmed the details.

'Just a – um – bit of business.' She punched out Jack's number. 'Heavy goods training . . .'

'For the lads?' Adele raised an unpainted eyebrow, and Nell noticed for the first time that her mother wasn't wearing any make-up. She looked soft and vulnerable. 'Only I thought they'd all been trained? I thought –'

'Er – Terry.' Nell blushed. She hated lying. There was no reason why her mother shouldn't know about Jack, was there? Was there? His mobile was switched off, too, and she gave a sigh of annoyance.

'Terry? Is he old enough? I thought –'

'Mum, it's not important. We've got a lot more important things to sort out. Like the money, the business. I mean, the paratrooper belongs to Sam. And if Claudia isn't coming back, then she's still entitled to a share of the overall takings. You and Dad ought to be seeing the bank manger or the solicitor or both and getting things sorted out.'

'Oh, Ross said he'd see to all that.'

Nell groaned. Of course he would. Ross and Danny would have it all neatly sewn up by the end of the day. Sam and Claudia would probably never see another penny from Bradleys – and Clem Percival would move mountains in the Guild to make sure that they didn't make a fresh start if Ross told him to do so.

Adele rubbed her eyes. 'We all ought to try and get some sleep. I – I don't really want to see Danny. Your father will have said all that is necessary. I can't believe he hit her –'

'He didn't. I'm sure he didn't. What he did was far worse really. He abused her – and frightened her and made her believe she was in the wrong all the time. And yes, OK, maybe there were faults on both sides, but she didn't deserve that.'

'No she didn't. Still,' Adele tried to smile, 'we've got your wedding to look forward to, haven't we?'

The birds were singing. The butterflies filled the air. Life was returning to even more normality; someone had started a generator and somewhere music was spilling from an open window. She couldn't marry Ross. She couldn't marry Ross and travel with Danny.

'I suppose so. Although I don't feel much like thinking about lifelong commitment and Happy Ever After at the moment.'

'No, I don't suppose you do. Poor Claudia.'

Adele closed her eyes. Nell could see the lines and the broken veins, usually so carefully camouflaged. She leaned her head on her mother's shoulder. 'I don't think Ross would turn out to be like Danny, Mum. But how the hell does anyone know until they've lived together?'

Adele pulled Nell to her. 'It's a gamble. But you and Ross have known each other for so long, I'm sure you wouldn't be taking any risks. Maybe that's where flatties have the edge over us. They test-drive their relationships first, don't they? Do you think Ross would agree to that? A sort of trial run?'

Nell wanted to laugh. Adele was the last person on earth to condone living in sin. 'It's more involved than that. It's having to stick with Danny, when I hate him so much. And I'd have to because Ross and Danny have already ordered extra Jessons machines – the expansion is well on course. If I want to travel on my own with the gallopers, then marrying Ross is the only way that I'll get the Memory Lane Fair on the road – unless Clem would give us the trucks as an "over the brush" present instead.'

But she knew that he wouldn't. So did Adele. With Clem's power it was marry Ross or face a life in the non-Guild wilderness.

'Clem was right,' Adele said bitterly, stroking Nell's hair. 'It is all my bloody fault. I wanted to bring you and Ross together. I interfered by buying the Crash'n'Dash – and look what's happened.'

'It's not your fault.' Nell's face was muffled in the pale pink cotton bosom. Her mother may not have had time for the make-up but she'd managed the earrings and the Obsession. 'It's not anyone's fault. It's just life. Full of ups and downs. Like a roundabout – swings and bloody roundabouts.'

She thought about the gallopers, about the Downland Trusters, about Jack. Especially about Jack. She'd let them all believe that she could make their dreams come true. She thought about the 'Petronella Bradley's Memory Lane Fair' emblazoned on the golden rounding boards, of the organ, of playing 'Paree' on that inaugural outing. There must be something she could do, some decision she could make, that would unravel this appalling mess.

'Ross always said he wanted a three-way split.' She looked at her mother. 'And maybe that's what he's going to get. I've got to go and see someone first though. Look, Claudia and

Sam will be in touch whenever they can. She's safe now. I don't give a toss about Danny – and neither should you. There are more important things to be sorted out. Would you like a visit back home?'

'Highcliffe? What for? Not until all the legal side has been sorted out. I don't think Peter and I should leave until that's been done and –'

Nell was scrambling to her feet. 'Not Highcliffe. Fox Hollow. I want to show you my part of the business.' She hauled Adele after her. 'Let's go and get the slap on. Let's leave the boring legal and business side to the men, Mum. Let's go and have some bloody fun.'

Adele still looked bemused as Nell rattled the Volvo into the yard at Fox Hollow. They'd made a fist of showering and putting on some make-up, although weariness meant it wasn't as effective as usual. The yard was deserted. The Roadster was missing. Nell was fairly relieved. Much as she wanted to see Jack, this visit would be easier without him.

She unlocked the shed, switched on the lights and waited for her mother's reaction.

Adele walked slowly towards the again-dismantled gallopers, looked at everything, lifted the tarpaulin on the Gavioli, stroked the immaculately decorated horses, then finally stared at the rounding boards. She didn't speak.

Nell was overwhelmed by the essence of Jack. His living quarters were still between the ghost train and the caterpillar, although Adele didn't appear to have noticed; the smell of him was everywhere. A pair of paint-splashed black jeans and a blue T-shirt were screwed up by the music cupboard and Nell picked them up, meaning to put them on the bed. She bunched them in her hands and laid her cheek against them, closing her eyes.

'Nell,' Adele's voice penetrated her thoughts. 'Nell, it's wonderful – incredible. I had no idea – and keeping them here. Ross and Danny kept ringing me to find out where they were. I would never have thought –' She touched Nell's arm very gently. 'This is it for you, isn't it? Not Matterhorns and white knuckles? Oh God, Nell. What have I done to you?'

Nell bit her lip. A thousand emotions were tangling inside her and if she gave way to one of them she'd probably howl. Yes, this was her life. This was her future. The Memory Lane Fair was all she'd ever wanted, and now she was so close to realising the dream, she couldn't and wouldn't let it go.

Claudia had been brave enough to throw away her security. Claudia had eventually found the courage to change her life. Could she be as brave as Claudia? Could she take that final, irrevocable step? Nell thrust Jack's clothes on the bed and put her arms round Adele's waist. The Body Beautiful had ensured that it was trimmer and firmer, but it was still the waist she'd clung to since childhood. 'Oh, Mum. I really need a hug.'

'God, Nell. I should have let Danny have a bloody smaller Jessons ride – and Sam have whatever he wanted – and paid for you to have trucks and things for this lot. I should never have splashed out every penny on the Crash'n'Dash! I should have found out what you all wanted – not decided what you should have. I should have *thought*. Instead I barged in and messed everything up.'

'You haven't. You've been kind and generous – and you thought you were acting for the best. I've been thinking – Once the gallopers are on the road, I don't have to travel with Danny, do I? Sam can sell the paratrooper to the new Bradley–Percival amalgamation and start again somewhere. Things always work out . . .'

Adele didn't look convinced, Nell knew as she pulled away from her mother and dashed the back of her hand across her eyes. 'Anyway, now you've seen all this I hope you'll understand. I still don't want anyone to know where they are. Look, I've just got to leave a note for – for one of the guys who has been helping with the restoration, and then I think we should get back to the gaff and make sure that whatever Ross and Danny have decided to do, Sam and Claudia don't lose out. OK?'

Adele watched as Nell scribbled a note for Jack, with details and dates of the HGV course, and pinned it to the fridge door in the kitchen. She knows, Nell realised. She knows, without reading it. She knows it's not for Terry.

'Mum, there's something else –'

The something else was drowned by the roar of the Roadster out in the yard. Nell's heart turned over. A shiver of excitement zipped through her body. She stood in the kitchen doorway, her mouth dry.

Jack, of course, knew she was there. He'd seen the Volvo. He was running his fingers through his hair, swinging the skid-lid, grinning, as he walked into the shed, looking for her. He was wearing the clean black jeans and a faded denim shirt. Nell melted.

Gathering her senses, she arranged her face into a welcoming smile. He looked so much better. He was happier, calmer, obviously coming to terms with his loss.

'Hi. You look lovely. This is a brilliant suprise. I thought you weren't coming over today, otherwise I'd've waited and whisked you off to the Maybush. I've been into Newbury. Made appointments with –'

Adele appeared in the doorway behind her. Nell took a deep breath. 'Mum, this is Jack Morland – he's done all the painting. Jack, this is my mother –'

They eyed each other warily, then smiled, and said all the right things.

Nell wiped her damp palms on her jeans. 'Jack, I've – er – left a note about Big Wheelers. They – um – can fit you in on Monday. Will that be all right?'

'Great. Thanks.' Jack was still looking at Adele. 'I know this must come as something of a shock. I hope you're not too disappointed. I mean, Nell explained about your plans for the expansion, but this is where her heart is.'

Adele straightened her pale-pink shoulders, and jangled her earrings. She looked from Nell to Jack and back again. Then she smiled. 'Yes,' she said quietly. 'I've just realised that . . .'

327

CHAPTER TWENTY-NINE

It was probably one of the strangest weeks of Nell's life. It had taken on an *Alice Through the Looking-Glass* quality: nothing was quite as it seemed.

No one had heard from Claudia and Sam. Their phones were still switched off, and even the travelling grapevine had failed to pick up on their whereabouts. Nell wasn't unduly worried. If – and she believed Adele on this one – Sam loved Claudia, she knew that he'd cherish her. He'd make the right decisions for them both, and use his gentleness to heal the scars.

Jack was away on his HGV course. She hadn't phoned him. Nor had she returned to Fox Hollow. There were a million other things she had to do.

Adele had said very little after her impromptu excursion to meet the gallopers – and Jack. They'd returned to Monkton Regis in the Volvo, and Adele had perked up enough to sing 'His Latest Flame' quite chirpily under her breath for most of the journey. By the time they got back to the gaff Clem Percival had left. Peter, Danny and Ross had contacted the solicitor, the accountant and the bank manager and seemed relieved, petulant and smug in that order. Nell hadn't asked any questions. She knew what she was going to do, and the fewer people she involved, the better.

Her parents left for Highcliffe just before the fair opened. Adele had hugged Nell. 'Ring whenever you want to talk. I do understand, now. Really. It's not what I wanted, of course, but I honestly wish you all the luck in the world.' She eased herself into the Gucci loafers and paused before clambering into the Jag. 'He's gorgeous, Nell. Such a pity he's a flatty –'

Ross, as she'd suspected, had taken control during the remainder of the fair's time at Monkton Regis. He'd reorganised the staffing, brought in spare Percival workers, installed the preening pair of Mackenzie twins in the hoopla, and no one outside could have spotted the difference. He and Danny took it in turns to staff the Crash-'n'Dash and the waltzer, and spent nearly all their spare time together.

Danny's face was spectacularly swollen – and beginning to change from red to blue and yellow.

'He matches the Bradley paintwork a treat,' Nell said to Terry as they worked the dodgems. 'Pity Sam didn't have time to livery the rest of him.'

She hadn't spoken to her brother, and he avoided her. It couldn't go on, Nell knew, any more than the constrained atmosphere between herself and Ross. Things would have to come to a head. Very soon.

They were due to pull out the following day and move once more towards Oxford en route for St Giles' Fair. Making sure that Terry was OK on the dodgems and that he understood that, should anyone ask, she'd be back shortly and no, he couldn't say where she'd gone, Nell drove away from Monkton Regis in the gathering twilight and headed for Chipping Norton.

It was a sultry evening, with the sky marbled lilac and pink and gold. Clem's Jessons rides dominated the horizon for miles, adding to the rainbow. Nell parked the Volvo in a side street and pushed her way through the fairground crowds.

Marcia, taking money on the awesome Ice-Breaker, drew back her lips in a sort of smile. Her teeth, Nell thought, looked as though they were about to take on a life of their own.

'Ross with you, Nell? He didn't say –'

'No. He's far too busy. I've just called over to have a word with Clem.'

'Everything all right? Between you? I mean, after all that awful trouble. I always said that Claudia was no better than she ought to be – and Sam! Well, I know he's your brother, love, but he was always so *dreamy*. I often said to Adele that I thought it might be drugs – Nell? Nell!'

Nell skipped quickly down the Ice-Breaker's blue-and-silver steps before she could help Marcia's teeth in their bid for freedom. Melody and Clementine and their husbands were toeing the Percival line and working their pristine socks off on the other white-knucklers, she noticed, fluttering her fingers at them as she passed. Smug cows, she thought, knowing that they expected to be matrons of honour – Marcia had even suggested that they'd look really nice in varying shades of pink. Not that that was going to be an option now. Oh, the joy of liberty, she grinned to herself, expertly side-stepping the crowds. She'd never be able to thank Claudia enough.

Claudia had had the guts to put up with Danny – but still made her own decision not to have a baby; Claudia had been bravely knocking back the pill; Claudia had inadvertently set her free. And if Claudia had had the courage to gamble on a dream, then she could do it too.

Nell finally found Clem barracking a couple of unfortunate gaff lads who had been foolish enough to think that dehydration meant they could skip off for five minutes and have a drink. She touched his arm. 'Sorry to interrupt. This won't take a second, but I wondered if I could have a word?'

Clem, like Marcia, immediately ignored her and looked over her shoulder for Ross.

Jesus, she thought, it's happening already. We're a pair, a couple, you don't get one without the other. 'He's not with me. He's far too busy wheeling and dealing with the Bradley–Percival amalgamation.'

Clem nodded. 'Ah, right. So, what can I do for you, Princess?'

She led him away from the relieved gaff lads; from the blinding neon lights; from the roar of the music and the thump of the generators; and finished up on the outer limits of the fair where a pair of very elderly travellers – even older than Mr and Mrs Mac – were trying to entice teenagers into the Fun House.

'I want to stop the trucks order.'

'You can't.' Once he was·out of sight of his family, Clem immediately lit a cigarette and inhaled indulgently. 'They're practically done and finished. Christ, you haven't changed your mind about the gallopers and stuff, have you? We've got 'em ready. All the wagons. Ross reckons that the old-time stuff will go a bomb – I've already got you some tentative bookings. Bloody hell, what is it with you Bradleys? Why can't you just make money like everyone else? Something else taken your fancy now, has it?'

Nell said nothing.

Clem sighed. 'For Christ's sake, Nell. I haven't got all day. What's your game?'

'No game. I don't want to travel with Danny any more. I want the Bradley–Percival amalgamation to buy me out with the dodgems. I want to know if the money raised from the sale of the dodgems will pay for the trucks. I'm also not going to marry Ross – although I haven't told him yet. And –' she added quickly, watching Clem's face change colour beneath the onslaught of pulsing lights, 'I don't want you to. All I want to know is where I stand if I don't marry him.'

'Where you stand?' Clem bellowed, scaring a hot-dog-eating couple out of their wits. 'I'll tell you where you fucking stand! Out in the cold with that slag of a sister-in-law and your poncey brother – that's where you stand! Understood?'

'Perfectly. Thank you. It's nice to know I've made the right decision. So, if I don't marry Ross then I can't go anywhere except non-Guild sites, is that what you're saying? School fêtes, village galas –'

'And then only if you're very lucky!' Clem roared again, this time even startling the deaf pensioners stumbling up the steps of the Fun House. 'And no, the money from the dodgems wouldn't go halfway to clearing the truck debt, so you'll have nothing to transport your junk around in anyway. No transport and no sites. No money. No life.'

Oh, I'll have a life, Nell thought, surprised at how calm she felt. No money maybe – and probably the dregs of the gaffs – but a life. My life. And how quickly the gallopers had changed from fortune-making preservation pieces into a heap of junk. And how very much Clem looked like Ross when he was angry . . .

She turned away, ignoring his bellows, hoping that she'd get back to Monkton Regis before Clem reached Ross on the mobile. Hoping that this feeling of serene euphoria wouldn't desert her before she did the most difficult thing she'd ever had to do in her life.

'Brilliant tonight,' Terry greeted her, showing her the takings, obviously keen for Nell to know that he hadn't pocketed any of them. 'I could get used to this. Running me own ride. Still, I guess that's just a dream, innit? I mean gaff lads don't own rides, do they?'

'Not very often, no.' Nell watched as he checked the cars for lost property, and deftly switched off the generator. 'Terry – can I have a word, please?'

'I never nicked nothing, Nell. Honest.'

'I know.' She took a deep breath in the darkness. 'It's nothing like that. Listen –'

She'd broken his heart, she realised that. Destroyed his dreams too. It didn't matter how many times she repeated that the dodgems would be staying – it was she who was leaving – and that he'd still have his job, they both knew he wouldn't. Danny hated him, Ross would collude with Danny – and Terry had always had a surprising amount of integrity.

That was it then, she thought, walking towards the Crash'n'Dash, as Ross closed down for the night. Adele had guessed – so Peter surely would have been told. Clem knew – so the whole of the Percival hierarchy would have been informed. And she'd told Terry. All she had to do now was to explain things to Ross.

'Me and Danny are going to open a bottle of malt.' He secured the pay-box. 'Fancy joining us? Letting bygones be bygones?'

She shook her head. 'I want to talk to you.'

'That makes a change.'

She watched him in the dusky purple light. He was so very handsome, she thought, and he'd always be rich. He'd expand Bradleys until it was up in the stratosphere of the Guild. She'd want for nothing. 'I think we should talk in private.'

'Suits me. My place or yours?'

'Yours.'

He couldn't even do that without explaining to Danny. He shouted up into the waltzer that he'd be five minutes and to leave some Laphroaig. Five minutes? Was that all she was worth? Walking towards her, he switched on his phone. It rang immediately.

'Don't answer it. Please. It'll be your father. Listen to me first.'

Ross switched the phone off again. 'I don't understand. Is it Claudia and Sam? Have you heard from them?'

'No. It's to do with us.'

'Great.' He slid his arm round her shoulders. 'My favourite subject.'

Why was it, she thought, that the words simply didn't ring true any more?

She sat uneasily on the edge of the pearlised leather, refusing a drink. Ross sprawled alongside her, relaxed, sipping whisky and ice from cut-glass, looking golden and glorious. She stared at the floor, at the ceiling – anywhere but at Ross – and told him that she wanted him to buy her out. That she wanted to leave. That she wouldn't marry him.

He didn't speak. He *wasn't* like Clem, she thought, swallowing tears. It would have been so much easier if he'd shouted and sworn and got angry. Then she would have felt vindicated. As it was, she felt guilty and shameful. He wasn't right for her and she didn't love him, but she had never wanted to hurt him.

'Ross? Say something.'

'It'll bugger up the nostalgia stuff a bit.'

'What?' She jerked up her head. 'No screams of betrayal and heartbreak?'

He reached out and took her hand. 'Nell, sweetheart, I don't hear any of those coming from you. Why should I be any different?'

Nell blinked. 'But you love me – don't you? You want to marry me? Isn't that what all this was about? The Brain-Scrambler and the amalgamation? You and my misguided mother plotting to get us together?'

Ross sat up, still holding her hand. Nell thought he looked as though he was going to laugh. She hoped he was going to laugh. She'd kill herself if he cried.

'That was your ma's idea, yes. It wasn't strictly mine. Jesus, Nell. I've known you for ever. We've always been good mates. And yes, I kept asking you to marry me – but only because I knew you'd say no. Shit, marrying you would be like marrying one of my sisters! There's no spark, sweetheart, is there? There's a good working partnership, but we'd be continually fighting for supremacy – and we know each other inside out. There'd be no excitement . . .'

She looked at him in amazement. He *was* laughing, the bastard. She shook her hand free and struggled to her feet. She poured a measure of whisky into a second tumbler and added water. 'So what did you do it for?'

He held out his tumbler for a refill and Nell topped it up. He raised the crystal in a mock salute. 'Cheers. I take it this is kiss, truth or dare time? OK, then. I went along with it to get away from my bloody parents. To gain my freedom. To stop being Mr Percival Junior and having Mother and Father planning my every move. The amalgamation was the only way I could see of escaping and preserving my sanity. Of being allowed to grow up – and if it meant having to marry you to cement the deal – well,' he grinned at her, 'I could have lived with it, I suppose.'

'You total shit!' Nell bounced on the pearlised leather with no regard for the mess or the expense as the whisky slopped everywhere. 'Why the hell didn't you tell me before?'

'How could I? I was under the impression that it was part of the deal. Oh, I knew you weren't exactly panting to tear up the aisle in virgin white, but I couldn't see any way out of it without alienating both lots of parents and screwing up my escape bid.' He hugged her. 'We'll always be friends, though, won't we? And now that you've told me all this, you'll stay?'

'Yes to the first, no to the second.' Her cheek was pressed against his shirt. It might as well have been her father. It was comforting and familiar. Nothing more. 'I've told your dad tonight what I'm doing. It nullifies the truck agreement and the gaffs, of course, as they were wedding presents.'

'Well, thank God for that. Oh, not the trucks, I mean that's a sod for you, but the fact that you've told him. Now they'll blame you for the split. I'll still be written into the Percival will.'

'You really are a conniving, entrepreneurial, unprincipled bastard, aren't you?' She kissed his cheek. 'So, will you? Talk to Danny and get him to buy the dodgems?'

'Might as well.' Ross wiped whisky from his fingers. 'We've already put wheels in motion to buy the paratrooper and put the money into an account for Sam wherever he is. I mean, he won't come back. This isn't quite how I'd envisaged the three-way partnership, but it'll suit me. But what about you? What will you do?'

Nell wasn't sure. Overwhelmed by relief, she was suddenly incredibly tired. There'd be money from the dodgems which would surely make some part-payment on the trucks. She was a Guild member herself. As long as Clem didn't have her blackballed she'd be able to apply for her own sites, wouldn't she? They might not be the prestige ones she'd planned, but they could start small – and grow . . .

'I'll be fine. Don't worry about me.'

'I never did sweetheart,' Ross said, and kissed her.

CHAPTER THIRTY

Claudia stretched and looked up from *The World's Fair*. They hadn't made the headlines – again. Nearly two weeks after their midnight dash, and there hadn't been one whiff of scandal. At least, not in the papers. No doubt the fairgrounds were alive with nothing else.

She curled beneath Sam's scarlet duvet, luxuriating that morning, as every other, in the long lie-ins, the breakfasts in bed, the cosseting. The living wagon, so overtly masculine with its red and dove-grey colour scheme, had become her haven. She'd had time to lick her wounds, probe her scars, and delight in the gradual healing.

Not that it had been all gentle, she grinned to herself. Sam was too intelligent to think that she'd need kid-glove treatment for ever. She'd expected to feel waves of guilt about walking away from her marriage, but so far she hadn't experienced the slightest twinge. Sam had told her that they would probably appear later, at irrational moments, when she was better able to handle them. He assured her that one's body had built-in healing mechanisms. That as she grew stronger, she'd experience things that she'd be unable to cope with during her present vulnerability. It made sense; and even if it didn't happen, the belief that it would, made each day a little easier.

Being with Sam was a revelation. She hadn't realised that

such relaxed happiness was possible. He seemed to enjoy spoiling her, and she certainly loved the attention. She knew he was weaning her away from the horrors very slowly. They'd teased each other and laughed a lot, and even had one row over a television programme. But it hadn't been the flinching, cringing battering-pulse-rate sort of row that she'd been used to. It had been quite grown-up really – it was a shame it had ended in a cushion fight . . .

And this, she thought, rolling out of bed in her pyjamas and peering out of the window, had been a stroke of genius. Sam's genius, of course. She hadn't even been thinking straight the night they'd left. Sam deciding to steer clear of travellers for a while, or at least until she'd regained her strength, had been brilliant.

After driving for most of the night they'd pulled the living wagon on to a tourist campsite in the Forest of Dean – having to pay two ground rents to accommodate its forty-foot length – and had lived like flatties on holiday. They were among touring caravans and frame tents, and apart from a few appreciative comments on the luxury of their accommodation, no one took any notice of them. It had been great. Joining in barbecues and drinking cheap beer every night in the humid clubhouse where sunburnt families laughed their socks off at rather blue comedians. Claudia had enjoyed every minute of it. But she knew that the time had now come to move on.

She wandered into the living room. Sam's bedding was still strewn across the sofa and she folded the sheets, stowing them with the pillows in the seat lockers. She loved him – he loved her – but there was no pressure. She was sleeping well for the first time in years, alone, safe and happy, knowing that he was only feet away from her.

They had talked about nothing but Danny that first night. They'd laid all the ghosts. There was nothing more to be said. No secrets left. They'd made a pact not to mention him again. They knew they would never go back, that their future was uncertain, and that there were still Adele and Peter to face. Sam had said there was plenty of time. They had also decided to keep their phones switched off for at least the first week. Claudia had ached to ring Nell, but felt that she couldn't do it until she knew she wouldn't cry the minute she heard Nell's voice.

The time was nearly right, she thought, as she switched on the kettle, set out the mugs, and spooned in instant coffee, ready for Sam's return. She was stronger, the nightmares were receding, and her belief in herself was re-emerging.

'Put that muck back in the jar,' Sam galloped up the living-wagon steps two at a time and waved a bottle of Moët beneath her nose. 'We're celebrating.'

'We are?' She kissed him. Tentatively, because she was still not quite used to it, and because she knew that he wanted her and she didn't want to be unfair. 'What exactly?'

'This.' Sam waved a piece of printed paper in front of her eyes, scrabbling in the cupboards for the crystal flutes at the same time. 'I've been to the bank –'

Claudia knew. It was one of the problems. Not having any money. They'd used Sam's credit card for food and petrol. Claudia, whose card had been linked to Danny's, had cut hers up and hurled it from the living-wagon window along with her wedding ring. Sam had been quite shocked about the ring – but she was absolutely sure that it was the final, irrevocable step. She considered herself no longer married to Danny. The ring that had bound them together now languished amidst burger wrappers and cigarette ends. It seemed fitting, somehow. It didn't, of course, solve any financial problems.

Oh, there was definitely money owed to them from the paratrooper, but they wouldn't touch that until they'd spoken to either Nell or Ross. They both had their own accounts with Bradleys, of course, but they wouldn't last for ever, especially if they had to start from scratch. In fact, between them they'd probably got enough money for one medium-sized machine that went out of fashion last season and a couple of joints. Claudia felt guilty about Sam leaving the paratrooper behind. It had been his inheritance; his only form of income apart from the divvying-up of the annual profits. He'd left everything for her. It didn't matter how many times he reassured her that it was what he wanted, she still experienced hot waves of shame.

Then there was the question of gaffs. They wouldn't be able to join the usual circuit, and Claudia was adamant that she wouldn't return to her northern family. They'd scoured the last two weeks' *World's Fair*s to see what opportunities were available. With rides, there were several – without, none at all. Unless, of course, they wanted to be gaff lads. They'd decided that this would be their final option, should all else fail.

Smiling, she watched him pouring the champagne. After years of practice, she wasn't counting any chickens. Sam had made an appointment at the local branch of the Midland – the Bradleys' bank – that morning. He had said he wouldn't hold his breath. Neither had she. She'd experienced one miracle, to expect two would be just plain greedy.

'So?' She raised her glass to him. 'I gather it went well?'

'This well,' Sam showed her the bank statement.

'Jesus!' The champagne slopped over her fingers. 'It's a fortune! Where did that come from?'

'The paratrooper, apparently.' Sam's grin was ear-to-ear. 'The guy at the bank was ace. He rang through to Oxford, confirmed that I was who I said I was – and they faxed me this. He asked all the questions for me. It seems that Ross and – um – well, the Bradley–Percival amalgamation has bought me out. Our wheel ruts must still have been damp when they decided to cut the cord – the greedy bastards. The cheque was cleared a couple of days ago.' He kissed the tip of her nose. 'Get dressed, chicken. We're going shopping.'

The getting dressed was a private joke. She had still only got the jeans and T-shirt she'd flitted in, and had been wearing rolled-up jeans of Sam's and the more shrunken of his shirts on chilly days, and just his T-shirts cinched in with a belt on the gloriously warm ones. She had never felt happier. The make-up had been an entirely different matter. She'd insisted that they break into their savings for mascara and lipstick – and a kohl pencil – oh, and some blusher. Claudia was adamant that however slobbily she was dressed, there was no way at all that she was sticking her nose outside the door without the basics.

They drove into Monmouth in the Shogun and Sam chattered about the bank and how things had to be on the up, and Claudia nodded and wondered if the bank manager in Oxford had been the same one that had put the sparkle in Nell's eyes. She wanted to talk to Nell. Very much. She wanted to thank her for giving her the courage to make that final decision. Nell had always been so strong, so principled, Claudia thought. Nell didn't want to marry Ross – and no amount of financial temptation or family pressure had persuaded her otherwise. She'd always had the dream about the gallopers and about falling in love, and against all odds she'd stuck to her guns and held on. Oh, sure – she was going to marry Ross now, but only because she'd fought for what she wanted, even if it meant abandoning the hearts and flowers. Nell, Claudia thought, was probably the bravest person she knew. After Sam, of course . . .

She thought she might ring her tonight. After all, Nell would know about the paratrooper deal by now. But Nell was part of Bradley–Percival, and because of that she'd probably never see Nell again.

After parking in the town centre, they had spent a small fortune on clothes. Claudia had been reluctant at first, insisting that it wasn't her money – it was Sam's. But Sam had waved away all objections, saying it was theirs – or, more excitingly, Bradley–Percival's. And therefore he couldn't think of a better way to spend it. They'd laughed at the irony and Sam had been brilliant – liking whatever she chose, whether it was sassy or smart, tarty or tasteful. They'd deliberately picked out one outfit as a 'cock-a-snook at the past and thanks for the cheque'. It was Lycra and tight and vivid crimson and Claudia adored it, promising him that she'd wear it whenever – if ever – they needed reminding of why they were together.

Walking back to the Shogun, Sam caught her hand. 'What's up? You're looking down again. Not regretting this are you?'

'I was just thinking of Nell. We used to have a blast buying clothes. I really miss her. Could we ring her? Tonight? We did promise –'

'Yeah,' Sam grinned and detoured into a rather swish restaurant. 'Lunch first, I think, courtesy of Bradley–Percival. We did promise. And we will. Actually, I think Nell might be our salvation.'

They discussed it over lunch. It made a lot of sense. Nell was going to be travelling with the gallopers and her other nostalgia rides, so if they spent the paratrooper money on a machine that would fit in, they could join her at whatever gaffs were available. Nothing to do with Ross and Danny. Nothing to do with Bradley–Percival. They'd be starting out on their own. OK, they realised that it would be pretty small-time compared to what they were used to. But it was so exciting – the challenge . . . They grinned at each other across the table, unaware of the other lunch-time eaters smiling at their enthusiasm.

When they got back to the campsite they scoured *The World's Fair*, made lists, dismissed some machines as either too modern or out of their financial league and others as too heavy to transport and build up – bearing in mind that they'd be flying solo to start with, finished the champagne, and nearly wore out the batteries on their phones making enquiries and offers.

By the end of the afternoon, Claudia and Sam were the proud possessors of a slip and a small big wheel. They'd bought them from the same owner, in Gloucestershire, who was selling up due to retirement and who was more than happy to include an elderly Foden wagon and drag in the price. Sam could drive the loads while Claudia drove the Shogun and living wagon. Sam agreed to put the cheque in the post that afternoon and that they'd collect the rides a week later as soon as it had cleared.

They sat on either end of the scarlet window seat and smiled at each other in triumph.

'Now we'll phone Nell,' Sam said, practically wringing the last drops out of the Moët bottle. 'And we won't tell her anything until we meet up. OK?'

Claudia nodded, fizzing with excitement. 'You speak to her, then. I'll only bawl. Oh, God, Sam – I'll never be able to thank you enough.'

'You already have,' he looked at her sparkling eyes, 'a million times.'

They met Nell two days later at the Fox Hollow winter quarters.

'Sneaky cow.' Claudia had grinned when Sam told her where Nell had hidden the gallopers. 'So bloody obvious, and yet no one would have thought of looking there.'

Claudia was like a child on a trip to the sea. The drive from the Forest of Dean seemed to take for ever and, being a passenger this time, she jigged impatiently for most of the journey. When they turned into the leafy Oxfordshire lanes and the signposts proclaimed that there were only five miles to go, she clasped her hands with delight.

'I know how you feel,' Sam said. 'The break has been brilliant but travelling is in the blood. God knows how flatties survive, being in the same place for fifty weeks of the year.'

They spent the next couple of miles in silence, feeling heartily sorry for those who hadn't been lucky enough to be born into the travelling profession.

Nell's Volvo was in the yard and Sam had scarcely stopped the Shogun before Claudia had tumbled out and was hurling herself towards the shed. The doors were wide open.

'Holy shit!' Claudia stopped short in amazement. 'Jeez, Sam! Come and look at this lot!'

They gazed in disbelief at the gallopers, the uncovered Gavioli, the ghost train and the caterpillar, all of which gleamed with fresh paint.

'Wow! Some expert Nell got to do this! It must have cost a bomb. God, they look incredible.' He grinned at Claudia. 'We'll have to ask Nell's painter to do some work on our stuff, otherwise we really are going to look like the poor relations.'

They walked among the machines, touching, marvelling at the expertise. No wonder, Claudia thought, suddenly overcome, Nell hated the thought of the Brain-Scrambler. This was simply perfection.

'Nell!' Claudia shouted. 'Where the hell are you?'

'Claudia?' Nell appeared in the doorway to the kitchen. 'I didn't hear you arrive. Oh – oh, bugger!'

They threw themselves into each other's arms and immediately burst into tears.

They both spoke at the same time, still crying, intermittently laughing. There were brief pauses for astounded exclamations before they plunged onwards. Claudia didn't reckon she'd caught half of what Nell said but it didn't really matter. There'd be plenty of time to fill in the gaps later. They'd got all the time in the world. They'd be together again. Travelling together. That was all that counted.

'. . . and so,' Sam was saying when he could get a word in, 'we've got a slip and a big wheel. It'll go great with this lot. All we need to know now is when do we start?'

'A slip and a big wheel will be incredible, but,' Nell's face fell, 'does that mean that you've spent all the paratrooper money?'

'Most of it. Well, it was two machines for the price of one, and the deal included a wagon and drag, so we've got transport –'

'Which is more than I have.'

Claudia wrinkled her nose, not understanding. The trucks were part of the deal, weren't they? Clem's wedding present?

Nell took a deep breath. 'As I'm not marrying Ross, I don't get the wagons or the automatic gaffs. It looks as though we're all out in the cold, doesn't it?'

'Not marrying Ross?' They looked at her in disbelief. If

344

Nell had said this earlier, they'd missed it in the eager gabble. 'Why on earth not?'

Nell bit her lip and told them.

There didn't seem to be any solution. Of course, Nell's money from the dodgems would, like Sam's, go partway to financing transport, but there was not going to be nearly enough for the gallopers and the organ and the other two rides. And even if they could afford lorries, where exactly were they going to go?

Claudia, leaving Sam and Nell discussing the various possibilities, wandered away to the back of the shed and stroked one of the horses. What incredible names they had. There was even one called Petronella. Someone had poured heart and soul into this. Oh, shit, she thought, we've come this far – we can't be beaten now. She was stunned that Nell wasn't marrying Ross; amazed that she'd cut loose from the Bradley–Percival amalgamation, and devastated that things might not work out because of this last small obstacle.

Not, Claudia realised, that it was that insignificant. In fact, it was pretty bloody significant indeed. If they were all going to be blackballed, they really would be reduced to the least prestigious sites. While this might be a major problem for Sam and Nell, she thought that it was infinitely preferable to her previous existence. But why should they be treated like pariahs? They were all Guild members, weren't they? Clem couldn't really prevent them applying for their own sites? If only they could find someone with enough money to provide transport, then surely they'd be able to overcome the rest.

As she hurried back to impart this stroke of genius, it appeared that Sam and Nell had come to the same conclusion.

'Great minds think alike.' Nell hugged her. 'Yeah, I was aware I could go it alone, but I wasn't sure that I had the guts. Now, with you two with me – Bradleys on tour yet again – I'm going to sort things out with the Guild first thing in the morning.'

'And the transport?' Claudia asked. 'I mean, I know it's a bit delicate, but what about the bank manager? I mean, you and he were quite pally. Hasn't he got any money? Couldn't you ask him for a loan, off the record, or something?'

Nell looked blank for a moment, then she blushed. Aha, Claudia thought, she's still torch-bearing! There may be hope here. She winked at Sam who looked mystified.

Nell shrugged. 'Actually, he – er – the bank manager is currently as skint as the rest of us. And I haven't seen him for a while. He's – he's currently on an HGV training course.'

CHAPTER THIRTY-ONE

It was probably ridiculous, Jack thought, folding the piece of paper carefully into his wallet, but he felt more proud of himself now than at any other time of his life.

The five-day driving course had been intensive, and despite feeling fairly confident about handling large vehicles, he had been intimidated by the forty-foot monster they'd introduced him to. However, as he'd hauled himself up behind the wheel on that first morning, he knew there was no way he was going to let Nell or the Memory Lane Fair down if he could help it. He'd indicated to his instructor that he was ready to go, had switched on the engine, and had moved – pretty smoothly, all things considered – into the final stage of achieving his dream.

But there had been times during the five days when he'd had time for reflection. Amidst all the euphoria was the nagging, dragging feeling that when all this was over, when he was as near to being a traveller as he was ever going to get, Nell would be marrying the man who had made it all possible.

It was ironic that just when he'd regained his single status, Nell should be announcing her engagement. Still, he'd reckoned, confidently cruising at motorway speed, Ross Percival would be far too busy travelling with the Crash-

'n'Dash and the other hydraulic machines to want to interfere in the Memory Lane Fair.

He'd liked her mother. He was sure he'd seen recognition of their situation in Adele's eyes. Though of course she'd never have accepted him as a son-in-law. And now he'd be with Nell as often as he wanted but not able to do anything about it. Look but definitely do not touch. Keep off. Property of Ross Percival. Jack had groaned and braked sharply and earned a reproach from his instructor.

There were still problems to overcome, he had realised as he mugged up the highway code in his hotel room, the evening before his test. Things like living accommodation. He couldn't stay at Fox Hollow indefinitely, and certainly not during the winter months when her family would be pulled into the yard and he'd be able to watch Nell and Ross together every day. He'd have to ask Nell about purchasing a caravan. Oh, no, he'd laughed, imagining her censure – a living wagon. Caravans were for – what was it she called him? oh, yeah – flatty holiday-makers. He was going to have to learn an entirely new language.

The driving course, and the preceding time at Fox Hollow when he'd painted himself practically into delirium, had salved his pain. He was more rational now about the loss of the baby. He didn't think of Fiona at all, and only occasionally thought about his parents. He had been to see his solicitor on the day Nell and her mother had come to the yard and organised that the deeds of the house should be made over to Fiona as sole owner. He'd changed their bank account into her name. He felt he could do no more.

And now, on the morning that he'd become the proud holder of a Class I licence, and was bursting to take Nell to the Maybush and tell her just how clever he'd been, there was this bloody summons from his father.

The message on his mobile had been terse. 'Meet me in the office. Ten on the dot.' Not even the softening of a greeting or a farewell. His father, it seemed, had not forgiven him for either of his defections. With some reluctance he headed the

Roadster towards Newbury, when everything in him wanted to be going the other way.

Bill Morland was not in the best of tempers. It was hot, the air conditioning was limping, and the new secretary who greeted Jack with the widest of smiles and the shortest of skirts, had apparently created some faux pas the previous day by putting letters in the wrong envelopes, leaving his father to field the incandescent telephone calls.

'Sit down,' Bill, shirtsleeves rolled uncharacteristically to his elbows, barked without looking up. There were three desk fans fighting a losing battle with the humidity.

Jack sat. He wanted to tell his father about the driving test, about his success. He knew he wouldn't bother.

'You're still unemployed then?' Bill turned it into a statement, raising his head for the first time. 'I've had no employers asking me for your P45 or pension details. No one contacting me regarding references. Have you even tried to find work?'

'I've got a job. I told you. I'm painting and –'

But Bill was in no mood for listening to anyone's aspirations, least of all his son's. 'That's not why I asked you to come here, anyway. It's really no concern of mine how you ruin your life.'

'I only came because I thought it might be something to do with Mum.'

'Your mother is fine. Heartbroken about the cancellation of the wedding, of course, but she and Fiona are still very close. They're even planning a little holiday together, I believe, so some good may have come out of this débâcle.'

Jack sighed. So his parents didn't apportion any blame to Fiona for the abortion or the break-up. They simply blamed him for walking away. 'Why did you want to see me?'

'To give you this.' Bill opened his desk drawer and withdrew an envelope. 'I'm buying you out of the partnership. God knows it grieves me to have to give you money that'll probably end up in a needle. No, don't look so

349

disgusted, I've seen boys with an excellent education and brilliant prospects drift off into some weird alternative lifestyle and end up on the streets. Friends of mine have been devastated – totally devastated – when their sons have gone off the rails and ended up in the gutter.' Bill frowned at the rather convoluted mental image.

'Dad, I'm not planning on becoming a drug baron. I'm a painter, and I'm joining a fair. I've just passed my HGV test and –'

'My dear Lord!' Bill slammed his perspiring hands down on to the desk. 'Don't tell me any more! And never let a word of this reach your mother's ears! You're becoming a member of the underclass!'

'No I'm fucking not.' Jack could imagine regaling Nell with this story at the Maybush, hearing her gurgle of laughter. He grew even hotter. 'Look, I wasn't expecting a pay-back from the firm, but I won't pretend it's not welcome. You've taken on a new partner, then?'

'Yes. A very bright and ambitious young man from Tay Homes. He's already started and looks extremely promising. He has drive and commitment, things which you sadly lacked.' Bill handed the envelope across the desk. 'This severs your ties with Morlands, Jack. I hope you realise what you've thrown away.'

'I do, yes.' Jack tried not to smile as he stuffed the envelope into the back pocket of his jeans. 'Just in case you think I'm totally fecklesss, I've seen the solicitor and the bank manager about making sure Fiona's OK in the house.'

'I know. She told me. I've actually paid off her mortgage for her. I felt it was the least I could do. So, as there's no more to say –'

Jack stood up. He'd been dismissed. Filed. Business completed. He stood awkwardly for a moment, wondering whether he should shake his father's hand, thought better of it and walked out of the office.

The forever-legged bimbo was painting her toenails. Her desk – Margaret's desk – was covered with highly coloured plastic bowls that seemed to serve no useful purpose, and several fluffy toys. Jack winked at her as he closed the door.

The Volvo was in the yard. Jack, trying not to grin too broadly, parked the Roadster beside it and rushed inside. Nell was perched on the pile of galloper tilts, her mobile phone tucked beneath her chin, a laptop computer beside her. She was wearing denim shorts and a pale blue cropped-off top, and her hair was piled into a silky, straggly bundle on top of her head. She was sitting with her legs crossed beneath her, and the scorching heat had increased her freckle-ratio. She hadn't heard him arrive, and Jack luxuriated in simply looking at her. Ross Percival, he decided, was the luckiest man on earth.

'Oh, hi,' she grinned in welcome, placing her hand over the phone. 'Won't be a sec. How did you get on?'

'Celebrations at the Maybush are now in order.' He waved the certificate at her. 'No problem at all.'

'Brilliant. Congratulations. You are clever. Not that I doubted you for a moment, of course.' Her eyes gleamed below the heavy fringe. 'Oh, hang on –'

She was talking rapidly, tapping things into the computer with her free hand, her hair escaping down her neck in silky, red-gold tendrils. Jack wanted to stroke the strands back into place and had to shove his hands into his pockets.

'Fine.' Nell snapped off the phone, and uncurling herself, walked towards him. 'God, I've got so much to tell you. But first let me see the hard-copy evidence of your brilliance.'

He waved the pass certificate above his head, drowning in her evocative floral scent. Almost as tall as him, she reached up and grabbed it. Her nearness made him ache.

'There is of course one huge drawback now.' She looked at him, the light in her eyes momentarily dimmed. 'You can drive the lorries – but the lorries no longer exist.'

'What? Oh, don't say bloody Percival the Elder has pulled the plug at the last minute? The bastard! Christ, Nell – what's happened?'

'About a lifetime of things. Do you reckon the Maybush can cope with a saga?'

'No doubt about it.' He reached beneath his pile of bedding. 'I bought you a present last week, in anticipation of this occasion –' He handed her a brand-new black crash helmet.

Nell moved it round in her hands. 'Jack Morland, you are in serious danger of becoming boring. This is a very grown-up piece of kit. And just when I'd got used to being a reckless law-breaker, too.'

'I just thought we should be legal, especially now we're a going concern. My obligation was totally for the business, you understand – not your skull or my licence.' He watched her as she pushed the silky bundle of hair into the skid-lid. 'We *are* still a going concern, aren't we?'

'Maybush,' Nell said with mock severity, pulling a face as she adjusted the visor. 'I'll tell you all about it when I've had my first ten pints of shandy.'

The journey was over far too quickly. Even though he'd driven more slowly than usual to savour the feeling of Nell's arms around his waist and the impression of her cheek against his shoulder, Newbridge humped into view long before he was ready for it.

Their table on the terrace was free. Jack was pretty sure that if it had been occupied by the business-lunchers he'd have asked them to move. Nowhere belonged to him and Nell more than these wooden benches and the sound of the river.

'You first then.' She placed her glass in the dead centre of a beer-mat. 'Although this is like a replay. We really should keep in touch more. Then we wouldn't have to have the reprises. And although I don't want to open old wounds or anything – you're looking a lot better. Have you come to terms about – er – the baby?'

'Yes, thanks. I just needed time on my own to sort it out. And, Ms Bradley, there's no way that I'm going to say anything before I've heard why we haven't got any transport. Have a heart, woman.'

'OK,' Nell shrugged, drawing her finger through the condensation on the outside of her glass. 'Are you sitting comfortably? Then I'll begin –'

He was never sure afterwards how he managed to listen to the whole tortuous story without interrupting her. His heart alternately rose and sank – with far more effect, he reckoned, than any ride on the Crash'n'Dash could have caused. At the part where he realised that she wasn't going to be marrying Ross Percival after all, he wanted to leap up and punch the air in triumph; the fact that it meant they'd lose Clem's lorries as a result was a mere hiccup in comparison, but he managed to control himself and even contrived to look sympathetic. The Sam–Claudia–Danny story was all a bit too *EastEnders* to be true – although he expressed complete support for her decision to leave that obnoxious bastard. And the fact that they'd be travelling with the Memory Lane Fair and bringing a helter-skelter – no, sorry, a slip – and a big wheel, was fantastic news.

This was almost toppled from pole position by the information that Clem Percival had not, as Nell had feared, interfered with her Guild rights.

'So,' Nell finished up, 'the incredibly wondrous news is that I've spent ages talking to the Guild, following up adverts for sites and – we've actually got our first gaff.' She crossed the fingers of both hands. 'At the weekend. The steam rally at Broadstone is desperate for an olde tyme fair – they've been let down at the last minute because someone had double-booked – and, after a red-hot telephoning session, we've got four or five definite bookings and two provisionals to follow on. These should see us well towards the end of the season, and by next year we'll be part of the scene and on the road permanently.' Her excitement had tinged the creaminess of her skin the way the sun never could. 'All we need now are some lorries – well, not any lorries – we need, as far as I can see, at least five numbers and the bonus thingy in the lottery to buy the wagons that Clem had commissioned.'

'No problem at all then.' Jack leaned back. 'But honestly – our first real gig? This weekend? Jesus.'

Nell smiled. 'I know. That's how I felt. That's why I've transferred my office to the shed. I didn't want anyone else to know what was going on. I'm going to move my living wagon over tomorrow – and that'll be my final break with Bradley–Percival.'

He touched her hand gently. In friendship. He understood. Cutting the umbilical cord was never easy.

But any day now, depending on the provision of transport, of course, the gallopers would be built up, the organ would play 'Paree', punters would ride – and every dream he'd ever had would come true.

He looked across the table at Nell and realised just how much his dreams had changed since that day they'd met at the Downland Trust auction preview. How much both their lives had changed, simply because of the other's existence. Hell, much more introspection and he'd be questioning the existence of Fate, the meaning of life – he might even get on to crop circles.

'I've got my money from the sale of the dodgems to Ross and Danny,' Nell was standing up, ready to buy refills, 'but that won't be enough. I mean, they paid me a rock-bottom price because they knew I wanted to go quickly, and I wasn't going to haggle. But these lorries of Clem's will cost a small fortune. My money might buy one of the Seddon-Atkinsons and maybe – at a pinch – the second-hand ones, but we're still looking for a huge amount. Same again?'

Jack nodded. It was one hell of a conundrum. He pushed his hair from his forehead and watched a family of moorhens diving and squabbling in the shallows, and the willows dripping lazily into the river. Christ! What the hell was he thinking about? He'd sat there, beaming like an idiot over the news that Ross Percival was no longer on the scene and that the gallopers would soon be on the road, and had allowed Nell to go and buy the next round. And she'd bought the first one, and he already owed her a fortune for the HGV test. He didn't mind her knowing he was broke, but he'd hate her to think that he was a free-loader.

He reached into the back pocket of his jeans for his wallet and drew out the Morland-logo'd envelope. Turning it over in his hands he realised he hadn't given his pay-off a second thought. Overcome by Nell and her news, his father's severance token hadn't been important. Idly, he slit the envelope open.

The figures on the cheque made him rock on his heels.

He folded it again, stuffed it back into his pocket, and finding a rather grubby fiver in his wallet, pushed his way through to the Maybush's bar.

Several of the Downland Trusters had arrived at Fox Hollow by the time they returned. Nell must have been busy, Jack thought, watching as she shook her hair free from the crash helmet. She had phoned them all, telling them the news – good and bad. Percy and Dennis, Fred and Harry, had arrived and were scrambling between the ghost train and the caterpillar – with scant regard for Jack's living quarters – checking that everything was as it should be.

'Piss awful news about the lorries,' Fred said candidly. 'We could've done without that.'

'Don't worry,' Percy bellowed across the shed. 'Summat'll turn up, Nell, love. Summat always does. What time have you been given for the Broadstone pull-on?'

'The steam rally is on Saturday and Sunday but a lot of people arrive early, so they're letting us on to the field at ten in the morning on the Friday. I thought we'd load on Thursday night and pull out of here as soon as it's light on Friday – transport, of course, permitting.' She grinned. 'Reckon you can complete building up the gallopers – and the rest – in time for a six-o'clock opening Friday evening?'

A chorus of 'no sweats' indicated that they could beat John Carter hands down.

Butterflies of excitement were already beating their wings in Jack's stomach. It was really going to happen at last. And if

Nell could get at least some of the wagons, they could do double runs if necessary, surely? He knew that wasn't how showmen worked normally, but when had any of this adventure been normal?

A shrill blast of Wagner sliced through the heat of the afternoon and Nell whipped her mobile out from the back pocket of her shorts. She said yes and no and nodded and Jack watched the sun spinning golden cobwebs in her hair.

'What was that?' he asked when she snapped the aerial down. 'I've heard mobiles playing Mozart, but I've never heard Wagner before.'

'It's the Ring Cycle.' Nell was laughing. 'I thought it was appropriate – and that was Eckstrucs. Clem's dealership mates – they've accepted my offer for one of the Seddons and the second-hand trucks. They'll be ready at the weekend. That only leaves the remainder of the galloper wagons to finance, but who cares? God, I can't believe this is actually happening – can you?'

Jack was paralysed by her. He wanted to kiss her, to touch her, to love her. He took a deep breath, trying to control the shaking, and grinned at her. 'It's really going to happen at last, isn't it? The Memory Lane Fair is actually a reality? If only we could get the other trucks by this weekend.'

'God!' Nell laughed, scrambling to her feet. 'You want jam on it, Jack Morland! Just be grateful for small mercies!'

'Oh, I am.' Jack stood up, his smile matching hers. He reached out and pulled her towards him. 'And before you go and tell the others the good news, why don't we have a small celebration of our own?'

CHAPTER THIRTY-TWO

Nell groaned for the three-millionth time. How could she have made such a fool of herself? Getting so excited? Snuggling up so close? She had clearly read every sign incorrectly and, expecting Jack to feel the same way, had probably only succeeded in frightening him away. Absolutely bloody brilliant, Petronella.

Of course it was obviously far too soon for him – after Fiona and the baby and everything. Just because she'd escaped from marriage to Ross, it didn't mean that everyone else had the same zinging sense of relief after the break-up of a relationship. And he was a flatty – he'd had a house and a garden – he was only bloody playing at being a traveller, after all. What the hell would he want with her? He probably didn't even find her attractive. She was tall and gangling and freckled, and that damn Fiona had been petite and blonde. Nell moaned with mortification.

She'd just been so sure that it was right. So sure. They'd become such friends; they'd grown so close. She didn't know whether to laugh or cry. After all these years – all the conversations with Adele – all the late-night chats with Claudia – when she'd told them that she would know when she'd met the right man. And she had.

The feelings she'd had for Jack Morland had, just as she'd

known they would, hit her smack between the eyes with trumpets, fireworks and a deluge of rose petals.

When Jack had pulled her towards him, she'd been convinced that this was it. The moment for his declaration. The moment when she could tell him how she felt. She'd all but thrown herself at him. She squirmed at the memory. And he'd simply hugged her, kissed her cheek, told her again how brilliant it was about the lorries and how he'd love to stay, but there was still something that he had to do, and then leapt on the Roadster and roared away.

It was Thursday evening at Fox Hollow. The Downland Trusters were doing their Munchkin act again, loading the ghost train and the caterpillar into the Eckstrucs wagons that had been delivered that morning. Nell had managed to pay for them with her money from the dodgems, but now not even the dream-come-true sight of the gleaming maroon trucks, so carefully liveried with 'Petronella Bradley's Memory Lane Fair' in gold leaf, could dilute her sense of humiliation. Not even the fact that the one brand-new Seddon-Atkinson that had been specially designed to take the platforms and the lighting spars, the swifts, the tilts and every other piece of the Savage that could be dismantled – apart from the horses, the rods and the rounding boards – now stood in the yard, could lift her embarrassment.

She sat on the steps of her living wagon, knowing she should be helping but feeling that if Jack wasn't here then her heart wouldn't be in it. They should be doing this together. Their dream had been symbiotic. And the worst humiliation of all was that, when she'd arrived with her living wagon, every trace of him had gone from the shed. The bedding and the clothes, the paints and the Beck's, had all evaporated. Even the scent of him had vanished. It was as though he had never existed. Oh Christ, what had she done?

'Come on then, Nell, love.' Harry paused in manhandling a corner of one of the galloper platforms, perspiration trickling down his delighted face. 'Give us a hand. No time to lounge about looking glamorous. We're great believers in sexual equilibrium. Come and grab a corner.'

Nell grabbed. She heaved and strained and sweated with the rest of them. It should have been the happiest moment of her life.

'I reckons,' Dennis wiped the ubiquitous oily rag round his face when the platforms were loaded, 'that we can do this. If we get this lot dumped off first thing, then come back for the horses and the rods and the rounding boards – oh, I know they should have special trucks – but if we work with what we've got for the time being –'

'We don't have much choice, do we?' Nell didn't want to disillusion them. They were wonderful. They were so delighted. And they were right, it was possible in theory. Maybe. Perhaps. And it should be quite easy to do it in two or even three journeys if necessary – especially now they had another Class I driver – if, of course, he ever turned up. She swallowed the stupid tears and grabbed a trailing corner of the tilt.

The Trusters sat on the loads puffing while she made tea, this time in her own kitchen in the living wagon. She could make tea. Tea didn't remind her too much of Jack. The Downland Trusters had arrived in every conceivable form of transport, some with tents, others with small caravans, and had pulled them round in the yard like a wagon train. Tomorrow morning the whole mobile village would move to Broadstone. They were talking, smoking, laughing. None of them mentioned Jack's absence.

The ghost train and the caterpillar were loaded. The first part of the gallopers was almost finished. With help from Dennis and Percy, Nell had rigged up the Gavioli truck behind her living wagon, and the music cupboard had been dismantled and packed into Fred's trailer. There probably wasn't any more they could do.

Claudia and Sam were going to be driving directly from the Forest of Dean to Broadstone in the morning with their stuff.

Nell had had a good-luck phone call from her parents and, most surprisingly, an Interflora bouquet with 'Fingers crossed. I know you can do it' on the card from Ross.

The evening was turning to musky twilight. The sky was skeined with vibrant colours heralding perfection for tomorrow. The Trusters had brought primus stoves and baby barbecues and the air was redolent with the scent of burgers and bacon.

'Stone the bleeding crows!' Fred choked on his sausage sandwich. 'Hark the herald angels – or what?'

Nell, who was sitting with Percy and Dennis, not eating because of the dry lump of disappointment lodged in her throat, listened with the rest of them. The low familiar rumble of a large lorry was Doppler-effecting its way along Fox Hollow's high-banked lanes. Nell felt a slight surge of optimism. Sam and Claudia must have decided to start early and come straight to Fox Hollow. They'd made good time. At least she could cry on Claudia's shoulder tonight.

She scrambled to her feet. 'Oh, my God!'

A small white Eckstrucs van skittered into the yard followed in stately splendour by two brand-new Seddon-Atkinson lorries purring regally. Gleaming in maroon and gold, perfectly liveried, the convoy pulled to a halt beside the wagon-train encampment. The Trusters were all on their feet.

'The remainder of your order.' The driver scrambled from the white van and brandished the paperwork towards Dennis. 'Horse truck and forty-footer. On time I hope. We knew it was an urgent job – but of course we had that blip in the middle. Still we was told to carry on with the job and get 'em here before midnight – and here we are.'

The two lorry drivers had already dived back into the white van for the return journey. The van driver was obviously also eager to go. 'Sign here then – safe delivery and all that. Nice piece of workmanship. Like this old stuff, meself.'

Nell, working saliva into her mouth, shook her head. 'I'm

really sorry but they'll have to go back. The original order was cancelled. I've bought all I can afford. I can't pay for these. I thought it was understood that it'd be all right to cancel.'

'All paid for according to my info.' The van driver was still impatient to get away. 'All you got to do, my duck, is sign the old paperwork. Completion of order, delivery on time, and all that. Here –'

'But who paid for them?'

'Not my business. All I knows is that nothing leaves our yard without the money being in the bank first, so I don't worry about it. Now, could you just sign me chitty and let us get off, duck? There's football on the telly tonight.'

Nell bit her lip. 'Look, I think there's been a mistake.'

'Just sign the man's docket.' Dennis and Percy seemed to be manipulating her arm. One of them handed her the forms, the other a pen. 'Go on, Nell. Maybe Clem Percival changed his mind. Who bloody cares? Just sign.'

Nell signed. Oh, God, she wasn't going to turn them away now. She'd have to sort it out later.

The Eckstrucs driver vaulted across the yard and while he was still tucking the paperwork into his pocket, the white van tore away. The Trusters, their suppers ignored, were swarming back into the shed.

'No time to waste.' Percy looked like he was about to burst. 'Let's get the rest of the stuff loaded.'

'It won't matter if we works all night,' Dennis beamed. 'We've got the trucks, gel. We're going to be all right.'

They lifted and strained the brass rods and all of the rounding boards into the wagons. Working with them in a state of dazed confusion, Nell was pretty sure that Clem Percival was going to storm into the yard at any moment and demand his money back.

It was late. The evening had melted into black velvet, the shed's huge exterior lights casting pools of brilliance across the yard. Nell, who was helping the Jims, Bobs and Bens shoulder the horses towards the doors, heard a whoop of delight from the Trusters outside. One truck successfully loaded, she thought, and one to go. Surely, if they were loaded, even Clem would allow them to be used just this once? She wondered vaguely just how much it was going to cost her to get them un-liveried.

She walked into the yard to check that they were ready for the horses. 'We're OK in here, Dennis. You ready for us?'

With the other Trusters she started to lift Petronella and Vincent, Miranda and Caliban into the horse truck. After the fourth journey Dennis was leaning back against the tailgate, wiping his forehead, while the others had disappeared into the shed for the next phalanx.

Nell took a deep breath. 'Dennis, have you heard from Jack? I thought he'd be here tonight –'

'Jack had other things to do. Things to see to, he said. Accommodation to sort out. I think he's buying a new house or something. He'll definitely be here in the morning.'

They worked until well past midnight. Nell had never known such pain. She lifted and loaded, knowing that her muscles were screaming and that her body was dropping with exhaustion, yet feeling none of it. The only agony was inside.

They'd all teased her about Jack's absence, saying that he was a fair-weather fair supporter and that, owing to his obviously being work-shy, he'd have to do the bulk of the building-up. Nell would have to crack the whip when he turned up tomorrow, wouldn't she? They didn't seem aware of any of this causing Nell pain, but then, why should they? She'd gritted her teeth and smiled and told herself that they'd got the lorries, they'd got the gaff, they'd got the Memory Lane Fair. What the hell else was there to want?

'Get a move on!' Harry yelled up into the horse truck. 'Only three more to load and old Perce has got his barbie going. Mind, I reckon we'll drop dead the minute we finish building-up tomorrow – I've never worked so hard in my life.'

'I'm really grateful,' Nell said, smiling at the Trusters, still wanting Jack to be there. 'I couldn't have done this without you. Without any of you . . .'

They sat around, eating again, drinking, talking of their families who would be coming to cheer them on in the morning. Nell had made yet more tea in the living wagon, handing cups over the open top of the door.

'Dennis said Jack was sorting out accommodation?' Fred and Harry had swapped places on the back of the galloper truck and she was sitting beside Percy. She had to say something. Maybe Dennis had got it wrong. 'Is he?'

Percy nodded. 'So I understand. He said something about it.'

She clutched the final straw. 'So, he might be bringing it with him tomorrow?'

'Doubt it, Nell, love. Bricks and mortar don't tow too well.'

So that was it. Her head reeled. How could she have misread it so appallingly wrongly? 'So he's planning – planning to settle down again?'

'Search me, but it sounds like it.' Percy drained his mug. 'He took all his stuff out of the shed a few days ago, so I suppose so. He'd had a bit of a rough time lately, by all accounts. Do him good to put down some new roots.'

'Yes. Yes, I suppose it will.' She swallowed the lump in her throat. 'I'm – um – glad that he's found somewhere else. Somewhere permanent . . .'

Nell knew that she should get up, walk away, call a cheery goodnight to everyone and tell them not to be late in the morning. She didn't, simply because she wanted to talk about Jack. She wanted to talk about Jack all night. But Percy wanted to talk about the gallopers. She nodded and shook her head and hoped that her yes and no answers were in the right places.

She and Percy still sat together on the tailboard as, one by one, the other Trusters gave in and crawled off, triumphant and exhausted, to their various quarters. The night closed in with a multitude of stars. Nell would have stayed until dawn. She knew she was waiting to hear the Roadster's roar.

CHAPTER THIRTY-THREE

It was, Nell thought, as perfect as she'd always dreamed it would be. A glorious golden September day; the fair field ringed by chestnut trees; a fat brown stream bubbling haphazardly through the middle of silky tufts of grass; a handful of honey-coloured houses hidden behind a haze of golden rod and Michaelmas daisies.

Most of the lorries, all proclaiming 'Petronella Bradley's Memory Lane Fair', were pulled into the gateway. The horse truck, because they were a driver short, was still at Fox Hollow. She'd have to go back for that. Her living wagon was parked under the chestnuts' dappled canopy, and the Downland Trusters were buzzing with excited anticipation.

It was everything she'd ever wanted.

Funny, she thought, scrambling backwards out of the Volvo with vital spare fuses and masking tape, how you dreamed and schemed and planned to accomplish something – and then, when you achieved it, there always had to be a piece missing. Her perfect jigsaw of attainment was lacking a pretty vital chunk.

Still, there was no point in thinking like that. The fact that Jack hadn't arrived at Fox Hollow this morning by the time they pulled out – despite her dallying and dawdling and leaving as late as possible – really should tell her something.

It was a pity that she wasn't listening.

The steam rally was gathering itself together on the other side of the field. Huge showmen's traction engines in maroon and gold, and their smaller agricultural cousins in less flamboyant green, were chugging into position, sacks of coal were being delivered, and a hundred craft and market stalls were being erected. The Downland Trusters were nearly frantic with expectation.

After long consultations with the rally organisers, the pitches were allocated, leaving spaces for Sam and Claudia's slip and big wheel. It was a shame, Nell thought, that they didn't have some old-fashioned side stuff and a set of swings. Still, once she'd become established she'd be able to advertise for the future, wouldn't she? She tried not to think that right now the future, which should have been beckoning and jolly, looked a bit gaunt and jaded.

A screech of brakes and the roar of an engine made her turn her head. Oh, God. At last. The Roadster was rocketing across the field towards her, and slewed to an unsteady halt. Despite her intention to remain cool, Nell felt giddy at the sight of him.

'I'm so sorry.' Jack wrenched off his helmet. 'I was still awake when it was getting light, and then I knew I ought to be getting up – and I immediately went to sleep. You must have been convinced that I wasn't going to turn up, especially after I missed yesterday.'

'The thought did cross my mind.'

He looked, Nell thought, as though he hadn't slept at all. Well, that made two of them.

'Anyway, I'm here now, and ready to atone for my sins.' He had the nerve to grin, damn him. 'What do you want me to do?'

'Go back to Fox Hollow and drive the galloper truck over here. You can stick the bike up into the back. After all, you might as well make the most of your licence since I've paid good money for it.' She stopped and wished she could have sliced off her tongue.

Jack winced visibly. 'I hadn't forgotten. Here.' He delved into the pocket of his black jeans and handed her a rather crumpled cheque. 'One HGV course – paid in full. I should have done it yesterday. I know I should also have been at Fox Hollow to help you. I wanted to be there, believe me. It was just that I had other things on my mind. Other things to sort out.'

'I heard. Still, as you can see, we managed without you. Did – did you get everything done? Everything you wanted to do?'

He nodded briefly, ramming the skid-lid back on, the beautiful eyes disappearing behind the smoked visor, and kick-started away across the field. Nell looked down at his cheque, tore it across again and again and hurled it into the air. She'd got the Memory Lane Fair. She'd just have to get used to the idea that she wasn't going to have Jack.

The Downland Trust built up the ghost train and the caterpillar first as they were relatively simple. It was a good-natured affair, very unlike any build-up at Bradley –Percival. Danny's bad temper and Ross's impatience seemed to belong to another life already.

The gallopers had attracted a mention in *The World's Fair*, and quite a crowd of devotees was gathering to witness this momentous occasion. Thanks to the dummy run in the yard the Trusters were not only fairly confident of getting it right first time, but also of beating John Carter's record hollow. The centre was ramped into position, this time to be joined by the Gavioli. Nell, screwing her hair into its scrunchie on top of her head, tucking her dark green vest more securely into her jeans, and trying not to think of Jack, got ready to work with the rest of them.

The horse truck rolled smoothly through the gates an hour later, just as they were unsheeting the organ from its tarpaulin. Nell stopped, shielding her eyes. Jack looked totally at home behind the wheel. Obviously, her money had been well spent. He pulled confidently into line with the other lorries and dropped from the cab. He could have been doing it all his life. Nell's heart thumped miserably against her ribs.

'Here, Nell,' one of the Jims shouted. 'You might be taller'n most of us, but you're probably the lightest! Get up here and sort this out!'

'This' was the centre pole, the one-time chimney from the days when the machine was steam-driven, which folded flat, but needed to be erected on top of the centre truck to support the tilt and the swifts and lighting spars, and eventually the rounding boards. A dozen pairs of hands pushed Nell's bottom upwards as she scrambled on top of the centre truck. Jack's, she noticed, weren't amongst them.

The build-up was going well. The top was completed. Jack had joined in passing her spanners, grinning at Percy, joking with Fred. His eyes gleamed with delight. Nell's embarrassment and pain had to be put on hold. The absolute surge of delight as the gallopers started to take shape simply obliterated everything else.

She stood beside him, looking up at his incredibly intricate artwork, looking at the wording he'd so carefully inscribed for her. Remembering. Nothing could spoil this. She knew he was watching her. 'It's unbelievable, isn't it?'

Jack nodded. 'The stuff of my dreams.'

Almost the stuff of hers.

The sun was clambering hand over fist into the sky, dazzling across the field. Fortunately a buffeting breeze stopped the temperature from rising to frying levels, but even so, they all looked as though they had been dunked in buckets of water. Oily water at that, Nell grinned to herself, thinking of a long, cool shower and clean hair.

Claudia and Sam arrived just before midday. Nell bounded across the uneven grass towards them, exclaiming in delight at the wagon, hardly able to wait to cast a professional eye over the rides. She had never seen either of them look happier. Claudia's short, spiky hair had been coaxed round her face and she seemed to have combined two totally different images, with dramatically heavy make-up and a long, floaty voile dress. Sam looked as though he'd walked on the moon.

'Everything OK?'

'Very OK.' Claudia hugged her. 'More than very OK. Absolutely sodding fantastic, if you want to know. Oh, wow!'

Nell beamed with delight. 'Is that wow because you've at last discovered gentle, tender, and mutually satisfying sex and are unbelievably in love with my younger brother? Wow because the gallopers even half built up are far more stunning than you'd even dreamed? Or wow for some other reason?'

Claudia nodded. 'Right with all three. Who on earth is that?'

Nell turned round slowly, although she didn't need to. 'Oh, him? He's the bank manager.'

'Holy shit.'

Sam drifted across, unable to stop smiling; unable not to touch Claudia's cheek very gently. Nell sniffed happily.

'The gallopers look tons better than the Brain-Scrambler,' Claudia said, tottering exaggeratedly against Sam. 'And he –' she wrinkled her nose across the field at Jack ' – is a million times better than Mr P.'

'Yeah,' Nell said quietly. 'I know. But like Ross he's not going to be a permanent emotional fixture.'

'Come off it,' Sam said. 'Why on earth not?'

'Jack's a flatty. There's no chance –'

'Don't be so bloody archaic. If Claudia and I can make a go of things, why on earth shouldn't you and a flatty? For God's sake, Nell, you're the gaffer now. You make the rules.'

She knew. But it wouldn't be enough to make Jack give up his bricks and mortar.

'We'll get built up, then give you a hand if you need it.' Sam looked around and sighed with pleasure. 'God, Nell. This is quite amazing, isn't it? Only one thing mars the proceedings. My Mazda is still wherever Bradley–Percival is at the moment.'

'St Giles.' Claudia and Nell spoke together.

'Probably being joy-ridden at this very minute, then,' Sam said mournfully. 'I'll have to get Ross to bring it over. You wouldn't mind?'

'Not at all.' Nell shook her head. 'He sent me flowers to wish me luck. Oh, look, I think I'm wanted. See you later – and you can borrow any of the blokes when you need them. They'd be glad to help.'

The gallopers were already transformed. The shields were up, the rods – the hardest and heaviest job – had been hung, and the horses galloped at last, suspended high above the ground, three abreast. Nell could almost sense their freedom.

'We've put Petronella in between Jonquil and Valentine,' Jack said, 'because she's the only centre-row horse with a front rod – so that children can ride alone safely. I thought you'd like that.'

She did. She smiled at him. She couldn't help it. She just wished she still didn't want to kiss him quite so much.

It looked spectacular. Even the jaded aficionados were oohing and aahing, snapping off lens-covers, hoisting up camcorders. Only the platforms and the steps to go. It was potentially back-breaking, but they were mob-handed. It was going to be OK.

'Don't want to interrupt you when you're so busy – but have you got room for a little 'un – or ten?'

Nell nearly dropped her bit of the platform. Mr and Mrs Mac beamed from their lorry cab. The rest of the Macs' vehicles appeared to be bouncing across the field behind them.

'Do you mean it?' Nell slid down to the grass. 'You've left Danny? You want to travel with me?'

'Well, we missed you,' Mrs Mac grinned gummily, 'and you, Sam and Claudia were allus the pick of the bunch. And we're not too happy with that new fangled-stuff. We thought our swings and bits of side stuff'd fit in a treat with your machines.'

Nell wanted to kiss them too. In fact she wanted to kiss the entire world. 'Build up wherever you like. You can see where we are – Sam and Claudia are over there. God, this is perfect. Brilliant. Oh, Jack – these are the Mackenzies. This is Jack

Morland – he did all the restoration painting –'

'Bloody fine job, too.' Mrs Mac beamed. This was high praise. 'Nice to meet you. No doubt we'll be seeing a lot more of you.'

Jack nodded and said he hoped so.

Mr Mac removed a cigarette from the corner of his mouth. 'Spoke to your dad last night, Nell, 'bout this. Him and yer ma are coming tomorrow to see you in action. They're right proud of you, gel. Sent their love.'

Nell sniffed again. She'd never been a crier – but today she reckoned she'd keep Kleenex in business single-handedly.

As the Macs' cavalcade moved away towards the outer edge of the field, Rio leaned from the window of her parents' wagon. Her eyes devoured Jack and she laughed at Nell. 'Christ – I can see why you didn't want to stay with Mr P. You lucky cow! Oh, and by the way, Mercedes and Nyree-Dawn aren't with us. What?' Rio peered back inside the wagon at her mother's apparent rebuke. 'Oh, stuff it. Nell won't care. Not with a lush squeeze like him.'

'What won't I care about?'

'That the twins are staying on to travel with Ross and Danny – offering – um – all the comforts of home . . .'

Bloody hell! Nell stared after the departing procession of Mackenzies and laughed out loud. Mercedes and Danny? Nyree-Dawn and Ross? Incredible! She couldn't wait to tell Claudia.

They worked on. Exhaustion and exhilaration had ignited fires in Jack's eyes. The Downland Trusters had been unbeliev-able. They had all worked so hard. Then at last it was over.

The gallopers were ready.

Nell stood down on the grass with Jack beside her, and gazed at them. She was crying; she thought they were probably all crying. It was the most emotional moment of her entire life. The machine towered above her and all around her, gorgeous and gaudy.

'Half an hour then,' she looked at the Downland Trusters through her tears. 'Just to give us time to clean ourselves up a bit, and then we'll have a dress rehearsal before we open tonight. We'll want to make sure we're inch-perfect for all the punters who are coming for the steam rally barbecue and fireworks display.'

They all synchronised their watches. They'd be back on the gallopers in half an hour. Ready to go? Too damn right. The Downland Trusters roared their approval and swarmed away to prepare.

Nell swallowed and looked down at the black cables which snaked away to the throbbing generator. Jack was still there. 'I honestly never thought this would happen.'

'Neither did I. Nell, there's something I need to say. Can we talk?'

She didn't want to talk about his return to bricks and mortar. She didn't want to talk about her feelings. 'Yes, of course. But I need a shower and a drink before I do anything else. I'm absolutely filthy.'

'You look great to me.' He smiled. 'I'll see you in twenty minutes, then.'

As Nell walked towards her living wagon, a red sports car bucketed through the gate and slalomed its way through the rides. Jesus! Not Ross! Transfixed to the spot, she watched as the car braked sharply, almost burying its nose in the ground. It wasn't Ross's Ferrari.

The door of Sam's Mazda flew open. 'Hiya! Got any good gaff-lad vacancies?'

'Terry,' Nell stared in astonishment, 'what the hell are you doing with Sam's car? Have you nicked it?'

'Nah, course not.' Terry, in skintight jeans and very little else, handed her the keys. 'I knew he'd want it back, and I want a job.'

The steam-rally ladies, who had been ogling Jack, were now joined by their teenage daughters who couldn't take their eyes from Terry.

'Couldn't hack it,' he grinned at her. 'It wasn't the same without you and Claudia. Danny's a bastard. I know this old-fashioned stuff is a bit tame, but Ross said you might need a hand on the ghost train.' His eyes gleamed. 'I reckoned there'd be a fairish opportunity for my various talents on there.'

Nell was delighted to see him. 'Consider yourself employed, then. We're opening tonight. We haven't got a Beast Wagon yet, but you can kip in one of the trucks until we get something sorted.'

'Brilliant.' Terry was already making eye-contact with the teenage girls. 'Anyway I thought I might get a little trailer of my own – for when me and Karen get married next year. I'll go and say hello to Claudia and Sam, then. And,' he leaned over and kissed her cheek, 'I know I'm not supposed to do that, but it's bloody great to be back. I've really missed your cooking. See ya.'

The sun was hot on the top of her head, and she felt ninety-per-cent elated. They were all back together again. She was, as Sam had said, the gaffer. The Memory Lane Fair was no longer a dream. Ninety per cent, she reckoned, wasn't bad . . .

She'd showered and washed her hair and was tugging on her clean jeans and vest top when Jack knocked tentatively on the living-wagon door. Maybe she should have been wearing the green shorts suit. She squirted on some Anaïs Anaïs and hoped it would do. 'Come in.'

He'd obviously begged washing facilities from one of the Trusters. His still-damp hair gleamed and he was wearing a peacock-blue collarless shirt over the black jeans. Nell's body completely dissolved.

'They're all waiting for you. I can't believe it's really going to happen –' he stopped and stared.

Oh, well, she thought – maybe she didn't look that bad. Then she realised that he was staring at her living wagon. It was decorated in shades of blue and cream, with apricot rugs on the polished floors, and Limoges porcelain against the pale wood. She always took it for granted.

Jack, gazing at the cushions and comfort, shook his head. 'It's incredibly beautiful. And so are you . . .'

Nell was rooted to the spot. She knew she was blushing.

Every damn freckle was probably twinkling like a midsummer-night constellation. 'Jack – about yesterday –'

'I blew it. I'm sorry. I let you down by not being there.' Jack was tracing the outline of one of the rugs with the toe of his boot. 'But I was so determined to get everything else cleared up before – well, before I started on this. And I behaved like a complete idiot at Fox Hollow the other afternoon, rushing off like that with no explanation. But there was something that simply couldn't wait. And, after all, you're a traveller –'

'And you're a flatty.'

'And two wrongs don't make a right.'

She swallowed. He was grinning again but it wasn't going to work. He'd bought a damned house to prove it.

'Come on, you two!' Percy and Dennis were beaming up into the living wagon. 'Tons of time for the hearts and flowers later! Let's get this show on the road!'

As Nell started to walk towards the doorway, Jack touched her arm. 'Before we do this, there really is something I want to explain to you. About being missing yesterday –'

Yesterday. Nell didn't want to talk about yesterday, and she really didn't want to hear any more about his flatty exploits. 'I know you've bought another house. I do understand. But maybe, if you're going to travel with us, you could let it out during the season or something?'

'I haven't and I couldn't.' He moved towards her, and reached out and removed her damp hair from its scrunchie so that it slithered coolly over her burning shoulders. 'I haven't bought anything – well, I have, but they're outside.'

Nell didn't understand. Jack was tracing the splodge of freckles on her nose. It made concentration impossible.

'Last week I bought the remainder of the lorries with my pay-off from Morlands. I sorted it out that day when you found out about the rest of the order, but Eckstrucs said they would only take cash because they'd been messed about, so I had to wait until my cheque had cleared. I thought it was the least I could do –'

'You? You bought them? You mean, I won't have to give them

back? Oh, you're brilliant! You did that – for me?' She was probably going to cry again. 'I'll never be able to thank you enough.'

'I hope you might, actually. And it wasn't just for you, it was for us – for the Memory Lane Fair. I had to make some input – I couldn't leave all the financial burden to you.'

He'd continued the freckle-tracing on to her shoulders. She tried not to wriggle delightedly. 'And the new house that you've bought? The bricks and mortar?'

'A bit of an untruth. After the lorries I didn't have enough money left over even for a pup tent. I've been bed-and-breakfasting at the Maybush.'

'Jack Morland! I totally hate you!'

'God Almighty!' Percy and Dennis, who had been kicking their heels outside, finally snapped. 'You've got the rest of your lives to get this sorted. We've got the gallopers to try out – and that's far more important.'

Nell bit her lip and laughed. They were probably right.

The gallopers shone in a rainbow of glossy reflected colours. Nell's mouth was dry. Jack, walking behind her, was silent. They pushed their way through the expectant, excited crowd.

'Ready?' Jack's voice was husky.

'As I'll ever be.' She gave him a shaky smile, then she grinned at the others. 'Come on then – let's find out whether we're in business.'

With the banshee wail of children on the last day of the summer term, the Downland Trusters, the fairground fanatics, several steam enthusiasts from the traction-engine scene, Sam and Claudia holding hands, Terry and practically all the Macs, scrambled on to the horses.

Nell, again with tears streaming down her face, swung herself through them into the centre, followed by Jack.

The Gavioli was poised, ready to entertain. Percy had transferred all the music books to the wooden shelves behind the carved centres. Nell, her hands shaking, lifted 'Paree' from the top of the pile and placed it on the key frame.

'It's now or never,' she whispered to Jack. 'I'll do the music – you do the remainder of the honours. And thank you –'

'And you . . .' Jack ran his fingers through his hair, took a deep breath, switched on the power and released the brake.

The electricity surged. A thousand light bulbs twinkled, reflected a million times in the cut-glass mirrors. Then amazingly, gradually, the whole giddy, incredibly beautiful hurdy-gurdy started to revolve. Nell, shivering, snapped shut the key frame. The bosomy shepherdesses, the moustachioed soldiers, and Harlequin and Columbine were imperceptibly awakened. Nell felt the sheer excitement shoot up from the soles of her feet and prickle along her spine.

The first sonorous notes of 'Paree' echoed mellifluously and, oh so slowly, before bursting into the most stirring, toe-tapping traditional riding tune of all time. Unable to see anything except a kaleidoscopic whirl of colour as the horses rose and fell, gathering speed around her, Nell stared at Jack.

'We did it.'

'I always knew we would.' His voice was low, and despite the roar of the music, she could hear every word. 'Oh God, Nell –'

He pulled her into his arms and kissed her. Fired by the roisterous melody, the swirling circle of colour and movement, the dream come true, and the absolutely sheer gorgeousness of him, she linked her fingers in his hair and kissed him back. Fused together, hearing the faint whoops of delight from the riders every time they passed the organ side of the centre, Nell swayed in his arms.

Eventually, as 'Paree' skipped and trumpeted towards its climax, she pulled away from him. Not looking at him, her hands trembling, she reached for another book and fed it into the frame. 'Sabre Dance' rampaged its way through the banks of notes, zig-zagging into the air.

The riders cheered and hollered as they galloped onwards. Nell curled herself back into Jack's arms again. His eyes were miles away. She put her lips very close to his ear. 'What are you thinking?'

He kissed her freckles. 'Oh, just that the Bradley–Morland Memory Lane Fair will be quite something to leave to our grandchildren.'